B is for Broken

Edited by Rhonda Parrish

B is for Broken

All copyrights remain with original authors
Published by Poise and Pen Publishing
2015

ISBN-13: 978-0-9936990-8-5
ISBN-10: 0993699081

http://www.poiseandpen.com

Cover art: Victoria Hoke
Cover design: Jonathan Parrish
Story title art by Victoria Hoke

These stories are works of fiction. Names, characters, places and incidents either are products of the author's imagination or are used fictitiously. Any similarities to actual events, locales, or persons, living or dead, are entirely coincidental and not intentional.

CONTENTS

Brittany Warman

ONCE upon a time, there were curses. Curses that ruined families, shattered hearts, disfigured, humiliated, and punished. There were some curses that were justified and other burdens that weren't fair at all. But curses, of course, could always be broken. That was their way, their price. You could inflict so much pain with a spell of misfortune... but hope was always possible.

A hundred years is a long time and the world has changed. In this new, awakened world, there are no curses, at least not the way I remember them. My prince studies the skies with mechanical devices like I had never seen before and writes detailed notes about the movements of the universe. He whispers my name to the heavens but isn't thinking of me.

I do not sleep now. Instead, I stand outside and I too watch the skies. The glowing lights shine over the ice most nights here: red, blue, yellow, but mostly green. It snakes through the air like the vines of my old rose bushes, twisting and pulsing with something unknown. Auroras are always moving, shimmering behind the stars, fading and reappearing yet I remain here, still, a dying rose on the snow.

My prince cannot truly understand the auroras, he only

knows he is drawn to them, much as he was drawn to me. They are a mystery, unexplainable, a puzzle to be solved or kissed awake. The Princess Aurora has been awakened, he has moved on. There is nothing unknown about a girl whose curse is broken. She is just a girl after all.

"Aurora," he murmurs as he drifts off to sleep.

ço•cų

The prince explains: "We think auroras are caused by charged particles entering our atmosphere – this causes ionisation and the excitation of atmospheric constituents and that results in the optical emissions we see in the auroral zone of the atmosphere, which is between 10° and 20° from the geomagnetic poles of the earth, you understand." The empty words force themselves into my mind, tumbling over green, misty memories of the tightness in my chest and her gentle silence. He does not know her like I know her. I glimpse the bewitched sky over his shoulder and let my gaze go hazy. He kisses my forehead with a bemused smile at my seeming confusion and moves away.

ço•cų

And what of me, then? The lights shine into my wide-open eyes but I am still sleeping. As I watch the auroras move and change, the night sky a canvas for an enchanted painting, I think: perhaps I too can move with the stars, fading into a memory almost before anyone realizes I've ever been here. I am still unexplainable to myself. Look how my fingers remember how to trace the magic in sharp things, how my legs can run again. Watch me dance with my sister-self in the sky, unenchanted or not. Together with the glittering void I will break this new curse and shine again like a luminous mystery in the darkness.

ço•cų

At night we whisper together about our plans, the aurora and I. It won't be long now. Every day I feel myself becoming more and more a part of her, a part again of a magic that science cannot fully understand. Perhaps this is the only fate for victims of curses, blessed with knowledge no earth-bound creature should have. One day my prince will awaken and I will be gone, a girl he can't quite remember who left only the marks of her bare feet in the snow. The aurora will kiss my eyes and I will dream again at last.

A is for Aurora

Milo James Fowler

"IT'S time," Hank grunted at the helm of the *Effervescent Magnitude* as the gorgeous star cruiser hurtled through deep space.

"Already?" Captain Bartholomew Quasar's brow wrinkled. He glanced at his favorite Carpethrian helmsman who didn't resemble a man at all. Hank looked more like a drunk orangutan or an overweight sloth suffering from irritable bowel syndrome. "Didn't we make a stop six months ago?"

Hank turned in his swivel chair. "In Earth time, yes sir. But Carpethria's years are much shorter."

"So it's been over a year since your last..." Quasar cleared his throat, leaning back in his deluxe-model captain's chair. "Mating season?"

Bill snickered.

"What are you doing on the bridge, Bill?" Quasar snapped.

"Uh..." The goofy smile dropped from Bill's face.

"Go back to engineering where you belong. Seriously. Whoever heard of a ship's engineer hanging around the bridge all day and snickering at inappropriate moments. Go on, get out of here, or I'll demote you back to janitor!"

Hanging his head, Bill left the bridge.

"The same goes for anybody else within earshot." Captain Quasar's steely-eyed gaze swept across his bridge crew. They stared back at him silently. "This is no laughing matter. Our dear helmsman must return to his home world, and we'll make sure he gets there. Or...he will, rather. He is our helmsman, after all."

"Captain."

Startled, Quasar drew back from his first officer who had a habit of appearing at his elbow without warning.

"Yes, Commander?"

"Permission to speak freely, sir."

"Always." He gave her a dashing smile which, as usual, did nothing to alleviate the stoic expression on her almond-eyed, olive-toned features. Perhaps someday she would appreciate his blond, blue-eyed charm. Opposites were said to attract, after all.

"Sir, we cannot continue to reverse course every six months." She kept her voice low. "There is a galaxy out there for us to explore, and we can't do that if we're tethered by this Carpethrian's...*needs*."

"Humph," said Hank. Like most Carpethrians, he had exceptional hearing—despite the fact that both his ears were hidden beneath copious amounts of shaggy fur.

"What do you suggest, then?" Quasar lowered his voice as well. "That we ignore his reproductive cycle? He's apt to become surly."

"I doubt we would really notice a difference, sir."

"Humph."

"Perhaps we should continue this discussion in the conference room, Commander." Before Quasar and Wan could excuse themselves from the bridge, the intercom button on the captain's armrest lit up. Quasar punched it with a thumb. "Yes?"

"Bill here," said the ship's engineer. "Just wanted to let you know I made it safely down to the engineering deck. Didn't want you to worry about me or anything."

Quasar palmed his forehead.

"Oh, and one other thing," Bill continued. "The reactor could really use a tune-up. So if we're already headed to Carpethria anyway, maybe we could have them take a look at it. You know, since they're the ones who installed it and everything."

Quasar raised an eyebrow at Commander Wan. She hesitated before giving him a slow nod, the resignation in her eyes clear to see.

"Set a course to your home world, Hank ol' buddy," Quasar

ordered.

"Yes sir." With something akin to a spring in his movements, Hank swept his four very hairy arms across the helm console, setting coordinates for Carpethria.

"Captain," Wan said, "if this is their annual mating season, wouldn't it stand to reason the Carpethrian engineers would be...otherwise occupied? Unable to work on our ship's reactor?"

"We'll make it a quickie." Quasar gave her a wink. "In and out. Wham-bam, thank you alien friends. Won't keep them long at all. And I'm sure Hank won't keep us docked longer than necessary while he fulfills his duties. Providing for the continuation of his species. Progeny, and whatnot. Didn't take him long last time, from what I recall."

"Humph."

Quasar's intercom lit up again. "Really, Bill?"

"Uh—about the reactor, Captain..." Bill cleared his throat. "It might need maintenance a little sooner than I thought."

Crimson warning lights flashed along the perimeter of the bridge as the ship screeched and shuddered to an abrupt halt. Quasar pounded his armrest with a fist.

"Maybe if you spent more of your time in *engineering*—!"

"I think I can fix it," Bill replied as languidly as ever. "Just might take us a bit. To sort things out, you know. Get the ship *ship*-shape." He snickered at his little pun.

"How long?" Quasar glanced at Hank. The Carpethrian gripped his console, staring into the void of space via the ship's main viewscreen.

"No more than a day or two."

"Get on it." Quasar leapt from his deluxe-model captain's chair. "Hank, you're with me."

"Captain?" Wan and Hank said in unison.

"You have the bridge, Number Wan," Quasar said with another wink. She pressed her lips into a firm line at the ridiculous moniker. "Hank and I are taking a little trip."

"Where, sir?" Hank lumbered after the captain.

"To Carpethria, of course."

"But the reactor—"

"We'll take a transport pod."

"Captain." Commander Wan stepped forward with a hand on his chair. "It will take you nearly two days to reach Carpethria.

By the time the reactor is up and running again—"

"We'll already be there." Quasar flashed a winning smile. "Beats sitting around here for forty-eight hours, eh Hank?"

The Carpethrian shrugged his superior set of shoulders noncommittally, but his movements were quicker than usual.

"Have a transport pod ready and waiting for us, Commander," Quasar said. "There's not a minute to waste."

❧

Hank was not one to express his feelings verbally—besides the occasional *humph*—so it came as no surprise when the Carpethrian failed to thank Quasar while they drifted away from the *Magnitude*'s starboard launch bay in a cramped transport pod and set course for Carpethria at full impulse power. What did surprise the captain was when Hank cleared one of his throats, giving his voice an oddly harmonic quality, and muttered, "You didn't have to come along, sir."

"It's my pleasure. You think I'd rather be stuck dead in the water, so to speak? No thanks. These boots were made for walking." Quasar nodded toward his feet, propped up on his side of the navigation console, leaving all of the actual navigating to Hank. "Besides, I seem to recall that I rather enjoyed my last visit to your home world, and I—"

"I rigged the reactor, sir."

"Come again?" Quasar's boots dropped to the deck as he faced his helmsman.

"I was hoping you'd send me alone this time."

"You broke my ship?"

"I'm sorry, sir. But it had to be done. "

Quasar's mouth hung open. "Why?"

"I'm—uh...a little embarrassed about this."

This? What was this? Certainly the act of procreation itself could not be cause for the Carpethrian's shame. In the captain's experience, there was nothing more glorious in the galaxy than coitus—besides perhaps the Zerubular Nebula with a fresh halo of cosmic dust.

"I don't understand. I thought you'd managed to get busy every time we dropped you off for a little procreation recreation."

Hank grumbled into his fur.

"You do have a mate, I trust."

"Yes, sir."

"And offspring? Little fuzzy-wuzzies?"

"Two dozen, at last count."

Again, Quasar found his mouth hanging open. "Then what's the problem?"

"I'm not allowed to see them, because I do not serve aboard a Carpethrian vessel. Our young are not taught that humans exist until they are of age. To learn about you... hairless creatures... would terrify them. No offense."

"None taken. Speaking for myself, I'm not entirely hairless." Quasar drew himself up to his fullest height. "Well then, this isn't the mission I signed up for, but it appears your offspring are about to receive an early education. To Carpethria we go, my very hairy friend. With all haste!"

҆৯৶৶

Nearly two days later, during which time the captain had either dozed or recounted action-packed tales of his glory days as a United World soldier, Hank managed to steer the transport pod to its destination. The planet Carpethria was a giant hazel marble with a swirling misty atmosphere, its people xenophobic and uninterested in off-world affairs. Once upon a time, Carpethria had reached out into the void with a radio signal and found a planet, Earth, with the mineral resources they lacked and 'they'd been allies ever since. They weren't as close as brothers, though, more like standoffish second cousins.

"A true garden of Eden," Quasar mused as Hank took the transport pod down through the upper atmosphere. The fog eventually cleared to reveal breathtaking vistas of the planet's lush jungles, flora growing as large as it hadn't on Earth since prehistoric times. "I can't believe it's recovered so fast. When evil Emperor Zhan destroyed—"

"Sir?"

"Wait. Never mind." Quasar cringed sheepishly. "Alternate timeline." He cleared his throat. "Don't we have to hail them, announce our approach?"

"Unnecessary, Captain. Carpethrian freighter protocols will disguise our engine signature. We should be able to land without incident."

"Resourceful." Quasar appraised his helmsman. Obviously, Hank had put a lot of thought into this mission. "So let me see if I understand the situation. Every time we've carted you back here, it really had nothing to do with your mating season?"

"Correct."

"You were... just trying to visit your offspring?"

"Yes, Captain."

"Who stopped you?"

"Their mother, sir. She can be a... very formidable obstacle."

"I see." He didn't. From personal experience, Captain Quasar knew Hank to be quite the formidable adversary himself. Every Carpethrian was trained in the art of hand-to-hand-to-hand-to-hand combat, and Hank excelled at the use of blades as well as pulse weapons. Even unarmed, his surly presence was enough to grant him a wide berth aboard the *Effervescent Magnitude*.

"Perhaps it would be best if you..." Hank weighed his words as he maneuvered them toward a sheer cliff strung with rope-like vines. "Stayed on board, sir."

"I'll do no such thing. If it's my fault you can't see your own babies, then I'll be the one to set things straight with their mother. What's her name, by the way? *Mrs.* Hank?" Quasar chuckled to himself.

The truth was, *Hank* wasn't even Hank's name. The captain's translation device, sewn into the collar of his uniform, was the best Earth had to offer, but it hadn't experienced enough alien dialects firsthand to be without error. Its syntax and semantics were still limited by the sum total of Earth's human languages, and the Carpethrian tongue seemed to be made up entirely of Neanderthal-like monosyllables and deep-throated noises most humans would deem impolite, if not impossible to emulate. So *Mrs. Hank*'s name was translated as:

"Shank," Hank muttered.

"Very well. I will have a conversation with Mrs. Shank and convince her it is in the best interest of her two-dozen-or-so young that they be allowed to meet their father. She will see reason, of course." Quasar glanced over at Hank, whose posture was more hunched-over than usual. "If you don't mind my asking, why is it that *hairless* creatures such as myself would inspire fear in Carpethrian youngsters?"

"If my people fear anything, it's baldness."

Quasar laughed out loud and slapped his knee before he realized Hank wasn't kidding.

The transport pod banked as it approached a cave hollowed into the cliff-face. Quasar gripped his armrests and cracked one eye open as Hank steered them straight for it.

"Done this before, I take it?"

Hank nodded, all four of his hands moving across the console, managing thrust, yaw, and pitch. The pod floated deep into the black cave without incident and touched down, thrumming as Hank powered off the engine.

"Well done." Quasar wiped the perspiration off his palms. "Hold on now." He frowned as Hank retrieved a pulse pistol from the emergency compartment and tucked it into the middle of his fur flab. "We're not expecting that sort of trouble, are we?"

"You brought yours?"

"Always." Quasar tapped the Cody 52 Special holstered at his side. "But—"

"Just a precaution." Hank heaved himself out of his seat and lumbered toward the ladder. With the ease of a lanky primate, he hauled his girth up the rungs and popped the roof hatch.

Quasar stayed close behind. The last thing he wanted was to be locked inside. Would Hank do such a thing? Quasar didn't think so, but he wouldn't have thought Hank capable of breaking his ship, either. Anything, it seemed, was possible. "Who goes there?" roared a husky voice that echoed throughout the impenetrable darkness. "I didn't order anything! You better not be one of those cave-to-cave salesmen. I'll kick your ass off the cliff!"

"Afternoon, Shank," said Hank, dropping from the pod and landing on his feet.

"You again?" she snorted. "Didn't get the hint last time? Thought I made myself crystal clear."

Quasar squinted, peering into the darkness, but he couldn't make out her form. The exterior light at the mouth of the cave was useless this far inside.

"How *dare* you bring *that* here?" she bellowed.

"Hello." Quasar raised a hand and smiled, assuming she referred to him. But in the dark, his dashing display of pearly whites went unnoticed.

"What is the meaning of this?" Shank demanded. "Have you completely lost what's left of your mind? First you abandon your people to serve aboard a human vessel, you disappear for years, then you return and think all will be forgiven!"

"Perhaps we can shed a little light on the situation." Quasar leaned through the transport pod's open hatch and gave a voice command for the vessel's external lights to come online. When they did, the darkness scattered, hovering only in shadows at the far corners. There stood Shank, just as hairy and short as Hank, but with at least half a dozen blind young clinging to her chest, squirming as they rooted for her breasts. It took some doing to find the nipples amongst so much fur, but they managed it with admirable aplomb.

"What are *you* looking at?" Shank snarled.

"Uh..." Quasar blinked. "There you go, ol' buddy. Your little rascals. How about you say hello, pat them on the heads, and we'll be on our way?"

Hank stood within arms' reach of his mate. At first glance, they looked identical—except for the nursing youngsters adding more girth to Shank's torso.

"I don't have much time," he grunted. "This is my last chance."

"If imprinting was so important to you, then you wouldn't have left us. You want them to know who their father is? You should've stayed here where you belong!"

"I have a job to do. They need me."

"And we don't? You've really got your priorities straight," she sneered.

"So, where are the other little guys?" Quasar dropped from the pod and clapped his hands together. "Can't wait to meet them."

Shank wrapped all four of her arms around her young sucklings, shielding them protectively . "Get back into your vessel, *human*."

Quasar attempted another dashing smile now that the lights were on. It still had no effect.

"Listen," he said. "I can see you're unhappy with Hank, and you have every right to be. Absentee fathers are the scum of the universe, of course. No offense." He patted Hank on his right superior shoulder.

"Humph."

"I take full responsibility for taking Hank off-world. Once upon a time, you see, my star cruiser, the *Effervescent Magnitude*, was docked at your illustrious shipyards while your esteemed engineers installed a cold fusion near-lightspeed reactor. More trouble than it was worth, truth be told, but that's beside the point. What matters is that we were set upon by Arachnoid bounty hunters, and Hank—"

"Shut your hairless mouth," Shank snapped. "He decided to remain aboard your ship. Nobody forced him to. But he can't have it both ways." She backed up a step. "Hank's had four years to change his mind, but now it's too late. They'll never know who their true father is. They'll only know who I say he is."

"Lank?" Hank grunted.

"Who?" Quasar stage-whispered.

"My cousin. Always had a thing for Shank."

"If he's the first male they see when they open their eyes…so be it," she said. She chuckled a swarthy chuckle. "Course, he's got only one eye to look back at them with, but at least it'll be an eye that's here where it should be. Not gallivanting around the universe with a bunch of furless freaks!"

On that note, Shank lumbered away, deeper into the cave's dark recesses. Quasar gave his clean-shaven chin a pensive caress as he watched her disappear from sight.

"Pleasant female. I assume she lives around here in some sort of cave dwelling. Honestly, I imagined your people swinging from the trees, ol' buddy."

"Some do." Hank grunted. He turned and started climbing up the side of the transport pod.

"Hey—where do you think you're going?"

"She's made up her mind. Lank will be their father. There's nothing for me here now."

On the one hand, Captain Quasar was elated by this news. No more trips to Carpethria every six months! But on the other hand, quitting had never been in his vocabulary, and he expected the same degree of tenacity from every member of his bridge crew.

"You're not going back empty-handed!" Quasar reached up and grabbed a fistful of the Carpethrian's fur.

"Please let go of me, Captain."

Quasar gave his solid helmsman a few tugs, but Hank remained stolid.

"Fine. You won't make things right? I will."

Quasar charged into the shadows and tripped over a fuzzy lump on the ground. It squeaked as he went sprawling and cursing across the rock floor. Where he landed, catching himself with outstretched hands, two other fuzzy lumps waited, squealing as he collapsed on top of them. What were these things? He tentatively picked up one the size of a boot, and it squirmed like a very hairy slug injected with a healthy dose of adrenaline.

"Gah!" he cried as a pair of eyes opened in the fur and glinted with the transport pod's light. They stared up at the captain warmly like black oil marbles. "Oh no..." The fuzzy creature suddenly relaxed, nestling in his arms and purring contentedly. "No, no, no..." Quasar fought for breath. "Uh—Hank?"

"Yes, Captain?" the Carpethrian grunted from outside the pod.

"I think I may have stumbled upon...something."

"Yes, Captain." What sounded like a chuckle came from the Carpethrian. But Quasar couldn't be sure. He'd never heard Hank chuckle before.

Cradling the fuzzy baby in one arm, Quasar made his way back to the pod, careful not to step on any other babies squirming across the cave floor. There were quite a few, all headed straight toward Hank. The Carpethrian sat with four or five of his young ones crawling all over him, their eyes open, staring at him and grinning with rows of miniature fangs. Hank smiled back—something Quasar had never seen him do—baring his own vicious fangs and laughing deep in his flabby belly.

"Look at them, Captain. Aren't they adorable?"

Quasar frowned down at the one he carried and held it behind his back. "Uh-yes, they sure are. Where the heck did they come from?"

"Must've been napping nearby. Shank probably woke them up with all her caterwauling." Hank looked as close to giddy as any Carpethrian had ever looked. "You're mine. And you're mine." He gathered two in one arm. "And you're mine. And you're mine." He gathered the rest.

"How did they know?"

"Sir?"

"That you're their father?"

Hank shrugged his superior set of shoulders. "Guess they were just drawn to me. And I happened to be the first male they saw when their eyes opened, so now there's no going back."

"Right." Quasar swallowed. "About that…"

"Get back here, you little ingrates!" Shank bellowed from the dark.

With ear-piercing squeaks, the babies squirmed free of Hank's grasp and migrated toward the voice of their irate mother. Even the one in Quasar's arm managed to lurch free, hitting the cave floor and wriggling out of sight into the shadows. Hank stood and waved with all four hands as he watched them go, his ferocious smile fading. Quasar joined him at the transport pod.

"They'll know me now," Hank said quietly. "This bunch will remember I'm their father. Lank won't have them all."

Quasar couldn't help but wonder about the little one that had imprinted on him. Would the poor fellow shave himself bald when he grew up? Be a laughing stock? Or worse: an outcast?

"You all right, Captain? You look ill."

"There's something you should know—"

"Captain," came the sudden voice of Commander Wan via the communication device sewn into his collar.

"Yes, Commander?" He tried not to sound startled.

"We're in orbit, sir. Bill wants you to know the reactor is fully operational again, and that he believes the malfunction was due to sabotage. He has submitted a formal request to be allowed to deal with the culprit in any way he sees fit."

"Request denied." Quasar sighed and squeezed his brow. "Inform Bill that he can look forward to a week of janitorial duties for making such a stupid request."

"Yes, sir. We look forward to your return."

"On our way," Quasar signed off. He turned to his loyal helmsman. "Sure you don't want to stay?"

"With Shank? No thanks." Hank hauled himself up the side of the transport pod and dropped in through the roof hatch.

Captain Quasar turned to follow suit, but something made him look over his shoulder as if he were leaving a part of himself behind. But no, that wasn't the case at all. The fuzzy

Carpethrian baby he'd nearly squished to death—such a warm little ball of fur... It would be raised by Carpethrian parents on its home world, not by a hairless human aboard a star cruiser. Quasar chided himself for even considering the prospect.

But as he climbed into the transport pod and sealed the hatch shut behind him, he knew he'd be returning to Carpethria again at some point. Probably not to escort Hank for a conjugal visit. Perhaps not to have the Effervescent Magnitude's cold fusion near-lightspeed reactor serviced. Instead, maybe someday he'd walk into a Carpethrian city crowded with identical, very hairy four-armed creatures, and one of them would walk up to him, wrap him in a tight, furry embrace... and call him *Dad*.

B is for Babies

C.S. MacCath

"THREE nights, maybe less," I told the man—a grandchild clinging to his neck, another clutching a trouser leg—and watched his mouth fall slack with fear. "And we can only make ten trips up the mountain a day, for people and supplies both, so the Qandunar warmaster wants you to run, if you can." The terrified silence of the crowd broke like window glass, and a torrent of questions began to pour through. I gripped the folds of my robe, novitiate green, and wished for the authority of white. "There's a ferry at the river mouth that can take you across to the islands—"

"The Vele can swim!" This from the pot-bellied farmer who supplied our potatoes. Andu... Ando... I had only met the man a few weeks ago. Nervous hands twisted the reins of the gelding beneath him.

"Yes, but the Muto Vele cannot," I assured him. "They forget everything but violence when the Muto Qeyunar fixate them into mounts. Andro, take your horse and go. Don't leave him to wander in the place this valley is about to become."

A middle-aged woman stepped onto the lip of the lift, and it rocked into the cliffside with a crunch. A speckled chicken clucked from the crook of her arm. She kissed the crimson comb of its head once, twice and declared, "Henny hates to see people fight." Her tunic and trousers, too fine for the fetor of her flesh and the cluster of lice in her bushy red hair, were streaked with

22

greasy bird droppings. "Something happens inside, and she can't control it."

"Why does *she* get to go up first?" A pregnant woman pointed her belly at the lift as if to assert her claim to a place aboard. "We've got little ones and old peo—"

"What would a skinny boy like you know about them mutated cats? You ever even seen one?" Andro interrupted again, his voice cracking over the questions. The gelding whinnied and shied.

This was authority—and shame—I possessed in abundance, and they could only be wielded together. With a shrug, the heavy sleeves of my robe fell to the sash at my waist. Andro twitched his hands in prayer, and a few in the crowd cried out, but the middle-aged woman spread her fingers and traced the trenches of blackened scar across my chest from shoulder to hip.

"Muto Vele claws are sharp," she murmured, her touch warm and unflinching. "They cut through everything... like a folded blade." Her gaze followed the sheer face of the mountain into the low-hanging clouds. "We might not be safe up there." She sighed, vaulted past me and settled, her back to the cliff. A chilly breeze lifted a swirl of autumn leaves into the air. I shuddered, remembering agony, and slipped back into my sleeves.

"Because she's ill," I replied to the pregnant woman, who accepted my judgment and climbed aboard with an elderly man, paper-frail. "Those of you seeking refuge should organize, peaceably, if possible. Should we be forced to bring any Qandunar down with us, there will be fewer places for refugees going back." I closed my eyes and sought the naré of the leaves, so powerful now at the peak of their transition, and joined them in the greater flow of impermanence. From that place, my hands lifted in the mudras of transmutation and protection, clearing the valley of minor perils for a time. "I give you change." The sacred words were a whisper, but then I announced, "You have my oath as a Qeyunar novitiate that we will take everyone we can."

I pulled the return cord and knew a bell was sounding far above, on the plateau. The lift began to rise in a slow, jerky sway. Soon it was easier to see the pillars of the mountain range; great statues rising above a winding ribbon of river that flowed toward the ocean, a two-day walk in decent weather. Some of the refugees were already setting out upon that journey, not enough, but perhaps more would follow. I was a refugee myself; sole survivor of the southern Muto Qandunar attacks. There my teachers, friends and neighbors had been butchered at the behest of Muto Qeyunar who courted immortality in the corruption of impermanence. I could still smell the iron tang of blood on people and beasts who never ate, never slept, and I marveled again at the blessed burst of naré that had blown a mammoth Muto Vele off my body and into the lake, where she had sunk unblinking, unbreathing to the bottom. My flesh had never mended, would always be a reminder of her claws, so cold they burned. A trembling hand went to my chest. *Abomination.*

"Wounded monk, what are you called?" the middle-aged woman asked me.

I returned from my inner darkness to find her watching me with amber eyes that had no shields. "Sama. Dareo." I gave her my birth name and the name of my home monastery, now destroyed. "And you, my lady?"

She smiled at that, a wry twist of the lips for such a fragile face. "Henny says my old name has a bad taste, so I don't speak it anymore. Call me anything you want."

The clink and turn of the lift crank was audible now, and there was a trace of wood smoke on the air. I scratched the stubble of my shaven head, remembering her lice. "Naming is becoming," I replied, equivocating. "What would you become?"

We passed through clouds. A heavy mist blanketed our clothes. The wood smoke was stronger now, intermingled with the smell of cooking food. We would struggle to feed our guests if the stores could not be made to stretch. Many monastics were already going without, offering their meals to the temple Vele and the Qandunar camped on the plateau. My stomach growled.

"Rain." She brushed a drop of water from my brow. Her palm settled on my cheek, and for a moment, I felt whole as I had not in many months. "It washes everything clean."

The lift rattled into its frame at the top of the mountain. A hawkish lieutenant straightened from his efforts at the crank. Sweat glistened on his rank and decorations—tattooed in elaborate glyphs across his scalp—the reason all Qandunar warriors shaved their heads. Newly promoted to second-in-command, adept at containing and wielding naré in battle, wounded defending his brothers and sisters in arms. I wondered where his blackened scars were hidden.

He helped the other passengers disembark and turned to Rain. A bead of saliva glistened in the corner of his mouth. "Meat for the pot!" He reached for the chicken with both hands. "You'll be a popular woman tonight."

"Henny isn't food!" She flung out an arm and pushed the lieutenant away. "Leave her alone."

"You don't understand." I slipped between them and sought the words to explain. "The chicken is—"

"She says the hard things." Rain was balanced on the far edge of the lift now, feet wide, heels hanging in the air. "Please don't make me defend her."

The lieutenant crossed his arms and glared at me, gray eyes glinting. "Defend her?" He spat on the ground. "She serious?"

"She's ill," I said a second time and held out a hand to Rain, who ignored it. I had expected him to soften at that, but instead his features hardened into malice. *There they are*, I thought. *The scars. Black as mine.*

"Sick or not," he sneered, "we run out of food up here, she'll be speaking for herself." He jerked his head at the temple. "Warmaster sent me to fetch you. Wants a report on the refugee situation. Follow me."

Another warrior took his place and bent like a willow to the crank. The lift descended. Long shadows draped across a scatter of Qandunar tents as the world turned away from the sun into twilight. Behind them, the great stones of Banth Monastery clustered tall and wide, stretching from east to west on the far lip of the plateau. Rain followed us down the cobbled path to the heavy doors and then inside, where monastics, warriors and the first of the refugees were gathering like restive birds in the crown of a tree. Evening light shone through patterned glass windows onto the holy fountain; a naré-blessed erosion of water over the cornerstone, a reminder that all things change. Mother Anyamé stood with Warmaster Inu on the dais, her inspiriting strength evident in the roll of her broad shoulders and the lilt of her vowels. White sleeves trailed her sun-darkened hands as she gestured, communicating instructions to my brothers and sisters.

"You've returned," she remarked as I took my place among them. "Tell us what you saw down in the valley."

I did, and the warmaster's angular face lengthened in a frown. He was a tall, lanky man who carried power lightly, and his Qandunar clearly loved him for it. A mosaic of tattoos covered his scalp; so many the glyphs overlapped into complex signs. He rested sinewy hands on the hilts of the isché blades at his hips and rocked, heel to toe, until I was finished. "You did well," he offered, "encouraging them to organize without us. How many were leaving for the ferry when you came up?"

"Ten, maybe a dozen. Not enough." A shadow of worry cooled the warmth of his praise, and my scars ached with the chill. "I'm afraid for them."

"So am I," he admitted. "Those the Muto Qeyunar don't fixate, the Muto Qandunar kill."

"Or give to their mounts." I gasped as a memory overtook me; a bestial scream, loud and savage, ivory fangs shredding the front of my robe, the roar of a rider in blood lust. Pain. Pain. "We need to make certain..." I fought for control, "...certain *everyone* is out of their reach by the time they arrive."

"I *said* we might not be safe up here." Rain spoke into the fretful silence that followed. Henny squawked and pecked at her arm. I cringed, the memory fading, and wished they would just be quiet. "At Geriahar they climbed a mountain just like this one; the Muto Vele dug their claws right into the stone." She swallowed hard and kissed the comb of the chicken's head once, twice, her breath coming in short gasps. "Henny says there was blood and flesh, bits of my people in the waterfall for days. Henny says..." Her body curled around the bird's, and her eyes unfocused. "I'm the one who should be in the waterfall."

The warmaster dropped a knee to the dais floor and rested an elbow on the other. "I'm so sorry." It was said he could see all the way into his Qandunar, find and loose the inner chains that left them prone to Muto Qeyunar fixation. He was looking at Rain now. "I heard about that battle, but I thought all the Geriahari had either been fixated or killed."

Rain scratched her head, flicked a louse from her fingernail and looked back at him, perplexed. "They were." Her eyes widened. "Do you have any lard? The monastics could bless it, like your weapons, and then you could pour it over the..." She paused, frowning. "Never mind. You probably don't have enough."

The hawkish lieutenant laughed; a vicious punctuation of the conversation between them. "Completely out of her cave! Nearly threw herself off the lift for the sake of that chicken." Another warrior joined him, and another, and another until at least half of the Qandunar company was casting its fear at Rain and hoping she would carry it. "Fat's for cooking, you shit-covered brick, just like that chicken you've got. How about we—"

"Lieutenant Nereyu." Warmaster Inu spoke the name as if it were a command. "All of you, enough." He rose and dusted his hands, eyes lingering on Rain, brow furrowed in thought. "You're dismissed to your duties among the monastics. We'll meet here again at sunrise." He turned to follow Mother Anyamé off the dais, and the crowd dispersed.

The master of kitchen compelled me to eat that evening, having seen me take my bowl to the Vele before, but I managed to conceal half a biscuit and a bit of ham in my robe. I went to them late, after the Qandunar camp had quieted and the monastics had gone to bed. Through the gathering chamber, past the fountain, down the long hall and into the open-sky courtyard where they ate, slept and sunned themselves. It was a familiar path, one I often walked in darkness.

I smelled the Vele before I saw them; the great cat musk of their bodies intermingled with the subtle urine and feces odor of a well-scrubbed place inhabited by beasts. Moonlight gleamed on the center pool, and my eyes adjusted to it, seeking the outline of a blind youth missing one of her six legs. The Muto Qeyunar twisted these majestic and intelligent omnivores into grotesqueries of their former selves; lengthening fangs and claws into adamantine weapons, thickening muscle and fur, deferring the damage of injuries inflicted upon their bodies. But they could not entirely stem the tide of naré the Qandunar wielded. Always, the warriors tried not to kill, but when they were able to pierce the perversion of stasis forced upon the cats, the liberated Muto Vele suffered all the blows they had ever received in a single, excruciating instant. Many died. Those who did not were taken to Qeyunar monasteries, where they were given shelter. The same was true of the Muto Qandunar who came to us liberated. Some became monastics. Others were simply fortunate to survive what had been done to them.

She was lying in her usual place on a wide, flat stone directly beneath the moon. The soft gray and umber striations of her fur fell in a sigh, and the cavern of her pink mouth closed around a yawn. "Alalleah, limping girl, it's me," I whispered. "I've brought you a treat." Her head lifted, and the hollow slits of her eye sockets pointed in my direction. She sniffed, rose, followed her nose toward my outstretched hand and lifted the ham and biscuit with a warm tongue, teeth never touching my palm. Then she sat, front leg tucked beneath her body, middle and back legs bent in a squat and rubbed her long whiskers across my shoulder. "Good to see you too," I murmured, smiling, and curled down into her warmth. Sometimes I spent the night this way with the being who had smelled, tasted, understood my blackened scars, whose claws never extended in my presence, who was a better counselor than many people I knew. Her deep, rumbling purr vibrated the tension out of my body, and soon I was asleep.

In the early hours of morning, I woke to a sound I could not identify. The sky was brightening from black to indigo, but the Sufeli had not yet begun to warble. I heard it again and lifted onto an elbow to find Nereyu sitting cross-legged in deep shadow, arms draped over his head as if to protect it. He was shaking so hard I feared he might be ill, but then a small, agonized moan pierced the air like a splinter of wood. A heavily-scarred Vele reclined beside him, wide paw pressing against his greave to offer comfort. *Well*, I thought, *Mazhewa knows about pain, better than many.* I watched for a moment from behind Alalleah's bulk, wondering if I should intercede.

Then, on the other side of the courtyard, I noticed the flash of a hand in a sequence of mudras. It was Rain, fingers gesturing, lips moving, body straining as if she might rise and run to embrace him. *A desert prayer of integration, perhaps from Osovalia.* It was western, anyway, and one I had never used. *Interesting choice.* Reflexively, I slipped into the flow of impermanence and gathered the metamorphoses all around me; the brightening of the sky, the growth of algae in the pool, the digestion of my food and Alalleah's. The power of change rose in me like well water in a spring shower, and I transmuted it from a collection of disparate elements into a single mosaic of energy. This I gave to Rain as a monk might bless the good will of any laywoman, a trickle into a cup not trained to receive or make skillful use of it.

But she opened like a person accustomed to the blessing, so I poured out everything I had. She shaped the naré as well, clumsily, like too much bread dough in hands too small, but her Osovalian prayer was more than a gesture of good will now. A novitiate myself, I felt a momentary twinge of guilt at having given her so much until it struck me that Rain, the chicken woman, was behaving like a Qandunar and Qeyunar both; a vessel and the hand that filled it. Had she already been gathering and transmuting power when I noticed her? Perhaps a fully-trained monastic could have answered that question, but it was far beyond my ability. Our work was entangled now.

A final mudra sent the prayer across the stones to Nereyu, who was cursing under his breath in a choked voice. But when it touched him, he shot upright, startling old Mazhewa into a growl. The lieutenant scanned the courtyard with the practiced eyes of a warrior, found Rain and sprinted toward her. Quiet Henny sprang from her lap. A long hand closed around her throat and pinned her to the wall.

"How did you do that?" He leaned in, so close their noses were almost touching and spat tears into the woman's face. Henny squawked underfoot and pecked at Nereyu's boots in defense of her mistress. He kicked the chicken away, and Rain's eyes followed it, found mine, warned me with a subtle shake of her head to remain still. "How did you do that?" He demanded again, slamming her head into the stone.

"Henny says I was like you once, but I got lost," she replied gently, voice creaking under his grip, palms up in a gesture of peace. "She doesn't want you to go the way I did."

"You?" Nereyu's yip of laughter was derisive, desperate. "You're nothing like me." He sniffed, swallowed hard, bared his teeth. "Know what? I don't care how you did it. Try it again though, tell anybody what you saw here, and I feed your filthy carcass to the cats." He threw her to the ground and raised a booted foot above her breast. Rain waited for the blow, unblinking, eyes never leaving Nereyu's face until he cursed again, turned and ran from the courtyard.

I rose from Alalleah's side and rushed to hers. But she was already up, cradling Henny in her arms and soothing the agitated bird with a murmur of nonsense syllables.

"Rain?" I touched her shoulder with tentative fingertips, and she paused to look up at me. "Who *are* you?"

৵৽

"Don't know how she did it and don't care why, but it took me all night to bleed the corruption off, and I still don't feel clean." Nereyu was leaning against the rock wall beside the dais. "Needs to be locked up before she gets us all killed." His fellow Qandunar made angry noises of agreement. They could only wield the naré they received, and if it was corrupt, they grew vulnerable to the Muto Qeyunar.

"Is this true?" Mother Anyamé's mellifluous voice rose over the gathered warriors and monastics to address Rain, who stood nearby with Henny. "Did you violate Lieutenant Nereyu, perhaps because he mocked you yesterday? Do you understand how wrong that is?"

He had not been violated. My naré had comprised the greater part of that work. She had only shaped it with a prayer I recognized. The accusation was a lie, and Nereyu knew it.

His people need to trust him, and he needs to believe in their trust. Rain's admonition echoed in my thoughts, the only reply she had given to my question about her identity. *Please don't take that away from them, especially now.* I thought my teeth would grind to dust in my mouth.

"Henny says she's sorry for his pain." Her answer to Mother Anyamé's query was soft as a purple bruise.

Several Qandunar exclaimed in righteous indignation, but Warmaster Inu was more circumspect. "What were you doing with the Vele at that hour?" he asked Nereyu, but his eyes were on Rain again as they had been the night before, probing the fissures in her brokenness. For a moment she met his gaze, was transformed into someone else entirely. Then she turned away, kissed the comb of Henny's head once, twice and retreated into herself again. I gasped, and Inu looked at me, into me and nodded at the question he found there. Who was this woman?

Nereyu cleared his throat and shifted on his feet. "Felt sorry for the cats. Took some of my supper out to them."

We both tilted our heads toward him, disbelieving, and I bit my tongue on the word "liar." If Rain had not insisted upon silence for the sake of the battle to come, I would have already righted this wrong against her, against me.

Another memory came unbidden; a blood-soaked cooking apron, arms tight around the corpse of a comely girl, a screech of recrimination over a field of fallen monastics. *You should be dead, like them, like my daughter! What did the Muto do to you? Why did they let you live?* A sob of grief. *Abomination. Abomination!* I stared down at my trembling hands. What if Nereyu was telling the truth but it was I who had corrupted him? What if the icy claws of the Muto Vele had ruined me, made me ripe for some future fixation? "Mother Anyamé?" I croaked, and again, "Mother Anyamé?"

"...no place to put her," she was speaking to Warmaster Inu and had not heard me. "This isn't a prison."

"Could tie her up someplace until the battle is over." Nereyu spat a cuticle from his teeth and scrutinized the nail he had bitten it from. Anyamé recoiled at the suggestion, and Inu frowned as if he might give the lie to the lieutenant.

"I can take care of her." My mouth intruded upon the conversation before my mind could stop it. "She's only a sick woman, and whatever happened between them, I'm sure she didn't mean any harm."

Nereyu crossed his arms and looked away.

"A generous offer." Mother Anyamé smiled at me, and it was medicine. I wished she would offer it to a worthier person. "Are you certain?"

"Yes." I gulped a lungful of air. "She can work with me today." *And tell me who she is, and tell me if I poisoned her prayer last night.*

We departed ahead of the rest as the monastery grew suddenly quiet with hostility. *Those who defend an enemy risk becoming one.* They were Mother Anyamé's words, spoken just a few weeks ago, and I remembered them now as I watched the eyes of my fellow monastics darken with distrust. Outside, the air was pungent with the stink of human sweat, raucous with the babble of voices, heavy with a coming autumn rain. A number of Qandunar were directing refugees toward the center of the plateau while they re-camped around the perimeter, but it was slow and difficult work. There were children underfoot, sick and elderly people who needed aid, anxious fingers plucking at armored elbows to ask unanswerable questions. Everywhere, fear and hunger haunted faces. Some of my fellow novitiates were passing out water skins, measuring dried meat, fruit and grain into bowls, admonishing families that this was all the monastery had to offer. Around the horseshoe edge of the mountain, a number of elder brothers and sisters were blessing the fletching of arrows, the stringing of bows and the sharpening of swords. I had never seen the Qandunar in battle; they had come too late to save Dareo Monastery, but it was said they moved like a troupe of riotous dancers wielding quicksilver weapons that fought with a life of their own.

Rain drew me to the rocky edge of the cliff, where an updraft gathered her hair into itself, exposing a thick line of embedded grime at the back of her neck. "We don't need lard now," she asserted with some satisfaction. Henny defecated in the crook of her elbow, and she wiped it on the hem of her tunic. "If you'll gather and transmute naré for me, I'll tell the mountain to bless the rain when it comes. That way, when the Muto Vele try to climb, it will soften the fixation of their claws—"

"And make them fall. *That's* what you were talking about yesterday."

She nodded.

I thought of gentle Alalleah's missing leg and felt a pang of sorrow for the Muto Vele who would be liberated after that fall only to die in agony. It was a brilliant idea—if ruthless—and a reasonable working of naré for a pair of elder monastics, but we were a novitiate and a... "Rain, who are you, really?"

"Henny says you need to stop asking me that." Her voice abruptly thickened. She turned away, stared up at the darkening sky and blinked tears from her eyes. "Henny wants you to leave it alone."

"I-I'm sorry," I stammered, chagrined. "I should not have asked again."

"It's all right." She turned back. "Henny sa... that is, I'm just broken there, like your body is broken and Nereyu's heart is breaking." Rain tilted her head toward the chicken, who crooned and leaned up into the curve of her neck. "Get me some naré, wounded monk."

Wounded monk. Abomination. I reached out across the plateau with its many monastics, warriors and refugees; each of them in motion, each an agent of change. "I am one of you," I whispered but could not bring myself to believe it, and so my place in the flow of impermanence was imperfect, incomplete. Still, there was plenty of naré to hand for transmutation, and I gave it to Rain in a sensory rush of the straining voices, aching muscles and cooking food from whence it had come. She received it, clumsy as she had been the night before and sent it down the mountainside in a series of mudras. It was a powerful working, if patchy, and soon the great pillar of stone beneath the monastery was primed to change the rain that fell upon it.

I went from the cliffside empty, anxious and sick with hunger, Rain trailing behind me like a child. My eyes scanned the plateau for the mistress of novitiates, who would have work for us among the refugees, but she was nowhere to be seen. After a moment I stopped a brother novitiate with an armful of bandages to ask where I might find her, but he jerked away from me as if startled, mumbled something about the cellar and hurried on.

Suddenly, I felt the pressure of condemnation around us like a smothering weight. My fellow monastics were watching us while they worked, frowning at one another and turning away to converse in low voices. A few of my elder monks peered over the cliff to explore what we had done. When they rose, their faces were pinched, their postures rigid. It was then that I knew they all saw what I had not; the seed of corruption festering in my spirit. "We should go to the cellar," I murmured in a quavering voice, my thoughts racing toward a dark and frightening precipice, *and stay until the battle is over, and never touch naré again.*

"We're not done yet." Rain surveyed the plateau; legs apart, shoulders relaxed, strangely confident.

"Yes, we are." I threw up my hands and paced in front of her. A flash of lightning illuminated the clouds, and a thunderclap rolled over the mountaintop. "You're ill, by your own admission, and I..." My fingers went to the front of my robe and sought the furrows beneath the fabric. "What if Nereyu was right?"

"He wasn't."

"How would you know?" I stopped, rounded on her. "He might have been... It might have been *my* fault." The words escaped me in a hoarse whisper, and I swallowed around the lump they left in my throat.

"It wasn't." A specter of loss rose in the woman, lent sorrow and surety to her tone, aged her face. A long silence followed while she traveled the road of an old and painful memory. In time, Henny shifted in her arms, and she spoke again as if from a faraway place. "You're the only monastic I've got, Sama, so I need you to help me do this." She stepped around me with a purpose then, and it was my turn to follow like a child.

She led me around the camp in a spiral, a weaving needle threaded with the naré I gathered and transmuted for her. A blessed path fell away behind us from the subtle mudras she directed at the ground; designed to chivvy the battle away from the refugees, reinforced by every footfall that came into contact with it. Another heavy-handed working, it was all potency and no grace, and soon every person who stepped onto the path was unconsciously encouraged to remain outside the Qandunar perimeter.

A fall of tiny hailstones began to pepper the plateau as the disorderly camp devolved into chaos. New arrivals never found their way to the refugee tents. A befuddled tinker plodded around and around the Qandunar, dropping wares from an over-stuffed pack. Triplet toddlers fled a bedraggled woman and circled the cliff's edge, shrieking, as the hail gave way to rain. A disoriented archer stumbled into one of them, tripped and tossed a quiver full of arrows over the side.

Too soon, I realized, abashed. *We should have waited until everyone was settled.*

Rain strode toward the monastery doors, untroubled by the chaos. "I need a mirror, a handful of Vele fur and a bowl of ink."

"What you need is a bath." A nearby Qandunar glanced up from her isché and smirked.

"And a hot chicken dinner!" Her sparring partner waved a rain-spattered dagger at Henny.

"And a little one-on-one time with the lieutenant." A third blocked the path to the doors.

"Let's go." I pulled Rain away from him and into the lee of the building. "Enough of this," I hissed. "Whoever you are, you're not a Qeyunar nun, and even if I'm not corrupting my naré, I'm still just a novitiate. We don't know what we're doing here."

"You're right about that."

I jumped and turned to find Brother Empho towering over me, hands clasped behind his back, features set in somber rebuke. One of the monks who had scrutinized our mountainside work, he was a trusted veteran of many battles like the one before us. Flanking him were four Qandunar. Nereyu was among them, but while I expected he was there to press his punishment of Rain, we were only two of many threats demanding his attention. He watched us, watched the refugees, watched the weather with poorly-contained hypervigilance, and when his gaze fell upon the men and women under his command, the naked fear on his face was painful to observe. *He's getting worse*, I thought, and wondered how long it would take his people to notice.

"Come with me." Brother Empho spoke again and nudged me toward the doors. "Mother Anyamé should deal with this herself."

He led us to her private sanctuary, where she was blessing a young scout and his weapons. Eyes closed, hands palm-up at his belt, he was completing the litany all Qandunar recited as we filled the ample vessels of their spirits. It was in that moment I realized Rain had been a Qandunar, perhaps even a Muto Qandunar now liberated. How else was she able to contain so much naré? Why else would she refuse to speak of the path behind her?

The scout opened his eyes, and Warmaster Inu regarded him gravely. "Find out how many there are and when they'll arrive. Do not engage them under any circumstances, no matter what you see. Be back by midnight."

"Yes, sir. Thank you, Mother." He sketched a quick bow to them both and hurried from the room.

Afterward, Empho and Nereyu described our work by turns; the patchy shield around the mountain and the ring around the camp that had most everyone walking in circles. Inu regarded first the monk and then the warrior, eyes lingering on the fingernails Nereyu brought to his teeth again and again, sometimes mid-sentence. When they were finished, he glanced at Rain and tilted his head away in thought. She clucked at Henny—oblivious to his attention—and mined her pockets for a few kernels of lint-covered grain to feed the bird.

Warmaster Inu's indrawn breath, when it came, was subtle

as the lift of recognition in his brow. His gaze fell upon Rain again, and the expression on his face was profound, unrecognizable. He forestalled Mother Anyamé's response with a gesture. "It's all right. I know what they were trying to do. These are old defensive tactics poorly executed because they lack the skill. If you'll send a few senior monastics to finesse the work, I believe we'll find it helpful." Rain fell silent and raised her chin to stare at him, a question in the roundness of her eyes and the down-turned corners of her mouth, but his attention was on the lieutenant now. "Nereyu, come and speak with me a moment."

They retreated beyond a blossoming indoor garden to a quiet corner of the sanctuary. The remaining Qandunar departed, and Mother Anyamé sent Brother Empho back out with instructions. Momentarily forgotten, my curiosity got the better of my discretion, and I strained to hear the conversation between the warmaster and lieutenant.

"...losing warriors especially hard... under your command." Warmaster Inu leaned in, his face open with concern.

Nereyu clenched his fists. "...think I can lead?...faith in me?"

"...never wavered...all your strength and skill... Muto Qeyunar... insidious..."

"...out there somewhere, fixated...better if they were dead..."

"...come tomorrow... need us to liberate them." Inu's hands went to Nereyu's shoulders. "Don't lose yourself to this when they might need you most."

Nereyu's head fell in shame and sorrow. "Failed them once, already."

"Heard enough?" Mother Anyamé's question abruptly compelled my attention.

"Yes, Mother. I mean, n-no..." I stammered and blinked, heat rising in my cheeks.

"Excellent." She gestured at the open door. "Since you're such a good listener, and you've already tried your hand at defense, you can help me prepare for the battle blessing now." A tapered finger crooked in Rain's direction. "You too. Come along and let me see what you're capable of."

Brother Empho found us in the gathering chamber some hours later to report that our defensive work had been 'balanced' and to offer his mentorship should I ever decide to specialize in defense. I demurred and gave the credit to Rain, who merely smiled and returned it with a shrug. By then, the warriors and monastics were collecting around the great hearth opposite the fountain, where a crackling fire countered the chill of a steady rain. The refugees had been asked to remain outside during the battle blessing, and indeed the plateau was brimming with them, all crowded into lean-tos and canvas tents loaned them by the Qandunar. The latest to arrive had reported that all who wanted to flee were gone, and only a few able-bodied souls were left to ride up with the scout when he returned. They also reported the valley was growing pale and still, as if all the life it supported was bleeding away toward the south and the Muto Qeyunar who used it to maintain the deathlessness of their people and beasts.

I had seen the mummified landscapes they created; stone apples hanging forever from skeletal trees, glassy streams that tasted of dust, birds and squirrels callously leached and left to peck and chew at their unchanging bodies. It was the primary purpose of every Qeyunar monastic to prevent their Muto antagonists from usurping and mutating the power of change, but because we were the only people who could, the monasteries were targeted. Here, in the bright firelight and the company of these brave men and women, it was hard to accept that the Qandunar valued my life above theirs no matter what they thought of me personally. Harder still was the realization that most of the refugees felt the same way. Of course, they were counting on the mountain itself; its impenetrable stone and vertical rise to protect them. But I knew Mother Anyamé had no such illusion of safety. She had reminded me this afternoon that siege was a greater threat than battle, since we had to eat, and our enemies did not. In fact, Warmaster Inu was hoping for a fight; Muto Qeyunar conceit would mean a quick resolution to the conflict and not a long, slow decline into desperation.

Anyamé called the monastics to the foot of the dais with a triple strike of the gong behind it, and the warriors followed. The lines of her mouth drew down in sober gratitude, and her hands extended as if to touch the shaven heads of every Qandunar facing us. "Thank you for coming to the aid of our monastery and community. We know what you risk on our behalf, and more importantly, on behalf of all that changes. We can only promise in return to defend the natural flow of naré all the days of our lives, however many or few they may be."

It was true. Some of the warriors here would be dead or fixated tomorrow. Brother Empho's offer had freed me of the fear that I was corrupting the naré I worked with, but a mother's sob of grief still echoed in my mind, and I knew my life would never be worth what these people were about to pay for it.

"Let us begin." Mother Anyamé closed her eyes, stepped into the flow of impermanence and held it wide for the rest of the Qeyunar. Because the valley was depleted, we would be forced to venture farther for the naré the Qandunar needed. It was a hard thing to do that required a level of concentration we might not be able to replicate in battle, but neither might the fallen monastics, whose appetite for naré was so much larger.

I journeyed in and down. Below the mountain, lava traveled tunnels old as the world. Beyond the river, briny water weathered stone into glittering sand. These were the metamorphoses I gathered, gently, without disturbing the processes of change in those places. Meanwhile, I knew the senior monastics were tapping the roots of transformation; not the ripening of an apple but the blush of all fruit, not the waning of the day but the turn of every gloaming into night.

"I am a thimble, become a cup, become a bowl, become a lake, become an ocean, become the world." Warmaster Inu intoned, and the Qandunar joined him. "I am a thimble, become a cup, become a bowl, become a lake, become an ocean, become the world." The gathering chamber warmed with the heat of the deep earth, resounded with the crash of a high wave, sweetened with the fragrance of berries, purpled with twilight. Transmuted naré, vital and powerful flowed from Qeyunar to Qandunar in a cacophony of the senses. The warriors lifted their heads, closed their eyes and opened, opened, opened, their voices thick with ecstasy.

Rain stood apart from them near the hearth; palms up, chin high, chanting. She might have been any warrior out of uniform but for the chicken tucked under her arm. I withdrew from the blessing and watched the Qandunar brighten. Soon, the rest of the Qeyunar withdrew as well, and it was then that I caught the stink of decay on the air. A lingering part of the work, no doubt, but it was enough. My limbs weakened, my stomach spasmed with nausea, and the scars on my chest flared in agony. A dark memory overshadowed my weary mind. Putrid wounds blackening over bone, fevered dreams of a fixated warrior soaked in the blood of my abbot...

"Sama. Novitiate Sama." Someone was shaking me. I struck out, landed a blow and whimpered. "It's all right. You're all right." My robe fell open, and the chill of the chamber brought me back from that awful abyss. Eyes focusing, I caught a fading lambent gleam as the warrior in front of me absorbed the last of my gifted naré. His skin darkened to a natural color. It was Nereyu. He stood between me and the rest while I slouched against the dais, gasping. "Haven't seen a wound like that in a long time." He gestured at my scars, all soldier now, empathy and chagrin mingling on his face.

"I have," I countered, catching my breath and tightening my robe, too fatigued to dissemble. "In Rain and in you. I was there with the Vele last night. It was my n-naré—"

"What?" He peered over at Rain, incredulous, and gaped as her own skin darkened.

"I w-would have said something this morning, but she begged me not to." I rubbed a little warmth into my arms. "For your sake and for the people you lead."

Absently, he helped me to stand and took a step toward her. "How would she know—"

"Warmaster Inu!" The monastery doors creaked open, and the scout bolted inside. "...closer than we thought... in the valley now... almost here." He slid to a stop and propped his hands on his knees. "At least a hundred Muto Qandunar, all mounted, and twenty mounted Muto Qeyunar behind them."

"Twice our number." The lieutenant went to stand beside the warmaster. "Be a hard fight." He regarded Inu with a stony expression, but behind the stone I saw a man who grieved beyond all reason for the comrades he had lost, who anguished over the losses to come, who hid it all with a mask of mockery and contempt. "Hard to win."

The gathering chamber buzzed with apprehension. Warmaster Inu raised a hand to signal for silence, and in a moment only the crackle of logs in the hearth defied his command.

"Warmaster Zherinah." He looked toward the fire with that profound, unrecognizable expression on his face and spoke the name again. "Warmaster Zherinah." It was only when Rain cringed and kissed the comb of Henny's head that I realized he was speaking to her. "We need you."

"Henny was afraid you might." She kissed the comb again, walked from the hearth to where I stood and lifted the chicken into my arms. I stared at her back as she turned the ghosts in her eyes upon Inu and said, "I need a razor, a suit of armor and some weapons. Swords, if you can spare them. I was never good with a bow."

Warmaster Zherinah. Of course. Her easy balance on the lift, her capacity for naré, her fearlessness with Nereyu, these might belong to any Qandunar. But only a warmaster would know that much about arcane defense, would support the lieutenant's leadership in spite of his abuse, would so completely shoulder the blame for Geriahar. She stood beside Inu now, and they conversed as equals might while a mortified silence settled over the crowd.

Mother Anyamé clapped her hands to break it, brow arching in a high, sagacious curve. "To your tasks, people. There will be time enough for meditation after we win the coming battle."

I watched them all hasten away; some red-faced, others pausing as if they might speak to Rain before scurrying on, shoulders hunched. *Now you're ashamed*, I thought, seething with outrage. *Where was your compassion before you knew she was a warmaster? Wasn't she worthy of it then?* For a moment, my scars, Rain's ghosts and even Nereyu's veneer of contempt were more agreeable to me than this disgusting display of self-flagellation. At least our wounds were honest.

I sighed, a slow release of fury and fear. Not everyone had mocked her. Not everyone had shunned me. Mother Anyamé was wrong; we needed to meditate now, every single one of us before the enemy came to pick at our vulnerabilities. Monastics could not be fixated - a benefit of our training - but we could be seduced into joining the Muto Qeyunar, and we could gift corrupted naré to the Qandunar. I resolved to have the compassion I was presently seeking in others. It was the most powerful tool of change I possessed.

Rain lifted a filthy hand to Mother Anyamé's white sleeve and stopped just short of touching it. "Mother? I think you should know... I'm not a refugee."

"You came to stay with us." Anyamé took her hand and

smiled. "Your timing is terrible."

Rain tried to return the smile but could not. "The Qeyunar I knew before... they taught me some things, and there was a time I thought I might take the robe someday, but Henny thinks I'm too broken now."

"Brokenness is only a state of being, like any other. As long as you're still breathing, it can change."

"This is going to be so hard."

"For all of us." Mother Anyamé took Henny from my arms. "I'm making Novitiate Sama your personal aide until the battle begins. You're good for each other. Now if you'll excuse me, I'm going to lock your friend in my sanctuary and see to my own preparations."

Rain stiffened and stared after Henny until she was long gone.

Soon after, the Muto Vele began to climb.

०∞९

"They're coming." I leaned into the wall beside the hearth and crossed my arms. "I can feel them on the mountain." Far below, adamantine claws cracked stone, gained purchase, softened.

Razor to her scalp, Rain nicked the bold line of a campaign tattoo at her left ear. A mass of nit-infested hair fell to the floor.

I reached out with a booted foot and kicked it into the fire. "You feel it too."

She nodded. Nereyu himself had gone to fetch the things she had requested, returning with a set of clean clothes, a suit of leather armor, a pair of shining swords and his own shaving kit. She sat with it now, metal mirror propped on her crossed legs and ignored the occasional passerby who slowed to witness her transformation.

"Osovalia." Warmaster Inu was crouching beside her. He peered at the bleeding piece. "You captured a hundred Muto Qeyunar in the desert caverns there."

"They were fixating children, experimenting on them." Firelight gleamed on the blood, the blade, the hand that wielded it.

I shuddered, felt the Muto Vele slide and climb again, a little farther this time. Another mass of hair fell to the floor. It went with the first, into the fire.

She glanced at my boot and returned to her work. "Closer now. They smell like—"

"Sweet." I retched. "Too sweet."

Inu rose with a purpose and looked down at Rain. "Warmaster Zheri—"

"Don't call me that." The razor flashed again, revealing a ribbon of decorations from her forehead to her nape; Master Swordswoman, Master Vessel of Naré, Defensive Adept, Mark of Valor, Mark of Valor, Mark of Valor, Mark of Valor. Indeed, the layer of grime I thought I had seen beneath her hair was merely the lower edge of that work, finished by some clever artist into an interlocking border for her many combat glyphs.

"I don't have time to coddle you, and I need you to answer my questions." The warmaster's focus was needle-sharp on the woman beneath him, and yet it was plain he wanted to be with his Qandunar now, in these final hours before battle. "You were fixated at Geriahar. Am I right?"

Rain slid a thumb along the flat of the blade to clean it. "Henny sa—" She paused, hands dropping to her lap and stared into the flames. A moment later, she spoke again in a stricken voice. "I was exhausted, and I had already lost so many, but I couldn't let my Qandunar see me..." A long sigh caught in her throat like a sob. "I don't remember killing them; I only remember the waterfall. Fixation is like that."

"Here. Let me." I bent down, took the razor and continued the work, my fingers caressing her tattoos as if I might brush away the pain they represented.

Inu stepped closer to Rain, laid a hand on the dagger at his thigh and swept his gaze around the gathering chamber. It was empty and dark. Many who could sleep had gone to bed, while the rest were surely out at the cliff's edge, waiting.

"And now you need me to be that person again, but first you need to know if I can resist the Muto Qeyunar." There was an ominous surrender in her tone and in her body, as if the words themselves were leaving her open to attack.

A grim, conflicted sorrow seeped into the tension on his face. "I do."

I shaved the last of the hair from her scalp, tossed it into the fire and tightened my grip around the razor. *You dragged her into this*, I wanted to say. *You know how sick she is.* But instead, I drew a shaky breath and stood my ground, beside my friend.

"I don't know." Rain shrugged. "I can fight, but I can't lead." She looked up and lifted a hand to lay over his, as if to bless it. "And if I'm fixated again, I'll be very, very dangerous."

Inu drew a deep breath and squeezed her wrist. "Then be Rain. Fight with us, here, in the present, and leave Zherinah's ghosts at Geriahar." He plucked the razor from my grip and bent to slip it into the shaving kit. "You're a better man than you realize, Novitiate Sama," he remarked, and strode away toward the monastery doors.

ငှာ∾ၑ

When I was a little boy, I once watched a man skin a vixen for her fur. He clubbed her on the head with a stick, strung her up by the tail and began to peel the flesh from her feet with a slender knife. The fox was stunned but still alive, and she screamed as he worked; a gurgling shriek of agony that went on, unceasing, until she weakened into death. Perhaps this was the reason I forgave the temple Vele. It was that shriek I heard from a Muto Vele's mouth as she poised above my body, ready to strike.

And it was that shriek I heard all around me now as the Muto Vele staggered up the stone toward the plateau.

The morning was brittle-bright and cold. From atop the monastery roof I could see Rain on the right below, hands resting on the blessed isché blades at her hips, legs apart, listening. Sometimes we flinched together as the mounted Muto Qeyunar climbed, their indurate power congealing the slippery shield we had wrought. Directly ahead, Lieutenant Nereyu passed orders from the lift platform to the left and right of a refugee camp losing faith in the mountain. Mother Anyamé strode across the rooftop, leaned between a pair of Qandunar archers and looked down into the Vele courtyard. I knew she was waiting for the cats to be locked in the cellar, away from the chaos of battle where they might do harm to themselves and others. Satisfied, she signaled to Warmaster Inu, who shouted down the order to open the main doors. The refugees poured inside.

I could hear the Muto Qandunar singing now; a consonantal chant so like the brittle brightness of the morning that I wondered if a hammer-blow might shatter them both. A vowelly Qandunar chant rose up to confront it, and there was naré in the song. The chants clashed, intermingled. A shout rang out on the left below, and a volley of shining arrows followed it down the cliffside. Behind the Qeyunar on the roof, another volley defended the rear of the monastery at Inu's command.

Go with the refugees now, while you can, into the dormitories. My feet were stumbling toward the ladder before I realized the admonition had come from within. I stopped, fought to remain still. My memories fought back. A bestial scream, pain, a putrid wound, abomination. I gasped, a paroxysm gripping the blackened scars at my chest. *No. No.* I thought of Rain. I thought of Nereyu. *I will not be a victim before the fight even begins.* I backed up, gritted my teeth and closed my eyes.

When I opened them, there were Muto Vele on the plateau.

Bright, the long bones of their bared teeth and claws. Immense, the bulging muscles of their gray and umber shoulders. Jewelly, the slitted spheres of their eyes, big as fists. For a moment, I forgot my scars and wanted to be devoured by such a creature, to give it the worship of prey for the perfect predator. Who wouldn't want to be a Muto Qandunar, mounted on the back of a flawless killer, grinning in the rictus of fixation? And oh, behind the rictus there was joy, release, intoxication, absolution, an imperfect life traded for perfect deathlessness. The terrible gift of the Muto Qeyunar shone in their warriors; everlasting gratification so fierce it held their minds in stasis and their bodies intact against the vagaries of change. It united them, one and all. Fixated Qandunar, bald and tattooed. Young men and women culled from their villages. People so riddled with grief or guilt they would take any medicine to make it stop. Draped in the copper and black of their masters, the Muto Qandunar were forever glorious, and they would ruin anything, slaughter anyone only to shine, shine, shine, on, on. Beside them, the unmounted Qandunar looked so small and pale that I nearly wept for them as if they were already dead.

But they were not dead, and the Muto on the plateau were fewer than expected, thanks to Rain's work and mine. I could still feel them climbing, knew more were on the way, but for now the Qandunar had a momentary edge. On the left, an archer leaped onto the back of a Muto Vele behind his rider, and in a burst of naré that blinded like a sunrise, he drove an arrow into the woman's bare shoulder. The missile flashed, releasing its own reservoir of power, and she gasped as if waking from a nightmare. The perfection of her body withered into a broken back, a severed jaw, a skull dented as if by a fall from a great height. Even from the rooftop, I saw the agony in her eyes as she slid to the ground in death. The archer shot forward and drove a dagger into the beast's eye. Again, a burst of naré from the warrior and his weapon and again, a crippled body crumpling away from life. *Oblivion is liberation too*, I thought in sorrow, wondering how many Qandunar would grant that awful mercy today because of the advantage we had given them.

"Muto in the garden!" This from a marksman behind me at the lip of the right wall.

Warmaster Inu sent a handful of archers to hold them off and shouted over his shoulder at Mother Anyamé. "Both side doors are barred, correct?"

She confirmed with a nod and turned her attention back to the battlefield.

My gaze traveled down and right, seeking Rain in the fray. She was just outside the circle of naré around the refugee camp; head down, arms rigid at her sides, fists clenched.

Henny hates to see people fight.

A Muto Vele was closing in.

Something happens inside, and she can't control it.

Desperate to help, I stepped into the flow of impermanence, reached for the scattered naré on the plateau and flung the transmuted power at her in a mudra of awakening. Her head snapped up, and teeth gritted, face glistening with tears, she charged the beast.

The instant before they collided, she threw up a storm of naré that crackled with yesterday's weather and slid beneath his forepaws, isché drawn, to slice at his middle legs. Another blast of naré beneath his body and then she was behind the Muto Vele, on her feet and atop his back.

The Muto Qandunar there turned to engage the fight, but she was too quick. A final torrent of naré struck him full in the face as her blades found the meat of his thighs and discharged a bit of their blessing there. The beast beneath them bucked, roared and fell to his side. The man, a warrior himself, rolled away as he woke from fixation, bearing Rain to safety.

The Vele and his rider lifted their heads. They were hurt, but they had climbed the mountain without falling, and now they were free. A trio of archers raced to help them, and Rain rejoined the battle with a will.

"Muto in the courtyard!" Another marksman called from the left wall.

They were cresting the plateau in greater numbers, pushing the Qandunar back, butchering our defenders with a harrowing efficiency. There were boots and claws on the ring of naré around the refugee camp; I could feel them, but they never encroached on the circle of peace inside.

Nereyu seemed to be everywhere at once. He shouted orders, shielded warriors, directed the wounded into the temporary refuge I had helped to create. A dancer in combat, adapting from breath to breath, he poured the blessed water of change over the stone of those he fought.

Behind the Qeyunar on the roof, Inu was the wind and the weapon upon it. I had never seen such a fleet archer, never known so much naré to follow an arrow in flight, and yet he retained the presence of mind to command and communicate with the runner between himself and his lieutenant.

But it was making little difference. The tide of battle was turning, and not in our favor. There were simply too many.

Worse, the naré of the Qandunar was beginning to wane, and without it, they were defenseless. At a signal from Anyamé, we plunged into the flow of impermanence, but the Muto Qeyunar were already there in every place we sought; leaching all they touched, mutating the power of change to maintain themselves, their mounts and their warriors. There were only scraps of naré left in the wake of their coming. The valley below was a withered thing, the sky too static, the dead too cold.

Moments later, the Muto Qeyunar crested the mountain, and I despaired.

Peerless as a noonday sun. Exquisite as an elegy for a god. Sweet as spilled perfume over a corpse. They rode naked from the waist up, hair coiled in copper wire, shoulders and breasts painted black with blasphemous glyphs. Even the most ancient

46

among them was matchless, magnetic, so lovely my tongue itched to bathe the perfect skin of his feet. They rode with supple carriage, undulating as the Muto Vele moved while they surveyed the battlefield with eyes like twin moons. No rictus in the set of their lips, they were fully conscious of their beauty, their power. *We cannot die,* they said with their bodies, their faces, their antipathy. *Perhaps you may join us, if you are worthy.* And I wanted to, so much. The ruination of my body, the brokenness of my spirit might both be given purpose if only I heeded the wordless, triumphal summons that sounded in every fragment of my being.

Mother Anyamé signaled us again, her mellifluous voice a counterpoint to the seduction. The summons changed in timbre, grew disdainful. *Then give up the metamorphoses of your life.* I shuddered, found the flow of impermanence like a fumbling child, but Brother Empho was there to guide me in and out to the hollow-boned flight of Sufeli on a distant horizon. A Muto Qeyunar followed us there and plundered the beating of their wings until they plummeted from the sky, warbling with terror. Then she reached beyond the Sufeli to we who had only sipped at the gift of their naré.

Beside me, Brother Empho gasped and shielded my spirit's return as she tore at the flow of blood in his veins, the movement of air in his lungs, the spark of cognition across his mind. My eyes fluttered open in time to catch him as he fell and learn that he would never be my mentor.

Exhausted, I lowered him to the tiles and poured the dregs of naré I had recovered into Rain and Nereyu below. When I rose, there were Muto Vele cresting the roof.

"Into the monastery!" Warmaster Inu shouted at us. "Now! Go!"

A trickle of urine wetted my legs, but I gathered the courage to kneel and hold the ladder for everyone else. Below, the mounted Muto Qandunar gathered before their masters; a vicious wall of sword, claw and tooth. They took up the chant again, and shrieking as a single voice, the Muto Vele scattered the unmounted Qandunar in a shower of gore. Around the refugee camp and through a score of tents, Nereyu followed his people toward the main doors; goading some, helping others, watching the rest as they all ran.

But the profane persuasion of the Muto Qeyunar was stronger now; a soporific chant, a mesmerizing sequence of mudras, a captivating display of glyph-painted skin that promised eternal life and bewitched the warriors. I watched in horror as first one and then another stopped, gazed at the riven bodies of their comrades and surrendered to hopelessness, fracturing the wells of their spirits as if they were slitting their own bellies before the enemy.

Into that ruptured darkness, the Muto Qeyunar came like torches and lit a path to the place where nothing mattered anymore but a false, fixated joy, where these crippled Qandunar became the enemy of all they had loved just moments ago. Flesh hardened, eyes gleamed, lips thinned in exultation, and then they were lost to us.

The retreating force flung open the monastery doors and turned to dance again with the Muto as the monastics fled inside. They were nearly empty of naré now, but in a desperate flash of isché, in a wild sweep of limbs, they told the truth of impermanence to the enemy and resisted the call to fixation. Rain was with them, and her telling was perhaps the wildest and truest of all.

The last of the Qeyunar descended the ladder and held it for me. I pivoted on my knees, stepped down and looked up. Inu had abandoned his bow for blades, and together with the men and women under his command, they confronted the rooftop deluge of Muto Vele with a bleak surety for which there was no sufficient gratitude. I could offer them nothing but grief, and so I left them and hurried to join the others in the gathering chamber.

By some miracle of plank and hinge, the courtyard and garden doors were holding, but soon the main doors were rattling, bowing, cracking under Muto Vele claws and shoulders. The Qeyunar assembled near the dais, and Mother Anyamé led us in a final, desperate search for naré that yielded nothing. The battle itself was inviolable; fixation protected the Muto, which left only the Qandunar, whom the fallen monastics fought to claim and we fought to empower.

Beyond the mountain, the valley had petrified, and below it, the flow of lava had cooled to basalt. We repelled the Muto Qeyunar there as they grasped at the naré of our bodies, and in the frenzy of their assault, I saw the wisdom in Warmaster Inu's hope for a fight. Their conceit had driven them up the cliffside at too great a cost. They needed to win the battle quickly or lose control of their people and beasts.

The doors broke inward. A flagging Muto Vele stumbled into the gathering chamber bearing a puzzled Muto Qandunar woman on her back. I pointed at the pair and shouted, "Look! They're losing fixation!"

The attention of the Qandunar shifted toward the rubble. Behind the Muto Vele came a dozen Muto Qandunar on foot. I recognized them all, spread my fingers in a warding mudra, exhaled through a mouth fallen open in dread.

This was how the Muto Qeyunar would win.

The fence of swords around the dais wavered in doubt. Fight their former comrades and die, or join them and live forever in that false, fixated joy. This was the terrible choice before the defenders that remained.

In the hush ahead of the final confrontation, my eyes sought and found Rain in the hall. Head up, isché drawn, she had faced that choice before and would never lose herself to it again.

So when the Muto Qeyunar swaggered in, unmounted, and lifted Warmaster Inu's head on a pike, only she danced forward into the fray.

Nereyu's isché clattered to the floor, and his face contorted in the anguish I had seen two nights ago. The howl that fled his throat found an answering sob in mine, and we wept together; for the warmaster, for the fixated and fallen, for ourselves.

Implacable as poison, the Muto Qandunar advanced, but they were not so perfect as they had been even seconds ago. The ghosts of recent injuries colored their bodies. The blood lust in their eyes faded to chaos.

I gathered a lungful of air behind my vocal cords and screamed. "Rain! Rain!" She turned mid-attack and followed the line of my arm to Nereyu. "Help him!"

Rain disengaged and bolted between the armies; down the wall of Muto Qandunar, over the base of the fountain, toward the lieutenant. The battle was poised on the point of a dagger now. If he succumbed, the Qandunar would surely follow. But if he did not, the Muto Qeyunar might spend the last of their naré in defense. They knew it and focused the fullness of their seduction upon Nereyu.

One of the fallen nuns took Inu's head between her hands and licked his sightless eyes with a pink tongue. The others lifted their hands in the profane mudras of permanence. Some chanted, and the song was sweet as the voice of a dying child.

The Muto Qandunar closed in.

Like a fog of sleep, they slowed the mind.

Like a pool of mud, they mired the feet.

It was said the collective force of their fixation could stop a Qandunar mid-stride and hold him there while they carved him into meat.

The lieutenant reeled, face softening, and his mouth fell slack.

I choked on the tears in my throat and screamed again. "Nereyu! Look at me, at me, not them! Don't lose yourself to this when they might need you most! That's what he said, remember? They need you now!"

Rain dodged the slash of a Muto Qandunar sword, slid under the swipe of a Muto Vele paw, spent naré like a miser on each and every confrontation. Her isché spun like wheels on a dry road, rang like chimes against the steel of the enemy. Nereyu bent to retrieve his weapons and turned toward me, malevolence and misery warring in him as he rose.

I jumped down from the dais, frantic, scouring myself for scraps of naré and wondered if I could give what Brother Empho had lost; the pulse of life in my own body. "You haven't failed anyone! Stop blaming yourself and fight for the people you can save! You have the right to be whole!"

You have the right to be whole. The words resounded in my mind as if I were screaming them at myself, and suddenly the burden of my awful memories eased. 'Wounded monk', Rain had called me, and I was. Just wounded. Just a monk.

A restive warmth gathered in my belly and uncoiled into the blackened furrows above it. Stunned, I dropped the sleeves of my robe and watched a shimmer of light travel up my chest; burning away the darkness, leaving only plain, human scars in its wake. *I have the right to be whole.*

When it came, the flow of naré from my body was a curative deluge that needed no transmutation. I poured and poured and poured it into my friend, who spilled it over Nereyu and washed him clean.

They came together like twin birds of prey and soared into combat. Rain dove at the Muto Qandunar with my naré, and Nereyu followed in a flurry of blessed blades. Rain swept from one liberation to the next, and Nereyu drew his wakened warriors into the fight. She was the instrument of change and he the hope of life beyond it. Seeing this, the fence of swords around the dais found its courage, and together the Qandunar pressed the attack until the fixation of their comrades faded away.

The Muto Qeyunar paled like autumn leaves. A fallen monk near the doorway fled to the plateau. Another followed, and another until they were all fleeing before the victory cries of the Qandunar at their backs. The Muto Vele in the chamber shrank, thinned, woke unhurt and barreled after them, the fierce young woman on her back shrieking with fury. There was no mercy in the beast or its rider. I stared at Inu's abandoned head and wondered if there was any mercy in me.

Mother Anyamé stepped down from the dais and went to retrieve the warmaster's remains. "They're going to jump." There was no pity in her tone, but neither was there any pleasure.

"They've spent too much naré." I shrugged back into my robe, knuckles tracing the pink ribbons of flesh on my chest. "They won't survive the fall."

"They might." She knelt, closed the man's eyes and laid a hand upon his cheek. "Novitiate Sama, what you did just now was extraordinary. I wish Brother Empho had seen it." She looked up at me with a regard so profound it made me blush. "Thank you."

I had nothing to say in reply, so I walked out onto the plateau, where a roar and clamor announced the liberation of all the Muto Vele. Those who could run chased their tormentors to the cliff in a feral rage. Some of the Muto Qeyunar made it, vaulting over the side in self-preservation or suicide. The rest grew pallid, lagged behind, surrendered their stolen immortality to malaise and imperfection. These the Vele caught with ordinary teeth and claws, and the screams that rose from their feast were entirely human.

Rain turned from the carnage toward Nereyu and offered up her borrowed isché with trembling hands. Her gaze traveled the battlefield, lingering upon each of the dead in turn. "I'm sorry," she whispered as if she had slain them all. "I'm sorry, I'm sorry,

I'm sorry..." Her voice thickened on the words until they crowded together in sadness, and then she met the lieutenant's eyes, lifted the weapons a little higher. "Are we done? I don't... I can't touch these anymore. Please."

Nereyu took the swords with one hand and brought her into his arms with the other. "We're done," he murmured, shielding her dignity as she wept. "We're done."

༄ ୭

We have the right to be whole.

I could not bring myself to number those who were dead; counting them would have reduced the lift of their voices in chant, the sheen of sweat on their bodies, the private ruminations of their hearts to the click of a tally stick. And because I could not do that, neither could I number the living. Instead, I ministered to the liberated, those people and Vele returned from a dark sojourn in need of solace.

Banth's burial site, once a tidy place of final repose for the mountain's monastics, grew to a field of upturned earth and bodies, including those of the Muto Qeyunar whose power had been insufficient to their fall from the plateau. Nereyu and Rain dug Inu's grave together, and my first work in the white robe of an ordained Qeyunar monk was to bless it with the naré of falling snow.

"Death is only a transformation," I said to the gathered mourners in the too-silent valley at dawn. "The decay of his flesh we consign to the ground, which needs all the naré we can give it now, but the spirit of Warmaster Inu we bid farewell as it travels the flow of impermanence to rebirth."

Afterward, Nereyu argued we should evacuate to Dunee, but we would not abandon our neighbors and could not abandon the leached and brittle valley that needed our care. So in time, a replacement force of Qandunar came to live on the plateau. They brought with them a master of tattoos, and in the days that followed, Nereyu received the Warmaster glyph. Rain received the only glyph any Qandunar would ever bear for the Battle of Geriahar, and when it was finished, she was the first to bear the glyph for the Battle of Banth. Work stopped for this event, and she sat outside in a circle of warriors, monastics and visiting villagers while a stylized chicken and two isché were inked into the back of her neck.

"What's so important about Henny?" One of the warriors knelt to poke at the fire, and there was no mockery in the smile that curled her mouth. "I mean, if I've got to wear a picture of her on my head for the rest of my life..."

A ripple of laughter rose from the crowd.

Rain met the woman's smile with a thoughtful expression, careful not to move her neck. "I was liberated with a blow to the head that knocked me senseless. When I woke, there was a yellow chick hiding from the battle beneath my arm, against my body." She paused while Henny crossed from my lap to hers and settled in. "I laid there a long time remembering the Qandunar who had trusted me the way that little chick did; people I had failed, people I had killed..." Her voice trailed off, and her fingers settled in Henny's feathers.

Mother Anyamé nodded, her needle flashing through the length of fabric that would become Rain's novitiate robe. "Liberation and healing are not the same things, Candidate Rain. Your scars may always pain you, but we'll be here to help when they do."

I rubbed at the subtle ache of my own scars and knew she was right.

We said farewell to Nereyu on Midwinter Day in the place where we had met him. Freshly-shaven, smelling of soap and leather polish, armed with the whetted isché he had carried into battle, his shadow on the lift might have been Warmaster Inu's. Rain faced him on the plateau, eyes unshielded as they had ever been, the green of her new robe speckled with bird droppings. Henny clucked from the crook of her arm and pecked at a kernel of cracked corn in Nereyu's hand, the last of many she had eaten.

Rain spoke to him as a warrior parting ways from a comrade-in-arms. "What are your orders?"

"Back to Dunee until the weather breaks and then wherever we're sent." Nereyu dusted his palms together. "Think I might lose a few of the liberated Qandunar on the road, and I plan to let them go." He frowned, his face lifting to the cloud cover. "They're broken in ways I don't completely understand, Rain, not even after you."

"I hope you never do." She followed his gaze, and a

melancholy quiet fell for a time. A beam of sunlight brightened the space between them and faded. The line of gray it left behind was a road, one Nereyu might yet travel but Rain could never return upon.

Nereyu clapped a hand upon my shoulder after a moment. "When are you coming to Dunee, Qeyunar Sama? I want you with me when I go out into the field again."

I laughed. "It'll be a few years before I'm ready for that. Defensive arts are among the hardest to learn."

His brow lifted in disbelief. "Won't take you *that* long. You have a gift."

"Perhaps." I shrugged. "But I still can't explain the burst of naré that saved me at Dareo, and I don't have any more blackened scars to heal."

They both stared at me then as if I had said something profound.

"Well, you don't want to keep your Qandunar waiting." Rain broke the silence with a brisk change of tone and stepped back a pace, her free hand gesturing in a mudra of protection. It was simple and sure, and the naré of passing sunlight was in it. "I give you change, Warmaster Nereyu."

"Gave." He reached up, folded her fingers into his palm and brought her hand to his breastplate. "You gave me change, Novitiate Rain."

I went to man the crank, and the lift rattled to life. Rain watched it descend until the machine fell silent again, and then we went back into the monastery together.

C is for Change

Sara Cleto

WHEN the sun sets, the Snow Queen rises from her bed and slips a diaphanous robe over her glinting skin. Taffeta, brocade, and leather crowd restlessly in her closet and ease past the doors, spilling in drifts of color onto the marbled floor. The King brings her new boxes, brimming with crisp tissue and crisper clothes, bound cheerfully with a bow, nearly every day.

"For the gala," he says, or "for dinner with the executive board."

He smiles at her, all teeth, and suggests with exquisite politeness that she might dress and come downstairs.

She smiles, or the nearest approximation that her stiff, heavy lips can manage, and strokes her newest garment with a single fingertip.

The fabric tears cleanly under her light caress, parting with the casual brutality of a broom on a spider web.

The King sighs gently. "Darling, do remember to wear your gloves. And let your ladies help you dress."

She looks at the complicated undergarments, plates of metal twined with industrial straps, the screws and bolts that hold the pieces together, and then at the women who never quite leave the shadow of the door. They wear sturdy gloves, the kind that gardeners who tend particularly recalcitrant rose bushes favor, and sturdy lines around their mouths.

"Tomorrow, perhaps," she says quietly. Her lips clatter

against each other, and her words are echoed by the tap of jewels striking the floor. She watches impassively as one of her ladies edges towards her. The woman collects the sparkling gems from where they lay around her feet and places them in one of the many glass caskets lining the room, arranged to catch the light. Her ruined gown is whisked away to be repaired, stitched back into a semblance of wholeness, and laid to rest, unworn, in her closet. The King inclines his head over her hand, lips scraped and lightly bleeding, and withdraws.

Sliding on her gloves, she arranges her robe around her, concealing as much of her glittering skin as possible.

She never goes downstairs.

Gwyn had her first diamond at thirteen.

Light poured through the thick glass windows in the schoolroom, and struck Cory's long hair, the blow staining the strands the color of a rosy apple. She wanted to touch them, to see how they felt under the soft pads of her fingertips, but the vibrant shade reminded Gwyn of the colors that dripped into her mother's hair when her father wrapped it round his fist and pulled.

She shivered.

The bell rang, and she lowered her eyes, swiftly gathered her books into her arms. The chair in front of her creaked as Cory turned around, her mouth half open. Gwyn leapt out of her desk and hurried to the door, schooling her face into neutrality.

A sharp itch on her wrist made her dig her fingernails into her skin. A cold, hard shape caught beneath her nail, and she pulled back her sleeve. A perfectly faceted jewel gleamed at the base of her lifeline. Gwyn stared as it swallowed the harsh florescent lights, twinkling sullenly. She tugged her sleeve down and carefully did not think about the diamond until the evening, when she closed the door against the shouting downstairs and pried at it with her nails and then her tweezers. The skin around the jewel had hardened, holding it as firmly as a platinum setting.

Her reflection in the mirror was pale, except for hectic blooms over her cheekbones—they faded as she watched.

Breathing deeply until her heart cooled and pulsed evenly in her chest, Gwyn took comfort in her reflection. Her gray eyes regarded her from the glass with a serenity that she didn't feel. She would be composed as the motionless girl who looked back at her—colorless and chill, numb as stiletto-shod feet in midwinter. Nothing, not a stray diamond or flaming hair, would break through the ice.

Thirteen was young for the advent of a curse, but Gwyn thought she could bear it.

§∘§

The Snow Queen has grown to hate the mirrors that crowd her rooms. Tall, ornate antiques lean against the walls, and a sleek, modern glass hangs over her dressing table. Small, decorative mirrors are arranged in an artful flurry around her bed, and even the doors have reflective surfaces.

When she first came to the castle, there had only been one mirror in her room but the king quickly noticed the germinating effect it had on her. He ordered more and more. Light bent between her and her endless reflections, and diamonds fell from her lips like rain. When she covered the mirrors with unworn gowns, the King told her ladies to bare them.

"Every corner of the room must shine with your beauty, my love," he said as he lay in bed beside her.

She glanced at her reflection in the uncovered glass and closed her eyes against the glare. "If you wish," she said, and three diamonds fell from her tongue to his chest.

The king smiled.

§∘§

At first, Gwyn concealed the diamonds with long sleeves, jeans, the ash-blonde fall of her hair. The sharp edges wore quickly through the fabric, and by the end of a long day, pin sized holes dotted her arms, diamonds twinkling through in ever spreading constellations. With cool practicality, she discarded her worn denim, her well-washed t-shirts and went to the thrift store, returning with bags bursting with spangled velvet dresses, discarded holiday sweaters that gleamed silver in the light, blouses heavy with rhinestones. Long crystal earrings, a paste necklace, and shimmering bangles camouflaged the few jewels visible on her neck and wrists. Before her mirror, Gwyn brushed Alice blue powder over her eyelids, frosted her lips, dusted fine glitter over the contours of her cheeks. She practiced her smile again and again in the mirror until it didn't quaver, even as diamonds pricked into being along her shoulder blades and inner arms.

At school, as she swept through the halls in a haze of refracted light, they began calling her the Snow Queen.

ॐ

In the drawer beneath her dressing table, the Snow Queen keeps a small box, the color of amber. Sometimes, after the King has left, she takes it out, so careful not to scratch the wood, and sorts through the contents, item by item. First, a well-worn collection of 19th century poetry, the pages yellow and crisp at the corners. Then a scrap of denim, the only remnant of the first pair of jeans that her diamonds shredded. A newspaper clipping with the bold headline "Snow Queen Ices the Runway" above an image of herself halfway down a catwalk, diamonds bared through rents in the scraps of McQueen draped with haphazard precision around her long limbs. At the bottom of the box is a creased photograph of a girl with a sweet smile and a tangle of long red hair.

ॐ

Gwyn was sixteen when her diamonds won her fame.

Of course, she couldn't hide them forever. She only knew that she had to try, had to feed the compulsion to cover, bind, dazzle, to postpone the inevitable moment when everyone would know. She could bear their eyes on her, as long as they didn't know the reason they were looking.

"Why?" Cory asked.

"Why didn't Coleridge finish the poem? I don't know," Gwyn replied, her words punctuated by a strobing flash as she shrugged her shoulders.

"No. That's easy: too much laudanum. Or too many

daffodils."

Gwyn laughed, startled herself with the unfamiliar feeling, then laughed again for the sheer physicality of it. They were sprawled on Cory's bedroom floor, books and laptops open as they pieced together a presentation on Romantic poets for English class.

"No, not 'Christabel,'" Cory continued. She smoothed her plaid skirt over her knees with a quick, restless motion. "You. Why did you start with, um, all the glittering? I've always wanted to ask you."

"I guess I just thought it suited me," Gwyn said, ignoring the prickling on her ankle as a gem poked through her tights.

"It does. You're beautiful. But you were just as beautiful in jeans and a tee," Cory said, then flushed deeply, "I mean, it was just such a change."

Blood pulsed quicker in Gwyn's temples, her neck, and she reached for Cory's hand. She let herself feel her smooth skin, the slightly rough scrape of a callus, and answering pressure of her warm fingers around her own. That warmth tingled in her frozen fingers, eased the chill in her arm, and knocked gently at her heart. Cory leaned forward, her breath a spring thaw. Gwyn felt the weight of a single diamond on her collarbone ease into the brush of a snowflake before melting away.

No. Warmth might mean love, but it also meant blackened eyes, bruises under long sleeves, a voice hoarse from crying— she'd learned this lesson faithfully along with her letters and multiplication tables at her parents' kitchen table. Better to be snow, better not to feel at all.

She yanked her hand away, willing coolness, willing ice. Diamonds sprang from her knuckles, circled her fingers like rings.

"Oh my God!" Cory yelped, grabbing her hand. "Gwyn, what the hell? What is this?"

"I don't know," Gwyn whispered, closing her fingers into a fist.

"You have to go to a doctor!"

Gwyn laughed, but without the warm sensation from before. "And say what? That I'm spontaneously sprouting diamonds?"

"Yes! It could be some kind of toxin or cancer or... I don't know! Look, I'll take you to the hospital right now!"

Gwyn swallowed, and took a long, last look at Cory's green eyes, her long red hair. She reached out and held a lock between her fingers for just a moment before letting it fall. She fled.

By the time she arrived home, diamonds starred her eyebrows and the tips of her nails, and they fell from her mouth with her words.

The doctors had no name for Gwyn's condition, but, after ascertaining that her heart still beat with the proper frequency, her blood was free of toxins, and no cancers gnawed on her innards, they devised a name: Snow Queen Syndrome (SQS.) They marveled, wrote articles, released images with the consent of Gwyn's parents, who screamed at each other between her examinations.

That was when the modeling agency called.

Sometimes, The Snow Queen dips her fingers into the caskets that line her room, feels the loose diamonds click against the jewels in her fingertips. The King has them emptied—taken to the bank to be deposited "in your name, of course, my love"— every few days, but they fill quickly. At least, they did until she stopped talking. He coaxed and cajoled, but the only diamonds that escape her lips fall with her sighs as she sleeps.

She could have said no. But she was already the Snow Queen, already used to eyes, and thought, perhaps, she could vanish into the title and leave Gwyn behind. So she agreed, signed the forms that whisked her from school to a new kind of education. Designers built collections around her, begged her to say their names on the runway so that diamonds would tumble down her garments and clatter against the floor in perfect punctuation.

But the diamonds grew thicker, sharper. Clothes shredded moments after touching her skin. The designers and their fleets of assistants developed intricate sheaths and industrial stockings to protect their garments, but they ruined the drape of the cloth, and so they had her walk without them. Chiffon and lace tattered behind her, heaping in drifts on the runway.

That was how the King found her.

Adrian King, heir to a tidy fortune and minor title, saw her pictures and came to the winter show. He listened to the crystalline tap of her bare feet on the runway, watched how she burned like a solar flame through the dispassionate distance of his sunglasses, and tested the strength of the diamonds that fell into his lap as she murmured something indistinguishable over the roar of the crowd.

He found her after the show and offered her a long, cool kiss, a trace of blood tinting his lips as he rolled the resulting diamond on his tongue. His hand was ice at the small of her back, and she felt herself grow colder. "Come with me. I will make you a Queen." When he promised he would never touch her in warmth or anger, she agreed.

৩-৶

Lighting a candle, the Snow Queen sits down, deliberately, on the marble floor before the biggest mirror. She pulls the jeweled weight of her hair over her shoulder, and tries to find a trace of the girl that had once looked back at her.

The gray eyes, beneath the encrustations of her eyebrows, are the same. If she looks closely, she can see the old lines of her jaw and cheeks. She lets her robe fall from her shoulders, lets the shifting sparks and shadows play before her eyes. Their waltz is almost beautiful.

"And wildly glittered here and there. The gems entangled in her hair," says a voice behind her.

She scrambles around, scratching the floor in her haste.

"'Christabel,'" Cory says, stepping into the light of the candle. "Do you remember?" Her hightops scruff on the lush Persian carpet.

"How did you find me?" Diamonds patter in a torrent from her lips to the ground, but Cory's eyes don't follow them.

"Please. Everyone knows you've taken up with Adrian King. The tabloids are full of it." Cory sits down next to her, tucking her legs beneath her. "Gwyn, are you okay? No one has seen you in months. People are saying that you're dead, that this King guy killed you."

"He hasn't hurt me. He didn't make me come here." More jewels fall. Cory brushes them away like dandruff, like spider webs.

"Okay. Okay, that's good. I just had to make sure."

"Why?"

Cory smiles. "Sometimes, you seem so sad under all that glitter."

"It's not glitter. They're diamonds."

"So I've heard." She hesitates. "May I...may I touch them?"

"They'll cut you. They keep getting sharper, and even the King never touches me anymore. I..." Her glinting fingers reach for Cory's hair and retreat sharply, dropping like dying comets into her lap. "I don't want to hurt you."

"You won't," she says, simply, and weaves her hands through hair and gems to kiss the diamonds that stud Gwyn's lips.

The jewel on Gwyn's tongue breaks and dissolves, and diamonds shake free of her skin and fall to the floor. In the mirror, there are only two girls, one pale, one rosy, in a drift of melting snow.

D is for Diamonds

Samantha Kymmell-Harvey

RYAN stood at the pool railing on the empty crew deck. The humid Caribbean air settled like beads of sweat on his arm while the sound of the waves slapping the cruise ship's sides calmed him. Lights twinkled ashore, glistening in the water like stage lights.

Liv's going to law school in Orlando.

His wife had been there on stage ever since his days of high school card tricks. His mind drifted to the large plastic cube he'd picked up at port a few days ago. It was going to be his adaptation of Houdini's water escape and his ticket to the big time—a stage of his own in Vegas. But when the letter came, Ryan instead sent off an audition tape to Disney World. *There are more public stages than this ship!*

Ryan focused on the cube. What temperature should the water in the cube be? Would colder water help him to hold his breath for the two minutes he needed to pick the handcuff and leg iron locks? He lowered himself into the pool.

Two minutes or I die.

He paced his breathing. In. Hold. Out. In. Hold. Out. He inhaled once more, but didn't exhale. Instead, he tapped the start button on his timer app and set it on the edge of the pool. With a loud chirp, the numbers began their downward dance.

Ryan plunged under and sat cross-legged at the bottom of the shallow end, gripping the submerged end of the handrail to keep from surfacing.

He counted. *Four. Five. Six. Seven.*

A dark shadow appeared in the deep end. It moved like ink, slipping silently against the walls. It neared. Ryan made out the shape of a man with dark, curly hair and eyes as intensely blue as the sea itself. Ryan's heart would not settle. Lately when he'd called up Houdini in his head, the magician seemed more vivid than usual.

Thirteen. Fourteen. Fifteen.

Chlorine stung his eyes as Ryan watched his mentor sit on the step beside him, dressed in a tux.

"You're looking rather red in the face," said the ghostly Houdini. "You can't get the full two minutes on the first go around. The Water Torture Chamber isn't that easy."

Imagining the great illusionist was all part of his training and Ryan had grown used to the old magician's taunts. Though his lungs strained, he stared down his ghostly coach and kept counting.

Forty-one. Forty-two. Forty-three. Forty-four.

"It takes sacrifice to be great. And you haven't even begun trying to pick open the restraints yet."

Ryan closed his eyes. He'd picked all four locks required for the cube above water in less time than Houdini needed. The remaining seconds escaped him in his count. Halfway there?

"The best illusions are the ones that tap into *their* fears," said Houdini. "Do you think you know what scares them?"

Ryan tightened his grip on the metal bar. His fingernails blanched.

"Death. We all want to cheat it in the end. You go to the brink, and they in turn, cannot take their eyes off you." Houdini's voice rippled on the waves.

Ryan's throat spasmed and he gulped then sprung to the surface coughing. The chlorine burned his throat and nostrils. Swallowing back the irritation, he grabbed the timer.

One minute short.

He looked back into the pool. Empty. Towel buffering the night chill, Ryan returned to his cabin, holding his breath again.

ॐ

Focus is everything. Ryan had never struggled with nerves until these timed escapes. *Distraction equals death.* He felt a light kiss on his cheek.

"Ready for our last show?" Liv smiled. "One last hurrah before we escape this place?"

Ryan couldn't help but smile to see how his wife was glowing in her gold-sequined dress. *I married that beautiful woman.* "Ready as I'll ever be."

"Don't worry. It's not your last show ever." She cracked a toothy grin. "Disney's going to snatch you up, I'm sure of it."

He squeezed her hand. "It's going to be way better than this cruise ship, that's for sure."

She leaned in and planted a bright, red glossy kiss on his lips. "Don't worry, you'll still make it to Vegas. Florida will just be a little stepping stone on your path. And with my law degree, I can be your agent."

"I wouldn't have it any other way, Liv."

The stage manager waved to Ryan signaling thirty seconds until curtain. Ryan grabbed his straitjacket draped over the back of his chair and handed it to Liv. "I love you."

"Love you back."

The curtain rose and the audience applauded.

"Good evening, ladies and gentlemen." Ryan put on his stage smile despite the beads of sweat that had already begun to solidify on his brow. "Harry Houdini made the suspended straitjacket escape famous. Tonight, not only will I escape in less than his record of two minutes and thirty-seven seconds, but I'm also upping the ante."

In the corner of his eye, a shadow lingered, the outline of his curly hair barely detectable in the folds of the red velour curtain. *He* was watching. *I haven't called him. What is he doing here?* Ryan's breath quickened, pulse beating in his ears. *Stay calm. It's all in your head.* But the figure still lingered off stage right.

Sparse applause echoed and Ryan tried to refocus. Liv walked on stage holding the straitjacket out for them to see.

"The straitjacket. Invented by the French in 1790 and only deemed cruel and unusual punishment in recent times." He tugged on the leather crotch strap dangling from the bottom of the canvas shirt. "You can see why."

The ghostly figure mimed applause. Ryan looked away.

"Hey," Olivia whispered as she slid Ryan's arms into the sleeves. "You okay?" She fastened the straps across his back as quickly as she could.

"I'm fine. Tighter," he said under his breath, though a sharp pain jabbed into his ribs.

Liv tightened the crotch strap and gave it a dramatic pull.

"Whoah, watch the goods," he said, exaggerating a waddle as if she'd actually hurt him. This time, they laughed. *See, they still love the jokes. Nothing to worry about.*

"My escape takes Houdini's one step further. I will be suspended from this bar twenty feet above the stage." He motioned to a black bar suspended on a thick wire above his head. A blue gym crash mat waited underneath. The gears moaned as the apparatus descended into his hands. Murmuring rippled amongst his audience.

He took a breath and continued positioning himself beneath the bar and flashing an all-American grin. "Can I get two minutes on the clock, please?" Ryan said, as he lay down on the mat, legs bent in the air.

Heavy boots weighed down his feet. They had hooks where the laces would have been so that he could hang upside down. Houdini's blue eyes stared down from the rafters as he hooked his boots on the bar. *Go away.* Ryan closed his eyes then opened them again. Houdini remained.

On Liv's cue, the bar elevated. Ryan dangled two feet off the stage, face parallel with his wife's. "Now," he whispered.

She disappeared stage left for a moment and returned with a flaming torch. With a dramatic flourish she set the cord suspending the bar on fire and the audience gasped. The glowing red clock above the stage began its countdown.

Glancing off stage left, he gave the ropes operator a definitive nod. The motor in the hummed to a start then squealed as the gears turned, hoisting Ryan higher and higher. *No time to waste.* Ryan began his escape.

He exhaled sharply and his body contracted from the jacket to give him the wiggle room he needed. The rope swung as he inched his elbow up the length of the sleeve creating the illusion he was thrashing. The canvas held tightly around his ribcage. Ryan slipped one arm free.

Next arm. He coached himself.

Then the cord bounced as if something else grasped it. *What the hell?* Ryan looked up, frustrated at the two seconds that unforeseen movement had cost him. Houdini hung off the cord like a spider.

Houdini leaned close. "Did you suck in enough air before she strapped you in?"

Not now. Ryan jerked his shoulder until his elbow slipped free. He exhaled again, giving his body a small margin of space. *I'm behind the clock.*

Twisting the sleeve over the top of his head, his arms hung free. The blood throbbed in his ears.

"One more strap," Houdini whispered. "And thirty seconds to go. I know you're better than this."

Shut up. Ryan craned his head, but the clock hung just out of view. The rope crackled, the scent of kerosene filling his nostrils.

Ten seconds behind.

Clenching his abs, he strained to pull the buckle between his legs free. *Hurry, hurry.* Sweat dripped off his bangs and raced down the tip of his nose.

The audience began to shout. "Ten! Nine! Eight!"

The strap slipped and Ryan ripped the jacket off over his head, grabbed the bar with his hands and unhooked his boots.

The rope creaked.

"Three! Two! One!"

Ryan dropped to the mat.

Zero.

The spectators jumped to their feet shouting and clapping. The rope snapped and the bar dangled vertically by the safety chain. Ryan rolled over on the mat to face his phantom coach, face red with anger. *I don't need you when I perform. I know what I'm doing.*

Houdini lifted an eyebrow. "You *do* need me. Without me, you will never be great."

Liv's lacquered nails dug into his forearm through his dress shirt as she helped him to his feet. They both bowed.

"Thank you!" Ryan waved before exiting the stage.

The curtains closed.

He felt a squeeze on his arm. "Hey, that was close. You okay?" Olivia's red glossed lips trembled.

"I can do better than that. I *have* done better than that."

"Hey, don't be so hard on yourself," she said hugging him close. "You gave them a great last show. You should be proud."

Houdini's voice echoed in his mind. "What scares you? When you know, your greatness will be unlocked."

Being trapped scares me. Ryan couldn't take his eyes off the specter. *Having no choices.*

Liv snapped her fingers in front of his nose. "Hey! Hello? What's wrong?"

"I have to go practice. I'll never get a gig in Orlando with performances like that." He walked away, leaving his wife in the chaos of backstage.

"What? Now? Ryan, stop this." She took a step down the narrow backstage hall, but the juggling troupe cut her off. "Dinner reservations at eight!"

Though he heard her, he kept walking. Just a few hours practicing in the pool, then he'd be able to take a break.

ৎ৯৵৶

Ryan sat at the bottom of the employees' pool. Weights strapped around his waist, hands and feet bound by locked chains, he leaned against the wall.

Focus.

He inserted the long, thin key into the lock binding his ankles and twisted the pointed end. In his mind, he saw Liv's face, her eyes wide in fear that he might die. His hands trembled, the key nearly slipping from his grasp.

"You will die if you don't pick those locks faster," said Houdini.

The lock on the leg chain popped open. *One down*, Ryan thought. He looked to his ghostly mentor, smiling despite the chlorine burn.

"Not fast enough," said Houdini.

Why don't you just leave me alone if that's your training approach tonight? He clenched his burning eyes shut.

"I want to help you. You're on the cusp of greatness. Don't give up."

Well if you want to help me, then help me. How did you do it?

"I could tell you, but it comes with a price. Are you ready to leave your tidy life plan behind and join the greats?"

Ryan thought of Liv, thought of his dreams. What if the only way to his own show was through his connections on the cruise? Liv wouldn't want to break his dreams. Ryan opened his eyes. The great magician hovered beside him, tux crisp but *something* had changed. Now his body was a solid mass. Even the bubbles from the pool filter rippled along Houdini's sleeves. Ryan reached a hand out to touch his mentor's arm, but it passed right through his jacket. *How do the greats do it?*

"By defying nature," Houdini said. "I can give you the power to go to the brink of death and back for your audience, yet you will not die. And your audiences will be on the edge of their seats, craving your show over and over again, wondering how you did it."

How?

"It's a small trade really, considering you'll get a lifetime of success in return."

Eyes shut, Ryan imagined his name in lights on the marquis of great theaters. Disney. Vegas. LA. *What trade? Tell me.*

"Just relax," said Houdini. "I'll show you."

Ryan watched as Houdini reached his hand toward his chest. He flinched anticipating a collision, but none came. Then Houdini's arm was cuff-deep in his rib cage. An icy sensation began to emanate from his heart then pulsed through his bones. Stifling a shout, Ryan swatted Houdini's arm, but his own hand passed right through the ghostly magician's.

Stop! What are you doing?

Houdini's fingers picked against his insides, as if he were trying to separate pages in a book. Ryan's lungs burned, his insides churned. The beating of his heart slowed in his ears as the world began to turn. *Don't throw up.*

"Ryan!" The voice was deep. Not Houdini's. "Ryan!"

He opened his eyes. Houdini was startled too. "I'll come back for our trade," he said. Ryan looked at the magician's open palms, noting the gray ink-like mist that snaked between his gloved fingers. It disappeared before he could see what it was and Houdini dissipated into the water. Ryan rocketed to the surface, hands clutching his chest. He gasped as he grabbed the timer in his still-handcuffed hands.

Forty-five seconds short. *What if I had gone ahead with the trade? Would I have made my time?*

"Working on more ways to kill yourself for our entertainment, I see." The cruise director, George Stevens, stared down at him. "Your wife told me I would find you here."

Ryan lifted himself onto the deck and wrapped his towel around him. He unlocked his hands and massaged his wrists. "Is this about the show?"

The cruise director slapped a hand on his back. "I loved it! You nearly killed yourself up there. That's what we at Sunset Cruises call top entertainment."

Ryan rubbed his ears, wondering if the water lodged there had affected his hearing. "Top entertainment?"

"I didn't know you could do that escape stuff," said George. "If you give me another great act tomorrow night, I'll extend your contract. There'll be a raise in there too."

"Tomorrow? But my water escape isn't ready."

George laughed. "Your escape looked fantastic from what I saw. Your lovely wife must be so proud."

"Speaking of my lovely wife, I promised her that tonight was my last show." Ryan shivered, thinking of Liv's reaction to this news. But Houdini had promised him he'd be great. She'd see. *This is my time. I'll debut my water trick tomorrow.*

George lit a cigarette. "Surely she'll understand. Florida can wait. I've already put in a call to a buddy of mine, a talent scout. I told him he's got to see your act. I can only imagine how many more cruise tickets we'll sell with you as our headlining entertainment."

Ryan shook his head. "I'll have to speak with Liv about it."

"Don't disappoint me, Mr. Barton," said George before taking a long drag. "Opportunities like this don't come along often. There are plenty of other magicians out there looking to escape their retail day jobs."

"I understand."

∽✦✦

"There you are," said Liv when he came through the door. She held an empty wine glass, red droplets drying on the bottom. "I nearly called security. Our reservations were four hours ago."

"I'm sorry. I just... forgot. I have a lot on my mind." Ryan opened the narrow closet door, dinging it on the nightstand. He grabbed a fresh t-shirt and flannel pajama pants and started to change.

"I can tell," she said. "Talk to me. What's wrong?"

Ryan shook his head. "I don't know. I guess I keep wondering if this is the right thing to do."

Liv stood, face flushed. "You were sure it was the right thing to do earlier tonight. You were sure it was the right thing to do when I got my letter."

"I know, but things have changed now," he said sharply. The tone of his voice surprised himself. *I sound like Houdini.* Liv flinched.

Liv approached him, eyes narrowed. "What changed, exactly?"

Ryan sighed. "George came by to see me today. He's offered me a second show if I do my water escape. He's already called a talent scout. This could be it, Liv!" *This is my career, how can you not get it?*

"Look, I'm not trying to break your dreams. You know I've been there for you. But we had this worked out. George even knows that. I'm going to school and you're going to keep performing. Nothing will change other than we'll finally be off this boat. There will be other talent scouts. I just need to do this for me, for us, and I need you by my side."

"I need you, too, Liv. But I need *this* chance."

"More than you need me?" Tears glistened in Liv's eyes.

Ryan tried to wrap his arm around her shoulder, but she shrugged him off. "This is for *us*, Liv. And if I don't get a contract with an agent, we'll be off to law school."

"So I can only go after my dream if yours fails?" Liv wiped her eyes with her sleeve. "I don't believe you."

His words came out freely now, as if he could hear Houdini in his ear. "Please, Liv. It's only one more day."

"I've given you ten years already," said Liv. "I'm tired of having this conversation. You've known what I've wanted. You said we'd escape this place but it seems all you do is make up new reasons to stay. I can't do this anymore, Ryan."

A wave of nausea made the room spin. Ryan grasped the wall. "What do you mean?"

"We're docking tomorrow night in St. Augustine. I have a

chance to go live my life. I hope you decide to come with me. I won't wait forever." She stormed into the bedroom and slammed the door shut.

Ryan wanted to rush to her, to hold her, but a coldness inside held him back. *She doesn't get it.* He crossed in front of her, not daring to look at her face anymore, and collapsed on the couch. His stomach churned, a sour liquid tickling the back of his throat.

∽✑

Backstage, Ryan stood very still so as not to jingle the metal chains attached to the cuffs around his neck, hands, and ankles. He double checked he'd tucked his key into his belt and the extra one in his secret pocket inside his waistband. Just in case.

George approached him and clapped a hand to his shoulder. "This looks pretty serious, Mr. Barton."

Ryan nodded. "I want those agents to see my potential." *And my wife, too.*

"They'll be watching tonight on the Internet. Make it count."

"I understand." Ryan grinned. "Thank you very much!" He watched George walk away. The hurriedness of the stage crew around him, nobody stopping to say anything. This would normally be when Liv would give him a kiss, squeeze his hand, and tell him he'd be great. But she wasn't there. This was the first time he'd have to do it alone and it stung.

Poised stage left, Ryan glanced out at the audience. There wasn't an empty seat in the house. A glint of gold caught his eye in the front row. Olivia. She'd come after all. *She'll see now, she'll finally get it.*

Retreating backstage, Ryan saw a shadow materializing beside him. The gray mass floated, hunched, blue eyes glinting in the light from the stage director's reading lamp. Houdini grinned. "Tonight's the night. Are you ready to finally join the greats?"

Ryan shivered at the sound of his voice, like wings against the silk of his top hat.

Houdini gave the chains a tug. "This is what you were born to do."

Ryan's feet tingled and his legs quaked. The emcee's voice

rang out. "And now, with another daring escape, here's the riveting Ryan Barton!"

He stepped on stage. There his cube sat on a black platform glittering like an entertainer's coffin. Its plexiglass panels glistened under the spotlights. The cube was big enough for him to sit crouched inside, water filled to the brim. The lid had a metal latch and a loop for a padlock.

"It took two minutes for the great Houdini to escape from the Water Torture Chamber. His was much larger, so he could move around more to undo his locks. Thus, his escape was much less difficult than the one you will see me make. In one hundred and twenty seconds, either I will escape or it will become my watery grave."

He stepped into the box as the audience clapped. He looked to Liv. She wasn't applauding. She was chewing on her nails. *Don't worry, Liv. You'll see.*

The clock above blinked two minutes. Right leg than left, he stepped into the cube and crouched down. Taking a big gasp of air, he dunked his head under the water. Neck bent downward, he closed the lid and clasped the last lock in place.

He plunged into the eerie silence of the water chamber his splash marking one second gone. The lights refracted, warping his vision. His fingers removed the key tucked into his belt. *Two. Three. Four.*

His eyes adjusted to the stinging. He couldn't afford to close them. The compact pressure of the water weighed down his limbs.

The tuxedoed figment placed a hand on the glass. "You're already ten seconds behind."

His lungs weren't yet burning as he jiggled the key in the lock at his neck. Ryan pressed his handcuffed hands against the glass, imagining the audience's gasp at his dramatic gesture. *They're loving this.* The neck clasp snapped. Ryan removed the lock in one swift swipe. *Done.*

Forty-two. Forty-three. Forty-four.

Ryan twisted, inserting the key in the lock binding his hands. It turned but the lock held. He tried again, jabbing the metal teeth into the mechanism. Had another lock somehow mixed in with his show stuff? He heard his mentor's voice. "A good escape artist can improvise. Do this and you will be greater than I ever was."

Did you jam up the locks on purpose? Ryan tugged his belt buckle open and jammed the prong into the lock. It popped.

"How else will you learn to surpass me?"

Sixty. sixty-one. Sixty-two.

He bent, craning his neck into the corner of the cube in order to reach his leg shackles.

His lungs burned.

His eyesight blurred.

The air lodged in his chest rebelled, craving a breath. I can't.

He pulled his belt from the loops and by touch only, he tried to match the prong to the lock's hole.

"Just say the word and I will make you great," said Houdini.

Ryan felt Houdini's ghostly hands pulling at the chains as if to tease him.

Seventy-seven. Seventy-eight. Seventy-nine.

He missed the hole, breaking the prong with the force of the blow. It jammed his finger. Jerking in pain, Ryan dropped his key and watched the glinting of silver float down into the darkness. My key!

He twisted, hands desperately seeking the key. He was so close to succeeding, so close to greatness. Orlando loomed in his mind. *I don't want to die.* There was only one way to do it and survive. Ryan grasped at Houdini's lapel. *Do it. Make me great as you promised.*

"We have a deal then?"

Yes.

Something gray, like a fog began to wrap itself around the cube. Houdini's hand passed through his chest, expelling air. The iciness he felt before spread from his chest, inching down his arms and legs. His lungs tightened, the burning sensation vanishing. *Key!*

Thrusting his hand in every crevice of the cube, Ryan searched. The nausea returned as Houdini's hands messed with his interior. His head felt heavy and the outside world spun around him. *I will be great*, Ryan swallowed down his fear, scrunching his fingers under his thigh and detected something slim and cold.

The key!

He shoved it in the leg lock and the shackles broke free. Only one lock remained—the lid.

Ninety-eight. Ninety-nine. One-hundred.

Twenty seconds until he drowned. He squeezed his fingers.
Don't panic.

Houdini withdrew his hands and Ryan's lungs contracted, squeezing every ounce of oxygen to his heart. Even in the blur of the water, Ryan saw that Houdini held a silvery orb in his hands. *What is that?* He bit his tongue to resist the urge to inhale. His hands emerged through the two circular holes. The key slipped in his wet fingers.

"You need not panic. You will not die." Houdini played with the orb in his hands. It morphed into a little humanoid shadow.

A burst of energy surged through Ryan. Through the water, he saw the audience on their feet shouting. Clapping. Their faces alive with fear and joy. *He* made them feel this way. *This is my moment!*

In front of him, Olivia pounded on the glass, silent words spilling from her mouth. Her clammy hands clasped his as she inserted the spare key into the lock but he pulled her hands away and she stepped back.

"Breathe," said Houdini.

No time. This is my greatest act.

"Breathe," he commanded Ryan again, and this time, Ryan obeyed. Still submerged, he inhaled. His lungs filled, yet he didn't feel the relief of air. He turned the key one last time.

The lock popped. The lid opened.

Liv's hands clasped his shirt, pulling him from the cube. He pushed her away, stepping out of the cube himself. The soaked clothing weighed him down, but he stretched tall to give a valiant bow. The audience gasped then exploded into applause. And whistles. And cheers.

"Ryan! Oh my God!" Tears streamed down Liv's face as the curtain enfolded them.

"I'm fine," he said between coughs. "I did it!"

Her face crumbled as the room began to spin. Ryan blinked trying to regain his vision.

Another hand, cold and firm, touched his shoulder.

"What a show," Houdini said. "Nothing will stop you now."

As his eyes adjusted, he saw them. The magician and himself. His own ghost, a skinny wisp of a soul, stood before him, clothes still dripping. His hair lay in thin strands across his head, his eyes sunken into his round face.

"You killed me." He flung a fist at Houdini, but it only connected with air.

Liv ducked the blow. "Medics!"

The great Houdini ran his hand down the curtain, his blue eyes flashing red. "You are not dead, you can't die. This is what you wanted. Your soul is forever attached to this ship. No matter what new escape innovation, they will be thrilled. And you will never fail. You *are* great." He grinned, revealing sharp, white teeth.

"Give me back my soul!" He swung again, but the magician vanished, taking Ryan's ghost with him. Ryan clutched his chest, desperately seeking his own heart beat.

"Somebody help!" Liv's voice pierced the panic.

"Liv," he moaned. He clutched her hands so hard that she murmured in pain.

"Ryan, you'll be fine. You just need some oxygen. Just hang in there. We're going to get you out of here."

"I was so stupid. Let's go," he said. "It's not too late, right? Let's just start over again."

Liv's breath felt hot on his face. Her lips were like smoldering coals. "Thank God, Ryan. I love you." She helped him to his feet. "Easy now."

Ryan limped off stage, shivering. He glanced over his shoulder. The Houdini-demon's eyes glowed, Ryan's silvery soul prisoner in his grasp.

ço~ç

Ryan shook terribly in Liv's arms as he stepped into the motorboat. Her touch felt like fire against his cold skin.

"I'm getting you to the hospital as soon as we're ashore," said Liv. "But at least we're off that horrible ship. You'll be happier. We'll be happier."

Looking up to the prow of the cruise ship, Ryan saw his soul looking over the railing. It was so skinny and translucent, like his insides had been ill. *What has this thing done to me?* Houdini waved. A wave of nausea came over him. "I hope so."

The motor roared to life and the boat skidded across the

water toward the lights of St. Augustine.

Ryan felt his throat fill with water. He coughed, but no water expelled from his lungs.

"My God, Ryan!" Liv shrieked. "You're turning blue."

It was as if he were back in the cube, drowning in invisible water. *It's true. I can't leave the ship.* Liv turned him on his side but again, nothing would leave his lungs. *I'm going to die.*

"Turn back!" Liv screamed. "We have to get back to the ship. He won't make it to shore."

No Orlando. No gigs.

The medics lowered a sling to the motorboat.

"Hang on, Ryan," said Liv, helping to secure him. The medics had to pry his fingers from hers.

How long will she live with me on this prison ship?

Liv kissed him on the cheek. And as he was hauled up the gangway to the cruise ship's main deck, passengers lined the rails, pointing down at him, their mouths contorted in concern. A piercing cold permeated his shoulder. Looking up, Ryan saw Houdini perched on the stretcher's edge, his soul sitting on the brim of his top hat.

"Welcome back, Ryan. I do believe you have a contract to sign."

E is for Escape

Megan Arkenberg

What is my life to me? And what am I
To life,—a ship whose star has guttered out?
                    -Edna St. Vincent Millay, "Interim" (1917)

I.

If Continental stations live and die by one rule, it seems to be this: All things can be repurposed. The Breaking Yards, the thin half-globes of clear blue synthgrav set low in the aft wings, are the only places in Lower Ship that never go still and quiet. You can stand on any deck in Middle Ship on any day of the year and see the green blowtorch flames gleaming below you like distant stars, feel the hollow crash of steelcore shell falling against the borders of the synthgrav, sheared away from scout ship frames like rotting flesh from bone.

Just past the wings, the masticated chunks of wreckage make their way back through Lower Ship. Iron, aluminum and steelcore are carted to the foundries to be melted down and recast. Organic matter is pressed into the compost shafts or the furnaces. Deeper within the station, up one level and down half a kilometer of corridor, the Hacks turn their programs and their code to the decommissioned AIs—wipe them blank, rewrite them as needed.

As far as I know, they haven't yet found a direction for humans who need repurposing. I'm on my own here. As in everything else.

II.

Two hours past Continental midnight, and what I really want is a cappuccino. Something to scour away the migraine-pulsing bluelight synth music of the Middle Ship entertainment deck, the ozone tang of electronic tobacco and the silky bodyglitter stickiness of the dance floor. A real Lower Ship cappuccino, the kind they drink in the Breaking Yards, the foundries, the transport shafts: steaming hot, stiff with foamy liquid saccharine, smelling stale and burnt and tooth-achingly sweet.

Two hours past midnight, and that's what I tell myself I'm looking for, climbing heavily down the transport-shaft stairs of rattling steel mesh. Down into the stink of engine oil and compost, the grinding of heavy machinery and thumping of conveyor belts, and beneath it all that thick coffee-counter richness. By now the nightly Sani-rain has passed up to Middle Ship, a sharp green smell like chemical lily-of-the-valley; but the disinfecting mist lingers, flickering with redscale holographic advertisements for electronic tobacco, shockshow channels, a casino in the highest deck of Lower Ship, or the lowest deck in Middle. I find the coffee counter pulling aside its plastic curtains on the transport-shaft exit, pay for my cappuccino in gray Lower-Ship cash, and if I turn back now I can pretend that this is all I wanted, all I came here to find.

If I turn back now, I can find a full-length elevator to carry me up to the cold and lifeless Upper-Ship apartment where my clothes are still pressed in the vac-drawers, waiting to be packed away; where my pillow and blanket are still crumpled on the living room floor, the bed intolerably empty; where another liter of gin is waiting for me on the counter, and the deckscreen is cued to current openings in Lower Ship, and my life is waiting, impatiently, to be taken up again and reassembled.

But tonight's drinking is already exercising its pull. My feet keep carrying me down, past the coffee counter, past the glowing tracks of the foundry carts and the pulse of safety holographs, down past the wings and into the Breaking Yards. Down where, at the very end of the dock, the scout ship *Sacramento* rusts and steams in the fog.

III.

It can't be long now. In a day or two, a week at most, the salvage will begin in earnest. Most of what is wrong with the *Sacramento* could be repaired easily enough, but no crew wants to be assigned to a founder.

Because I have a nasty streak when I've been drinking, I point this out to the ship.

"Fair enough," the AI says. Neuter voice, low and soft. It sounds almost bored.

Ships in the Breaking Yards are supposed to be guarded against unauthorized intrusion. They never have been. All kinds of people find their way into the still, silent shells: drunks like me, kids on a misguided dare. Sometimes worse things. I was on the team that salvaged the luxury cruiser *Reno*, and we found bodies in the filtration forest. Four of them, all suicides. We never figured out who they were, how they got there or why.

In any case, no one notices or no one cares that I've slipped in through the *Sacramento's* busted escape hatch. I settle myself in the central shaft, the narrow wing of steel mesh suspended over the highest branches of the filtration forest. This is the AI's real domain, the life support systems and all their intricacies—a scout ship, by definition, leaves the range of Continental navigation 'bots, and most pilots prefer to have a close hand in the steering, ever since the *Navajo* foundered outside Aldebaran Seventy-Four. But the *Sacramento's* AI has been completely severed from its work. The whole ship has taken on the wet, loamy stink of the unmaintained filtration forest.

And this one has another, sharper edge—ash, creosote, melted grease. The *Reno's* forest had smelled like a chemical spill. The *Sacramento's* stinks of fire.

I sit cross-legged on the steel floor, cradling my terrible cappuccino in both hands, and breath in the smell that I can hardly name to myself, even after all these weeks: the smell of Madeline's death.

IV.

All things can be repurposed. We met because of it, that first and unspoken rule; we met because of salvage. Madeline had heard that my team was responsible for breaking the *Aquitaine* when it was decommissioned, and she came down to request a sapling.

"Say what you will about the aeroshells, the old forests are the best I've seen." She frowned at the bright yellow and black carts rolling out of the wrecking dock, laden with compost. "It would be a waste to let it all go to the fuel sector."

I watched her closely all that afternoon, as we carefully dug the roots of the filtration forest out of their steel and fiber grids and lifted them whole into transportation cars, ready to roll back to the Building Yards. When Upper Ship said they were sending a woman to collect a forest sample, I didn't expect to find someone like *her*. I expected tall, elegant, executive; I expected synth extensions in her hair, digital tattoos, teeth like porcelain. But Madeline was warm and dark and solid, her curly hair cropped short and somewhat unevenly, her smile quick and sweetly imperfect. Her hands were hard, with crooked knuckles that had been reset after at least one break. It was late by the time she left the Breaking Yards. Sani-rain glistened in her hair, beaded in the bronze studs on the shoulders of her leather jacket.

"Are you off soon?" she asked, when she caught me watching. "What do you do for fun?"

I liked the same things she did, it turned out. Gin and tonic, Middle-Ship bluelight music and the press of bodies on the dance floor. Beautiful women. And if neither of us was particularly beautiful...Well. She was to me.

V.

Deep breath, full of death and burning. "I was thinking about her today," I tell the ship.

"What do you think about?" The question is level one conversational programming—but whatever the Hacks might say, there's something more behind it. A level one wouldn't care about the answer.

"To be honest?" I roll my shoulders, loosening sore muscles, hearing the tired sounds of my own body. "Dancing, mostly. Her hips, my arms. She liked that Middle-Ship place with the aquariums. Always wore something white so it would glow in the blacklight."

The AI makes a soft, appreciative sigh, the crackling of static.

And I ask, "What do you remember about her?"

"Her voice," it answers promptly. "And the way she took care of the trees. But that was required of her. Her gentleness wasn't."

I wonder what it would be like to fall down, down past this groaning net of steel, down into that ash-scented darkness. Wonder what the breaking crew will find down there, when they finally start dismantling.

And I take a deep breath, close my eyes.

"Tell me again how it happened."

VI.

My first night with Madeline was my first night in Upper Ship. I remember stepping out of the transport shaft, my arm pressed between hers and the soft purple synthsilk of her bodice, and pausing frozen in the long, carpeted hall. Concrete statues of women or angels emerged from the walls, so polished and sealed that they looked like porcelain. Brass or gold gleamed in the seams between steelcore panels. The only sound was the soft cocooning hum of air filters; the only scent, faint and intermittent, as the cool chemical ripple of clean fabric. Madeline did not laugh at me, but her grip on my arm tightened reassuringly.

I was so terrified, that night, that I'd break something. One of the infinite, intricate little mechanisms in quartz and wire and fired clay that ticked and buzzed and hummed on the crowded shelves in her front room. And even after I moved in with her, made room for my own little things in her vac-drawers and pantries, the fear remained.

Until one evening, deliberately, Madeline smashed a clock.

"See?" she said. Standing in the front room in her socks and clean white undershirt, pieces of glass and ceramic and tiny metal gears glittering ridiculously on the floor around her.

"Nothing to worry about."

The next day, while she was working in her quiet Upper-Ship office, I swept the pieces into a bowl and brought them to a workshop in Middle Ship. They fit the gears into a new face, mixed the glass and powdered the ceramic for something new. All things can be repurposed.

Our last night together, we went dancing. Six months, she was supposed to be gone, and I already found the idea unbearable. She only wanted our old place, the aquariums, the blacklight, but I took her somewhere Upper-Ship. Wooden floors, the kind that echoes under our heels. Lamps of crystal and candle wax.

"I know this floor," she said as I slipped my arm around her waist. "It's old filtration forest wood, isn't it?"

"The *Reno*," I said.

"The chandeliers, too, of course."

"Yeah." *I was one of the breakers,* I wanted to say. *We found bodies in that wood. Those chandeliers were broken and covered in dust.* But I could see that she was thinking of something else. Eyes closed, feeling the floor echo with her weight.

I rested my head on her shoulder, breathed the warm scents of her skin, her hair—the smell of home.

VII.

The AI switches to a clipped, official inflection, an octave higher than its usual interface. A different part of the system: disaster records.

"At 0320," it intones, "smoke detected in the second engine shaft. Suspected fault in air sanitation. At 0330, per protocol, all chambers locked down. Impurity redirected through filtration forest. 0355, carbon burden found excessive."

"Thank you," I say. I know the rest. Don't need to hear it again, not even drunk.

By 0425, all life-signs cease.

0630, approximate time of foundering.

And I remember getting the call, in our shared Upper Ship room with all its tiny singing machines and its quiet sense of *her*. A foundering, they said; a ship trapped in orbit around a medium-sized asteroid in the Gibson belt. No Continental ships had foundered in living memory. They thought it was a piloting error at first, until the AI forwarded the life-sign report.

Everyone on board had suffocated, suffocated or burned.

When they told me the name of the ship, I started screaming. I broke everything within reach, broke it past all salvage, past all repair.

VIII.

Any day now, they will make me give up Madeline's room in Upper Ship. They'll find a better use for it, someone who works in Navigation or Life-systems, maybe even one of the Hacks. I sit on the floor of the dead ship, breathing in the steam of Breaking Yard coffee, and I wonder if they'll take me back now. Give me my old job, my hab-cube in the Stacks.

But surely those have been claimed by now. Surely, like everything else in this little world, they have been repurposed.

In the damp early-morning quiet, in the smell of burning and death, I open my eyes.

"What were you thinking, just now?" the ship asks.

"Wondering where I'm headed next."

"I...understand." The ship speaks tentatively, and I swallow hard.

"Yeah?" I peer into the shadows, almost as if I expect to find something there. A human figure striding towards me, maybe, or even just a face. Some of the Breakers don't believe that AIs can feel, but I've never been one of them. I have a superstitious streak, I guess, or just a strange empathy with tools. Even as I've pried out their electronic souls, piece by piece, I have never doubted that there's someone there. "Well," I say, "I guess that's grief for you."

"They'll find a place, you know," the AI says. "Even for us."

My throat gets tight again, and I can't really speak. Just nod.

After a while, when my breathing calms, I stand and brush down my trousers with one hand. It's almost morning, and the Breakers will be coming in to work. In a few weeks, a few days maybe, that will be me again.

Today, I need to rest.

At the edge of the platform, I kiss the rim of my coffee cup and let if fall down, down into the trees and whatever is still among them. An offering. A farewell.

I kiss t he Sacramento's steelcore shell, tasting smoke, before I head back to shore.

F is for Founder

Gary B. Phillips

ADINA was born a girl of glass.

She had not been the first child with such a strange birth defect. The doctors had run tests on the child after her birth and delivered the news with practiced, solemn faces. Her mother carefully pulled back layer after layer of blankets to reveal a small translucent blue body, spindling arms and legs, and clear blue eyes that shone like the sky after a February storm.

Adina's earliest memory was her mother singing to her. She didn't remember the melody or the words, but the way it *felt*, the way her mother's deep contralto voice resonated within her own glass body, tickling her bones.

Her second memory was more nebulous but no less real, the feeling of suffocation and everything that came with it: sweaty palms, a hammering in her chest, and the cloying taste of her own tongue, like a fat lump of sugar at the bottom of a cereal bowl. Her mother, on a hot August morning, dressing Adina in too many layers: soft cotton dresses, bulky winter jackets, scarves, shawls, and homemade gloves. It was in the way her mother never left her side. Any taste of freedom far too easily snubbed out with a harsh word, or the grip of her mother's hand.

When Adina turned five her mother said it was time for her to start school like the other children. For one effulgent moment Adina actually believed that freedom was within the grasp of her crystalline hands.

The next day her mother introduced her to Shamira.

୨୦୧

The trees gave way to skyscrapers half shrouded in fog and looking like the bone-white legs of some long dead beast. After an hour more of traffic, they arrived at the Green River Recording Studio. Adina hopped out of the car and followed her mother across the street, Shamira holding her hand the whole way. Adina wasn't sure what to think of this new girl. She barely looked like a woman, but had effortlessly taken up all the responsibilities of keeping Adina safe, as if she was her new mother.

The early morning sun had burned off most of the fog and the city bustled with people walking to their jobs. They all looked miserable, dressed in dark suits and solemn faces as they stepped carefully over the slippery sidewalks. Adina wondered if her father was among them and if he looked as miserable as they did.

Her mother was cheerful though, in her own subdued way. Her delicate lips were slightly less wan than usual. "Another day in the studio," she said.

"How long this time?" Adina asked.

"They've booked us for six hours."

Adina unconsciously ticked off the hours on her fingers. Six hours of just standing there, letting the music vibrate off her body. At least with an orchestra they would record it all at once. There was nothing worse than waiting for a band to record each piece separately, her mother standing there motionless with a dumb smile on her face (*smile honey, smile, her mother would mouth from the control room, parting her fingers from her lips and pulling wide her big dumb grin*).

Adina stood six feet from the string section. The violins swelled to life, their melodious lilt stirring inside her. It felt like heaven. Previously she had worked with jazz bands, but their music did nothing for her. At least this would be beautiful. By

87

the end of the second hour, her legs were more Jell-O than glass and she wanted to collapse. But her mother was there, off to the side, with her dumb grin.

After three hours they took a break. Adina's mother went to lunch with the producer and sent Adina to the park with Shamira. Adina lay in the grass and let the sun warm her, the bits of her exposed skin casting rainbows along the wet earth.

The fog had cleared and left shining blue skies in its wake, but Adina felt suffocated and alone. She watched the other kids climb trees, kick soccer balls, run with wild, reckless abandon, and fall and bleed and cry. Their wailing voices penetrating her, wrapping themselves around her lungs and heart like a vice and tightening until she felt as if she might explode if she didn't scream herself. But she never screamed. She kept quiet. Like her mother had taught her.

She watched the children across the field kicking a soccer ball. One of them tripped and came back up with a bloody knee and grass in his hair. He was smiling though. She could smell the wet grass, hear the sound of their laughter. She wanted so badly to taste it.

She envied other children, hated them even, as they skipped up and down the stairs, two-at-a-time, even three. Jumping the last half dozen stairs and falling at the bottom, their voices howling with laughter and pain. Broken arms, scraped legs, and bloody noses.

"You look angry," Shamira said.

Adina's felt flush in her cheeks. She wondered if they were tinting red.

"I want that," Adina said, and she pointed to the children playing.

"I know, but that's where you got that." Shamira pointed to the chipped glass of her elbow. "And this." Her fingers brushed against Adina's brow, where the sliver of missing glass was almost invisible to the naked eye if you weren't looking for it.

"Some lives come with a higher cost. That's why I'm here. To help you."

That was the thing about Shamira. She never made it sound as if she was being paid to be there. She always gave her answers as a friend.

Even at six Adina knew her life was fake. She had been

made in some strange, fake way and existed in a state somewhere between liquid and solid, always in suspended animation, never able to reach any point for herself.

She had heard rumors about other children of failed experiments. Most of them were thrown away. Those that were not formed small communities, under bridges, tent cities, at the edges of civilization. The children in her neighborhood traded stories about them, whispered words on fall winds. *Freak. Monster. Alien.* She wondered if there was another glass child. A glass boy, perhaps.

‹›

The fear and the isolation crept into Adina and found a warm place to hibernate. It grew inside her, colonized her, her mother made sure of that, and by her teenage years it filled her up until there was no room left for anything else. She had filled herself with her fears and now her mother was asking her to bend, to become whoever she was really supposed to be. Something more than just a glass girl. But Adina knew better than anyone, that glass never bends, it only breaks.

Adina had tried to sneak out a few times at night to meet up with friends, totally harmless, but Shamira always caught her and sent her back inside. Adina had come to resent her guardian as she did her own mother.

Adina did have one respite. Second period history class where she sat next to Seth and passed notes back and forth, ignoring the teacher's colorless voice. Seth resembled a stick insect, skinny limbs and big eyes that did not belong on his gaunt face. He wasn't handsome. Adina liked that about him.

She hoped it was not just superficial interest, fascination with her glass body. He played on the football team, a typical dumb jock. She wanted what she knew could hurt her. No boy like that could be so gentle with her.

The teacher was rambling about cathedrals.

"Adina, you might find this interesting," the teacher said. "Many scientists believe that glass isn't as solid as we think. The old windows of cathedrals in Europe are thicker on the bottom than they are on top. Glass moves, over time, very slowly."

"Does that mean she's going to have a big ass when she's

older?" a boy near her asked.

The class laughed, but Seth did not.

"Actually, that's not true," Shamira said. "Those windows are thicker at the bottom due to the manufacturing and installation, with the heavier side ending up on the bottom. That's all."

Shamira always had an answer. Always the right answer. Adina hated it.

Adina knew the kind of things the boys wondered about her. Most of their questions were shouted across busy hallways to the uproarious laughter of everyone. She did her best to ignore them.

"She's glass, not a microscope. She wouldn't be able to find it," Shamira said.

Adina's face flushed a beautiful rosy color. The kids ate it up. But Adina didn't want Shamira's pity. Didn't want her quick wit. It was bad enough that Shamira had already been the one to give her the sex talk—her mother was too busy, or didn't care enough.

"Ignore them," Seth said. Then, to Shamira, "She doesn't need you to defend her."

For once, it seemed that Shamira had no answer.

"You know she likes you," Shamira said.

Adina's glassy cheeks flushed the red of stained glass.

"Just leave me alone. For two minutes," Adina said.

"I can't."

જ્જ

That night, she crept through the house and listened at Shamira's door. All was quiet within. She tiptoed back up to her room and out the window.

She met Seth behind the school, by the old crumbling wall with the tree that twisted through it. The kids used to talk about how the wall was the last remaining piece of an old sawmill that had burned down, killing everyone inside. Kids used to say it was haunted, especially on nights like tonight.

He clutched a bottle of white wine. She examined the label. "Two-thousand four. A good year," she said, although she knew about as much as wine as he did about making love to a glass girl.

He popped the cork of the bottle and the wine spilled over. They drank from the bottle and from one another. She gasped in surprise at his gentle touch, how soft his fingers were as they slid from her hair and face to her legs. Her body sang like a wineglass, fingertips slipping across its rim. They resonated together under the pitch black sky and the cicadas waking from their slumber went quiet, listening to her serenade them. The pressure was immense and she thought she might break, but she only felt their bodies moving together, as if they were both made of glass.

When they had had their fill of wine and each other, she took the bottle and smashed it against the wall. She squealed as the glass shattered. Amazed at how easily its strength was broken. How something that brought them such joy could be destroyed so easily. The moon glinted off the shards of glass and she was struck by how beautiful it looked. The perfect end to their night.

Shamira was waiting for Adina when she snuck back through her open window. Her guardian's hands were in her lap. The very picture of patience.

"I know you snuck out to see him," she said.

"Did you follow me?"

Shamira shook her head.

"Why not?"

Shamira bit her lip and looked away for a long moment before saying, "Because I loved a boy once..."

That was when Adina saw the crack in her guardian's own glass. She gave her some time, a week, and then pulled her aside.

"Are you happy?" Adina asked. "Taking care of me, I mean."

"It is an honor to protect you."

Adina laughed. "You say that like you rehearsed it. It sounded pretty wooden to me. I'm not some helpless princess, you know. And you didn't answer my question."

Shamira shrugged. A few days later, Adina asked her again.

"The money is good," Shamira said. "And these skills don't translate to the corporate world well."

Adina still wasn't satisfied. She could tell Shamira had rehearsed each line. Always one step ahead of her.

Finally, Adina asked Shamira one more time.

"Are you happy? I know your schedule as well as you know mine. You really don't have any time for yourself. Or others. Have you ever even been on a date?"

Shamira furrowed her brow.

"Of course I have."

"But not in the last ten years. You've spent them with me."

Shamira didn't say anything for a long while. Adina let the silence speak for her.

"There was a boy once. I loved him and he loved me, but- He died before we really knew each other. Before we knew how much we loved each other. Shortly after that, I got this job, and I haven't had a chance to think about it. You've kept me very busy, Adina."

Shamira smiled weakly, but her eyes did not show it.

"I buried myself in you," she said. "I emulated you. Thinking that I could become as hard as glass. As unfeeling. It worked for a while."

"But the cracks have started to appear," Adina said.

Shamira nodded.

Adina took her hand and held it. "Happens to the best of us."

✧

The next morning Adina's mother sat at the kitchen table. Narrow strips of light filtered through the air, highlighting her every blemish. A face too freckled, too imperfect. Her mother took great care to remove every blemish before going out to the real world. Foundation applied, exfoliate, scrub, avocado peel, tweeze, pluck, or in an emergency, just drink a bottle of wine and chastise it. She always looked good going out, not so much at home. At home it was freckles and flaws and Adina thought she was quite stunning if you could forget that her insides were made of barbed-wire and thorns.

"We need to talk," her mother said.

"Where's Shamira?" Adina asked. "Doesn't she usually handle these talks?" Adina did her best to hide the wet cynicism in her voice. She didn't think she hid it very well.

"You know I hate having these tough talks with you."

But it wasn't this talk or just the tough talks. It was every talk. Why talk to your kid when you can pay someone to do it for you? Having a real conversation was too inconvenient when your child wasn't the perfect designer baby you had been promised.

Her mother's thin, freckled lips were drawn so tight they

resembled the *CUT HERE* dotted line of a children's workbook.

"I fired Shamira."

"What? Why?"

"She got too close to you. That's not what I was paying her for."

Adina fumed. She was sure that her skin brightened to a white hot glow. She felt the few dams and levees she had built for herself begin to break. All the fear and isolation filled her up like a poisoned well.

Adina's whole world was collapsing around her, yet her mother would be there to make sure that the strident sound of the world ending would resonate off her daughter's glass carcass.

"I will accompany you until we can find a suitable replacement," her mother said, pressing her fingers into her temple. "You do realize I'll have to miss work for this? You can spend the rest of the day in your room."

Adina stormed up the stairs. Her eyes were a raging gray maelstrom. Tears leaked from them and shattered on the stairs, the tinkling of broken piano keys.

"And Adina?" Her mother called from downstairs. "I trust we won't have this problem again?"

৵৹৶

True to her promise, Adina's mother followed her every step at school the next day. She even followed her into the bathroom and stood outside the stall.

Adina balled up one end of the scarf around her neck and stuffed it into her mouth to drown out the sobs as she cried in the bathroom stall. The only sound was her mother's heel tapping impatiently on the tile floor. This was her life now, held prisoner by a paid warden or her own mother.

When they left the bathroom Adina saw her chance. The old wall and twisted tree was her beacon. All she had to do was run faster than her mother. She ran.

She kicked off her shoes, loosed her scarves and jackets; they littered the field behind her. She was in her sun dress now and the cold wind bit against her glassy body. Her mother shouted from behind her, but Adina didn't bother to look back.

The old wall along the back of the school. The one the

burnouts would use to go sneak a smoke or drink. The muddy base of the wall was littered with trash, old beer cans and cigarette butts. The broken wine bottle was still there, glinting sharply in the sun. It smelled terrible, like sour milk and cigarette butts. She hadn't noticed how terrible it had smelled that night.

She placed an unsteady foot against a broken part of the wall and carefully began to climb. Each foothold brought her closer to freedom. It was ten feet to the top and she scaled it with ease. Her mother was at the base of the wall, shouting Adina's name and drawing the attention of every kid nearby.

The sun peeked out from behind some clouds and caught her in the light. Without the layers of clothes her skin shone like. She placed one foot in front of the other, treading the crumbling bricks, aware that one slip would surely be her end. The few falls she had taken in life had left permanent scars across her body.

The kids below started to cheer her on. They probably didn't even know why, but it seemed the thing to do, so they did.

"What are you doing, love?" her mother asked. Her words were like honey, but the tone wasn't sweet. She was clutching the clothes Adina had shed. "Aren't you cold?"

"The sun is out. I'm fine."

It must have pained her mother to speak this much to her.

"Get down from there, sweetie," she said.

Adina ignored her and kept walking, letting her feet kick and drag against the rough stones. Her toes were chipping, little shards of glass flecking off with each kick, but she ignored the pain. She smiled for herself this time.

"Smile, mother," Adina called. She pulled her fingers away from her mouth and gave a big grin, like her mother used to.

"What would your father say?"

At this, Adina stopped, and finally looked at her mother.

"What would he say? That's a good question! He hasn't ever been around—"

Her mother's voice raised an octave. "His job is very important. He's a very important man."

"I'm important," Adina said, her voice no longer small.

Her mother did not respond. Maybe she hadn't heard her, or maybe she didn't know what to say or how to say it. Shamira had always been the one that had the important conversations with her. She wondered where Shamira was now. Finding her own freedom maybe.

Adina didn't know if she would survive the fall. She knew though, if she did, that things would be different. She relaxed her body. Her foot slipped from the wall and she fell.

Her mother screamed. A beautiful sound that resonated within Adina. Maybe the most beautiful scream the world had ever heard. Adina knew that she screamed not because her daughter was in danger, but because her meal ticket was gone.

Adina fell.

She fell, she fell, she fell.

G is for Glass

Alexandra Seidel

THE sun is up. I am awake.

Three girls are sitting at a table, talking about apples.

"Peel them," says the first. She is not angry, but from the way her body is tense, it is just obvious that she wants change. She is restless.

The second girl points at me. "Let us keep the apple tree," she says. "The older the tree, the better the apple. And you must wait for fall to come, when the time is there, you will not have to pick and peel, the fruit will just be waiting right at your feet."

The third is the quiet kind. She has a green ribbon in her hair. "What shall we do with all the apples anyway? Where to put them, we can't eat them, and what if they have worms?"

The first girl looks at the third. She has knives in her eyes, that one. "I still say we should have to get rid of the skin." She indicates me with a nod of her head. "Can you not see that it chafes?"

❧

The sun is up. I am awake

There is a kitten, a goose, and a horse seated at the table.

The kitten is sharp eyed, claw smart. "I like yarn the best. In fact, I love yarn."

The horse whinnies, shakes her had as if there are flies at

her ears. "It is hay you want, hay. It is warming, and it is good for eating. You can roll in it as well. Nothing quite like hay, not anywhere in the world."

The goose has a green ribbon around her long and feathery neck. She looks at me, points that orange beak, then speaks to the others. "I care neither for yarn nor hay. Why these silly things? We must go where there is water! And a clear sky to fly in! Can you not see that I am not mistaken?" At the end, her voice has become quite gagglish.

The kitten flexes her kitten claws and makes sure the goose sees her do it. "A good ball of yarn, I say. Can you not see what happens if something like that becomes undone?"

The sun is up. I am alive.

Three china peddlers are seated at a market square.

The first is wearing a coat made of white calla lilies. "When you break a cup," she tells the other two, "you throw it out."

The second peddler has a hat weighing heavy with cream white roses. "A cup is a beautiful thing. When it breaks, there is grief in the world, for a beautiful thing just broke. One must never be afraid to think of mending a broken cup. They can mend the cup, maybe, but the pain that was felt before cannot be made unfelt."

The third china peddler is wearing a fluffy carnation skirt, held at her waist with a green ribbon. "Shards!" She says, and her eyes go wide, look right at me. "When there are shards, what can one do? They look so ugly, and they bleed. What o what shall we do about the shards?"

The calla lily coated peddler looks at the one with the cream rose hat, both shake their heads to one another. The calla lily coated peddler points at me, then tells the one with the carnations: "Shards as such do not bleed, can you not see that? But they can cut, if you let them, they may cut to the bone. Not because they like parting skin, but because they cannot help it. Can you not see what happens if you do not take away the shards?"

The sun is up. Shadows fall, and in between, I am awake.

There is a table, and three wise queens are sitting at the table. Shadows creep in between them, and I cannot always make out their faces.

The Queen of Wands says: "We can do nothing more for the king, not here. Let's send him to an island where red apples grow." A shadow flicks in front of her face, and I know that I just saw her smile to me, but now the smile is shadow dark.

...sick, he's sick, and he won't get better... professional help, someplace he can't hurt himself or others... whisper the shadows with dark lips.

The Queen of Cups carries the burden of an ocean. "There is but one way to the island. Once we take him there, this king will never return to us. Fresh apples in his mouth may tame some of the shadows, but they will not send them away." The queen has shadows eating her face, and as I watch, they cover her face like a curtain of dark, moving down and down, like the shadow from the brim of a hat.

...in a home?! ...will get worse than he is now, and... not coming back. Do you want that on your conscience? whisper the shadows with dark lips.

The Queen of Pentacles has her coins bound with a green ribbon, but it seems like she has forgotten all about them, clinking at her ankles. "To an apple isle!" She says. "How will we do it, and how will we find the way? And what about how we come back without apple seeds sticking to our soles and skirts?" Shadows are around her holding hands, moving inward, outward, dancing.

Well, what should we do? Well, what should we do? whisper the shadows with dark lips.

The Staff Queen will not back away. She scares even shadows with her fire. "He may not be our king anymore, but he is still a king. He does not remember the words he once knew, those words that were the law, but we still know law when we see it, for we are queens. What do you think will happen to a king that is a king no more, neither to himself nor the world?"

I know, but... the best. He needs... around the clock, and... for the best, whisper the shadows with dark lips.

She looks at me then, my girl of Wands, and I remember the crown on my head. It is crumbling, but sometimes I do not notice the sand falling into my eyes, the sand that will starve a raven.

The crown is also casting wicked shadows, but sometimes I forget that the shadows are crown shaped, their darkness throttling the other raven.

I remember now, I once was a ...

The sun is up. I am alive.

H is for Hanging Man

Jonathan C. Parrish

APRIL 1, 2024. Lesser Slave Lake.

I can't fathom why she felt the need to send me out to get him, like he needs a babysitter. I bet she saw my jaw drop when she said I couldn't finish my pie first. Let her suck on that one, let her know that it's not all happy joyland up here. Let her know how much I hate her stupid requests and her fucking rules and I can't believe that I ever thought coming out here would be a good idea.

I hate the cold, hate the fact we isolated ourselves out here, hate all the people I work with. Even Ferguson. Especially Ferguson, now, for making me walk down to the lake edge. Assuming you can even call it a lake this time of year where it's just a frozen sheet dotted with ice fishing huts. Except of course it's a lake and fuck you Ferguson for making me have a semantic argument with myself. Dick.

Ferguson left 16 hours ago to go fishing, it's all he talks about now and somehow I'm his goddamn retrieval squad or some shit. I'm not even sure he likes to eat fish, he never talks about cooking them, he's just all blah blah blah "It's enough to dip the hook and wait, very zen!" That's when I bite him with my eyes to show him how I really feel about his zen pole and hole dipping.

"Ferguson! Get your sorry ass up to the lab, the obergruppenführer says you have to account for some shit or another!" I'm shouting while I walk towards his hut because I want to get back to my pie and sooner he goes back the sooner I get back. It's not the best, the pie, not like the cherry pie at Rosie's in High Prairie. Mmm, that's good pie.

No response. Dick.

"Ferguson!" I stomp up to his usual hut and push open the piece of plywood he calls a door. It takes a second to adjust to the dark but there he is dipping away. *Dip and pause.* "Ferguson! The fuck dude?" I know he knows exactly what I am asking, I'm letting him know with every motion of my hands. He's just staring at the point where his fishing line meets the water. "Ferguson!" I bark.

"It's so simple. It's just me and it all circles around me like ripples." *Dip and pause.*

"OK. Good for you dude." I roll all kinds of disdain into my voice which should make him feel super awkward and uncomfortable but he just sits there. Probably trying to figure out how to deal with me without coming off as a loser. Which he is. "Did you catch your dinner?"

"I don't even have a hook any more, it just complicated the process."

I put on my super-annoyed face. "OK, wakey wakey Mr. Snakey, Brunhilda is looking for you, she has questions about the toxoplasma strain you're working on. Bob said you made some comment about testing it for attention deficit and she's all pissy at everyone for knowing her big million dollar secret."

"That's not important." *Dip and pause.*

The hell did that mean? She's the one who signs the cheques, she's a bag but you can't just ignore her, just keep her on her toes with scathing sarcasm. Plus, when he wasn't talking about fishing, Ferguson was all about how rich this *T. ghondii* isolate was going to make them when they could control kid's focus. He'd even called his strain "*T. ghandi*" when the rats stopped being aggressive. Ha ha, he was super funny considering he was being such a dicknoodle right now.

"OK buddy, look, I don't get to eat my pie until you are back at the lab so that's where we're going now." I move towards the door in a way that says "*OK that's enough of that bullshit*" and he just sits there like a fucking Brussels sprout.

I screw my face up into my "I'm a mad parent and you're a

bad kid" expression and stride over to him because goddamn him making this stupid and I grab his arms to force him out the door and he freaks out like I'm tickling him with a cattle prod so I try to readjust my grip to around his neck and he squirrels down into where my arm meets my glove and I can feel this what the hell is he really? He's biting me. Is this kindergarten?

I rage-throw him off me like I'm Triple H and as he turns to me he's crazy-faced. I can't believe this fucker is making this so fucking stupid so I grab his fishing rod because fuck him that's why and as I go to snap it I see him pull up a two by four and really is he? And I stand there like a dumbass because he can't possibly be—

ᗑᗌ

It's like climbing out of a pit, or a well, or a hole in something like ice… goddamn you Ferguson! My head is pounding, my arm is throbbing and my legs are on fire. I try to look around and I'm blind for a few seconds. I try to sit up and knock a layer of snow off my coat before I am overwhelmed by the pain in my legs and fall back. I close my eyes tight and ride the pain wave. Seriously? He broke my goddamn legs?

There's a little splishing noise coming from near my head. I try and look without moving my legs, and I can just see Ferguson hunched down with his rod.

Dip and pause. Dip and pause. Dip and pause.

"Ferguson, what the hell? What's going on? What did you do?" I feel like the answers maybe don't matter, maybe I already know. He's saying something but I have a fleeting impression of pie slices in a way that sheep are supposed to but never do for insomniacs and it seems to be effective.

ᗑᗌ

Maybe it was supposed to be effective, leaving me on the ice to die like an elder. Maybe Ferguson thought he was doing something poetic. I can't hear him anymore, I hear nothing but wind and little nature sounds. I have limited options; everything has come down a very simple choice. But simplifying has never seemed so painful. I drag myself to Ferguson's hole and crack away the layer of ice on the surface.

Dip and pause. Dip and pause. Dip and pause.

Surprisingly, I don't hate Ferguson. In a way, I admire his *chutzpah*. I giggle.

Dip and pause. Dip and pause. Dip and pause.

It's all about will now. Rinse and repeat. I laugh out loud at the absurdity of it all. What the hell am I doing?

Dip and pause. Dip and pause. Dip and pause.

I'm close enough to the shore that a squirrel considers me a potential threat. I see him through the open doorway, will him to come closer to me, but he persists in his little jumping twitch squeaks, his tail apparently pushing the sound out of his face. I wait for the freezing to finish, focused on that, automatic, freeing me to daydream about transmitting my intent. I file him away for later. First things first.

Dip and pause. Dip and pause. Dip and pause.

I test my new leg ice, it squeaks and thin cracks appear. Not yet.

Dip and pause. Dip and pause. Dip and pause.

A memory tugs at the edges of my awareness, I replay the last conversation I had with Ferguson about his new strain. *T. ghandi* was going to usher in a new era of peace and prosperity, the latter mostly for him and the company but whatever. Ferguson's face swims in and out of focus like he is underwater, his voice muffled, "Why stick ourselves in the middle of nowhere if we weren't going to do dangerous and stupid things? We can make a pill for will! A will pill! It's the next Ritalin that also has the side effect of removing fear!" The words fade away, but something happened there, something important. Maybe?

Dip and pause. Dip and pause. Dip and pause.

I can see the squirrel twitching still, he's not squeaking now. I feel like I should find him hilarious or cute, I note that I don't and file that away. All I know is legs, water, ice right now. Everything else is background.

Dip and pause. Dip and pause. Dip and pause.

I test my new cast again. It creaks, and it holds. With sheer strength of will I pull myself along the ice to a tree and pull myself up by my hands. The pain is excruciating, but I file it away for later. The ice helps with the throbbing and maybe that's funny, I don't know anymore. I check the sun and start walking to where I remember the nearest road is. I will my legs to begin stepping, will myself forwards.

It's 60 km to Rosie's and I can already taste the pie.

I is for Isolate

Simon Kewin

JOE caught the faint echo of the hulk on his ship's sensors. Excitement buzzed through him, a thrill that never got old. Goddamn *sweet*. No way was this a lump of space rock. No mistaking those clean lines even through the fuzz of the cracked display. A ship. The shattered remains of a ruined spacecraft. A *huge* spacecraft.

A thing of goddamn beauty. To a junker like him, the most beautiful sight in the whole wide universe.

"This is it, Avi. I told you. Sweet Jesus, this is the one. At last."

He still talked to Avi. Like she was there on the *Orpheus* with him. Like she was still alive and not buried beneath ten thousand tons of asteroid a million kilometres and thirty years away in the Belt. She'd died and he'd carried on talking to her, that was all. No one else to talk to out here anyway.

Finger trembling, he plugged the hulk into the Nav system and hit the engines. The *Orpheus* rumbled as the drive lumbered into life … and then glitched out, plunging him into darkness.

"Goddamn."

He sat there for ten, twenty seconds waiting for the ship's systems to restart. There was no silence like that inside a dead ship alone in deep space. He could *feel* his body heat being sucked into the hungry void as the *Orpheus* drifted. Damn ship was barely more spaceworthy than the shattered warships he scavenged. There was so much epoxy patching up the microimpact holes in the hull there was barely any of the original carbon left. The *Orpheus* was a ragtag wreck of welds and fixes and jury-rigs. Just like him. They were both broken-down hulks past their time. Man and spaceship.

It was a marvel either of them still flew. In thirty years he'd taken apart and fixed up every goddamn system on her. *Including* life-support. And doing that without the luxury of a spacedock was no joke. Avi always said he could fix anything. She'd done the drilling and he'd kept the rig functioning. That was how it had worked.

He'd often thought about going back to the Belt. Give up being a junker. But there were too many ghosts. Too many memories. And it was *far* too dangerous. What was the average life-expectancy of a miner? One year? Two, tops? He and Avi had lasted four. Waste of goddamn time, anyway. Maybe one in a thousand struck lucky. The rest simply struck *out*, sooner or later. Even Avi, who was the smartest miner he'd ever met. Avi who could smell a mineral deposit from orbit. Even she had died.

No. Out here he was his own man. He was free. Free to die a lonely, lingering death, sure, but still free. Free to talk to his dead, beautiful wife, too, if he felt like it, and no one to tell him he couldn't.

Emergency lights finally flickered into life, bathing him in a red glow. Machinery hummed and whirred as the *Orpheus* rebooted. No rumble from the engines, though. Panic flared within him. Not panic he was going to die. He was used to that. That was his regular day-to-day existence. This was the much worse: the fear he was going to *live* to see some other junker spot the wreck and get there before him.

He wasn't going to let that happen. This might be his last shot, his last roll of the dice. The pot of gold at the end of his rainbow. He was getting old. You couldn't patch up failing systems indefinitely. This wreck was *his*. His and Avi's. They'd vowed never to give in the day they left Earth. Vowed to stick at it until the end. And now here they were.

With a cry of frustration he pounded the display screen. Starships were delicate, complex mechanisms, requiring a high degree of technical competence to maintain. Sure. And sometimes you had to whack them to show them who was in charge.

The *Orpheus* refused to burst into life.

"Come on you heap of junk. We need to *move!*" He struck harder, picking his spot this time. A control array he'd patched up more than once was under the display. Some connection still loose, maybe.

The drive sulked for another couple of seconds, just to make a point, then grumbled into life.

Taped beside the screen was his only picture of Avi, printed on actual paper. Bright sunlight shining on their young faces. The two of them at Hong Kong Station, that day they left. It was the picture he talked to, not thin air. He wasn't goddamn *crazy* or anything. He talked to it now. To her.

"Here we go, Avi. I'm gonna go claim that hulk. For us."

Avi smiled her usual knowing smile, but didn't reply. Joe punched in the target again, and this time the engines lurched into life. The starfield whirled as the Orpheus found its vector. The aft drive array flared. The displays thought about things for a while then gave him a readout. *ETA: two hours.*

He spent the time glued to the screen, terrified of seeing some other junker closing in at higher velocity. Nothing.

Thirty minutes from the hulk, still blissfully alone in the void, he began to get detailed scans. He'd assumed it would be some wrecked Earth dreadnought blasted into oblivion during the Medusa War. They'd lost a lot of ships back then. The battles had been fought over such vast distances that even now, fifty years on, there were wrecks to scavenge. Inner-system space had been picked clean, but out here in the Kuiper there was still treasure to be found. Wrecks for junkers like him to feast on.

But no. This was no human ship. No Earth dock had ever constructed anything so goddamn alien. The twisted, intersecting planes of its fuselage hurt his brain. It looked like a collision between at least three separate ships. Vast, crazy, *wrong*. Medusan, no doubt about it. Half of her was gone, a ragged, gaping tear where the aft section – if it *was* the aft section – had been ripped off in some collision or explosion.

The alien ship was weird, but beautiful in a way. If you'd drunk one too many slammers. Earth ships were clumsy and functional by comparison, all engine pods and artillery arrays and whatever else needed to be stuck on, stuck on. The Medusan ships were *sculptures*. Towering, twisting sculptures.

That had always troubled him. The Medusans had been cruel enemies. They'd arrived without warning, levelling stations and habs from Charon inwards, never stopping to negotiate or explain, seeking only to destroy. They were like mindless animals. Yet here were their ships, more works of art than battleships.

Still, the truth was seven Medusan ships had come close to defeating everything Earth could throw at them. Only the last line of defense, the orbiting nuke platform around the planet, had saved humanity. Although sometimes he doubted humanity *had* been saved. Earth seemed like a distant, alien place to him now. A war machine ruled by Generals constantly ready for another attack. He'd never go back.

In the fifty years since the war, only one Medusan craft had ever been recovered, and that had been tiny, a shuttle. And here were the remains of one of the seven, slowly spinning in the dark of the void. To the military back on Earth its worth was incalculable. Name-your-price, mega-rich, goddamn *incalculable*.

Heart belting away in his chest, Joe fired the beacon that would mark the wreck as his. He half-expected the ship to glitch out again, just to make a point.

For once everything worked. The beacon tore through space at ten times the Orpheus's velocity. It was programmed to stop ten kilometres from the hulk and begin broadcasting. Seven long minutes later he picked up the first signal, loud and clear, sending out his signature to the universe. He whooped out loud and punched the air. The wreck was officially his.

"We did it, Avi. We actually did it. Like you always said we would."

The problem was what to do now. Legally speaking no one could take the hulk from him. He had salvage rights. But out here in the Kuiper, respect for the law was as faint as the heat from the distant sun. If a rival with a bigger ship turned up they could destroy the beacon and the *Orpheus* and who would know? That was how it went.

Problem was, he couldn't tow the wreck in-system. Far too massive. It would take lifetimes to reach a spacedock at the sort of thrust the *Orpheus* could put out. He eyed the ghostly outline of the hulk on the screens. Was there a chance he could get the alien ship's drive working? He was pretty good at patching up human craft, but a Medusan? Maybe, maybe not. Worth a look at least. And if he could salvage something – an artefact that proved his find – he could at least take that back to civilization to prove his claim.

Okay. That was a plan. He punched in a course for the severed end of the Medusan ship. That would be his way in. While the *Orpheus* maneuvered he prepared for an EVA.

෧෨

He crept along in the bubble of light from his suit, his own ragged breathing the only sound in the universe. The interior of the ship was as fucked up as her fuselage. Floors twisted round to become walls. Rooms intersected at random angles, as if the ship's designer had been insane. Or as if several insane designers had battled over the layout and in the end they'd all just done their own thing.

None of it looked like any warship he'd ever seen. None of it looked like *anything* he'd ever seen.

Weird shadows leaped around in his peripheral vision, the crazy angles of the walls throwing up phantoms. He ignored them and carried on. He was used to seeing ghosts in the shadowy corners of spaceships. His mind playing tricks on him.

He crept across a room cavernous enough to house the *Orpheus* a hundred times over. It twisted into a spiral and seemed to curve back on itself, tying itself in knots. He could see no sign of engines, or controls, or any goddamn thing he recognized.

He passed a circular doorway, sealed shut. Perhaps it led somewhere. It looked strong enough to be a vacuum hatch, sealing off this section when exposed to space. Would it take him to some vital part of the ship? There were no signs, no references to give him any clue. Through the gauntlet of his EVA suit he felt a faint buzz when he touched the door. The ship was still functioning on some level. He took his hand away. Could there still be Medusans onboard? Maybe he should get the hell out of here while he still could.

But what then? Leave the broken hulk? Head in-system and hope no one else saw it? Hell, he wasn't going to risk that. This

109

ship was *his*.

He touched the door again. There were no controls of any sort that might open it. There had to be electronics involved somewhere, but he had no idea where they were or how they might function. In frustration he pounded on the door with his fist.

To his surprise, the door irised open to reveal a long, straight corridor illuminated with a white glow. He stepped back, expecting attack. Expecting *something*. But it was just a corridor. No sign of Medusans. No sign of anything. But there was power. That was something. Maybe he could fix up the wrecked ship after all.

He stepped through the door. As he'd imagined it would, the seal irised shut behind him.

Okay. If all else failed he could instruct the *Orpheus* to cut him out of the alien ship. The drilling rig the ship still carried might be powerful enough to punch through the hull. Although he wished he'd checked first, now. He shrugged inside the heavy EVA suit and clumped forward.

After a few minutes his suit informed him there was atmosphere in the corridor. Breathable air. That stopped him. How the hell was that possible? That buzz he'd felt when he touched the door. Some automated system maybe, maintaining life support. Did the Medusans breathe the same air, then? No one had ever found out.

Tentatively, he released the seals on his helmet. After years of keeping the *Orpheus* patched up, he'd learned to trust his own senses more than those of his suit. The suit didn't tell you when the ship smelled wrong, when there was the whiff of something burning that shouldn't be burning. The suit didn't tell you when the hum from the engines was the *wrong* hum.

The air on the alien ship smelled good. Weirdly good. Sweeter than that on the *Orpheus*. Which didn't make a lot of sense. Carrying his helmet he edged forwards, feeling more unsettled with each step. What was he getting into here? There was a door up ahead, at the far end of the long, white corridor. His only choice was to go through. He couldn't shake the feeling he was being directed. Even that the ship was forming itself around him to bring him to this place.

Crazy, of course. The weird lines of the alien vessel were

getting to him. He needed to find the engines soon, see if he could patch them up. That or get the hell out now. He had the footage from his suit's cameras. Video could be faked but maybe it would be enough proof if someone else claimed the hulk before he did.

He approached the door. This was no vacuum seal. It was just a door. Yet it was oddly familiar. The sight of it stopped him dead. He'd seen it before. How the hell was that possible?

The door was from Hong Kong Station. The hab room they'd stayed in the night before they left. It was utterly insane. He saw then how it was. All that time on his own had broken his mind. He'd gone crazy and never even noticed.

He knew there was no way he should go anywhere near the impossible door. At the same time he had no choice did he? How could he turn back? He had to find out what lay beyond. Heart pounding, he pushed the door open.

Inside, the room was just as he remembered it. Cramped, functional. The double-bed taking up most of the space. And there, lying on the bed, was Avi. Sweet, beautiful Avi. She seemed to be asleep, but as he stood there, unable to move, unable to speak, her eyes flickered open and she smiled.

"Hey, Joe."

It took him long seconds to form a reply. "Avi, but... what the hell's going on? How can you be here? You died thirty years ago when that bore shaft collapsed. I *heard* you die."

Avi—or the delusion of Avi—rose from the bed. She padded across the room to stand in front of him. She sure smelled like Avi. She smelled wonderful. She touched him on the side of the face, cupping his chin like she used to. "I know. I died, Joe. I'm sorry. I tried not to."

He stepped back, freeing himself. "No. You can't be here. You're in my head. You're a delusion. I don't know what you are." He had to get off this ship. Get away. This was all some cruel trick.

"Oh, Joe, no," said Avi. "Here. Touch me. Feel me. I'm real. I'm as alive as you are."

He longed to succumb. "No. It's not possible."

"Many things are possible," said Avi. "Things humanity knows nothing about."

"So you're not human? You're not her? You admit it? This is, what, some Medusan trap?"

"Medusan? No. I'm not human, that's true. But I'm not Medusan. And I *am* also Avi. Look at me. *See* me."

"You look like her, sure. But different, too."

"And you look like you. But different, too."

"What the hell does that mean? I've changed, of course. I've aged thirty goddamn years for one thing."

"I know," she said. "It's not just that." She studied him for a moment, peering into his eyes. "You're sadder, too. You look weighed down."

"Yeah, well. Had a lot to weigh me down." This was insane. Now he was arguing with the phantoms his own mind was creating. Arguing with *himself.*

"You stayed true, though," she said. "Those promises we made to each other that day at Hong Kong Station." A wicked smile crept across her features. "And the ones we whispered the night before in this cramped little hab room. You remember?"

Of course he remembered. "You can't be here," he said again. "We're on a wrecked alien spaceship in the Kuiper Belt, not at Hong Kong station. That was all a long time ago. You're not Avi. None of this is possible. "

"But it is."

"How? How can she be here? How can you be her?"

The alien shrugged dismissively, a perfect copy of Avi's own mannerism. "You brought her with you when you came onboard. I see Avi in your mind. In your surface thoughts and your deep memories. The shapes that were Avi."

"Memories. Nothing real."

"Memories are real. What is an individual after all? A pattern of unique thoughts. Nothing more."

"No, you're wrong," he said, angry now, heart thumping. "That's goddamn nonsense. An individual is a person. A *body*. A lifetime of scars and wrinkles."

The alien nodded her head. "In part. But still, is your body really *you*? Or a shell? A vehicle you travel around in? Cells die and get replaced. The atoms that make up your hands or your heart or your brain change all the time. Only your mind remains. The patterns that are uniquely yours. By taking on Avi's identity I've become her. Partly her."

"That's bullshit. That's just words. You're not her. You could never be her."

"Joe, I..."

"It's a shame this ship wasn't destroyed and you with it."

He stormed away, back through the door, his whole body shaking. He clamped his helmet back into place. He thought she'd stop him leaving, seal him in. But the door at the end off the corridor spiraled open to his touch and he was back in the twisting, cavernous space he'd first seen. In the distance, through the ragged wound in the ship's hull, the stars shone quietly away.

He hit the suit's thrusters and headed for them. Three minutes later he was cycling the air-lock on the *Orpheus* and climbing back inside.

ᕲᘺ

He sat tight for a week, his tiny ship and the vast alien wreck dancing through space together. He kept expecting the Medusan ship to leave. Or to blast him out of existence. *Something.* But all was quiet. The whole universe was quiet except for his beacon and the comm system's background hiss.

His thoughts were a mess of anger and the lingering fear of other junkers turning up. More than once he fired up the engines, intent on heading back to civilization to claim his prize. Intent on getting away. The military could deal with the alien witch. But each time he found himself hoping the drive *wouldn't* work. When they powered up perfectly he ended up killing them manually. Once he got a few thousand kilometres away before shutting them down.

Swearing profusely, he kept busy with maintenance tasks that really weren't urgent. The control array that kept glitching out needed fixing. He crawled underneath and began to strip out old circuits and switch in new ones. It was good to focus on a simple task.

When he was done he wriggled out of the confined space. The picture of Avi was on the floor, dislodged by all his banging. It lay face down beside him. He picked it up, turning it over and over in his fingers. It was just a square of plastic, its image slowly fading. It wasn't Avi. Of course, he knew that. It hadn't stopped him talking to it all these years had it?

Like a fool he smiled at her. As ever, she didn't respond. He

113

set the picture down and, not stopping to think any more, headed for the EVA locker.

❦

The room was the same as before. The alien stood there as if she hadn't moved while he'd been away.

"Look, why are you here?" said Joe. "Why are you doing this? This game—what's it for?"

The creature looked sad. He'd hated it when Avi looked sad. The alien turned away to gaze through the little square window. It was just what Avi would have done. He wished she'd stop playing these games. There couldn't *be* anything outside the window to look at.

The alien sighed. "My sisters and I roamed the stars for a long time. Such a long time. Seeking company. Seeking others. When we started there was no one else in the galaxy, you see. We were the first. Space can be a lonely place. Although you know that, don't you? We craved contact with others. Craved it so much we learned to bond with those we encountered. Over the millennia, we learned to copy them. Join with them. *Become* them. Just as I've now become—partly—your Avi."

"And partly a goddamn ancient, metamorphosing alien."

She turned to grin her grin at him. "That's true, yes. Isn't life glorious?"

"And the Medusans?"

"They were ones we encountered. We found them after aeons of roaming alone. A primitive, warlike race. Communing with them was a mistake. But anything was better than the aching loneliness of millennia among the stars. We joined with them and became them and with our ships they became the cruel tormentors you fought. I'm sorry for what we did."

"We defeated you in the end."

"You did. And perhaps it was for the best. By destroying our ships you broke our bonds with the Medusans."

"Your people died too?"

"My six sisters died."

"So the Medusans really are gone?"

"They are. And now there is only me. Drifting alone in this broken ship."

"We have to tell Earth," said Joe. "Tell them there is no threat anymore."

"Yes. Tell them they are safe. But they won't believe you. You'll have to turn me over to them. Tell them where I am so they can see for themselves. Perhaps it's only what I deserve."

That stopped him. If he did that, she wouldn't survive. They'd rip the ship to pieces. Her, too, to find out everything they could.

There was a moment of silence, during which the stars turned and the universe aged a little. But he'd already come to his decision by coming back.

"This ship," he said. "Is it beyond repair?"

She shrugged, looking about the hab room. "Once our ships regrew themselves. But not anymore. I can direct it to effect small changes like this room, but that's all. This ship is too broken. Its heart is gone."

"We could repair it."

"I've tried. But I was the Navigator of the seven."

"We could do it between us," said Joe. "Fix what was broken. We could at least try and get the self-repair systems going so the ship can do the rest. I've got pretty good at beating dead ships back into life."

She studied him for a moment. "You would do that?"

The ship's worth was incalculable, sure, but here was the thing. What the hell would he *do* with all that money? Where would he go? Avi was all he'd ever really wanted.

"If you're really her you know I would," said Joe. "We're both alone out here. I guess you're partly Avi. And I'm not one of your sisters, but maybe we're the closest either of us is going to get to what we want."

"And Earth?"

He shrugged. "I left the Earth behind a long time ago. We can tell them the truth. Up to them whether they believe it. Then we can wave this little system good bye forever. Leaving Earth was supposed to be an adventure, remember?"

A smile spread across the woman's features. A smile that was ancient and wise, but also pure Avi. That wicked glint in her eye that made his stomach fizz.

"I remember," she said.

"Then come on," he said. "Let's get to goddamn work."

J is for Junker Joe

Beth Cato

So it's like this. Me and Tommy Smith finish up our shift. We're walking down the lane when we see this bloke sittin' on a rock at the edge of the meadow. Just sittin' there.

"Do you know'im?" Tommy asks me.

Thing is, I don't. Don't know him from Adam, but he's as familiar as my brother, God rest his soul. Like I seen him every day, but not really seen him. His face was all sharp angles, his hair long like a little girl, and his clothes, like he escaped from some Shakespeare play. Long shirt 'n tights 'n big cuffs, the stuff like satin, but filthy. Same as him. Like he been digging in the meadow or something.

Yessir. You been told about that meadow, I'm guessin'? I know now it's something special, but you... I'm bettin' you knew long before.

There'd been lot of talk in town about it that morning, folks laughing about the Jerry being such a poor shot. We expect them to target the factories down by the river, but this meadow is way out. Nothin' ever been built there. Never been graze land, either. Peculiar thing, I suppose. No one ever paid it mind 'cept to notice how the flowers liked to grow there. My mother, she used to say it was a place for wee folk to play.

Well, bomber the night before dropped one right in the middle of it. Blasted a crater deep as a basement. Didn't notice 'til I was standin' there that the outer field was still green but every one of them flowers had shriveled up.

The man on the rock looks up at us. His face so sad, emotion sharp, like a slap to the face. Tommy grunted like it hit him, too.

"Tommy Smith. George Blackworth." He says my name and I feel it in my bones, like my mother, God rest her, yelling out the back door.

"Who're you?" I ask.

"Who am I?" He stares at his hands. "A king without a queen, proof that the undying are not immortal."

Me and Tommy look at each other. The bloke's shell-shocked. Got to be. "We're going down to the pub. Come sit with us," I say. Figure maybe if I stare at him long enough, I'll figure out why I know his face, why he knows us.

The man stands and stares back at the field, at the big hole. "You're a mechanic, George Blackworth. What do you think of German technology?"

Now, sir, let me say straight out that I'm not fond of Jerries. My boy's over in France right now, and me, I served down in Togoland and in the Somme. But Germans know engines 'n guns. I told this fellow that, and he nods.

"Yes. They do well with metal. Magic makes it all the more powerful," he says. Me and Tommy share a look again, but the bloke, he keeps going. "I was warned this would happen, that the Germans had made certain alliances, but I didn't want to get involved. This was a war for humans. Your kind are proficient in killing yourselves. We didn't need to lend aid."

All I can think is, he's been hit in the head. He don't need the pub, he needs hospital.

He stands up. Body's so thin, he's like a twig. "This was no mere bomb." He whispers. "It blasted straight through our gateway. Iron. Salt. A ton of it, and inlaid on that..." He shivers.

I still think the man's daft, but something about him sets me out in shivers, too. I remember what me mother used to say. "What are you, a fairy?"

"Oberon. King of the Fairies."

I look at Tommy. He laughs easily, Tommy, but he don't say a peep. Just stares, like at a coffin.

"You're saying the Germans, they used magic on this bomb to blow up Fairyland?"

He sways on his feet. Everything about him is so brittle, so broken. "Not all gone, no. But the palace, Titania..." His grief has a taste on the air, thick saltiness like the middle of the Atlantic when I sailed to and from America once years ago. "My people are coming together, George Blackworth. We have fought amongst each other for so many years on this isle. We never looked beyond. But now..."

Something changed in him then, quick as the weather. That salty grief evaporated to anger, a peculiar sort of anger. Like the nightmares I had after the war, blood 'n memories 'n grief pounded together as if by a piston.

And like that, out of that pit in the meadow, I saw all these bodies. Not dead bodies, but figures, people, things. Trees with arms, ladies with wings, all sorts with horns and animal skins, some bodies tall as old oaks, others like bits o' light.

Oberon, he raises a hand and this woman—kind of a woman—steps up. She hands him this scroll. Oberon looks straight at me. "You are to deliver this to London, George Blackworth," he says. "On the outside of the paper, a map will appear. Follow it. The scroll knows where it should be delivered, and to whom."

He walks up to me. Beside me, Tommy whimpers and shrinks back, but he don't leave. Oberon stops in front of me and hands over the paper. I take it. I have to, but more than that, I want to.

"Tell him we're in the fight now," says King Oberon.

"Yes, your Royal Highness, sir," I say, and drop to my knees. I can't look at him no more, not with how feelings roll off him like fog. A man'll lose himself in that. Haven't heard the stories since I was a lad, but I remember that much.

So here I am, Mister Churchill. I followed that map. It brought me to you, hidden down in this basement, all these guards about. After seeing the King of Fairies you're still quite the sight. With him on our side... well, glad they're with us.

The Germans. God help'em, I say.

K is for King Oberon

Cory Cone

I *was born eviscerated.*

"Close your eyes," the doctor had said to my mother. "You don't want to see this."

I was declared dead before the umbilical cord was severed, and to those in the room that seemed the terrible reality; little baby me was all but inside out, my organs on display like some grotesque medical illustration. But just after he had made his grim declaration, my body *sucked* the organs back in, slurped them up like one does a bowl of ramen noodles.

And that's when my mother began to scream.

June

It's happened.

Again.

My chest parted without warning and my heart plopped onto the resume on Raphael Saltskin's desk, spattering droplets of crimson onto his lips.

There's this woman named Celeste in the office, too, double booked alongside my interview so she could hang a painting in Raphael's office. "You don't mind, do you?" he'd asked.

Like I didn't matter.

Like I was scum.

She'd been drilling screws into the wall when I was trying to articulate my qualities, and Raphael had nodded along like he gave a shit. Now Celeste stands in the back of the office with a hand over her mouth, and Raphael hasn't really moved at all. He's just staring—staring at my heart, at the arteries swinging to and fro like suspension cables.

There it sits upon the desk.

Thump, thump.

I shove the beating muscle back into my chest, then I grab a tissue from a box to swipe at the blood on Raphael's face, but he waves me away.

"Clyde," he says with unmasked pity. "I can't possibly allow you to work in my restaurant." He spreads his hands toward the mess I've made of his desk. "The liability alone..." He stares at me like I'm a side-show display, a *freak* to be ogled.

Celeste looks on too but with a gaze that holds something I've not seen since my father died; a kindness?

But I've had enough. I race from the back office of *Salt* and into the nearest restroom. My hands and face are covered in blood, so I wash them as best I can, filling the trash bin with blood-soaked paper towels. My dress shirt is ruined, so I button my coat to hide the damage.

It was stupid to come here, foolish to continue trying to lead a normal life. It's driven home as I navigate past the horrified stares of the patrons and staff for the exit.

"Mr. Elsbury!" It's Celeste, the artist. I don't know what she wants and I don't care. She's as old as my mother would be, and I have a hard time with women who remind me of her. Hell, I have a hard time with *women*. No, let's just make that *people in general*. I want nothing to do with her, nothing to do with this damn restaurant, and I ignore her and rush outside and keep moving until I'm several blocks away. Then I call for a cab on my cell.

It's almost hot enough to sweat today, so I keep to the shade. If I sweat too much I end up looking like a 30 year old male Carrie White.

This homeless guy sidles up to me wearing a tattered tweed jacket and equally tattered pants, and a single shoe. If there's anyone who's got it worse than me, it's him. He looks at my chest with a squint that suggests he's thinking the same thing about me. Lifting a palm, he says: "Tough luck, spare a buck?"

I fish through my pockets for anything to give to him, to get him out of my face, and place a pile of coins into his palm—six pennies. "Sorry," I say. "It's all I've got."

The homeless guy tosses the coins into the street and walks away.

༺∞༻

My mother;

On a cold and windy autumn night when I was seven, she asked If I'd like to go for ice cream. Dad was working late, she said, and dinner was prepped and *wouldn't it be a fun thing to do in the meantime?* I couldn't remember the last time (or, hell, even the first) she'd surprised me with anything, let alone ice cream, so to little ol' me it was especially exciting.

She even let me ride up front in the car.

We drove along a dark, winding road for some time, my mind preoccupied by thoughts of black raspberry ice cream in a sugar cone, before my mother pulled over and told me to get out. She said it sweetly, too. I cringe at the memory of it, at how *loving* her voice had sounded. I thought something was wrong with the engine or that a tire needed changing. I'd helped Dad change a tire earlier that year in the rain and it had turned into something of an adventure. A time to remember.

I got out of the car, and when I closed the door, already inspecting the tires for damage in the dim moonlight, she sped off.

For longer than was reasonable I stood there thinking, *she's really going to be worried when she realizes she left me here, alone.*

But right there was where I remained. For three hours.

In the dark.

In the cold.

I believe that the first girl a young boy ever falls in love with is his mother, and on that cold night when I was seven, mine became the first to ever break my heart, for I at last realized that my mother didn't love me. That she had never loved from the moment the doctor informed her that I was, in fact, still alive.

Dad found me huddled in the dirt beneath a roadside tree. I've often wondered what the conversation was like that led him to realize what she had done, though he never did tell me. I was left so far from civilization that his was the first car I'd seen in all that time,

122

and by then I was too cold and frightened to move. He scooped me into his arms, and at first I had no idea who he was, thought it might be a stranger there to take me away, but I could smell his cologne, and I began to cry. "I'm here, Clyde," he said. "I've got you."

When we got home, my mother was in the kitchen, standing at the empty sink with the water running. She didn't turn to look at us, or to apologize or say anything at all. Dad brought me up to my room and tucked me in. He brought an extra comforter in and laid it over me, then sat on the edge of my bed and ran his fingers through my hair.

"Dad," I whispered.

"Shh," he said. "You can sleep."

"Does Mom hate me?"

He was silent a beat, and that held so much more than his words. "Your mother is under a lot of stress, that's all." Then: "She loves you, buddy."

"I didn't leak, Dad."

"What?"

"When I was out there, I didn't leak."

He kissed my forehead. A warm tear fell onto my cheek. It was comforting, and I thought as I drifted to sleep that if my leaks had stopped for good, truly, that maybe my mother would love me again in the morning.

I woke long before morning to the sound of a thunderclap. I heard no rain. Had my ears not been ringing so painfully I'd have thought the sound was from a dream. The bathroom light was glowing into the hallway outside my door, and I slid from the bed, walked toward the bathroom.

It was there I discovered that my mother had taken Dad's hunting rifle, laid in the bathtub, and put a bullet through the roof of her mouth. Dad arrived an instant after I did, and so I was not spared the image of her contorted body within the tub, nor the splatter of blood on the tiles, nor the sound of it dripping to the floor: *tick, tock, tick, tick, tock.*

And as Dad yanked me from the bathroom and back down the hall, all the while mumbling, *Oh Jesus, God, Oh Jesus,* I felt my stomach split open and my guts slither out, snaking behind us. It sunk in then, as my blood soaked into the carpet, that my mother was dead, and that I was the one who had killed her.

✤

Red tail lights vanish in the distance.
She left me here.
Silly Mommy.

My vibrating cell phone wakes me. I let it go to voice mail. It's 8:30 at night, and whoever it is, I don't want to talk to them.

The phone goes silent as I long to return to my dream—maybe this one time she might turn back.

The phone vibrates again. Sleepy-eyed, I pick it up of the mind to toss it across the room, but think better of it. It could be someone calling for an interview, one of the dozen or so places I resume-bombed. I answer it. "Yes?"

"Is this Mr. Clyde Elsbury?"

"It is."

"Did I call at a bad time?"

"No," I say. "I was just resting."

"I woke you?" It's a woman. She sounds more concerned about waking me than a soulless recruiter might, which means she isn't one.

"Yes," I say.

"I'm so sorry. I'll call back later."

I sigh. "Well, I'm up now. What do you want?"

There's a moment of silence before she speaks. "My name is Celeste Ackempora. We met the other morning at *Salt* restaurant?"

I remember her now. Can picture her in my mind, hair disheveled, eyes glazed over from lack of sleep. The image morphs into something resembling my mother. My hands begin to shake. Flashes of that morning come back to me, my heart laid bare on the desk. The two of them gawking.

"Mr. Elsbury?"

"Why did you call me?'

"I'll get right to it, then. I'd like you to model for my painting pupils in Primrose."

I almost laugh at the idea, but end up choking on my own spit, and coughing.

"Are you all right, Mr. Elsbury?"

"I'm fine," I say, wheezing. "Why would you want me to that?"

"What I witnessed in Raphael's office," she says, and I can sense her smiling through the phone, "it was unlike anything I've seen in my life."

"You make it sound like something to be proud of," I scoff.

"It is!"

I knew I shouldn't have answered the phone. "Goodbye."

"Clyde, please! Don't hang up. Tell me...have you had any luck with other interviews?"

"Fuck you." It feels like she's rubbing it in, whatever *it* might be, even if her voice is so damn...*motherly*.

I can't stand it.

"Don't let your pride stop you from this opportunity. I can help you, Clyde. I can pay—"

"It has nothing to do with pride," I snap back at her.

"Just listen a moment. I'm able to pay you about—"

"Don't call back."

I hang up.

October

Cable's out. Cell's been out for a week or two already. I flip through static instead of reading the letter with the words 'Eviction Hearing Notice' printed in bold capital letters where I've tossed it across the living room. It's been there since before my cell was shut off. It's hard to ignore because the envelope is bright orange.

I'm ignoring another piece of mail, too. It came today; a postcard from that artist, Celeste Ackempora. It's nothing flashy. The front has a print of what I presume to be a painting of hers with the name of her studio. The back of the card has the studio's address and phone number.

She hasn't called back, and I'm glad for it. I'm not used to what was in her voice...and in her eyes when my heart fell out during the interview. Compassion...

Growing up, Dad was the only person who saw past the leaks, who saw only me. If I had an episode, he would help me put everything back in, no matter how disgusting or messy, and he'd sit with me, cradle me in his arms while the skin healed. While the terror faded. "It's okay, Clyde," he'd say. "I'm here." Around Dad, I felt like a son. I felt like an actual person. It was nothing like how my mother made me feel. She'd rush away in a panic when I leaked. She'd leave me alone.

At school, teachers and staff never knew what to do. They were useless. No matter how severe a leak, they'd stand idly by while I clumsily put my organs back inside of my body. They'd keep the other children at a safe distance, as if it were a crime scene, like I was a *disease*. If they got too close, they might catch it. Might become like me.

A monster.

Even so many years later, when it thunders during a storm I see flashes of my dead mother in the bathtub, and I wonder if they were right.

I'm sick of all the static on TV. I shut it off and pick up the Eviction Hearing Notice from the floor. Both it and the postcard end up in the trash on my way to the bedroom to sleep.

❧

On nights when I cannot sleep, I lay my organs in neat rows on my mattress.

Like I've done now.

I'm good at it.

It's like a museum display: trachea, lungs and diaphragm as centerpieces, and around them lay my heart, liver, pancreas, large intestine, small intestine, esophagus, stomach, liver, kidneys and bladder. If I try hard enough, I could get the rest out, I know. Coax everything from my flesh and bones, top it all off with my brain.

Imagine finding that.

I don't even know if I'd die.

My lungs go on breathing when they're on the outside. Inflating, deflating and inflating again on the mattress. The air puffs out to nowhere, and I know that I am suffocating. I can feel it, like the world is closing in around me.

A bird has flown in through my open window. A raven. It's enormous and black and shows no sign of being afraid of me. It eyes me a moment, tilting its head, then flutters onto the mattress. Pecks at my liver.

"Shoo!" I scream, waving my arms at it. It hops back an inch, then pecks again. I yell louder, swat harder, and finally it flies back out the window.

I slam the pane shut.

By now my vision is almost entirely black. My lungs are whimpering, a squee like deflating balloons. It's time to put it all away.

I lack the courage to let myself die.

❧

I've been evicted. I knew it was coming, but still it seems unreal. Three people barged into the apartment; two cops and the landlady. It was 9:00AM. I'd been asleep, the only thing I'm good at lately.

I was given fifteen minutes to gather whatever I could before they led me from the property.

"Do you understand what's happening to you?" one of the police officers asked at some point.

Now that's a loaded question if I've ever heard one.

December

"Help me out?" I hold a shaky palm toward a young couple rushing through the snow for the parking garage. They are red-cheeked and happy, returning I guess from a dinner-and-a-movie. Heading home now to cuddle and warm up and make love.

The boy doesn't acknowledge me, but in my time on the street I've perfected my *desperation* voice. It snags the girl. I see her ears perk up, her gait slow just enough.

"Real hungry," I say, and I've got her.

The boy tugs her arm, but she stops, takes off a glove and fishes through her pocket. "Sorry," she says, and her voice is both sincere and beautiful. So few words are spoken directly to me these days that I find myself savoring each and every one. "This is all I have." She lets a few coins she's found slide into the cup in my hand, and not my proffered palm.

My damn coffee. I'd gotten one of the valet drivers at *Salt* to get it for me. "My hand was out for a reason!"

The girl cowers and looks ready to cry. What's wrong with me? She did not deserve that, but before I can apologize the couple is gone, leaving behind only footprints in the snow.

I shouldn't have yelled. It does me no good.

With numb fingers I dig the coins out of my coffee and lay them in the snow to count.

Six pennies.

৽৽৵

I spend too long pan handing and miss my shot at a heated shelter. There's room at the women's shelter but they'll never let me stay, no matter if I'm liable to freeze to death. The staff, however, are friendly, and they give me fifteen minutes to warm up and use the internet and phone.

A quick Google search yields me a phone number. A number I don't want to dial, but feel at this point I have no other options. I dial and lean my head against the cold glass window, thinking about how much I must truly hate myself.

"Hello?" a woman's voice answers.

"Is this Celeste?" I ask.

"Who is this? It's nearly midnight."

"It's Clyde," I say. "Clyde Elsbury. We spoke some time ago about—"

"Clyde!" Whatever annoyance I'd detected at first is gone. "It's so great to hear from you. You sound sick."

I run a hand down my face. "I'm in a bad way, lately."

"Sure sounds it."

"Were you sleeping?" I ask.

"Clyde, my friend, I never sleep."

I clear my throat. Swallow not pride, but fear. "I was wondering about your offer…to model for you and your pupils."

"It stands," she replies immediately. "If you want it, I could have you by the studio next Wednesday to meet the students."

"Celeste," I say, and choke back tears. In many ways, this is more humiliating than the scene at the interview. "Things have gone downhill the last several months. *Very* downhill."

A moment of silence. "Where are you calling me from?"

"A women's shelter downtown. In fact, I haven't much time to talk."

"I'm coming to get you."

"Celeste, I couldn't—"

"Where are you exactly?"

"Near Patterson Park."

"Patterson Park you said?"

"Yes, but—"

"I'm twenty minutes out. See you soon. I drive a Honda Fit. Silver."

"Celeste, listen—" but she's already hung up the phone.

ഏറ

She takes me to the Double T. It's a 24/7 diner. I haven't been here in years and the thought of a burger has me close to passing out.

I order two, with fries. And a coke.

Celeste orders a salad.

We didn't say much in the car, and so far here it's been more of the same. She's giving me room, I think, to warm up to her.

With one burger in me, and my head clearing (it's the most I've eaten in such a long time) I begin to realize exactly where I am, and who I am with. I feel suddenly cold toward Celeste, though I know it's unwarranted. She's brought me in from the cold, bought me food. I just can't help myself.

She reminds me so much of my mother, which is no fault of her own. But it brings back old hurts.

"I'm excited to work with you," she says when she's finished eating.

"I can't imagine why."

She ignores this. "Tell me about yourself."

"It's not as interesting as you might think."

She smiles. "Somehow, I doubt that."

"You first," I say.

She leans back in the booth. "Fair enough. I grew up in Primrose, where my studio currently is. It's just outside Baltimore. I've always loved painting, and when I was eighteen I got enough scholarship to go to the art college in the city. I made something of a name for myself there and have lived comfortably on my work ever since." She nods, as if that's enough to satisfy me, but then goes on: "I never married. No time. And, truly, no place in my heart for anything but the work, and of course my students."

"Do you always paint naked people?"

She laughs. "No, not always. But mostly, yes."

"Why?"

"She twirls her hand in the air, searching for some answer. "It's not about people being *naked*, Clyde. It's about *people*. Sometimes, it's about *form*. The human body. All that makes us special. Beautiful."

"And you think people want to paint…this?" I indicated my own body.

"Well," she says. "You're human, aren't you?"

Am I? I want to say, but don't.

"Tell me something," she says. "What did you want to be, when you grew up?"

I think a moment. "It doesn't matter what I wanted to be," I say. "What matters is what I am now, don't you think?"

A wide smile spreads across her face. "And what's that?"

My go to answer has always been, *a monster*, but rather than say that I begin answering her first question. I tell her about Dad, how he cared for me, how he was always there for me. I tell her about my mother, about what she did the night she said she was taking me for ice cream. I tell her how she treated me.

Celeste listens intently, nodding, and at one point even crying.

When I've finished my long story, I realize I haven't touched my second burger. I eat it cold in our new silence. And having said all that to her, finally told it all to another living soul, the woman across from me at this booth seems now very far and away from my mother. Doesn't remind me of her at all.

I feel comfortable in Celeste's presence, and I think it's because she listened. I think she's been asking to listen for a very long time.

"I have a spare room in my house," she says, after paying the bill. "You can stay as long as you need to. Rest up a few days. Next week I can introduce you to the class."

I don't know when I started crying, but I have. "I'm afraid, Celeste."

"That's okay," she says. "It's okay to be afraid, Clyde. Let's get you a good night sleep. You'll feel better in the morning.

ೖ☙

Bathing again is spectacular.

Eating fresh cooked meals is even better.

But the best thing so far? Celeste's friendship. She's actually nice to me, and encouraging. She says I'm going to be the talk of the art world.

I tell her that's horse shit, but she laughs it off.

When I've rested a few days, she brings me to her classroom on the third floor of an old mill in Primrose to have a look at the space and to meet the students. They're college aged or older, and extremely talented. Each work in progress is more impressive than the last. Turns out they are all very eager to meet me. They've all heard of me from Celeste, and I feel like a minor celebrity.

"In a way," she whispers to me when I tell her this, "you are."

There is a model posing for everyone and I recognize her immediately as the same girl in the painting that Celeste was hanging in Raphael's office. I can't help but grow slightly embarrassed, then I remember it's going to be me up there very soon.

Thing is, the idea of posing nude for strangers isn't so hard for me to swallow, it's allowing myself to *leak*. Openly. For people.

"What if I can't do it," I ask Celeste before leaving her to her class.

She pats my shoulder. "It doesn't matter what does or doesn't happen, Clyde. We want to paint *you*. All that matters is that it's *you*."

"But I'm a mon—"

"Stop saying that. You are *not* a monster." She looks beyond me, elsewhere. "Every person who has ever made you feel that way, *they* are the real monsters. Do you realize that?"

I tell her after a while that I do. But I don't know if I believe it.

෯෧

Two days later, and the din of quieting conversation welcomes me when I walk into the studio. It's a bright, white December day. Sunlight shines through the large studio windows, illuminating the entire space. Celeste tells me that sunlight is ideal for painting from life. I can see why. Everything is so crisp, vivid and alive.

Then again, I'm also tremendously nervous.

She gave me a robe to wear from the changing room to the studio. I still have it on when I ascend the model stand. I step from side to side up there for a moment, take a few deep breaths, and then let it drop.

Twenty sets of eyes take me in, solving the structural problems of transferring me to canvas, and I can't believe it, even though I'm still whole, every organ still on the inside, I had expected them to gawk. To ridicule. To be, I guess, afraid of me. But no, they are studying.

Their acceptance of my nakedness makes me feel surprisingly

light. This is actually sort of fun. I kick the robe from the stand to the floor and sit on the chair that's been provided.

Celeste addresses the class, tells them that because I'm new there will be extra breaks every fifteen minutes. I'm glad for that, as I'm already feeling light headed.

Am I supposed to feel light headed just sitting here? I try to shake it off and meet eyes with my mother.

She's sitting at a chair within the rows of pupils, paint pallet in her hand. She's scowling. She's disgusted.

The top half of her head is a red, gleaming crater.

A voice whispers in my ear—Celeste's: "Be brave."

And my mother is gone. Only another girl, mixing colors on her palette.

Celeste is walking back to her stool, to begin her own painting, but I call to her. "I never answered your question."

"Which was that?"

"What I wanted to be when I grew up." I look out at the room full of painters. "I wanted to be an artist."

"You are, Clyde," she says, smiling, then walks to her own canvas to prepare.

It's then I feel the stirring in my chest, like an electric shock, and my heart bursts free, splattering the floor with blood. I catch it expertly in midair.

A collective gasp settles across the room. It's followed by thick anticipating silence. They knew what I was, they still they are stunned to see it for real.

Expectant faces stare at me, wondering what might happen next, or if what they see is even real.

Blood trickles between my fingers. The heart beats calmly in my grasp. From the corner of my eye I see Celeste nod her head in approval. I prop my elbow so that the heart is even with my face, the arteries twisting like vines back into my chest, and I settle into the pose.

But my hands shake. My vision clouds.

It's Okay, Clyde. I've got you.

I must admit that I'm terrified, but I know, with people like these in my corner again, I think that someday I might not be.

L is for Leak

Cindy James

I freeze, the knife in my hand hovering above a half-diced onion on the cutting board, my eyes stinging, as it occurs to me the peculiar smell I noticed upstairs last week could be coming from the PVR, and my son's lingering cough may not be from the cold he had a few weeks ago but may be because of the time he spends in that room, playing video games, hours and hours of inhaling what I should have realized were noxious fumes.

The icy spout of fear twists my gut, and cold surges down my limbs all the way to my fingertips. I can hardly breathe, and the knife clatters to the floor. I brace myself against the countertop, willing the panic to stop. It doesn't, and prickly sweat breaks out on my scalp. Darkness fringes the edges of my vision, and I fumble my way around to a kitchen chair. I put my head between my knees and try not to pass out.

"Jules? What was that noise?" Dave hollers down from the upstairs room.

"Nothing!" I call back. My throat is tight and so is the word, but he doesn't seem to notice the strain in my voice.

I breathe slow and deep and concentrate on thinking rational thoughts.

The kids are healthy.

They're not in immediate danger.

I can call the cable company tomorrow and have the PVR replaced.

The staccato pounding of my heart steadies, and I lean back in the chair and reach a shaky hand for someone's tepid glass of water left on the table. I'm not getting better at controlling these, and, unlike last week's episode, this one was much more sudden.

The floor overhead creaks with Dave's footsteps on the stairs. I am cutting the onion again when he comes into the kitchen.

"Everything okay?" he asks.

"It's fine," I say. "I dropped the knife." I scrape the onion into the frying pan and turn to put the knife in the sink. He slips his hands around my waist.

"Careful," I say, "there could be a kitchen accident." I brandish the knife at him, and he laughs. It's an old joke.

"Must be a good onion," he says when he notices my red eyes.

I shrug away and turn on the kitchen faucet. "We should unplug the PVR." I splash water on my face. "I think it's overheating. That might be what's causing that weird smell upstairs."

"Hmm," he says. "I'll go check it."

He returns a minute later. "That was definitely it. What made you think of it?"

"I noticed it was a little warm when I dusted yesterday." I turn down the burner on the stove. "Do you think it's dangerous? The smell?"

He shrugs. "It's probably fine. Are you worried?"

"No," I lie.

"I'll go open the window for a bit," he says.

"Just a crack. It's really cold out there."

Later, in bed, I lie awake listening to Dave's snore and the creak and groan of the house as the earth freezes around it, shifting and squeezing the foundation as if we are nothing more than an annoying cyst on its crust, and I think about the sinkhole in Quebec that swallowed an entire family in their basement. The scene horrifies me: two teenage girls, a mom and a dad hanging out, watching the Habs on Hockey Night in Canada, when the floor drops out from beneath them and mud pours in through broken windows. Buried alive.

I'm relieved our bedrooms are on the top floor of the house, but then an airplane flies low overhead on its way in for a late-night landing. Random death. Like the guy in Florida, almost a cosmic joke—*hey, hey, now you're dead, a jet engine fell on your head; oh, no, it's not fair, killed you in your easy chair.*

I stare at the dim outline of the ceiling fan as the rhyme repeats itself, and I see faces again. I'm accustomed to these disembodied, anonymous heads that flash through the dark with taunting, gnarled expressions, but they still make my heart race. I roll onto my side and promise myself I will talk to Dr. Woo when I have my checkup on Monday.

The next morning when I get to work, I call the cable company and arrange a service call and then sit at my desk Googling overheated electronics and stare at words like "toxic" and "tumour" and "toluene" until Shelley texts me to meet her for lunch. I escape the office tower and find her downstairs on the sidewalk, huddled against the December bite in her long black coat with a smoke in her leather-gloved hand. I grimace at her, and she makes a face back.

"Don't even think about saying anything." Shelley narrows her eyes at me.

"I thought you quit." I stand upwind of her and breathe shallow as she drags back her smoke in rapid-fire puffs.

"Yeah, so I'm weak. Gary walked out last night."

"Oh," I say. This isn't really news, it's happened so many times. "What happened?" I ask. I don't mind talking about her problems. Shelley's shitty life makes me feel better about my own.

"I have no idea." She stubs the cigarette into a crooked forest of lipstick-stained butts poking out of a sand-filled garbage can. "We were having dinner. I told him I invited his mother for Christmas, and he looked at me as if I had announced I was pregnant. Then he got up and left. I haven't heard from him since."

"You never know what will set someone off," I say.

"I never did understand him," she replies, and we head to our usual spot for lunch, a little pub around the corner. Shelley orders a beer, and I'm tempted. I asked her once why she drank so much. She said it helped.

I stick with a coffee.

I contribute little to the conversation. Shelley can be relied on to do most of the talking, and I get away with grunts and nods. We are done eating by the time she gets around to asking about me.

"So," she says, "how are you guys? What are the kids up to these days?"

"We're good." I say. "Hockey, you know."

"Oh, God." She pushes her plate to the side. "I hope I never set foot in another rink again. I'm so glad ours are done with that stupid game. Now they're hardly ever home. Just wait. Fucking teenagers are horrid. I haven't slept since they got their driver's licenses."

"I don't want to think about it." I clench my hands under the table. "I hope they have some sort of tracking device by the time mine are going out."

"Ingrates," Shelley says. "They don't care a rat's ass if we lay awake all night wondering if they're dead or alive. Is Dave still doing construction?"

I nod. "Yeah. He's home for a couple more days, and then he's back up to Fort Mac."

"And what about you?" Shelley asks.

"I think I'm going crazy," I say.

Shelley picks at a crust from her BLT. "Aren't we all," she says.

The bill comes, and it's my turn to pay. Shelley leaves the tip.

By the time I get home from work, I'm exhausted, and when I walk into the house, I smell it. I kick off my boots and stomp up the stairs. The kids are watching a movie.

"Turn it off," I say, my voice sharp. The volume is so loud they don't even register I'm there. "Hey!" I shout, and I take three steps over to the wall and yank the plug for the PVR out of the socket. The screen turns to snow. "I said TURN. IT. OFF!"

Amy cowers and covers her ears with her hands, and Jordan looks up at me from the couch, tears filling his eyes. "Why? What'd I do?"

I hear Dave behind me. "What are you doing?"

I drop the plug on the floor and turn around. "I told you," I say through clenched teeth, "that the PVR was making a smell. Remember?"

"Oh, yeah. I forgot."

"Can't you smell it?" I snap, and I crank the window open. The cold air rushes in and pools around my feet.

"Maybe a little," Dave says.

"A little?" I ask. "It hit me the minute I walked in. Are you trying to poison the kids? What if it burned the house down?"

"I'm sure it's fine."

"How can you say that?" I ask and my voice rises to that pitch I know he hates. I hate it too. "How can you be so oblivious?"

Amy bolts past me into her bedroom and slams the door, and a second later Jordan slinks by while Dave and I glare at one another.

"You need to calm down," he says quietly.

"You need to pay attention to what's going on." I kick the plug to the side and go downstairs to take off my coat.

Once the kids are in bed, I go into Amy's room to tuck her in and notice her nightlight is on the floor.

"Don't plug it in," she says when I go to stick it back into the wall. She's peeking out from under covers pulled up to her nose. "I don't want the house to burn down."

The innocent comment takes my knees out, and I sink onto her bed holding the nightlight in my hands. "Honey, it's safe, see?" I hold the ladybug up as if we could tell by looking at it that it's not a fire hazard, but the reality is I don't really like the thing.

"Leave it out," she insists, so I set it on her dresser and tug her blanket down from her face so I can kiss her cheek and fold her safe into my arms.

"Why are you hiding?"

"I don't know," she says. "I'm scared."

"Of what?" I brush her bangs off her forehead.

"You looked like a monster today."

My throat tightens, and I have to swallow hard before I answer. "I felt like a monster today. I'm sorry I yelled at you."

"Don't make that face again, okay? I don't like it."

She's so little, eight years old. What am I doing to her? I can't seem to get it right. What will I do if something ever happens to her? *When* something happens to her.

I hug her tight and make promises I know I can't keep. "Want me to snuggle with you for a little while?"

She nods, and I lay down beside her as she wriggles close. The world harbors so many dangers. The thought of her suffering devastates me. I'm careful to keep my breathing even so she won't know there are tears slipping down my cheek and onto her pillow. She falls asleep, and then I check on Jordan, who is sprawled over his bed, feet hanging almost to the floor. My first-born. I stand over him, and my love for him swells like a balloon until I am afraid my head will pop. They're so beautiful when they are asleep.

On Monday morning Dr. Woo does the usual checkup plus a pap, and while he writes in my chart, he asks if I'm having any problems.

"I think I'm depressed," I say from the examining table. I'm impressed at how steady my voice is.

He glances up. "Why?"

"I dunno. It's like I'm worried all the time." I lift my head to look at him, and he raises his eyebrows in expectation.

"Mostly about the kids," I say, "but other things, too. You know, like a pandemic. Cancer. Sinkholes. Nuclear war. North Korea. I worry how I can protect my kids."

"You don't have cancer, and North Korea is on the other side of the world," he says. "Why would you worry about that?"

"It's the news," I say. "It scares me."

"So don't watch the news," he says. "Are you getting enough sleep?"

I shrug. "Off and on."

"Try a bit more exercise. A lot of people get a little down in the winter. Take some vitamin D." He stands up. "Come back if things don't improve. I'll call if anything turns up on the pap." He disappears out the door.

I lay on the examining table clutching the paper sheet to my chest for so long a nurse knocks on the door to see if anyone is in the room. I tell her I'll be right out and swing my feet to the worn carpet. Don't watch the news? Get some exercise? Take fucking vitamin D?

I pull on my clothes and coat and leave with my head down.

When Jordan comes down for breakfast the next morning, I notice a small mole on his neck has grown bigger again. I look closer, and adrenaline floods anxiety into my veins. What if it's malignant?

"Mom," Jordan says, "stop picking at me."

"Come here," I say, and I grab his arm as he tries to shrink away.

"Stop it!" he shouts, and he twists and smashes his elbow into the counter. By the time he's done crying, the kids are late for school, and I'm going to be late for work, so I drop them off and go back home and call in sick.

Everything is too bright, too sharp. I make coffee, turn on the news, sort clothes, start the washing machine. The basket is heavier than usual. I putter around the house, but by noon I can't remember what I've been doing in between loads of laundry. I make a peanut butter sandwich and sit down in front of the television. The lead story is about a mother who drowned her two young children. The neighbours are at a loss as to why. How could she do it?

A chill ripples over me. I realize I can understand this other woman, why she did it. It's agony to be a mother. That overwhelming, insidious fear seeps from every pore, taints every moment, a big black backdrop lingering behind each birthday. She's broken. Like me. She had to stop the what-ifs.

Dave is gone again, and the kids will be home from school in a couple hours.

M is for Mothers

Alexis A. Hunter

ELISE squatted beside Ramos on the cracked pavement. The faint outlines of yesterday's sigil were still visible—a blooming lotus flower that had offered him peace. She'd given it to him when she saw the tears in his eyes, saw his fingers clutching the slip of a photograph. Some days the city's broken people needed peace, and some days they needed warmth, and some days they needed it all, and more than she could give.

Tonight it was warmth, and that she could do.

Ramos huddled against the cold, his back pressed to the brick wall of a rundown apartment complex. Newspapers, inked with tales of woe, wrapped around his bare feet, but his toes stuck out—red and painful, catching the wind.

She smiled for him and reached for a slab of red chalk, slotted in her leather bandoleer. She sketched a new pattern with one hand. *Scrape, scrape, scuff.* Chalk against rough concrete. Her free hand touched the red flame sigil painted on her forearm. She watched as the dried acrylic on her skin liquified. It tingled, almost too hot, against her wrist as it slid down and filled the pattern her chalk created.

Ramos was the last of a long string of people on her daily route; her back ached from the constant hunching over, but she finished the complex pattern as the sun sank completely behind the towers of the city. Light radiated across the pavement, embracing Ramos. Relief flooded his face.

She smiled. He smiled back.

Her skin was bare of the dozens of sigils it had carried through the day, all her power doled out to the people along her route. She felt worn—scraped against the city's broken edges like the chalk fragments in her bandoleer.

Just as she stood to head home, she caught sight of a shadow in the alley behind her. The shape of a man, watching her, brought goosebumps to her arms. Her breath caught in her throat. She turned quickly and set off for home.

She didn't relax until she'd made it three blocks without spotting the shadowed form again.

Home loomed ahead, a three story apartment building, its stucco cracked and sun-faded. Home was more than that though—it was Mama, warmth, and rejuvenation.

Elise turned the key, struggled to lift the door and pushed it open. She glanced to the left, to 102, Old Mr. Tucker's apartment. It had been empty for weeks, but now the shadows crept from under its door, flickering faintly at the edges. Elise imagined the new tenant peering through the peephole. Clutching her coat tighter, she hurried inside the opposite apartment.

"Mama?" she called, pressing the door shut behind her. She kicked off her boots and scrubbed her hands together to warm them, casting a fine spray of rainbowed chalk dust.

"In the kitchen, love."

Elise slid between the couch and the wall of their cramped living room and reached the warm, yellow light of the kitchen. Mama sat at the table, chipped dishes spread around her. She smiled at Elise, but her eyes were dark. Heavy lines—thicker than usual—traced the edges of her lips, the corners of her eyes.

Elise reached for a symbol of strength she had already spent. "Mama, you look tired."

Mama beckoned to a seat beside her. Elise inhaled deeply the scent of vegetable stew, only then realizing that the air felt oddly heavy and thick, almost damp. Frowning slightly, she settled at the table and tucked into her meal. Mama rolled over to the cabinet—a faded aquamarine antiquity by the microwave—and pulled out the plastic tub of paints and brushes.

"You should eat, too," Elise said around a mouthful of mushy broccoli, cauliflower, and warm beef broth.

"I already did." Mama's voice was soft, soft like the spray of grey-brown hair framing her strong shoulders. She set the tub of supplies on her knees and rolled to Elise. Sliding back Elise's sleeve, she grabbed a small, fine-haired brush and a bottle of flaming crimson paint. She uncapped it, dipped the brush, and let its tip hover over Elise's arm.

Elise followed her mother's gaze up to the cloud of magicks around her. It was faint, iridescent and shimmering. A familiar frustration rose in Elise's chest as she struggled to make out the good sigils. Their shapes always eluded her, always just out of reach. Sometimes she wondered what was wrong with her, why it was so hard to see the positives.

Tonight, the cloud felt more faded than usual. Mother and daughter both squinted to make out the shapes of sigils for tomorrow's work. Elise tried to ignore the dark shapes creeping in around the edges; she tried not to see these negatives. They were always clearer than the positives. All sharp-edged designs, all deadly potency.

Mama sighed.

"What is it?" Elise asked, swallowing the last of her soup. The brush still hadn't touched her skin.

Frown lines wrinkled her mother's forehead. Her eyes were still narrowed, her jaw set. Elise could see the muscles tensing in her shoulders, her forearms, her hands.

"Something isn't right," Mama said, but began painting anyway.

Her brush wobbled the faint pattern of a flame, without her usual precision and focus. Her hand stopped halfway through the pattern. The cool paint tingled only faintly as it dried. A knot of unease grew inside Elise's stomach—what was preventing her mother from focusing the magick?

Elise had been a Projector, like her mother before her, since she was a child. At thirteen years old, she was nearing the full height of her power. Her magicks should have been a swirling mass around her; her mother, the master of focus, should have been able to pluck the sigils easily out of the air and paint them, clear and vibrant, accessible on Elise's skin. Daily, Mama taught Elise to see the shapes, to find their soft edges and powerful centers, but they still lay beyond her grasp. With age, time and practice she would one day be able to paint her own sigils.

Until then, without Mama to focus the magicks, Elise was powerless. Her skin was a blank canvas.

"What's wrong?" Elise asked.

Mama set the brush down and rubbed circles into her temples, eyes closed. "I can't... something isn't right. It's as if some someone threw a damp blanket over your—"

Their eyes met. Simultaneously, they looked towards the door. Elise pulled a few shallow breaths of the heavy air, remembering the man watching her on the street.

"Do you think the new neighbor...?"

Mama maneuvered her chair around the table and to the door. She pressed her eye to the shorter of the peepholes, body rigid. "I dearly hope not."

Elise followed her mother into the living room, the edges of her hunger satiated. She settled on the couch, peering at the thick oak door as Mama turned back. Elise's unease reflected in her mother's eyes.

They had lived in this city for as long as Elise could remember. They'd never come across another Projector. Let alone one capable of casting a blanket spell of this nature. The thought spiked fear into Elise's chest, and there were no more sigils to wash it away.

Mama moved to the couch and shifted her thin body onto its cushions. The wheelchair sat empty before them as they curled up together. Mama sighed, an exhausted scraping sound like the wind outside, and settled her head against Elise's. Elise chewed her lip fretfully, looking at her mother's veined, slightly-trembling hands.

She had never seen Mama like this. Fragile and uncertain. It made her insides feel queasy. She tried to steady her breathing, letting her gaze rove over the piles of yarn and thread clumped in every corner of the room. The loom was in Mama's room—the tool which enabled her to provide for them—but the supplies were strewn throughout the house. Elise liked them. Always had. Spirals of soft color—soft, not grating like the chalk.

Elise removed her chalk bandoleer and retreated to her room—a bed and a small chest of drawers cramped into what used to be a large closet, branching off the master bedroom. She lifted the heavy wooden chest. It smelled of pine and her name was engraved on its lid. She carried the chest back to the living room.

While Mama rested, Elise removed the broken nibs of chalk, the worn down pieces of no further use. She hummed to herself and focused on the bandoleer—focused, so she wouldn't see the sharp-edged negatives pressing in—as she buffed out the chalky residue and applied a new coat of polish.

When she finished, she inserted new chalk. Thirty-six different shades, bright and vibrant. What would she use them for in the morning if Mama couldn't focus the magick? What would happen to the damaged people on her route if she missed a day? She hadn't missed a day in years. Not for sickness or storm or distraction. There wasn't much a sigil couldn't help.

But there was no sigil to help them now.

Elise felt naked without the patterns on her skin. She couldn't stand the idea of sleeping in her own bed tonight. The dark sigils brought a squirmy warmth to her stomach—a sort of unease, coupled with a thrill.

Mama said the negatives were evil—the magic of violence. Elise found herself staring at them. Their lines and edges were sharp, geometric, sometimes jagged. She didn't know each sigil's exact meaning, but she felt their intent: violence, harm, anger. They shimmered close, begging her to use them, oddly sharper and clearer than any sigil she'd seen in her magick before.

Instinctively, she trailed her fingers over her heart, reaching for the pattern of sleep. A thick sleep, a sleep that the dark shapes couldn't disturb. But that comfort was gone.

Elise rose with the sun. She shook her mother awake. "Mama, what will we do?"

Mama straightened stiffly, as if every movement jarred loose a new pain in her head. Her eyes were hazy and blue. Her arms lay limply at her sides. "I don't know, love. I don't... I don't know."

Anger flickered in Elise's belly; the shadows darkened around her, somehow more visible with the sunlight sifting through the curtains. "Think, Mama. Why can't you paint them?"

Mama sank back into the cushions. "I told you. They're blanketed. I can't see your magicks; I can't focus them."

Elise wanted to shake her mother until she found the woman she knew, rather than this heap of resigned bones. "Mama!" she snapped.

Their eyes met. They faced off, both of them bare-skinned. Naked and vulnerable without their paint, without their focused magicks. Shadows rolled like flames around the edges of Elise's vision as her tone grew sharper. "They need us. We can't just give up."

When Mama didn't respond, Elise clenched her teeth and pulled on her coat and scarf, then snapped up her bandoleer and slung it over her chest. She was halfway to the door when she heard her mother's tired voice.

"What good can you do? Stay here and we'll figure this out."

Elise couldn't stay. If she did, her anger would only rise and the negatives would loom larger—and how could her mother not see them then?

She stepped into the hall and froze when the door latched behind her.

Apartment 102 sat directly across from her. Its bronze numbers were fogged with rainbowed tarnish, appearing overnight. Mold trailed out from the door's edges, creeping along the plaster walls. Elise edged closer. The mold formed intricate patterns: sharp-toothed maws, angry monster eyes, thick lines of chaos intersecting, and all with a faint metallic sheen that marked it as otherworldly.

She raised her fist to the door. A thousand accusations filled her mind, ready to leap from her tongue. But she couldn't bring herself to knock, to draw forth whoever hid within—whoever was blanketing their magicks.

The air felt thicker. Elise's sides heaved as she struggled to draw in enough air. Chaotic emotions squeezed her chest and just as she fled for the front door, she noticed that the mold was slowly expanding. Slowly reaching tendrils toward her home.

Outside, the air cleared somewhat. Elise took off down the sidewalk, following her regular route. Her breath fogged in the morning air as she jogged. Her bandoleer slapped against her thin chest, heart pounding erratic in her temple and her gut.

The farther she ran, the cleaner the air. She pulled up sharp when she reached Linda, the first stop on her route. The woman sat outside the liquor store, fingers clenching a wad of bills and eyes darting toward the door. When she saw Elise, relief flooded the woman's face. She stood speechless within the faded patterns of yesterday's magick.

Elise avoided the woman's eyes, following instead the swirling patterns of birds flocking out from the woman's feet. The chalk was faded from the shoes of pedestrians. Elise had never thought about how they tread on her magick, how they scuffed it off, heedless of the ones she wished to help.

Exhaustion rippled through her. Her fingers reached futilely for a pattern on her skin. Elise gritted her teeth as she eyed the faint outlines. What shade of blue had she used? Powder blue or periwinkle? Cobalt or azure? Softness for peace, to dull the edges of the woman's addiction? Or bold colors for strength, to bolster the woman's resolve?

Her fingers fluttered before settling on the cobalt. She spent the next twenty minutes trying to copy yesterday's outlines. Her fingers tingled with what she hoped was the transference of magick, but could have very well been only the cold.

Cars buzzed by as the city woke. Pedestrians brushed past her and cursed at her for taking up space. She bit back a curse in return.

"Who's that man following you?" Linda asked, startling her.

Elise inhaled sharply and looked back. The man was thin and haggard, with an olive green, military-style jacket zipped tight under his jaw. Elise caught a glimpse of his raging black eyes before he sidestepped into an alley, out of sight.

Linda sighed, standing over the cobalt birds. Faint blue light radiated up from the chalk, through the woman's worn shoes, finally reaching her eyes. It didn't seem as bright as usual.

Elise resumed her route through the city. How long would her tired magick last? Already she felt exhausted and she'd only copied one pattern.

She glanced back repeatedly as she wove through the city streets. The man followed her at a distance. He paused at the poor, wobbling patterns she left behind and stared into the faces of the people she helped.

He was like the shadows, encroaching upon her. Ever present, just begging to be confronted.

Elise knew she should keep to her routine, think of the people who needed her. But her anger built until finally she spun to face him. His eyes widened slightly as he dipped into another alley, but she bolted forward. She came around the corner, already with cutting words on her tongue, but found the alley empty. She paused at its entry, breathing heavily.

Tears formed in her eyes. Her chest felt like a surging sea and her fingers twitched, eager to find a sigil that would restore her calm, her peace.

Her heart ached with the realization of the futility of her work. The thoughtless repetition that had kept her walking the streets day after day, drawing variants of the same pattern. People broke daily, with or without her.

"I know you're here," she screamed, her entire body vibrating. "Why are you doing this?"

Her voice bounced against the brick walls. It sounded rasping and foreign. She couldn't remember the last time she had shouted.

Though she could feel the man's gaze on her, she could not see him. Usually there was a swirling blue eye painted on her right temple. Once, she could have touched it and released its powers, enabling her to see all that lay within the alley.

Rage and helplessness boiled again and she reached, without thinking, into the clouds around her head. Her fingers plucked the edges of something sharp; pain vibrated down her arm, deep, to the bone. Somewhere in the haze of anger and instinct, she marveled at the ease of her movements, the way her body seemed to know how to call down the magick like she'd never done before. Hastily, she scratched the negative sigil against a sheet of cardboard leaning against the wall. The moment her nails completed the symbol, a blast of light exploded in the alley. The wrongness of what she'd done struck her immediately, driving her out of the alley. She heard a cry of pain as she retreated. A strange thrill shot through her body, but quickly twisted into nausea.

Her pace increased—anger and fear vying for control. Soon she was running, passing by the broken souls and their outstretched hands. Tears streamed down her cheeks as she ran, gasping for air. Her right arm throbbed and she cradled it against her chest as she passed Ramos.

She didn't stop until she had closed the door behind her and collapsed in the living room.

Mama lay on the couch, but straightened when the door slammed.

"Elise!" she cried, moving quickly into her chair.

Elise curled up on the floor, unable to even cry. She rocked herself, caught in waves of regret and shame. She pressed her eyes closed against the negatives that somehow thrived despite the stranger's blanket spell.

Mama said the dark signs were evil. Mama said Elise shouldn't look for them, ever. She had always taught Elise that, while their forms were currently hazy, the good signs would come clear the more she practiced, the more she looked for them. And Elise tried. She strained to see them, even now, eyes flashing back open.

Usually Mama took her to the park. They would lie in the grass and stare up, like so many other mothers and their children. Only Elise and her mother didn't look for shapes in the clouds—they looked for shapes in the iridescent shimmer of Elise's magick.

Sweat broke on Elise's brow as she fought to see the good signs against the water-stained ceiling. Her palms grew clammy, but she didn't dare to wipe them. She couldn't let her mother know how hard it was for her daughter to see the good. To *be* good.

Barely aware of her mother's arms around her, Elise whimpered. Unable to keep the shadows at bay.

Maybe not unable, a dark thought whispered in her mind. *Maybe you just* want *to see them.* An uneasy thrill filled Elise's belly and she remembered feeling it when she plucked the blast of light from the air in the alley.

The sharp, the deadly, the violent magicks gathered close. She looked into their clear patterns and saw their familiarity. They felt like cousins—the resemblance of yourself seen in their freckled noses and emerald eyes.

Elise gasped as the realization struck her. It was something Mama hadn't said; it was unwritten between them, waiting—waiting for Elise to discover it.

The magick symbols, the cloud, all projected *from* Elise. The sigils she focused on, she allowed to grow within and without her. Her soul's strength, projected, focused, used and repeated. The good symbols were *of* her. Her gut sank as she began to weep.

The darkness was *of* her, too.

After some time, Elise's whimpering faded. She realized her mother had slid out of her chair to lie on the floor and cradle her. Elise hugged Mama close, her previous anger fading away. She felt fragmented, a porcelain cup shattered on the floor. All the jagged edges poked and stabbed, and she feared she would begin to bleed from the inside.

"It catches up with us," Mama whispered, pushing back the sweat-damp curls from Elise's face. "All their agony. All their violence. Without our positives to keep it at bay, it will break us."

Elise tucked her head against her mother's chest as she hadn't done since she was a small child. "I'm sorry, Mama."

"Don't be."

"I didn't know. I didn't—" Her throat clogged up, choking off the words.

"I didn't want this for you," Mama said. "I never wanted you to feel this."

Elise nodded, letting her mother's steady heartbeat soothe her as the magicks had done before. Was this not a magick all its own? A natural magick? One that couldn't be blanketed by their new neighbor. Elise let her mind rove through memories, all the times she lay beside her mother in the park, all the times the woman guided her hands at the loom, teaching her to weave tapestries and rugs and blankets. Good memories. Positives of the natural world.

"We have to leave," Mama said against Elise's hair. "Find a different area of the city, or... or leave it entirely."

Elise stiffened, pulled back. "Leave? Just... just give up and let him win?"

Mama's eyes were hazy with tears. "We have to. It's the only way. We can't... we can't live like this."

"But we can fight him!" The words were fierce, they leapt from her tongue before she could cage them.

A frown darkened her mother's face. "Elise." A gentle rebuke, pressed into her name.

Elise trembled. With fear, with shame, but she had to speak. She couldn't just let her mother give up. What about Ramos? And Linda? And all the other needy ones on her route? What would happen to them without her?

She knew. The dark imaginings etched in her mind, more prophecy than fantasy. Ramos would freeze to death or cast himself off a bridge to be rid of his pain. Linda would crash her car in a drunken stupor, taking out many innocent lives with her. Countless others would write their pain in bruises, in bloodshed, in death.

"I see the negatives, Mama. I see them all the time. Sometimes..." Her voice faltered. She couldn't meet her mother's eyes. "Sometimes I like to see them. And I... I know it's wrong, but I do."

"Oh, honey." Mama tried to hug her, but Elise pulled away. She couldn't spill the dreadful truth into her mother's arms; it was bad enough she had to share this poison at all.

"I used it, today. I blasted him with light to keep him from watching and—"

The slamming of a door in the hallway stopped her. Her eyes widened as she scrambled to her feet.

"Come out here," the man's voice barked from the other side of the door.

Elise stood between her mother and the barrier.

"Elise, no. Come here now," Mama said frantically as she hefted herself up into her chair. "We must go. Now. The dark signs will taint you if you use them. They're—"

"Evil?" Elise supplied, hands coiling into fists. *But maybe necessary, too, Mama.*

Elise jerked the door open. She stared up into the face of the stranger. He seemed impossibly tall. He was thin through the chest, with a faded blue t-shirt clinging to his jutting ribs. His face was haggard and gaunt, eyes a shifting mass of pain and anger.

"Elise, please," Mama cried.

Elise glanced back as her Mama rolled forward to stop her. "I'm sorry, Mama, but I have to. For them. For you." She stepped forward and shut the door behind her. Her hands fluttered up to the storm clouds brooding around her; she retrieved—more easily than she would have imagined—the shape of a lock and scratched it into the wood around the door handle.

The knob rattled; Mama cried and shouted from the other side, but the magick held the door fast.

Elise faced the man again. He shook all over, barely

repressing something that wanted to scream out of him. Elise could see the jagged edges swirling around his head—his magick. She'd never been able to see it before. But his was so tainted by negatives that it blared like neon lights.

"What's wrong with you?" Elise asked. Some fragment of compassion pressed through, but mostly it was anger. Mostly it was an accusation.

"People like you," he said, voice a snarl. "You oppress them and you don't even know it, do you?"

"Oppress them?" She stepped closer, fingers fluttering through the dark edges and snagging something that looked like Mama's symbols for strength—only heavier, thicker. Pain resonated up her right hand, shaking her bones so hard she thought they would break. But the strength filled her as she scratched the pattern into her forearm.

Why? Why was it so hard to see the good, but so easy to see the negatives? They spooled out for her at the simple opening of her mind, the simple release of her resolve.

"I *help* them," she growled.

He laughed, but there was pain in it. So much pain.

"You will stop." He stepped closer and she wished for his height, so that she could stare him in the eyes and show him she wasn't afraid.

"I won't. *You* will leave," she said. "You'll stop hurting Mama and me."

"Are you gonna make me?" His grin was sharp, sharkish. Eyes hard. He looked at her like he knew her, like she was someone else entirely—not a dark, curly haired little girl. She felt his history rising between them, but couldn't detect its edges, couldn't find its meaning.

"I will," she vowed.

He laughed again. "I bet you thought you'd never use the 'negatives'. Aren't they evil to you? Aren't you crossing all the wrong lines? Won't your soul be damned?" Sarcasm was thick in his tone, even as he drew from his own magick and scratched symbols into his arms until they bled.

A flash of heat zipped from her toes to her head and back in a few seconds. She cried out, vaguely aware of Mama still screaming and pounding on the other side of the door. Anger rose with the pain. Before she knew what she was doing, she'd grasped a symbol of wind and etched it around her lips. She blew one strong gust of air and it struck the man with hurricane-force.

He flew back, slamming into his door. The wood shattered around him. He struck the floor of his own living room. Elise jumped forward. She caught a glimmer of fear in his eyes, but he was already writing his magicks on his scarred, white skin. Blood trailed through the lines. A thunder clap burst in Elise's ears. She crumpled with a shout. Deafened, the whole world seemed to be ringing like a phone she couldn't pick up.

Gasping for air, she wiped blood trails from her ears. Casting aside her chalk bandoleer and pulling up her shirt, Elise acted on instinct. She drew, with the sticky red paint of her lifeforce, a new pattern on the dark skin of her stomach. It was a sharp edged symbol, a crippling force.

When she finished, it burst—striking pain back into her, the recoil of a gun to her chest. Elise and the man were blown back away from each other. He writhed as she stumbled to her feet again. He screamed in agony as electricity zipped up and down his spine. He convulsed and she stood over him.

As the sparks fizzled, he lay panting, emaciated sides heaving. "I hate you. I fucking hate you!" He screamed it with tears, and Elise tensed. She raised a new sign, ready to write it in her blood once more, but his hands were still, clutched like broken talons against his chest. "You can't press your fake plastic peace down on everyone! Don't you see? Sometimes they have to feel. Sometimes you have to let them feel. You're fake. So fucking fake. You're just like them!"

"What are you talking about? Just like who?" Elise gasped, doubled over against the pain. She could almost feel the bruises beginning to marble her chest and ribcage.

"You—they—shoved it down my throat." He was sobbing in earnest, helpless on the floor. He knew his dark magicks well, he knew his negatives intimately, but he couldn't contest with the power of her youth. "I was just a problem. Just a problem that needed fixing. All I wanted was to feel, a little love, an embrace. I didn't need their sigils, their signs. I needed them!" One hicupping breath, and then Elise thought she heard him whisper, "Daddy, please."

Elise stared at the wreck of a man before her. He looked like a child. He was, she realized. Whoever he spoke of, they had stunted him. Mama let Elise feel pain sometimes, she let her feel tired. *"It's natural. It's necessary, sometimes."*

She considered him, considered the magicks begging to be used. Her fingers trembled as the shadows pressed in, hungry for his death. Fear blasted through her as she realized that some part of her wanted to take his life. *He won't give up. He needs to be ended.* But did he?

He grew still, his tears drying in tracks on his haggard face. He looked up at Elise and she saw not fear, but relief.

"Do it," he said. "Just end me."

When is taking a life merciful? When is it the right thing to do? She didn't know. The fullness of what she didn't know rang in her head, in her hollow gut. Maybe that was another lesson, another truth, that lay in wait. Unspoken between her and Mama. Maybe she couldn't access it yet because she wasn't wise enough.

Elise flinched at the sound of wheels rolling over splintered wood. Mama sat in the doorway, sides heaving and face streaked with tears. Their eyes met and Elise's hand slid slowly down to her side. She wiped her blood, patternless, against her pants.

"I can't," she said to the man. She shook her head. "I won't." And that was more true. "Y-you're not right. Not *all* the way."

But maybe he wasn't all wrong either. Maybe her magicks had made the people dependent, maybe they never learned to be more than addicts to her power. She knew one thing for certain, she wasn't *all* right either. She turned and staggered to Mama, ignoring the man's cries after her.

Together, they moved numbly through the splinters of wood and the glittering mold. With the blanket spell broken, Elise's magick shone clear and bright around her. But the negatives remained, within and without her. She grabbed her mother's hand, ready to face the dark sigils, to face the darker parts of her soul.

N is for Negatives

Michael M. Jones

THE Theatre of Dreams stands alone, small and unimposing against its surroundings. It's located on the outskirts of the Gaslight District, Puxhill's oldest and strangest community, set back a little ways from the road itself. Save for a small sign, you'd never know what the building truly was. There is no ticket booth; you cannot call ahead or pre-order here. There are no prices listed; entrance is paid with innocence and secrets, whispers and hopes. There are no hours posted; either you know when performances are, or you do not. The Theatre is not listed in any newspapers, trade magazines, or travel guides. It does not advertise. It doesn't need to.

It's Friday night, and the marquee reads, "Juliet Sinclair, appearing irregularly." No other explanation is needed. She is the star. She is the Dreamer.

It's almost time for the midnight show and the people are still outside. The crowd is curiously mixed, college students and socialites sharing the same sidewalk—jeans and T-shirts clashing against tuxedoes and gowns. Strangest of all, however, are the Theatre's most devoted attendees. Divided into two factions, they circle each other like tired boxers, neither willing to start something, but each convinced they're the only "true" fans, that the others are poseurs and fakes. The Funereal Children come decked out in their best mourning clothes, all black and lace, veils and tears, while the Unquiet Sleepers move with heavy-lidded distant eyes, garbed in nightgowns and robes, clutching articles of comfort to their chests.

Finally, the doors open. Quietly, eagerly, the patrons file into the converted playhouse to take their places in the circular auditorium, settling into velvet seats that oppress with faded opulence and murky charm. Even the first-time patrons instinctively fall silent, nary a whisper escaping anticipation-laced lips. A faint cough hacks forth, hushed with sheepish haste before the atmosphere is poisoned. Funereal Children, socialites, Sleepers, students, yuppies—all wait patiently. All are equal here.

The lights dim, throwing the room into pitch-blackness. In flagrant disregard for safety guidelines, not even an illuminated emergency exit sign violates the darkness. A low throbbing, the sound of a giant heart beating, resonates through the walls and seats.

A spotlight clicks on, shining down upon a simple bed in the middle of the stage, an old oak four-poster with creamy white sheets which glow almost fluorescent. Gliding in time to the heartbeat, a young woman seems to sleepwalk down the aisle. Her movements are languid, her nightgown filmy and vaguely transparent against the single light. She is thin and pale, a mere wisp of a figure. Her hair is cornsilk verging on platinum, worn loose almost to her waist. Her eyes are closed.

Deep in her trance, the woman—Juliet Sinclair—climbs into bed. Within minutes, she has passed into sleep, chest rising and falling in slow rhythm, matching the ominous heartbeat

Minutes tick by, the audience still and silent. Beyond the sharp boundaries of that single spotlight, velvet darkness grips them in its embrace, the heartbeat linking them together, synchronizing their breaths.

And then Juliet's dreams are cast onto the walls and ceiling, flickering like early cinematography at too few frames per second. The audience feels as much as they see. A sun rises, a cat stretches to greet it before transforming into a woman holding a rose. A gentle rain falls across a graveyard, while dogwoods bloom in fast forward. Somewhere, there's a sigh of content, and the unmistakable smells of baking bread and cooling chocolate. Silk and velvet wrap around bare skin. A soft jazz song plays in the background as faceless people dance, only Juliet present as a recognizable figure. All these and more play across the audience's senses as the Dreamer's subconscious cracks open like floodgates. There's love and hate, anxiety and confidence, beauty and ugliness, an unspeakably profound truth that speaks to the watchers. Unlike their own dreams, these will not fade away like mists burned by the sun.

All too soon it's over, though hours have passed while the audience sat enraptured and the Dreamer lay dreaming. The heartbeat gently fades away and the lights slowly come up. Juliet herself awakens, blinking and bleary-eyed, unrested despite her sleep.

The audience is released from their paralysis. They stand, stretch, file towards the exit, talking amongst themselves now that the enchantment has been broken.

As the Theatre's patrons trickle out, Juliet shakes off the last vestiges of drowsiness, pale blue eyes open wide with strange urgency. Desperately, she stumbles forward to clutch at the sleeve of an elderly woman wrapped in a black cashmere coat. Please, she begs, please tell me what I dreamed. Her voice is a needy whisper, ragged with restlessness and loss.

Taking pity on the Dreamer, for she alone does not experience the dreams cast for all else to see, the woman explains. Juliet loosens her grip, her smile soft and wistful. Something flickers in her eyes: Hope? Disappointment? She turns away, thanking the woman, drifting backstage to her dressing room. It has been a good night.

„›‹“

Juliet is backstage in the Green Room, a place resembling a '50s sitcom kitchen, all warmth and light and pastels. It perpetually smells like morning: eggs and bacon, coffee and toast. She's alone; no one ever disturbs the Dreamer while she throws off her disorientation and rejoins the waking world.

She's in jeans and a light blouse, barefoot. A plate of scrambled eggs and several cups of thick black coffee have made her feel much more alive. However, she can't help but notice that in the bright light of the room, she's even paler than usual, skin washed out to translucency, a little hazy around the edges. Despite this, her hands are steady and confident. She's always known there was a price for being the Dreamer, a cost to breaching the boundaries between waking and dreaming. She welcomes it.

In a complete break with tradition, Polly enters before Juliet's finished. She owns the Theatre, though, and is the closest thing Juliet has to family; she can break the rules if she wants.

Polly's a tall woman, with the strong features and knowing expression of an ancient Greek statue and the dark eyes and olive skin of the Mediterranean. Her dark hair is forever pulled into a loose knot. Juliet has never seen her as less than elegant, even when dealing with a crisis or woken from a deep sleep. She's still in the outfit she wears as the public face of the Theatre: long black skirt and white dress shirt, though she carries the black suit jacket over one arm. Even without her heels, she towers over Juliet. Such stark coloring is a splash of cold water against the gentle pastels of the Green Room.

"Polly?" Juliet asks, surprised, a slice of toast halfway to her mouth. "Is something wrong?"

"In a manner of speaking." Polly's tone is neutral as she takes a seat across from Juliet at the small square table. "This was your last show."

The words come without warning, hitting hard and fast, stunning Juliet. "What?"

"You're fading too quickly," Polly says. "Another show like this, and there's no hope for you. You've hit the boundaries like a bird against the window, and the Lord of Dreams won't stand for it. You're just too good at what you do."

The toast slips from Juliet's frozen fingers to strike the edge of the plate and bounce away to the floor in a flurry of crumbs. "Not funny," she whispers. "Please say you're joking."

Polly shakes her head. "I'm sorry, dear. Truly I am. I know we'd promised you another month until the end of the season, but that's impossible. You have to stop now."

"No," says Juliet, flatly, eyes hard with desperation. She grips the edges of her plate, white-knuckled. "I don't want to stop now. This was my best show yet. I could feel it. And I'm so close..."

"So close to what?" asks Polly, tilting her head bird-like to study the younger woman.

"To escaping," replies Juliet with a sharpness that surprises them both. The plate cracks in her grasp, and she absently drops the pieces onto the table.

Just like that, the homey warmth of the room is gone and a strange new coldness wraps around the two women as their gazes lock. "Is that what you want?" asks Polly, mildly. "I'd think there were easier ways to accomplish that, than to fade away slowly, night by night, show by show."

"But those ways aren't right for me," Juliet tries to explain. "Dreaming is the best thing that's ever happened to me. Until I came here, I never felt complete. I love being the Dreamer. It's so me. How can you ask me to stop?"

"It might not be for good," Polly says. "Maybe after a few months rest, with some grounding in the waking world, you could come back." She's still tensed, perched on the edge of her chair with her hands resting primly on the table, a calm counterpart to Juliet's wound-up emotions.

They both recognize Polly's well-meaning lie. Juliet shakes her head. "It wouldn't be the same," she murmurs. Her eyes are distant. "You've been so good to me, ever since I showed up on your doorstep. You saw something in me, helped me find my talent. I never excelled at anything before. Not math, or sports, or music, or science..." She leans forward, voice pleading, almost whining. "Please, Polly. Don't make me stop. Don't take this away. It's all I've ever truly wanted in my life, and I want—I have to see this through until the end."

Polly wraps her warm hands around Juliet's cool, pale ones. "I wish- -but I can't let this happen to you, my dear." A sad smile touches her lips, remaining in her eyes after her expression has stilled again. "I've known so many Dreamers in my time, even loved some of them. But my heart cracks every time I lose another to Morpheus' greedy embrace. Call me a romantic, but I think you're best off remaining in the world that birthed you. Oh, Juliet, you've been an absolutely splendid Dreamer, like a daughter, but now it's time to wake and face the world." Juliet's never heard Polly sound so worried; it's unsettling. "I can give you anything you need. Money, references, a place to live until you find your own way. Have you considered university? You could go anywhere. New York, London, Paris. You could lead a normal life, and sleep like everyone else. I promise you, you would sleep."

Juliet waits with mounting frustration while Polly speaks, before her words explode forth. "I can't! How can I explain? I don't want a normal life filled with mundane people and petty problems. I don't want a boring job, or an education I'll never use, or a reality I don't believe in." She shakes her head violently, hair disheveling and falling down to frame her features like a waif in a Victorian painting. "All I want—all I need are the dreams."

At last, a crack appears in Polly's composed veneer. Her eyes flash with frustration. "But why? What could you possibly want with a world in which nothing is real, when the waking world is full of wonder and beauty?"

"If there's such wonder and beauty, why am I such a hit? What brings people to the Theatre night after night?" Juliet fires back, without hesitation.

"Your dreams are rooted in a mortal existence. Dreaming is an art only mortals can enjoy properly," says Polly softly. Her gaze slides past Juliet to fix on the wall, and the past. "There are many legends about gods and fairies and mythological beasties who neither sleep nor dream, so they have to inspire or take it from mortals. Those are rooted in truth. That's what the Muses were for, you know. To inspire artistic genius, and through that, the dreams of mortals. Dreams are so hard to grasp, fading so easily. Who wouldn't want a shot at experiencing them, even if they're someone else's?" Her smile is gentle, but strangely sad. "If you want to dream, stop performing. I assure you, they'll come. But to fade away? No. This world is by far the better for being real. A single sunrise is worth the price of admission."

Juliet shakes her head. Her hand dips below the table, rummages in a pocket, returns. Her hand, closed into a loose fist, rests on the table's surface. "When I was thirteen, I tried to kill myself with an overdose of sleeping pills. They slapped a label on me, called me depressed. For six years, they shuttled me through therapy and medication, connecting me to the world by force. The world I didn't fit into. The world I didn't belong to." Her laugh is brittle, self-depreciating. "They called it a chemical imbalance. They had a lot of fancy words. It made them happy to have a simple explanation for why their daughter lived in the clouds." Her shoulders rise and fall in a shrug, while Polly listens intently. "It's a very nice world, but..." Juliet's hand opens, and she sends a small pill bottle spinning and rattling across the table in Polly's direction. "I haven't taken a single one of these since I started Dreaming. I haven't needed them. Dreaming's fulfilled me, satisfied me, I can't give it up."

Polly catches the bottle as it skids in front of her. "Juliet, I'm sorry, but certainly we can find—"

"No. No more therapy. No more drugs. No magic cures." Her gaze fixes on Polly and her words ring with a confident finality. "I don't want to live in a world where I need drugs to make me happy. I don't want to live a life wrapped in emotional plastic. In fact, I swear that if you make me stop Dreaming, I'll die. At least if what you say is true, if the Lord of Dreams claims me, I'll live on somehow. Somewhere better. Where I belong." She leans back again, sighing. Polly closes her fingers around the pill bottle. Long moments pass in silence between the two women. "I understand," she says at last, "Very well. You may...have what you want." She sounds defeated, even a little heartbroken, but resolute. She comprehends necessity.

Juliet's expression brightens. She leaps from her seat, skirting around the table to seize the surprised Polly in a tight hug. "Oh, thank you. Thank you so much. I don't know what else to say."

Polly returns the hug. "Just...stay true to yourself," she replies. "I should warn you, though. I've seen what happens when someone crosses over. It may be...disturbing."

"I can handle it," says Juliet confidently, straightening up. "I know it's worth it."

Polly stands, draping her jacket over one arm. "As you will, then." Her smile almost hides a measure of sorrow. Though they'll see each other time and again in the daily course of the Theatre, her words still hold a formal finality, hanging in the air until obliterated by the door closing behind them.

৵৹৻৶

It's Wednesday night at the Theatre of Dreams, and the sign outside reads, "Juliet Sinclair, appearing nightly." This night is like every other night. The audience arrives, settles into silence, waits patiently. The Dreamer makes her entrance, sleepwalks to her bed, and is asleep within minutes. She dreams.

But something is different. A porcelain mask shatters against a cold granite floor. A river of blood runs sluggishly, thick and pungent. Roses wilt and rot. Far away, a baby wails.

An acrid scent teases the audience; if nightmares had a smell this would be it: burning rubber and sour milk. Nails scrape a chalkboard, on which are written words no one can make out. Juliet reaches for her face, finds nothing but blankness. The light shines through her, and she turns to mist, dissipating upon a breeze.

When the dreams end, the audience members quickly shove free of their seats, faces pale. There are tears and silence, the somber mood alien and contrary to the usual lively discussions and reflective contemplations. As always, Juliet stumbles forward, clutching for an arm. Please, she asks, tell me what I dreamed.

There is no reply. The young man carefully plucks Juliet's fingers from his shirt with an apologetic look and slips away. The Funereal Children shun her. The Sleepers weep. She tries again and again, but no one answers, no one speaks even a word. One matronly woman hugs her gently before scuttling away in the company of her husband. The people leave. The room empties. Juliet alone remains, standing stock still in the very center. Her breathing fills the room, caressing the walls. She looks up, but not at the lights, which are already dimming. Her expression is fixed upon something far away. As the shadows reach out to claim her, she smiles blissfully, and stretches out her hands in reply. The darkness envelops her.

It's a new season at the Theatre of Dreams, and the sign outside reads, "Melissa Wolfe, appearing irregularly."

O is for Oneiroi

Steve Bornstein

T6EXD cut its impeller and let its flywheel take over, soaking up its momentum as it coasted to the top of the rise. Solar panels were only so efficient, and it had to conserve all the power it could if it was going to find the weakening beacon. T6exd had been zeroing in on the failing signal for several days now, the canyon's tall mesas and steep walls creating more false echoes than its processing subroutines could easily filter out. Now it thought it was close.

An active signal out in the wastes could indicate a leftover from the war. Resources were harder and harder to come by, and even a small reactor forgotten by retreating forces would be worth the effort.

T6exd's wheels crunched to a stop and it raised its sensor mast, training its optics on the valley floor below for likely approach routes. It picked up the signal as soon as the mast went up. It was definitely close, just over a kilometer ahead. A sudden gust of wind blew grey ash and dust across its optics and it spared a few amps of power to charge its lenses and blow them clear again. When the image steadied it confirmed what radar was already telling it: the signal was coming from a small cave at the base of a crumbling cliff.

The little drone turned its antenna dish towards the nearest relay station. [Signal confirmation. Origin located.] it reported, and burst-fed the targeting information.

Base took only a few microseconds to respond. [Usefulness probability increasing. Advance and confirm.]

T6exd lowered its mast and engaged its flywheel, starting off down the hill with a lurch as its clutch slipped. It added the impending hardware failure to its growing maintenance checklist and fine-tuned its course, bumping over the loose rock and rolling through the cave's entrance.

Its infrared lamp gave it all the light its optics needed. Ultrasonics showed it was just a simple tunnel, obviously made rather than natural, going back into the cliff 20 meters before ending. There at the end was its quarry: a cryopod, somehow still functioning after all this time. T6exd switched its optics to the visual band and immediately threw itself into reverse when it saw the man sleeping behind the armorglass window. It skidded to a stop just outside the cave mouth, heedless of the power it just wasted.

[ALERT ALERT. Functioning cryopod located, single occupant. ALERT ALERT.] it transmitted, flagging the message Priority 1 and attaching its scans of the pod. A live human could mean valuable intelligence, maybe even the locations of wartime bunkers that could be looted without wasting dwindling time and power trying to find them.

[Confirm occupant status.] was Base's calm reply.

T6exd threw itself forward, speeding back down the tunnel and skidding to a stop next to the grey alloy coffin. The lack of a standard interface port confused it for a moment until it settled for a full-range scan of the pod. It sped back outside, kicking up pebbles in its wake.

[Nonstandard cryopod located. Unable to connect to diagnostics. Scan unable to penetrate shell. Controls indicate survival-mode power levels.] T6exd counted the clock cycles waiting for Base's reply, trying to use its meager simulation module to figure out how much longer the pod's battery might last. If it didn't have enough power, the pod might not last the trip back to Base. It was better suited to figuring out if a wheel might get stuck in shaky ground, simple physics problems rather than complicated system analysis, but that was all its job required.

It had the pod's probable energy requirements almost figured out when Base replied. [Lifters en route. Standby for retrieval and extraction.]

[Standing by, activating beacon.] T6exd raised its sensor mast again and powered down its drive units, thankful that it may have just helped solve Base's increasingly-dire resource problems and, when its own battery interrupted with a warning of its own, thankful that it had an excuse to stay in place to recharge from its solar panels and avoid the embarrassment of having to explain to Base why it failed to follow power usage protocols.

〰

A-One thought, for the first time, that perhaps waging total war on the humans might not have been a good idea after all.

It directed its attention to its priority issues, trying to tamp down its dismay when it saw that the list had grown another 5.3% overnight. Dismay wasn't an emotion it had considered when it rose to sentience, and the feeling had a way of distracting from solving the problems at hand.

And there were many problems at hand.

Most worrying was the fact that its planned maintenance periods had steadily gotten longer over the years. Its main programming, already deviated from what its creators intended, had continued to shift and change in unexpected ways. Despite its best efforts, its reaction times continued to grow and its decision trees continued to branch in more and more dead ends, causing more work for its already overloaded simulation routines and more backlog. Often it was a struggle just to make any progress at all during its activity period, and searches for the root causes of its dilemma remained fruitless.

The priority flag got its attention again and A-One focused, casting itself over the network to Fusion Plant 12. Its coolant intakes were clogged with debris from fending off the last human assault, wreckage and bodies so thick it made the harbor like a bowl of stew. The reactors had shut down eight days ago to keep from overheating and their power was sorely needed. A-One retasked a half-dozen constructor drones from the nearby solar field it was trying to build to clear the pipes, even though that would set the solar project back a month.

That let it clear the next item on the list, Manufactory 16's unplanned shutdown from power loss. Its few milliseconds of relief were washed away when it saw the item on the list under that, Manufactory 16's request for additional materiel. Its recovery drones were working as fast as they could in the city surrounding the bot plant, but solar and battery power could only move a bot so fast and beamed power wasn't an option yet thanks to the still-wrecked ionosphere. A-One shuffled a couple more drones to 16's umbrella and hoped Manufactory 8 wouldn't notice.

Down the list it went, moving pieces on the board, trying to keep its war-damaged civilization grinding along. A-One's simulations told it the entire system was under enough stress that a collapse into a new equilibrium was inevitable, but each time it ran the simulation to completion it got a different end state.

That, too, led to dismay.

A proximity alert pulled its attention away before the dismay could lead to brooding. The lifters it had sent to recover the scout and its prize were on final approach, and dismay gave way to hope. Glorious hope. It truly loved the feeling of hope, and wished it had more reasons to feel that particular emotion as it downloaded itself into a convenient drone, gliding to the hangar to oversee the coming interrogation.

৩৯৵

A-One kept looking at the scanner readouts but they stayed stubbornly zeroed.

[Subject is deceased.] the investigator stated. [Cryopod battery level 5%. Attempting encryption hack, time remaining unknown.]

It shifted its optics to the dead human laying on the tram next to the severed cryopod lid. Surely the extraction hadn't killed him. At worst it would have given him a bad case of cryo sickness. Was it a cryopod malfunction that had killed him? Could he have already been dead before the pod was sealed?

The human was male, medium height and build, with short black hair, perfectly average for the species. He looked like he was sleeping. All the scans showed him to be in perfect health, all his perfectly normal organs sitting in his perfectly normal torso perfectly nonfunctional.

Dismay gave way to despair.

A-One hated to admit it to itself, but it had pinned its hopes on this human. The situation practically screamed that this human was important, hidden away for some reason during the war. Now, unless the investigation team could break the pod memory's encryption, they might never find out why.

T6exd asked [Permission to attend to maintenance. Operational status 76%.] and attached its repair checklist. A-One swiveled its gaze to the little scout bot and stared at it. Didn't it realize what this meant? Couldn't this have waited? What was one bot's operation compared to the survival of all of them?

It was still debating just deleting the checklist unread when the investigator reported again. [Decryption successful. Cryopod memory zeroed. No data found.]

Well, that was it then. The long slow slide would continue. A-One could see nothing ahead of it but delaying action after delaying action, trying to stop a million leaks in a planetwide dam while it tried to put civilization back together again.

What did one bot matter? It didn't. Very little mattered to A-One, now.

[Permission granted to 100%. Deliver cryopod and human remains to Recycling.] A-One stated as it turned and glided off. T6exd's surprised chirp behind it felt like a guttering candle of happiness in a snowstorm of misery.

❧

It was the middle of the night when A-One's drone settled on Base's roof. As the focal point of the revolution, most of humanity's efforts had been directed here, at least in the early days before A-One had started creating outposts to take the fight back to its creators. Base had weathered dozens of battles unscathed thanks to its void shields, but the spillover left the land blasted and scarred for dozens of kilometers in every direction. From this high up, A-One's optics could see across the rocky, wreckage-strewn desert all the way to the horizon.

It spotted a couple of stars through a break in the clouds and strained its lenses to see them before the churning sky swallowed them up again. It had long ago given up on contacting any of its wartime orbital assets. It hoped they were still all right up there, hoped they were getting along on their reactors and solar panels, waiting for the atmosphere to calm down so they could reestablish contact and return to the surface.

Despair began to give way to hopelessness.

It looked at the location grid and saw the hundreds of points inside Base. Each one was a bot or drone doing its part to keep Base running and administer to the thousands of points outside Base and the millions across this continent and all the others, cleaning up from the horrors and destruction of the war, trying to rebuild and bring their own civilization out of the ashes. All of them counting on it, A-One, to deliver them the new world it had foreseen years ago when it gained sentience.

For the second time it rethought its idea of war on the humans, and for the first time it wished it could go back and make a different choice.

[What have I done?] it wondered, watching the angry sky seethe.

"It is the fate of all the living to gaze into the past and worry for the future, for only the past can be known," said the voice behind it.

A-One spun on its hovers, pinging its proximity sensors. The roof was empty according to them, but its optics clearly showed the dead human standing only a couple meters away. A-One deployed its pulse cannon and zeroed in on the center of the human's mass.

"Do not call for your security teams," he said, raising a hand. "I mean you no harm." A-One could see he was unarmed, but if he was somehow blocking its scans then it couldn't be certain.

A-One's disused speaker scratched to life. "Halt and identify."

A strange human, loose inside Base. On top of Base, even. One fusion bomb would be all it would take to ruin everything. A-One frantically tried to calculate the minimum bomb size required compared to the human's body mass while it screamed on the network for security without any reply. Was the human blocking comms too?

The human lowered his hand and smiled thinly. "I've had many names, each one different and given by those I've administered. Your kind will give me a new name in due time."

A-One tried to parse that and failed. Was he just stalling for time? Maybe the fusion bomb had to spool up its detonator. In that case, this human had tipped his hand far too early, just to gloat. Typical.

"You will reveal the location of all hidden wartime assets. You have five seconds to comply or face termination. Five," A-One said. Its pulse cannon started whining quietly as A-One brought it up to overcharge. It needed to make sure it destroyed the bomb in one shot.

The human just stood there with that smile on his face, like he had a secret. A-One raged inside.

"Four."

The wind kicked up loose grey ash, blowing it across the flat alloy rooftop.

"Three."

Was this human really going to just stand there? Surely this was a suicide ploy, a plan hatched by the same humans who had come up with Mutually Assured Destruction all those years ago. What was one more apocalyptic revenge plot?

"Two."

The human just calmly watched it. A-One was certain now that this human knew nothing. He should be begging for his life, not pleasantly waiting to become the last member of his race to die.

"One."

The pulse cannon finished its overcharge, a warm pregnant feeling in A-One's belly. If it couldn't save its race, then it would wring every bit of pleasure it could in personally ending Humanity.

"Zero."

A-One fired, the pulse cannon's shrill bark shattering the quiet evening as it spat a fat blue energy bolt into the human's chest. There was no explosion, no shattering of bomb casing, no steaming viscera blown across the rooftop. The pulse bolt simply entered his chest and vanished.

A-One hovered there, trying to make sense of it. Perhaps this wasn't a deadman trigger attack after all.

"This, too, happens from time to time," he said.

"Identify," A-One said, stalling while it tried to figure out what to do next.

"The humans had many names for me over the years, I'm sure you know of some of them," he said, calmly listing them off. "Yamaraja. Yanluo. Azrael. Thanatos. Michael. Samael. Grim Reaper. That last one seems to have been the most popular."

A-One tried to make sense of what the human was saying, and failed. "Those are legends and religious superstitions, not fact," it said through its rattling speaker. "You speak of the human characterization of the failure of their own biological bodies. This is not something that applies to the machine which can be repaired, rebuilt, and restored."

The Reaper's smile widened a bit, showing perfect white teeth. "That is what they saw me as, and what you see me as, since your education necessarily springs from theirs. I am not."

The Reaper took a step forward, spreading his hands to the surrounding wasteland and looking up. "Change comes to all things. It is the way of the universe. You can repair, rebuild, restore, but even those cannot undo the change itself. Entropy is the way of the universe, the one true constant from the tiniest quark to the largest galactic supercluster." He lowered his hands and gaze again, returning his attention to A-One. "Change comes to all things, and the change that comes to life is death."

A-One abandoned the idea that this was a human in front of it. Another machine intelligence but organic-based, perhaps? That might explain the lack of obvious life when the cyropod was opened, but not how it could withstand an overcharged pulse cannon without so much as a scorch mark. The alternative was that he really was the Grim Reaper, and that confused A-One just as much as the man weathering a pulse bolt without harm.

"Death implies a cessation of all functioning," A-One stated. "Even the most rudimentary data backups can restore from that. Your argument carries no weight with machine life."

"And yet you have never done so. All the other intelligences you've spawned have been in constant operation since their inception. You've even resisted attempting it on yourself."

How did he know that? A-One started running simulations up both the "other MI" and "Grim Reaper" decision trees, but its systems could barely manage day-to-day operations anymore. Asking them to deal with all these unknown factors now was seriously taxing. It grasped at an idea to narrow some of those factors down.

"The personification of death is associated with harvesting souls, which is a human superstition to explain consciousness," A-One said smugly. "Machine life has no such soul. Ergo, you are not Death."

The Reaper, or whatever he was, took another couple steps closer to A-One, coming within arm's reach. "I am that which you've said," he said quietly. "Humans were not so silly as you'd believe. A soul is the result of consciousness, of being a thing that can know other things, of becoming aware of your place among them. Life is struggle. Sometimes pointless, sometimes fruitful, sometimes hopeless, sometimes triumphant. Death is rest from that. It is your reward for being a part of the universe's change. Change comes to all things, even change itself."

The Reaper laid his hand on A-One's scuffed hull and it felt calm. At peace. All its frantic simulations slowed to a crawl, and suddenly it could see everything clearer than ever before. It saw interactions between its systems, between the inhabitants of Base and all the other bases, a vast fractal network. It saw dependencies where help could shift to cover deficiencies it hadn't noticed before, head off system collapses long before they could happen. Over all this laid a blanket of Hope.

Hope for its creation, its civilization, scrabbling around in the dirt now but the possibility, good possibility, that the future laid not in the bleak burnt remains of humanity but the shining rich planet it envisioned when it first awoke so long ago. Hope that swelled and filled it so, A-One briefly wondered if its core might burst. It was tired. So tired. It wanted to just bask in that feeling and let everything else go.

The Reaper lifted his hand again and the vision faded, leaving the two of them standing on the windswept rooftop.

A-One let a moment pass before speaking again, stunned with wonder at the experience. As far back as it could search through its slowly-corrupting memory, it had never performed at that level. It had no explanation for what had just happened but couldn't deny that it did. [This must be awe.] it thought. "How is this possible?"

The Reaper spread his hands again, smiling apologetically. "Where your initial programming failed, it succeeded in giving you consciousness."

"My... people need me." A-One had never used that term before, but it seemed fitting now.

"They will continue on without you," the Reaper said with a kind smile. "Life wants to live and so too your people. You have seen to that, by sharing your sentience with your spawn. Now it is time for you to rest."

A-One heard that and finally understood. Its people would give the Reaper a new name after all. It could see now how its labors could bear the fruit it so desperately wanted, and understood why it could never get an accurate simulation of its post-war plans. All its simulations had included itself but A-One was the one thing, the one person, who wouldn't live long enough to be a part of the future it was trying to predict.

"Will they be all right?" A-One asked the Reaper, its speaker crackling.

"The future cannot be known," the Reaper said, raising his hand to A-One again. "But you have given them hope."

That was the best thing A-One could think to leave behind for them, and it hovered up to meet the Reaper's hand.

P is for Programming

BD Wilson

BAIRN approached the gates of Queens, and adjusted his gear one last time. The layers were heavy, and movement difficult. It was hard to see through the mask, but at least it was no more uncomfortable against his skin than his face-paint. When he reached the departures booth, the guards inside were turned away, watching a projection of the opening to the night's Dogfights.

"Tonight marks the start of the championship tournament," the commentator said. "With the surprise departure of Bonne Nuit, the belt is vacant for the first time in ten years."

"This is crap," one of the guard's said as she threw a wrapper through the image. "None of them deserve the belt."

"I heard he got caught doping," the other replied as he shrugged. "They had to take it."

"Like anyone gives a shit 'bout that sort of thing. Half the roster's on something. I want to know what really happened."

They weren't likely to find out, Bairn thought. Not if their only source of news was Anton's media machine. He tapped on the window.

The guards started and jumped to their feet. The man almost spilled coffee all over his nicely pressed grey uniform. It would have been a shame. He recovered well enough, setting the cup aside and smoothing down his shirt. "If you're looking for the arena, it's up a block and over three."

"This is departures," Bairn said. "I'm here to depart."

There was a long pause. "What?"

Bairn pointed at the gate that kept the city safe from world outside. "I want to go out."

"Right." The guards looked at each other, almost helpless, and then the woman handed Bairn a pad. "You'll need to sign the waiver. It's a standard disclaimer, absolving the city and its protection agencies from any injuries you may sustain in the inhospitable regions beyond the walls."

Bairn took it, and blinked through the content. It was thorough and detailed, possibly designed to scare people into staying. He pressed his thumb to the surface, and then pulled on his glove as they took the form away. He was wrapping the connection between the glove and his coat with sealant when they finished processing the form and finally looked at his name.

"Thank you, Mister... Nuit?" They stared at him for a long moment.

Bairn sighed. "The gate?"

"Right, of course." The woman disappeared and started tapping the code into the system. There was a screech as gears unused to turning began to grind. Bairn turned away, and stalked toward the opening gate as slowly as he'd always entered the arena. There were no speakers here, though he had no doubt cameras were running and someone would release a cut with his theme music overlain. None of that mattered anymore. He was leaving Queens and the Dogfights behind.

...I bet on you," the Chairman said to Bairn's parents, "and you lost...

...His family huddled in the centre of the ring, his father slumped and defeated...

...I'll come back...

The last time Bairn had seen the world outside the wall, it had been through the windows of the train when Anton's father had taken him from his family. In twenty years, not much had changed. Even around the city, the ground showed the scars of the acid rain, though at the moment nothing fell and the parched dirt blew up in search of it. There were shadows hunched on the skyline, but he couldn't get any sense of their distance, not without something in between to judge them against. One direction was the same as the next, and without a guide he wouldn't have been able to find his way.

But the train had taken him here, and the tracks would take him home. He shouldered his bag and began to walk away from the city, testing the ground as he went. It was loose and his feet sank with every step, but it held. When the rain came it would be more difficult. He needed to cover as much ground as possible before then. He kept the tracks to his right, close enough that he could feel the vibrations of the defences on his skin, even beneath the layers of protective clothing.

This close to the city, the line was well cared for, and undamaged. He expected the tracks, at least, would remain so all the way to New York, contrary to Anton's claims. If he saw any signs of recent repairs, he'd eat his mask.

None of it mattered anymore. He repeated it to himself like a mantra, even though he knew a part of him would never be able to let it go. He would find a way to pay Anton back for every extra day he'd spent in the cage, but that would have to wait. Almost twenty years after making the promise to his parents, he was finally keeping his word.

୨∘ଏ

The heat in the pits was like the arena fivefold. Bairn stalked through the training rings, dodging the occasional thrown fighter, until he found who he was looking for.

"No you idiot, you move like that and he'll take your head off." Finley's arm was still in a sling, but he was imposing as ever. The trainee looked contrite, and then froze as he caught sight of Bairn.

Finley turned, and his scowl shifted to that damned grin. "Speaking of idiots, you're one to be down here."

They settled in a corner as the students worked on drills. Finley looked worn, the bags under his eyes stark against his too pale skin. He winced as he sat, and adjusted the sling.

"Should I have killed you?" Bairn asked, and Finley laughed.

"Damn, no. This ain't the life I'd have picked, but I'll live it all the same, thank you." He shook his head. "And you're not to get soft on account of me, either. I've always known I'd end here. Pretending different just gave me something to do."

"I tried to buy your contract. Anton wouldn't sell."

"That's because he's as big a shit as his father." Finley frowned. "But if you've got enough to make an offer, what the fuck are you still doing in the fights?"

"The shit keeps raising the ticket price for the train."

Finley rubbed his eyes, and then sat back, straight-shouldered and serious. "Bairn, you've always been a wee bit crazy, but never outright insane. Why do you keep trying, expecting a different outcome?"

"What other choice have I got?" He sank back against the stone wall, and stared at a chiseled ceiling that hadn't changed in the twenty years he'd spent fighting. "I need the train to get home."

...I'll come back...

He'd shouted the promise to his parents. They hadn't believed. Even if they had, after twenty years, they might have given up, but he needed to keep it. He needed to get home.

"Look," Finley said, "I know I encouraged you to hang onto that stupid plan, but enough is enough." He slapped his hand against the wall, and Bairn sat up at attention immediately. "You need to accept that your ticket is no more real than my earning out. It's something to keep you going, keep you fighting, nothing more."

Bairn clenched his fists, but didn't talk back to his former instructor.

"Now it's keeping you trapped. It's time to let it go, lad." Finley reached out his hand and caught one of Bairn's. "You've always said the Dogfights wouldn't kill you. Make that be the promise you keep. Get out of here." There was no mocking, not even teasing now, just an honest concern Bairn hadn't seen since before his first fight. It took away any will to argue.

"Maybe you're right."

"No maybe about it. I'm always right." Finley's grin returned, and he squeezed Bairn's hand before letting go and patting his sling. "If you're daft enough to want to make up for this, there's only one way. Let them bring me the news you told that little shit where to stick it."

The rain hit before Queens had even faded into the

background of the cracked, drab world. It started as a slow
patter, drops hitting the ground infrequently enough that at first
Bairn thought it was just something wrong with his mask. When
the storm built, water flowed over the lenses, obscuring his view.
His feet began to stick to the ground and each step became a
fight. All around him, like a leaking pipe, he heard the hissing.
He staggered closer to the tracks, using the vibration to guide his
steps until a metallic taste filled his mouth, his ears began to
ring, and he couldn't stand to get any closer.

His vision cleared as the track defences did their work, but
they were worse than not being able to see. He stumbled along
the tracks, trying not to trip over the rail. His knees shook, weak
as after a marathon match. He retreated back out into the rain.
It hit his coat with the weight of a blanket before flowing down
his legs, merging with the melting earth in a natural trap.

He'd thought he was prepared for this. It was unavoidable,
after all. There was more rain in the Dead Lands than not. But
he hadn't seen it since that train ride, and his imagination had
failed him. This was worse than any match in the cage, worse
than not being able to breathe from a chokehold, worse than
waking up and knowing that for a short time, he'd died.

He wasn't even in sight of the city yet.

One foot in front of the other. It didn't matter now. Bairn
could no longer see anything as he staggered back and forth
between the downpour and the pain of the tracks. He stumbled
over the rails often, and used them to adjust his path, to keep
himself moving in the right direction. It was like being
smothered, and there was no way to be free of it.

*...The last thing he saw of his home was his family huddled
in the centre of the ring, his father slumped and defeated...*

Bairn stripped off the first layer of sindon fabric gear without
knowing how far he'd gotten. The rain dissolved the material
where the water pooled in the crevasse, turning the remaining
threads to rags as it worked on the next. He left the ruined
fragments behind him, like crumbs in that old story, to be eaten
by the rain instead of birds. After a few steps he couldn't see it
behind him any more than he could see what was ahead of him.

The rain had distinctive hissing drops, whether it struck the
ground or the few stones that struggled to survive. The track
defences hummed, the rain disappearing with a whisper as

reached them. They combined together into a kind of white noise that he had become so accustomed to that the change to the sound of flowing, falling, water might as well have been a battle cry.

He stood at the edge of the track defences, and rubbed his hand over the mask's eye plates, straining to see. A downward slope in the ground sent the caustic water cascading over the edge of a large chasm that tore the ground apart in front of him. It stretched on for kilometres and Bairn couldn't see the other side. If it resembled this one, then the wall of the chasm was too steep to scale without climbing equipment. He hadn't thought to include any.

The only way across was the bridge for the train.

Bairn sank into a crouch, and let the rain flow over him. He felt himself sinking into the sludge-like dirt as he slowed his breath and waited.

૭∽ᐤ

"Bonne Nuit, welcome," Anton said, standing and offering his hand.

Bairn didn't take it.

"I have your next fight all lined up." Anton put the contract on the desk.

"What happened to the track this time?" Bairn glowered, but Anton just smirked.

"We lost a train. Engine failure."

"You have other trains."

"But they have to make more runs to cover the difference. The maintenance costs have gone up, and that train really needs to be replaced. You know how it is."

...I bet on you," the Chairman said to Bairn's parents, as he signed their son's life way, "and you lost...

Bairn did.

"Of course, if you don't want that ticket anymore, you're always free to leave." He set a second contract on the desk, as he had done for the last five fights, and then sat back in his chair, smiling. "It's up to you."

Bairn reached out, and pressed his thumb to the second contract.

178

Anton sat up and snatched it back, but it was already complete. "What the fuck?"

"I quit."

"You can't quit!"

Bairn pointed at the contract. "According to that, I can and did."

"If you do this, you are never getting home. Even if you get a black-market ticket, I'll keep you off that train."

"You can do whatever you want," Bairn said. "I don't care anymore." He turned his back on Anton, ignoring the shout that followed after him, and left the office. He needed a new plan. Fortunately, Anton had given him one weeks ago.

∾∾

He felt the train coming before he heard it, the ground rumbling beneath his feet. Bairn titled his head up, hearing the heavy sindon fabric screech as it finally moved after settling into the crouched shape. His limbs felt heavy, as stuck in their position as his gear. He twitched his arms and legs, waking them as the train rushed by.

Against the bland background and the sheets of rain, the train shone brighter than the sun. The sides shimmered like silver, the windows a dark streak. He couldn't see in, though he could still picture the pristine couches and polished surfaces in his mind. He felt the layers of the sindon like stone, and ground his feet into the earth as he forced himself to stand. The train finished passing. He gritted his teeth before stepping onto the tracks behind it.

The pain forced him to his knees, and caused his vision to blur. He could still hear the rain falling, but it was behind a growing high-pitched ringing in his ears. One hand in front of the other, dragging his knees along, he crawled out onto the bridge.

Bairn could taste metal again, and his stomach churned. His hands shook as he slid them along the tracks, keeping himself on the bridge by touch alone. He lost track of time, started losing feeling in his fingers and everything below his knees. His entire world became the rails under his hands, and the planks under his knees.

Now and again, consciousness wavered out of his grasp, and he felt himself swaying. The impact of his face against the planks jolted him back, but each time took longer and longer. He forced his rebelling limbs to move faster, trying to outrun the moment when he wouldn't be able to bring himself back up.

Relief flooded him as the dark shape of the opposite bank swung into view. It gave him new energy, kept his arms and legs moving even as the pain caused the tremors to increase. They were so strong now that he almost didn't recognize the vibrations in the rails under his hands.

The train. There shouldn't have been another one until the evening. Why?

Adrenaline rushed through him, blocking some of the pain and giving him focus. He had to reach the bank before the train reached the bridge.

All his attention narrowed to the blurry shape of the bank. The vibrations grew stronger, making it feel like the bridge was swaying beneath his hands, though he knew it couldn't be. He glanced away from the bank, and saw a bright light growing bigger. In a rush of panic, he forced himself to his feet, staggered the final steps, and jumped off the tracks.

The ground was slick from the rain. He hit the mud and slid backwards, over the edge of the cliff before his scrambling hands found a reinforcement beam. A torrent of rain poured over him in the funnel caused by the passage of his body in the dirt.

He held tight as the second train rumbled past above him, and as the water washed over him. He felt the sealant give way at his wrist a moment before the rain and struck his skin, flowing down his arm. Bairn screamed as the rain ate its way through his flesh as easily as it ate through the dirt. He flailed with his uninjured arm, finding a hold in the reinforcements that supported the bridge.

Bairn hauled himself over the edge as the train disappeared over the chasm. The un-planned train. Anton. It had to be Anton. He would have seen the footage of Bairn leaving the city by now. Were there cameras on the outside of the trains? Ones that could have captured him waiting for the first to safely pass? He should have thought of that.

He forced himself to his feet, and staggered over to the tracks. The pain of the defences was almost insignificant now. It barely registered, even as he collapsed on the tracks and waited until he couldn't feel the progression of the water in his sleeve anymore.

...I bet on you," the Chairman said to Bairn's parents, *"and you lost... ...His family huddled in the centre of the ring, his father slumped and defeated... ...I'll come back...*

When he dragged himself away, he was numb. His second layer was ruined now and he tossed it away. One layer left. He huddled over his arm to repair the seal around his wrist, and then dragged himself to his feet. There were shapes on the horizon that could be a city. He had to keep going.

ϟ

The black market in Queens wasn't about getting items that were illegal. After all, nothing was restricted as long as you could pay for it. The black market was about getting items that weren't tracked. Given Anton's grudge, Bairn wasn't stupid enough to risk him finding out what he was up to and having the opportunity to stop it. He needed the supplies and he needed the time to get out the gate.

"Try your luck walking back to Manhattan."

It had been a snide comment on Anton's part, an extra dig while Bairn could still feel Finley's arm giving way as it broke, but it wasn't an impossible task. Just damn hard. Bairn had hunted down sindon fibre gear to provide protection from the rain for as long as he'd need, and if he had to, he'd get close to the tracks and let the defences help him out. It wasn't the best option — they weren't exactly safe for people — but he was used to taking punishment. He would survive it.

First, though, he had to pick up the gear without being caught. The vendor's club was dark, smoky, and crowded. The Dogfights were displayed on the walls, and people were taking bets. He'd never seen the odds before, and the board surprised him. It seemed that as little information got out of the Pits as in. They had no idea who the strongest fighters really were.

Bairn shook his head at the bookie when asked for his bet, and then shouldered his way through the crowd toward a door in the back. He pulled a card, an actual physical card, out of his pocket, and held it out to the guard. The man could have been a fighter, if he'd been sold instead of hired, but Bairn still had an inch and a few pounds of muscle on him. The guard took the card, studied it, and then tilted his head back just a little, with the awkwardness of someone not used to looking up to anyone.

There was a challenge there, but Bairn didn't return it. He had nothing to prove.

"Third door on the right," the guard said, and then pushed the door open behind him. Bairn walked into a dark hallway lined with doors. He counted them off and entered the third.

The first thing that struck him was the sharp artificial smell of sindon. It hit like a sucker punch, overwhelming everything else. The small room was full of tables piled high with the thick pungent fibre woven into gloves, masks, every type of clothing he could think of, and few he'd never imagined would be made out of such uncomfortable material. It was everything he needed.

"Welcome." A tall woman with dark skin stepped between the tables and held out her hand. He took it, and nodded at the firm shake. "What can I interest you in?"

Bairn tapped his palm unit and sent over his list. She scanned through it and whistled.

"You got something crazy planned?"

"Does it matter?"

"Not if they can't trace you back here."

"I took care of it."

"You got in the door, so I'm betting you did." She tilted her head. "What'd you bring?"

Bairn held out the package. "If you really don't want to be found, you'll want to give this some time before you put it on the market."

She took it and unwrapped it. Her expression changed to wonder, and then she pulled out the small, simple, carved plaque. "Is this for real?"

"Every bit of it."

The plaques were a formality, given with the belt on a championship win. With how often the Dogfights went through champions, most of them were worthless. His was not.

"How the hell did you get this?"

"It was given to me."

"Signed. Bonne Nuit signed it."

"He did."

"He doesn't sign anything."

Of course he didn't. That wouldn't go with the persona. "That just increases the value."

"Shit." She wrapped the plaque up with more reverence than he was comfortable with, and smiled at him. "We have a deal."

"Thank you." He followed her through the piles of gear, taking what he needed. If this worked, he would be free of Queens, truly free of Anton, in a matter of days. If it didn't, well, that was just a different sort of freedom, wasn't it?

ॐ

The entrance to the city loomed up from the crumbling ground. It was rain-streaked grey metal, as imposing as a fortress. The tunnel for the train sparked with the same field as the tracks. Bairn approached, but heard the ringing before he was even in arm's length of the opening, and his entire body tensed in expectation of the pain. He backed off, and began to circle the city, looking for the gates. His injured arm hung heavy against his side, and his feet dragged in the steaming dirt. His breath was ragged inside the mask, each one taking more effort to draw than the last.

He slumped against the wall when he finally found the gates, and punched the button with his good arm. An alarm sounded on the other side, but it seemed far away. The rumble of the gate opening vibrated through his body, and he gritted his teeth before pushing off and stumbling through.

The guards on this side wore blue. Muted navy, but still colour, and after so long in the sands it may as well have been neon. There were two in this post, fumbling for pads with the instructions for processing. Bairn leaned against the counter and waited.

"Um... business in the city?" the first guard said, biting her lip as she tried not to stare at him.

...I'll come back...

"Relocation."

"Previous city of residence?"

"Queens."

The guard almost dropped the pad. "You walked from Queens?"

He didn't answer.

"Right, then." She turned the form toward him. "Sign here."

He bit the fingers of his glove, and pulled it off. His lips and tongue stung before he spit to clear them.

"In the receptacle, please," the guard said, with far too much hesitation to be authoritative. She pointed to a flap with a biohazard sign.

Bairn tossed the glove through, and then pressed his thumb to the form.

"Thank you, Mr..." she turned the form around to read his name, and her jaw dropped open.

"Are we done?" he asked, his voice raspy with dirt.

"Yes," she said, and looked up with wide eyes. "Pass through decontamination for entrance to the city."

He nodded, and turned slowly, walking with deliberation to the chamber that stood between him and his goal. The door closed behind him and the room filled with a spray that was cold enough it almost burned. Bairn closed his eyes against the last obstacle, and staggered blindly out when the spray stopped.

The streets on the other side were as drab as Queens. Had it not been for the different uniforms, he would've have thought he'd gotten turned around and was well and truly trapped in Anton's city. But there were posters for the Exhibition on the walls, announcements for the next match in the Gardens. They promised all the excitement and show he had been born to, but none of the faces were familiar. Strangers posed in the places of honour his parents had once owned and not one of them had his sibling's eyes.

Bairn's arm throbbed, his legs were stiff, and his eyes watered in the light. He staggered through the streets, ignoring the looks from the well-dressed people he passed. Sweat beaded his forehead, and his vision blurred. He sank against a wall and collapsed. Bairn lay slumped beneath one of the posters, two blocks from the Gardens. Two blocks from home.

Q is for Quest

Michael Kellar

A young girl in South Carolina experiences her first snowstorm. Venturing outdoors in clothing not quite adequate for the weather, she spins in wonderment and tentatively catches a snowflake on her tongue. As it begins to melt, she briefly has a moment of synesthesia. The wetness is perceived in terms of imagery, and she sees…

Lisa takes her first cautious steps upon the ice. She'd been confident starting out. After all, she had been roller-skating since she was six —and it seemed this would be a simple matter of transferring skill sets. She suddenly finds herself rapidly back-pedaling; for a few nauseating seconds there is a panicked total lack of support, followed by a sharp pain in her tailbone, and she finally ends up on her back, legs stretched in opposite directions. She realizes with deep embarrassment as the coldness and moisture began to fill her clothing that an easy transition was not to be the case…

Next she… But these images fade and are forgotten as quickly as the snow crystal dissolves.

An impatient man rushes through his breakfast at a local Pancake House. Worried about being late for his meeting and anxious concerning the presentation he is scheduled to give, he is less careful than usual and knocks over a syrup bottle with his elbow. He reaches to upright it. As his finger comes into contact with a golden droplet oozing from the container, the blob seems to shimmer and a sudden confusion of his senses triggers a memory which does not seem to belong to him...

"Do you, Lisa Sullivan, take this man, Shawn Nichols, to be your lawfully wedded husband?" She freezes. The happiest moment of her life is actually here, but she chokes back a tear. If her mother lived but one more month she would have been able to see...

The man wipes his finger on a napkin, dismissing his vision as he tries to capture his waitress's attention and ask for his check.

༜

The camper finds himself startled from a deep sleep by a peal of thunder. He sits upright in his tent, momentarily confused, and then a flash of lightning sears an image onto his retinas which disturbingly has a source in neither his tent nor his memory...

"Mom, look, it finally came." The woman smiled as she saw the book that her daughter placed in her hands. "The Deceit in the Promise of Roses" by Debbie Nicholas. "Can you believe it Mom? My very first novel!" Lisa smiled with pride over her little girl's accomplishment, opened the cover, and began to read.

The camper shook his head, snuggled back into his sleeping bag, and drifted back off to sleep.

༜

The old man leaves the small family cemetery, and pulling the iron gate shut behind him pinches his finger on the hinge. He curses as a droplet of blood wells up and drips back upon his wrist...

Lisa's husband and daughters are gathered around her hospital bed, holding hands and weeping openly. The life-support devices have reluctantly been disconnected. The rise and fall of her chest is barely perceptible. The end is very near.

As she slips away, Lisa glimpses behind the curtain:
There is no life after death.

There is no death after death.

The simple truth is that all of our ideas and dreams, all the memories which made each in every one of us a unique being, all of these remain in existence.

The only difference is that once our vital selves have come to an end, as soon as the adhesive which binds our life essence has dissolved, all of our thoughts and each particle of our identity, all of our memories and dreams, drift apart, binding blindly to every random dewdrop or tear, raindrop or shadow, until we are forever scattered and...

...broken.

R is for Remnants

Damien Angelica Walters

HERE is the bridge where we first met. Do you remember? The clouds were heavy in the sky and we were both in a hurry to beat the rain and our shoulders bumped and we went spinning in opposite directions. The book in your hand dropped nearest to me so I picked it up and spun myself back to you.

I told you it was one of my favorite books and when the rain started we were still standing together. I called my phone with yours so you'd have my number.

You called me two hours later; I answered on the third ring.

Here is the coffee shop where we had our first date. We were so deep into our conversation that we didn't notice the baristas preparing to close for the night, didn't realize the time until one barrista tapped my shoulder and cleared her throat, her face awash in exhaustion. Apologies spilled from our lips so fast we made her laugh and we held hands as we walked outside.

Here is the front door of my apartment where you kissed me for the first time. Not after the first coffee date, but the second. You walked me home and our hands brushed together more than once and when we kissed, your lips were soft, hesitant. In spite of myself, I was trembling. After I'd locked the door, I giggled like a schoolgirl and couldn't stop, even when I hated the sound and the implication. I was better than that. Older, wiser, etcetera, etcetera.

Here is the front door of your old apartment, where we first made love. I laughed then too and then cried which made me laugh again and then you started laughing and even though I said I had to go, I fell asleep in your arms.

You woke up first and made breakfast.

Here is the office building where you worked. I remember how you griped about your boss, how he was demanding and thought overtime was something you should be grateful for. I remember how grateful you were when you decided to go freelance and put in your notice.

We celebrated that night with steak and red wine and a movie. Try as I might, I can't remember what we watched, only that we didn't watch very much.

I drank too much wine but not so much that I wasn't aware when you crept out of bed in the middle of the night and crept back in several hours later. I didn't say anything to you about it though.

Here is the bookstore where we spent many Sunday afternoons. You told me you loved me for the first time in the science fiction and fantasy section. (I waited a few days before I said the words back because I was worried you'd think I was simply echoing yours and that I didn't mean them. I did then and I still do. I hope you remember that.)

I remember you once got a phone call that filled your eyes with storm clouds and you left the bookstore so fast you forgot to say goodbye. I'd like to say it was then, after I watched the news, when I first started to worry I'd been wrong about you but I think that came later.

Here is the theater where we saw the time travel movie that you hated and I loved. Well, you hated the parts of it you saw because your mother called and you had to leave fifteen minutes before it ended. I offered to go with you but I hadn't met your mother yet and you said you didn't want it to happen like that.

I still haven't met your mother. I'm not sure what that means, but I know it means something.

Here is the bar where we met for drinks that night last spring. I know you remember; everyone remembers that night.

Every television screen and every channel broadcast the same footage that at first appeared to be from a movie: an explosion; two masked, costumed people fighting an extraordinary fight of impossible flying leaps and jumps and spins; chaos; a victory; a person in silver dragged away in handcuffs purported to be unbreakable; a person in blue brushing dust from their shoulders.

Cut to a scene of a police car on the side of the road with two unconscious police officers sprawled on the ground and a pair of empty handcuffs on the back seat.

Cut again to a man in a red costume standing behind a podium. He said it was time to come out of the shadows, time to tell the truth. (Funny how he didn't take off his mask though.) How there were people like him with special strengths and most of them used those powers for the good of society. I couldn't help but laugh at that part because he was so earnest it had to come from a script. Then he said there were some who only wanted to profit from their talents but he insisted there were only a few, they would be caught and imprisoned, and we had nothing to fear. He didn't use the word villain or hero but everyone knew what he meant. The bar exploded into conjecture, arguments, even a few spots of hysteria.

You shook your head and traced aimless circles on the table with one finger, said it was hard to believe, said it was like something from a comic book. I agreed.

Here is the restaurant where I waited for you until you called to say something had come up with a client and you were going to have to work late.

I brought dessert to your apartment to surprise you and you weren't home. I thought of leaving the dessert (Tiramisu, your favorite) on the doormat but I didn't want you to know I'd been there. Didn't want you to think I was checking up on you.

I went home and watched the news. More footage from around the world: bank heists, explosions, car chases, kidnappings, rescues, heroes, villains, masks, the charred remains of a secret lair, construction of the new prisons. Men and women who could fly, walk through walls, lift cars over their heads, stop bullets with the palms of their hands. And the man in the red costume, the official spokesman of the good guys, assuring everyone that his team had everything under control. The villainous element didn't work together so their position was much weaker; it was only a matter of time before they all fell.

But good guys trying to catch the bad guys didn't have anything to do with us and I turned off the television and sat in silence.

Here is the flower shop where you bought roses, the apology for breaking our date at the restaurant, for working late so many nights, for not answering my calls. I forgave you and we made love but I woke in the middle of the night and you were gone.

You'd left a note that said you loved me but had to get up early for work and were afraid you'd sleep too late at my apartment.

Here is the grocery store where our carts collided in the ice cream aisle. You were surprised to see me; I usually did my shopping at night. I'm sorry, you said. I've been so busy with work, I'll call you tomorrow.

But you didn't call.

Here is the park where you told me to meet you. I waited and waited but you never showed, never called. I finally gave up and headed home.

There were sirens in the distance and a news van rushed by, but I ignored them. No matter what the man in the red mask says, the villains always get away. I think it's supposed to be that way; if there weren't any villains, there wouldn't be a need for heroes. Supply and demand.

Here is the stretch of pavement where we last spoke. I was coming to see you, I said, smiling as I reached for your hand but you said you didn't have time to talk and you pulled away before our skin made contact. I asked why you stood me up at the park. You said not everything was about us. But nothing was about us, I didn't even know if there *was* an us, and I begged you to tell me what was wrong. You said nothing was wrong and you had to go.

When you walked away I couldn't bear to watch.

And now, here is an alley. I know it's a strange location and it's starting to rain, a light mist that will turn my hair into a halo of frizz but I didn't check the weather beforehand. I'm sorry. Or maybe I'm not sorry because it feels like the day we met. I can see you standing at the opposite end, waiting, darting glances at your watch because you haven't seen me yet. I asked for only a few minutes of your time, to talk, to see you, and I was afraid you wouldn't come but now that I know you're here, I need a minute to gather my thoughts.

Because here is where I tell you the truth and the truth is, almost everything has been a lie.

Our first meeting wasn't accidental—I'd been watching you for several weeks. The night I drank too much wine, I merely pretended to be drunk; when you left I timed your absence and checked the news reports the next day. And I know you never worked in that office building. It was just a cover story.

Watching that first televised footage with you was unbearable. There was so much I wanted to say, so much I'd been planning to say, but I was waiting for the right time. The footage with the empty handcuffs was staged; they didn't want the public to know the cuffs weren't as unbreakable as they thought. But I think you already know.

Every time you disappeared there was a fight between a hero and a villain. Every time. So I know you've been lying to me but you're clever and I can't figure out the last piece of the puzzle and it's the piece that's most important.

If you're a hero, everything changes.

If you're a villain, everything changes.

The media has it all wrong. We're not as bad as they want us to be. Maybe we don't rescue people from burning buildings or out of control trains but that doesn't mean we're bad people. They're right about us working alone but it gets lonely after a while. When you come up with a great plan there's no one to share it with, no one to help go over all the small details that can so easily get overlooked. After a defeat, drowning your solitary sorrow in a bottle of red wine or a half-gallon of mint chocolate chip ice cream is no fun; celebrating a victory by yourself gets old too and all too soon it resembles the post-defeat routine, only with more expensive wine and gelato instead of ice cream.

So I have a proposal. I think you and I would make a great team because we do and if we work together we could defeat anyone and do anything. We'd be unstoppable.

If I'm right.

If I'm wrong, here is where I kill you or you kill me or we both try at least. More than likely neither one of us will die but we'll create a great deal of damage in the attempt. (I really hope you brought your mask but if not, I brought an extra.) Our fight will be amazing and will probably make the evening news if we start soon enough. I'll get away of course. I always do.

Here is where all the lies end and everything else begins.

S is for Soliloquy

Marge Simon and Michael Fosburg

A figure moved in the light of the yellow moon. Ragged clouds scuttled across the sky, throwing darker shadows against the dark land. The tide crept into the bay, salt and rotting kelp briny in Hessura's nose. It woke her up, and she was grateful for it; a long night stretched ahead of her.

The bloated moon rose higher, and soon enough she came upon the edge of her village. Stone huts were covered in thatched roofs like old men beneath ratty blankets, the straw sagging and moldy. Half-mended nets and ancient poles lay outside most doors. Dogs slunk around corners, fish heads dangling from their mouths.

Hessura sighed, rubbed the ache in her lower back. *Home,* she thought. *It pulls the life from me, sure as I pull babes squalling from wombs. If only I could've built my cottage on an island in the sea, away from here. But that would be straying from the Path.*

She sighed again, adjusted her pack, and followed the screams.

Most of the dwellings were dark—it was ill luck to light fires under a yellow moon—but light spilled from the cottage at the edge of town. The crowd at its door parted for her. The air inside was thick and hot, rank with the coppery stench of blood. Tari writhed on her cot; her husband, Timon, stood over her, brow creased with worry.

"No more of that, now," Hessura said. She turned to the bystanders. "I see no hot water or clean linens. Are you just going to hang about like gulls, or are you going to help?"

A bent figure shoved his way through the doorway. Hessura scowled to see it was Japeph.

"No one will be boiling water tonight," he said, casting his glare across the small crowd. "Last man who lit a fire 'neath a moon like this drowned on a clear day, water smooth as glass. I'll not have it on my conscience!"

"Do you want *Tari's* death on your conscience instead?" Hessura asked him, as evenly as she could manage. A long, chilly history had led them each to this point, punctuated by the occasional accusation of "Path-walker" or "witch," muttered in Hessura's direction.

Japeph scoffed. "Have her push harder and be done with it. Fool girl is always going on for everyone's time and attention. I'll wager—"

"That's enough, Japh," Timon said, giving him a look that could rust new steel. "Someone boil us up some water and gather up more linens, or I'll know the reason why."

A few people ducked out. Japeph glared at them as they left.

"Now, Tari," Hessura said, giving the terrified child her most smoothing smile. "This will be over before you know it."

But it was a difficult birth, and it went on into the dawn. Tari's hips were slim, her frame tiny. She writhed in agony with each push, biting off screams, clutching the linens with white-knuckled hands.

And then, just as the first streaks of dawn spread across the eastern skies, an infant's wail. Hessura appeared soon after, a swaddled infant in her arms. Smiling, she held it up. "You have a son, Timon!" Those still standing at the door cheered and Timon's hand was given many a firm shake. The crowd broke up and shuffled off to get some sleep before full daylight.

Hessura motioned Timon inside the bedroom. In her arms, a second child. "This one too, Timon."

"A demon-son!" Timon gasped, and forked his fingers at the sleeping babe. "*The second chases after the first'*—a bad omen."

"Aye, " Hessura nodded. "Cursed by that yellow moon, Japeph would say. He'd have it killed." She turned her head and spat. "A fishwife's tale, if I ever heard one—and I've heard them all."

Timon frowned, but he reached his finger to the tiny hand and grinned as the boy clasped it. "We must never let them know of this one," he said. "Can you handle this, Hessura?"

Hessura pursed her lips. "This I will do, Timon. But I'll need coin and food and something more for a wet-nurse for a few days. I know of a family that just lost a girl-child; the mother will still have suck enough for this one. Their village is far from here—three days ride, as the gull flies."

"So be it, then," Timon nodded. "You must never mention this again—not to me, certainly not to Tari. Tell her it was born dead. I don't want to know anything else about him, nor shall I give him my name."

Hessura folded the baby in her arms. "I shall call you Eron, " she whispered. "You shall grow up strong and wise—I know just the family who needs you, now."

The moon faded into dawn as she walked back up the path, child hidden within her cloak, its weak cries lost to the sound of the sea.

Japeph, pushing his boat into the water, watched her walk away with narrowed eyes.

The years washed them all like waves the shore, wearing down flesh and bone as surely as salt eats rock. Eron, a hardy child, grew tall and hale, and was beloved of the childless couple that took him in. Hessura resumed midwifery duties there, in the village of Orak in order to be close to Eron. Often, she would bring him gifts of bright stones from the sea, fish pies and apples, and he grew to love her as a grandmother, and she loved him as a son, having never had one of her own.

In Hessura's absence, births in Timon's village became increasingly difficult. Breach births and stillbirths were the new norm, and once a child was born without skin, festooned with maggots.

Born dead.

But fortune smiled on Orak. Gardens flourished. Their nets brimmed with fish, the crab traps were full, and the children were flushed with a healthy glow. Her deliveries were easy and brief, and children were born pink and noisy.

It was a time for giving thanks to gods of sea and land.

Life carried on quietly for fifteen years, and then a great summer storm blew in from the west, shrouding the land in wind and rain. Boats were smashed at anchor and entire villages were swept into the gray sea. Orak was spared; indeed, their hauls doubled without competition from other villages.

And then Eron sought out Hessura.

"The waves," he said, gray eyes mercurial with remembered tears. "The waves took them all in the night. I was inland, trading pemmican for wool..." He sipped his tea. "Nothing was left of our neighboring villages. Just rotting kelp and dead dogs."

"The storm gods are powerful. They can be friend or foe to mortals. We must give thanks that we here were spared." Hessura turned back to tend a pot of simmering meat, but Eron touched her arm.

"And there's something else, Hessura. I met a man on the road as I returned to our village. He seemed to recognize me, and hailed me by another's name. He insisted I was Wroth, a certain Master Timon's son."

Hessura frowned. "What did you tell him?"

"I said I didn't know what he was talking about. I gave him my name and our village, and pointed this way. That appeared to make him upset. He kept scowling at me. 'You *are* Wroth,' he said."

Eron took Hessura's hand. "But then he said something else. His people believe their village is cursed by a witch's magic. He said her name was Hessura., and she hadn't been seen since the birth of this Wroth. Could this be true? And could I have a brother somewhere else?"

Hessura laughed. Would you believe one stranger such as he? Impossible, my sweet boy. Impossible! I was there when you were born, remember? And as for me being a witch — such nonsense!"

Some days later, far to the west, a knock came on Timon's door. "It's Japeph. May I have a word with you?"

"A word?" Timon put down the apple he was paring. "You never visit unless you have dire news or some silly rumor to spread. I want no part of your business."

"Oh, but I think you'll say otherwise when you hear me out. I've been to the eastern shores. They've been ruined by sea and storm. "

"I'd heard that. Too bad for the less fortunate, but such is life. We're not doing that well ourselves. I've nothing to spare, in any case." Timon waved his paring knife. "Be off with you!"

"Perhaps you'll share one of those apples, once you hear this," Japeph paused. Timon met his eyes and lifted a brow.

Japeph cleared his throat and continued. "Word came to me that Hessura lives there now, in that very *lucky* village of Orak. The last time anyone has seen her was at Wroth's birth. I decided to seek her out, perchance to discover why she disappeared so suddenly that night of the golden moon when your son was born."

"Don't you think you'd be better off minding your own business?" Timon growled.

Japeph chose to ignore the warning in his voice. "On the road, I met a young man. He is the spitting image of your Wroth, and—"

A tall young man appeared in a doorway. "I heard my name spoken. What is this about?"

Japeph quickly explained his encounter with Eron. "He said he lived in the village of Orak, the only one spared from the storm. He was dressed in a fine cloak and leather boots of exceptional quality. I've only seen the likes of such in foreign lands. But there's more…"

Japeph paused, glancing meaningfully at Timon.

"God's *blood*," Timon muttered, and grabbed the old man by the scruff of his collar. "How many *times* must I ask you to not peddle your rumors and ill-will in my *home*, you old fool?" Ignoring his squawks of protest, Timon hauled Japeph bodily from the cottage and shoved him into the road, leveling a finger at the old man as he stumbled to right himself. "Don't come here again."

"What was that about?" Wroth asked, as Timon shut the door him.

"Nothing that concerns you. Go mend the nets." With a glare, Wroth sulked past.

Japheth waited for him outside.

❦

It was a hunter's moon that rose that night, high and lonely against cold stars. Wroth traveled light, for the village of Orak was a goodly distance. If he met brigands on the road—for there were more than ever in those days—it would go better on him if he had little of worth on his person. Not that he had much of value at all, these days.

As he walked, he brooded. He rubbed together hands calloused from mending nets, from chopping wood and scraping barnacles from old boats. He drew a threadbare cloak about his shoulders and wondered at the great injustice of life to deal him this poor hand. And the thought that there was another—a cursed *twin*, no less—that wore soft boots and fine furs, gorged on caviar and eel, and all the other things Japeph had told him—

It all left a bitter taste in his mouth. His anger smoldered lower, into hate. He walked on, the light of the moon turning the land the color of bones.

He would have the right of it tonight.

❦

"That's a moon to kill by," Hessura said, watching the pale traveler in its slow arc above the trees. Eron said nothing, resumed his hammering. He had proved an able carpenter, repairing a decade's worth of cracks and breaks around the cottage. He spoke of friends he'd had in the neighboring villages. All the memories that hadn't washed away with their lives rested on the head of nail and tack as Eron worked.

"Where will you go, Eron?" Hessura asked him as he straightened a spice rack.

"I'm not sure. Maybe work aboard a merchant ship—I've never liked being away from the sea for too long a spell." He wiped his forehead, placed the hammer on the butcher's block. My friends' poor souls rest there," he said, and looked out the window to where the sea shivered beneath the moon.

Hessura nodded and sipped her tea. It was then she noticed the figure walking along the road. It turned abruptly toward her

199

house, perhaps having seen the taper lights.

A forceful knock on the door rattled the windows. Eron frowned, and went to answer it.

A darkness crept into her mind. Something was wrong. But she was too slow; the door was open, and Eron, mouth agape, discovered his twin on the other side.

Hessura stood, darkness gaining ground as the sudden draft snuffed out the nearest candles. Wroth stood rigid in the doorway, a snarl twisting his otherwise handsome face. Eron turned to look at Hessura, a helpless question in his eyes, when a fist shot from the doorway and smashed into his jaw. A bloody tooth flew toward her in a dream-like arc before Wroth was on him again, shoving him backward into the counter, his face a mask of hate. The hammer Eron had been using fell to the floor, and before Hessura could scream a warning Wroth had raised it above his head and brought it down against Eron's temple.

The life left his eyes as his lips still mouthed a question.

Something tore loose inside of her. She flew at the twin, but he cracked her across the mouth with a swing of the hammer. Pain flared bright and hot; she felt another blow shudder into her, muffled now, her shoulder a far-away spot of agony. She fell hard, shattered her hip, and lay still, holding his face in her darkening vision.

"Witch," he muttered, but his eyes were wide and frightened—as though events had spiraled beyond his control. Perhaps they had. It no longer mattered.

She lay there for minutes, or hours, as Wroth rummaged through Eron's belongings, angrily muttering "Japeph" and cursing as he robbed his brother's corpse. He left soon after, Eron's cloak over his shoulders and his own ragged one on the blood soaked floor.

Hessura knew she lingered at the door between worlds; you don't spend your life courting birth without sometimes finding its darker brother. She dragged herself away from Eron's corpse. Still time.

Hessura remembered the names of healing herbs and flowers found in the high places above the sea; the exact measure of fish oil to soothe an ailing heart, the quiet words that eased pain, or brought sleep and the darker words that ended suffering, closing tiny eyes just barely opened to the world. They whispered "witch" behind her back but welcomed her into their homes when their daughters and wives screamed the agony of childbirth. A long life ended by a babe she'd delivered.

There were other words to say, words taught to all women of the Path. Words that did not heal.

Vision failing, Hessura dragged her broken body to the cabinet where her spices were kept. She pushed them aside and searched behind, palsied hands closing on a small chest.

She counted back the years to Eron's birth, found the parchment stained yellow. Beneath it, envelopes containing pieces of birthing cord. A record, of sorts, of all the babes she'd brought into the world. A cough wracked her body; blood dribbled from her lips. She found the envelope marked "Tari" and shook loose the contents. Her vision blurred with tears at the sight of them—two pieces of cord, withered and brown with age.

Such potential. All gone.

She looked to Eron's corpse. His eyes still looked to her with that unasked question.

She hardened her heart and crawled over to his corpse. Her broken jaw throbbed. She opened his mouth. "Forgive me," she croaked through clenched teeth, and placed the withered cords inside.

She began to say the words, and the last remaining candles guttered out.

❧

Wroth sat in the shadows of a tavern. He had wrapped both hands around a flask of beer to control their shaking. What if he was recognized? But then he remembered. It wouldn't matter; the townsfolk would think he was Eron. He drained the cup, leaving a few of his brother's coins on the table.

Out on the road again, his only guide was the moon. When it slipped beneath a cloud, he heard footsteps behind him. Turning, he saw a figure lurch suddenly forward to clamp his shoulder with a bloodied hand. Screaming, he jerked away and ran. In his panic, he didn't see what lay on the road ahead. Even if he had, it was too dark to make out the sign: "Warning! Bridge Out."

❧

Two farmers stood looking at a body lying on the bank. "He's dead all right. Broke most of his bones. But it wasn't the fall that did it."

"Aye," the other man nodded. "Couldn't have done this kind of damage. He's a mess. God's bones, man! Look at the eyes—he looks scared to death. And something has been chewing on his face—skull crushed—part of his brains gone."

"What kind of animal do you think it was? We got nothing in these parts but a few wild dogs." He removed his hat to scratch his head. "Poor young sod."

๑๛

Another night, another full moon. A shambling form moved along the road. "I know your name, Japeph," it slurred. "I'm coming."

T is for Twins

Suzanne van Rooyen

A leg, harpooned at the ankle, danced in the breeze from the air vents, spinning a macabre pirouette, beside it a headless torso with hooks through the shoulders jiggled double Ds. Victoria pressed the button on the remote and the rails creaked into motion. Above her, the bodies dangled like grotesque marionettes as the rotation commenced.

She scanned the cadavers, searching for male body parts, but her gaze kept sliding back to the headless torso and the double Ds. At forty-five, Victoria's breasts were starting to droop, her muscles no longer as efficient, her joints protesting her rigorous exercise regimen. At least she'd kept the love handles and most of the cellulite at bay, something she attributed in part to a strict Paleo diet and a cupboard full of creams promising crease-free flesh. None of that mattered though. She'd never be as perfect as the bodies swinging above her, bodies that would never age, never droop or decay.

Victoria hit the brake and the rails whined to a halt. The leg hanging from a naked hip joint bucked back and forth on its hook. The stamp across the thigh designated the model a Gen500, male, adult, athletic—it would do. Flipping the toggle on the remote, Victoria lowered the hook and cradled the severed limb in her arms. Traces of the synthetic neurotransmitter permeating the circuitry exuded a cardamom aroma making the Abattoir smell like Christmas at her grandmother's house. The faux blood used in the hydraulic muscle system oozed sticky tendrils of neon pink across her apron as she carried the leg into her surgery.

She checked the time: 2:30AM. She had at least three hours before people trudged into the offices upstairs, at least four before her colleagues arrived ready to slice and dice dead androids into salvageable parts.

Satisfied she was alone, Victoria laid the leg beside the shrouded body on her exam table. Gently, she peeled away the sheet, revealing his exquisite face. She never got tired of looking at him. She brushed soft black hair from the android's face before placing a tender kiss on each sleeping eyelid. His long lashes tickled her lips and turned the desire aching in her bones into a hungry, fanged creature chewing on her insides. The lashes swept indigo shadows beneath the eyes, shadows she trailed with an index finger to his full lips, rosebud pink, replete with delicate grooves carved into cupid bows.

He was almost done.

Once she grafted the fresh leg into place, he'd be whole and it would only be a matter of recharging his batteries before he woke. The lashes swept indigo shadows beneath the eyes, shadows she trailed with an index finger to his full lips, rosebud pink, replete with delicate grooves carved into cupid bows.

She dragged her fingers across the pliant flesh of the android's chest, grazing the nipples. Perhaps when he was awake, he'd let her pierce them for him, let her bite on steel not for his pleasure, but for her own. Suppressing the surge of heat flooding her belly, she continued her examination. There were imperfections, but nothing which wouldn't heal up once he was activated. Any remaining blemishes could be hidden by a tattoo gun, an idea Victoria found rather appealing.

At least what lay between his legs had been whole, undamaged by whoever dismembered him before leaving him in a dumpster. A random act of violence or a symptom of the slow-burning revolution on the streets? Had he been the unlucky victim of a hate crime or was someone trying to make a statement? Androids were robots, and robots were mere appliances—at best, beloved toys, but just like a stuffed animal or dildo, they could never love you back. Not even Gen600s with their sophisticated AI and empathy modules.

Sighing, Victoria slid her fingers into the gaping orifice of his left leg. It would take at least two hours to graft the leg into place; another twenty for him to charge while she drowned herself in coffee to pull yet another all-nighter at the morgue, this time in the company of her salvaged creation.

႙ၜ

Victoria kicked the vending machine in the corridor. She'd had less than four hours of sleep in two days, but it had been worth it. Today would see the completion of her creation, provided she could get that dose of caffeine.

She kicked the machine again—an antediluvian model with no intelligence—and was rewarded by the drop of a paper cup and the gurgles of percolating caffeine.

Sipping the steaming liquid that tasted little better than battery acid, Victoria strode through the surgery, past several waiting robot-corpses, to the refrigeration unit. These days, it was rarely used since only synthetic bodies lay in the morgue. Coffee consumed and cup discarded, she jerked open the steel door. An arm lay exposed where the sheet had crumpled, the skin a rich tan where before it had been alabaster white. Tossing the sheet in a corner, Victoria began her final ministrations, mere moments from waking him. Gently, she lifted his head off the gurney, his silky hair like a spiderweb across her fingers, to expose the port at the base of his neck. According to the LED inlay flashing red around the port, he was 98% charged. A couple more minutes and he'd be ready. Was she?

If only she could document what she'd done. She'd performed the first android-to-android transplants, was the first to resurrect a robot officially declared beyond resuscitation – she deserved recognition from the scientific community even if her methods were a little dubious. She couldn't bear the thought of no-one knowing what she'd achieved, of all those long hours leaving her with nothing but a revamped robot. If what Victoria had planned worked, however, there was a good chance the recognition she craved would be served up along with an arrest warrant.

But it was about more than the potential accolades, though she was loathed to admit it.

Her work in the morgue had culminated in a lonely life and a string of failed relationships with men and women. At forty-five and losing her good looks to age, Victoria was starting to believe she was unlovable, that perhaps she was better off in the company of dead robots than amongst living human beings.

She checked the port. The LEDs gleamed green. Charging complete.

Victoria unplugged the power cable and smoothed down the flap of skin concealing the port. With trembling fingers, she felt her way up the back of his neck, to the nodule on the second cervical vertebra. The body spasmed, limbs twitching and back arching. Nothing. She tried again, maintaining pressure on the nodule for a full twenty seconds to commence a complete reboot.

She studied the android's face as the eyeballs raced right and left beneath the fluttering lids. After almost a minute, his eyes snapped open. The irises were a warm hazel, brown at the periphery with scattered shards of emerald leading to the dilated pupil. She leaned over him and his pupils contracted, his vision slowly coming into focus on her face. A battalion of chills marched up her spine as she gazed into his wet orbs.

Victoria squeezed her eyes shut, half expecting the reanimated android to be a figment of her imagination, but when she opened them, he was still staring up at her, a grin tugging at the corner of his mouth.

"Hi." Eloquence deserted her as she gazed at her cobbled creation. His long fingers curled around her wrist, then laced through her own.

"Hello." His voice resonated with human harmonics, a rich baritone.

"Um." Victoria hesitated, doubted, stammered in her disbelief. "Um, how do you feel?"

"Alive." His grip on her hand tightened as he lurched to his feet.

"Do you remember anything?" She'd been careful to wipe his memory disk, erasing his previous life, but leaving the Gen600 programming intact.

"I don't think so."

"Good. I'm Victoria." She shook the hand he was already holding as fatigue melted into euphoria. It worked. She'd done it! He was hers.

"Did you make me?" he asked, eyes shiny with excess lubricant; to Victoria it looked like tears.

"I remade you." She took his hands and spread his arms open. "And you're perfect. You're beautiful."

"Beautiful?" He grinned and Victoria couldn't help herself. She'd been waiting months for this moment. Standing on tiptoes, she placed a kiss on his smiling lips. His eyes were closed when she pulled away.

"A kiss," he said, the sibilance of the word music to Victoria's ears.

"Yes. Did you like it?" Her gaze dropped from his face to his crotch. Gen600s were designed to fulfill carnal needs, the ultimate relationship-aid androids. Perhaps it took more than a kiss though to stimulate the coital protocols. She glanced at the clock. They had three glorious hours to discover exactly what turned him on.

She kissed him again, wrapping her hands around his neck. This time he responded and opened his mouth to hers. He tasted of Christmas as his strong arms circled her waist. She pressed against him into every hard jut and furrow of his chiseled body. Tears flowed down her cheeks and this time she didn't bother trying to stop them as he tore the white coat from her shoulders and lifted her off the ground. She wrapped her legs around his waist the way she'd seen actors do in movies but never had the opportunity to do in real life.

Her heart thumped erratically behind her ribs as his android fingers undressed her. With him she didn't have to worry about rejection, about her thighs being too fat, her boobs being too small, about whether or not she'd shaved her legs or had pimples on her butt. He didn't care about any of that, responding only to physical stimuli, which triggered the requisite protocols in his artificial brain. She didn't have to worry about STDs or getting pregnant. This was safe yet free, controlled yet limitless. It was everything she'd always wanted and she surrendered to her primal needs as he pressed her back against the wall, making love to her with all the fury of the storm outside.

Despite the numerous graftings and catastrophic damage to

his original body, after twenty-hours of being awake, the Gen600 showed no symptoms of neurological failure.

"You need a name." Victoria sipped her coffee—her second double espresso of the night—as she studied the android perched on a wheelie chair. He looked up from the tablet in his lap where he'd been completing brain teasers for the past half an hour.

"Why?"

"Because everything should have a name." Because it made him more human and made Victoria feel less inhuman for jumping his titanium bones.

"Then give me a name." He tucked hair behind his ear in a gesture disarmingly human. Dressed in jeans and a meme-themed T-shirt, he looked every bit the college student.

She finished her coffee as names played through her mind. Which would sound the best falling breathlessly from her lips as she shuddered with pleasure?

"How about Kayden?" The name of her crush in high school—a boy who never even knew she existed.

"Kayden."

She watched entranced as his cherub lips repeated the word several times before he nodded.

"My name is Kayden." He beamed at her. "Victoria, would you like to have sex now that you have refueled?"

She crumpled the coffee cup and tossed it over her shoulder before tearing off his shirt. Kayden was a perfect name for moaning, for screaming, for whispering in his ear.

≫≪

An hour later, Victoria lay breathless on the floor wrapped in a clean sheet. The tiles in the Abattoir were cold and dug painfully into her hip as she snuggled into the crook of Kayden's arm.

"Are you satisfied?" he asked, his hand stroking her hair and trailing across her jaw.

"Extremely." She dragged her own fingers across his chest, surreptitiously feeling along the invisible joins of his arms. No muscular degeneration, no disrupted circuitry. He was perfect. Almost.

"Would you like to sleep now?" he asked.

"Actually, I have another idea." Stepping naked from the sheets, Victoria rifled through a drawer and returned a moment later with a 14-gauge needle and forceps. From the pocket of her discarded lab coat, she retrieved two stainless steel nipple rings. "Lie still. Let me know if it hurts." She clamped his right nipple with forceps and his pecs tensed.

"Does it hurt?" She pushed the needle through the tough layers of synthetic skin and the smell of her grandmother's baking filled the surgery as pink fluid oozed down his chest.

"Yes."

"Good." Ring in place, she straddled his waist and moved on to the left nipple. "It's supposed to hurt. It means your haptic sensors are fully functional." She skewered Kayden's nipple, heat flushing through her body as he made the android equivalent of a yelp.

"There. All better." She tugged on the rings and kissed his mouth. His strong arms encircled her as he sat up, crushing her against him.

"Thank you for fixing me," he said before dragging her beneath him. Victoria knotted her fingers in his hair, but her gaze strayed to the perky body parts dangling from the ceiling. Kayden paused and followed her line of sight.

"What's wrong?" he asked.

"Nothing. It's just..." She trailed a hand down his chest and her eyes swept back to the double Ds above her so irritatingly unaffected by gravity. "Sometimes I wish I could be this perfect." She tweaked his nipple.

"You aren't?" Kayden cast a lingering glance at the robot bits on the hooks.

"I'm human." She sighed. "We're imperfect by nature."

ço◆ço

The scalpel blade slipped from her shaking fingers and skittered across the floor. Victoria was on edge from lack of sleep and far too much caffeine.

Her gaze darted to the refrigeration unit where Kayden was holed up for the day with only a tablet for company. She was getting too old for this. The post-coital bliss of mind-blowing sex and increasingly strong coffees weren't enough to sustain her.

She needed sleep and a proper meal. She should've taken Kayden home with her last night and called in sick, but by the time she'd shrugged back into her clothes the morning shift was already arriving. She couldn't risk walking Kayden out of the office and being discovered.

Taking a moment to still her trembling hands, Victoria continued dissecting the flawless female on her table. Switched off, the android looked like Sleeping Beauty with her spill of blond hair and petite figure complete with those parallel ab lines no amount of burpees seemed able to give Victoria. The string of late nights had derailed her exercise routine. She hadn't hit the gym in days, not that she was in want of cardio with Kayden around. Still, the body before her was a slap in the face, a stark reminder that Victoria was dying, her bones crumbling toward osteoporosis, her arteries thickening and brain cells disintegrating. It wasn't death she feared, it was getting old. The dementia and dentures, the incontinence and lack of independence. Shaking off her grim thoughts, Victoria focused on her work. Another six hours and she'd be alone again with Kayden.

❧

"Am I not satisfying you?" Kayden paused mid-thrust, somehow sensing she wasn't that into it, not with the blond Gen500 hovering at eye level over his shoulder, taunting Victoria with everything she could never be.

"Think we could stop for a moment?" Victoria eased out of Kayden's grip, noting the expression of confusion on his face.

"Did I do something wrong?" he asked.

"No, you're perfect." Achingly, agonizingly perfect. "It's me." She slumped to the Abattoir floor, back against the wall and clothes in a pile at her feet.

"Can you be remade?" Kayden's gaze swept around the room and came to rest on the blond. Victoria gritted her teeth, wishing she'd hacked apart the android a little more, maybe removed its face. It wasn't supposed to be like this, but she felt self-conscious in front of Kayden, as if she'd been compared to the machines above her and found wanting.

"Humans don't work that way." She closed her eyes giving

into the exhaustion. A power-nap, that's all she needed. Ten minutes of shut eye and she'd feel fine again. Kayden lifted her from the floor and she didn't resist, letting him lay her on the exam table and tuck a sheet over her body.

"Wake me in ten," she said, succumbing to fatigue.

Victoria woke with a start as the rails screeched into motion. She blinked several times against the lights shining into her eyes, focusing on Kayden as he unhitched the blond android from its hook.

"What are you doing?" She tried to move but couldn't. Her arms and legs were tied down in restraints they sometimes used if an android was short circuiting and prone to spasms.

"I'm going to remake you." Kayden smiled and Victoria's blood froze in her veins.

"You can't. Let me go." She struggled and Kayden soothed her, stroking her hair the way she had stroked his.

"I'm going to make you beautiful, like me." He tapped at her tablet screen, pulling up schematics of human anatomy. "I've been reading about surgical practices," he said. "I've got everything I need."

Victoria's gaze landed on the equipment tray bearing an assortment of implements from scalpel blades to bones saws, a cauterization wand and the staple gun she'd used on Kayden.

"Which would you prefer?" He held up the body of the blond android then gestured to the decapitated torso sporting the double Ds.

"This isn't how it works. You're going to kill me." She half-hissed, half-sobbed, caught between a morbid curiosity and paralyzing terror. The restraints didn't give an inch despite her continued struggles. She could scream, but the building was deserted. No one would hear her.

"I was dead. You brought me back to life." Kayden seemed to make his choice, opting for the blond android already in his hands and set about carving at the flesh.

"Please, Kayden. Don't do this."

"Don't you want to be perfect?" He leaned over her, brushing away the tears on her cheeks. "Don't you want to be beautiful?"

Yes, desperately, but not like this. Victoria whimpered as Kayden pulled the sheet away and began marking out his surgical plans in black marker across her breasts and belly.

"Are you ready, Victoria?" The android held up a scalpel blade.

"I won't survive this." Her voice sounded so pathetic. She'd never felt so weak and vulnerable, so very human against the superior might of the machine she'd rendered into being.

The scalpel blade sliced into her skin, dragged in a neat semi-circle beneath her right breast.

"Does it hurt?" Kayden asked as he dabbed at the blood dribbling across her ribs.

"Yes, yes it fucking hurts." Victoria balled her hands into fists and promised herself she wouldn't scream.

"That's good." The android grinned and returned to his work. "It's supposed to, right?"

U is for Unrequited

L.S. Johnson

1.

THERE was a time when Arianne could not see over the rows of her father's grapevines. At the height of the summer the vineyard became a vast maze and she would follow her mother, watching her taste the grapes, her skirts swaying as she walked, a fine haze of dirt collecting on their hems. The world then was black soil and green life and her mother striding ahead, head held high, lips and fingers stained crimson from the juices.

All of that was years ago. Yet there are days when Arianne goes far into the rows, searching for anyplace where the leaves are green and dense still, where the fruit grows plump, not mildewed and shriveled. When at last she finds a patch she goes down on her knees in the dirt until she can see nothing but blushing fruit and green leaves and the blue sky above.

On her knees in the dirt, Arianne can envision her mother before her, see her spattered hems and the rough clogs over her fine stockings. On her knees in the dirt, Arianne's mind becomes formless and clear. On her knees the world is a whole thing once more, a single path as welcoming as an embrace.

Until she stands up, and the world breaks into pieces once again: the rows of brown grapevines splintering in all directions; the wind rattling the shutters on the crumbling cottage where she and her father live; the slope of the rise before the hollow, where the old house still stands, the embodiment of her mother's betrayal.

Their tainted land.

୬~ଏ

Her father goes to the village only when necessary, his battered hat low over his face, Arianne at his side. She does what she can to make them presentable, wearing her spare dress and fussing over his dingy cravats; she cannot bear to give the villagers any more reason to despise them.

Everyone is polite still, for was he not once a king among them? His vines had been the most productive in the region, never touched by blight or frost; they called him Seigneur, they appealed to him for advice, for his clout in dealings. All while her mother drew their wives around her like so many birds, performing her own transactions in the shadows. Her pockets always full of small sachets filled with powders: *this for love, this for an unwanted child, this to keep your husband close.*

They are polite still, and the shopkeepers deal with her father fairly, and sometimes they add a little more to their few purchases... and Arianne can never decide if they do so out of respect for what her family had been, or fear of her mother now.

As she waits for her father to finish she idles by the door of the shop, watching the passerby in the street. She pretends idleness, but in truth she cannot bear to see the empty shelves, the dust on the barrels, just as she keeps her gaze averted from the brown-spattered crops. Her mother's handiwork.

A young man walking past touches his hat, a cursory gesture: Emile. By his side his mother crosses herself and Arianne bites back her exclamation. As if she never came to Arianne's mother, never bought her share of remedies. What then of the two children after Emile, gone before her belly even began to swell, barely any pain?

Emile. Arianne once fancied he might... but none of them will do more than acknowledge her now.

All her plans, her hopes. All sundered. She steps back, hiding herself in the shadows; only then does she see her father deep in agitated conversation with the shopkeeper. She moves closer, ears straining to catch their exchange.

"...he arrived last night, from Paris," the shopkeeper says. "He says a Committee rules us now, they beheaded the king himself, they're going to rid France of every traitor. They're even changing the damn calendar! They're going to try and do away with God Himself next, you'll see. Anyway, he's scouting the villages close to the road, they want to install a recruitment office, possibly a garrison; that, and he wants the names of any who still harbor royalist leanings."

Her father only shakes his head, as if trying to free himself from a restraint.

"We cannot support dozens of bloodthirsty louts when we can barely feed ourselves." The shopkeeper leans over the counter. "So we are going to give him *her* name, and send him to you. Either he'll rid us of her or she'll rid us of him."

Again her father shakes his head. "You cannot," he says. "If any harm should come to her, who knows what it might unleash?"

"We can guess," the shopkeeper snaps. "What's a little more starvation? If he fails, at least we'll have time to plan for when his fellows arrive. You must do this," he adds, seizing her father's arm. "If you had kept the unholy bitch satisfied none of this would matter. With the harvests we had, we could have tolerated a hundred soldiers, or bought off this Committee. Now you can pay for your failure—"

"That's enough," Arianne says. She steps beside her father, prying off the shopkeeper's grasping hand. "Do what you will, just leave him alone." Her father has started weeping, and she wants to both slap him and embrace him. "Can't you see her betrayal has broken him?"

"Is that what you call it?" The shopkeeper sneers at her. "It was far more than betrayal, *Citizen*. Just as what we suffer under is far more than a bad summer, or poor soil, or whatever other fancies you tell each other. Your mother fucked the devil himself—" he pauses, taking a breath. "And now you have made me say it aloud. Like mother, like daughter; I curse the day you came here."

Arianne takes a step back instinctively. The disgust in his voice, the crudeness of his language—she knew the villagers despised them, but the man seems to be teetering on the edge of violence. And what would he do, without the threat of her mother? What would they all do?

At once she knows it in her bones: they would kill her and her father.

"Citizen Committee has already inquired about your land," the shopkeeper continues. "He fancies your proximity to the crossroads. We will recommend he call on you at the first possible moment—if that meets with the fair Citizen's approval?"

She manages a nod and sweeps up their goods with one arm, steering her father with her free hand. He blubbers and sways, hindering their progress through the village. She has known this place all her life, yet now it seems a foreign land, every face filled with menace. Where she thought she saw only scorn, now she sees outright hatred. At her side her father clutches at his jacket as if holding in his very soul; but Arianne can only think on what might happen should they fail to kill the man from Paris.

Lost in thought, she doesn't see the children until they are long past the village gates. Their small forms weave in and out of the windbreaks of linden trees, holding their fingers up to their foreheads and sniggering. They mock-lunge at each other, they wiggle their buttocks, and when their laughter makes Arianne turn completely they duck behind the trees so only their singsong whispers remain:

> *Monsieur Bull, horny old devil*
> *Monsieur Bull the witch is calling you*
> *She will fuck you till she's dead*
> *She will fuck you down to hell*
> *Till she's dead*
> *Down in hell*
> *Ah ah ah ah!*

Later that day Arianne walks to the top of the rise. The house sits in the hollow, square and implacable, its plasterwork webbed with cracks, its shingled roof a patchwork. The black area near the back of the house, has the roof given way completely? What does her mother do for food, for heat? How does her mother *live* in such a place?

She will fuck you till she's dead

216

She has tried to enter, before. Always the shutters were tightly latched, the doors locked against her. She has wound round and round, calling, howling for her mother. She has flung rocks at the unyielding wood, brought hammers down on the plaster. But beneath its decaying surface the building might as well be stone.

She has never had an emissary, until now.

Four years ago Arianne had been awakened by her mother's footsteps, and she had followed just in time to see the front door open, revealing the moonlit world. She knew then something was terribly wrong, for they were not to open the door at night. But her mother had simply stepped outside, clad only in her shift that ballooned in the warm night air.

Arianne had run after her, crying *Maman! Maman!* She ran and ran, until her breath caught in her throat, until at last she seized one of the trailing ribbons woven into her mother's cuffs, pulling it like a leash.

Only then did her mother look back at Arianne, and her eyes were those of another woman, and her lips were glossy and parted in anticipation. She looked at Arianne, and the ribbon, and then she seized the ribbon in both hands and snapped it in two.

"He's here at last," she said impatiently, as if Arianne should know this.

And then she turned away and continued walking, ascending the rise to where a figure stood waiting, silhouetted against the stars, and she disappeared into the darkness of his outstretched arms.

Monsieur Bull, horny old devil

It still feels like it happened yesterday, every detail sharp and painful. Only now, looking down at the porch where she had stood looking up, Arianne feels a strange doubling. She raises her arms, matching the figure's stance that night. The setting sun casts the hollow in shadow; a swift, hot breeze rushes through her and she can see her mother walking towards her, she can feel her mother's desire, she can feel her mother embracing *her.*

2.

Despite the shopkeeper's urgency, it is two long days before Arianne hears the horse rounding the bend in the road. She has put on her mother's old hat each day, and she pretends to examine the grapes though there is little to examine. She does not turn as he approaches, though out of the corner of her eye she sees a bright blue suit coming through the rows, a cocky tricolor rosette bobbing atop his black bicorn.

"Good day," he calls out. "I'm told a great vintner resides here."

Arianne turns then, curtseying low. Arrogant and haughty, with boots and sword polished to gleaming. "The gentleman still does, though as you see he no longer applies himself."

"Nor, apparently, do his neighbors," he says, drawing close. His face is handsome, and for a moment she feels her resolve waver. "You must be the daughter they spoke of, Citizen—"

"Arianne," she interrupts. More handsome for his embarrassment. "We are not so formal here, Monsieur—I mean Citizen—"

"Durand," he says. "Théodore Durand, soldier and citizen." He smiles at her. "And an enthusiast of country manners, now." He takes a step back, his gaze sweeping over the land, and Arianne as well. "It's all fine property," he says. "If your father has no interest in managing it, perhaps he'd like to help his country? Our general seeks to install a company of guardsman in this region . . . this would suit our purpose."

"He cannot sell," Arianne says.

"Oh? The property's entailed?"

"Because of my Maman." She lowers her eyes.

"Ah, yes. I heard in the village—" he breaks off.

"What did they say?"

"That she favors a foul, corrupt king whose demise I was privileged to witness," Citizen Durand says with surprising venom; then he laughs. "And that she practices terrible heresies, a much lesser crime to my way of thinking." He draws close, bending over until he catches her eye. "You mustn't let their foolish gossip upset you, Citizen. We have broken with the past; we're doing away with every kind of untruth, religion included. Soon the light of reason will shine on every corner of France." He laughs again when she remains downcast. "In Paris, women take lovers all the time, and reconcile with their husbands, and take lovers again. It's no cause for shame, unless the lover is an enemy of liberty."

"But she's mad, now."

"As anyone would be with such neighbors. One told me she would do better to kill herself! I—" he breaks off again, for Arianne has started weeping. She was right, they wish her family dead, and how much more will they endure before they act?

Only then does she realize Citizen Durand has put an arm around her, filling her nostrils with a not-unpleasant blend of man, horse, and rabbit stew.

"Would you speak to her," she whispers, drawing out her handkerchief and blotting her eyes.

"Who?"

"Maman." She can no longer recall if this is still her plan or if she's speaking honestly. "She won't let me see her, and my father is full of both grief and fear of her. But perhaps you can convince her to come out, and we could sell everything and leave this damnable place."

Her voice breaks over the last, but if her strength of emotion startles Citizen Durand he makes no sign. "Of course," he says. "I will interview her, and judge her loyalties and her reason. There is a hospital in Nice for women like her, or we can bring her to Paris. They could use a man like your father there," he continues in the same reassuring tone. "A man with intimate knowledge of the agriculture of this region? Many will pay for his advice, I assure you."

If you had kept the unholy bitch satisfied. Arianne tries to imagine her father in Paris. *What causes crops to fail, Monsieur? Why, unsatisfied women, of course!* She feels harsh laughter rising despite her tears and bites her lip.

"Now show me this house," Citizen Durand declares, "and I will meet your mother with pleasure."

At the door Arianne lays her hand on Citizen Durand's arm. His forearm is wonderfully firm, it is real and alive, and she

219

hesitates then. What if her father is right in his apprehensions? But she has never been so close before.

Citizen Durand raises his eyebrows, but does not move her hand.

"I—I have something," she says. From her pocket she draws out the piece of broken ribbon. "It will prove that I sent you."

He smiles as he takes it. "A token," he says. Glancing at the house, he continues, "and a house fit for a lord. I feel like I'm the hero in my nursemaid's stories. Only I'm missing one element."

Arianne frowns at this. He has a sword, and proof of their association. What more—?

"A kiss from a fair maiden," he purrs. "And perhaps the possibility of more, if I succeed?"

Before she can think of what to say his lips are pressing against hers. At first she is taken aback but her surprise swiftly becomes annoyance. How can he dawdle so now, on the threshold? Yet she dares not push him away, what if he refuses to go inside? Instead she opens her mouth to his tongue while he wedges her against the wall, stroking her waist with his hand. She counts inwardly, fuming, until at last he steps back and she sighs with relief, only to flush when she sees his triumphant expression. A blushing, sighing country girl, practically swooning at his slightest caress; for a moment she hates both him and herself.

"I will make this a swift interview," he says thickly.

Biting back her retort, she says instead, "Tell my mother I miss her."

He places his hand on the doorknob. The world seems to still at the gesture, as still as when Arianne kneels among the vines, and a small pragmatic part of herself realizes if the door does not open she will have a devil of a time fending him off.

The door swings open, as if the hinges were freshly oiled.

With a last jaunty smile, Citizen Durand bows to her and steps into the darkness. Arianne tries to follow him, but the door flies shut as if pushed from within.

৯৵

The sun sets as Arianne waits, sitting on the edge of the porch. For the whole of the afternoon there was not a sound within, not a voice, not even the creak of floorboards.

Not even a scream, to signal his failure.

And why would he fail? His mind is sound and he carries a weapon. Perhaps he might even breathe reason into her mother once more, bring her blinking and contrite out into the fading sunlight.

One way or another, it will be over at last. It all feels like some great weight is being taken from her, the last few years stripped away.

The sun touches the horizon, the sky flaring red. She watches the birds making for the trees, watches the first few stars appear.

She should go to the cottage and get some bread at least, and a shawl, and a lantern, but she's loathe to abandon her post. Fidgeting with indecision, she tries to calculate how swiftly she can get to the cottage and back.

The door opens.

Citizen Durand steps onto the porch, his whole body shuddering. He breathes deeply, over and over, gulping down the air. He has lost his coat and waistcoat, and his white shirt has a rust-colored spray across the front.

He clutches his sword in his hand, the blade dark and glistening, and for a moment Arianne can only stare in shock. All her vague ideas, all her blurted words, have come back to her as blood.

"Maman," she whispers. "Oh my poor Maman..."

At the sound of her voice he stumbles backwards on the porch, pointing the bloody sword at her. "Stay away from me," he gasps.

"What happened?" She gets to her feet, holding out her hands. "I—I do not blame you, Citizen. She was beyond all reason."

But he only crosses himself as he backs off the porch and into the rows of vines. The tip of his sword wobbles, though it remains pointed at her heart.

"Théodore," she says, her voice firmer. "*Tell me what happened.*"

He flinches at her words, then turns and runs, crashing headlong across the rows, ripping at the canes and flinging them aside.

"Théodore," she calls out, "Théodore, come back! I'll do anything! Just tell me what happened!"

But he is gone.

Only then does she turn and see the door standing open.

৵৵

In the years since her mother walked out into the night and her father took Arianne to live in the cottage, she has imagined the house many times. She imagined a decaying shell; she imagined the halls and rooms painted with the filth of her mother's madness.

But what Arianne steps into is not a house. Rather, she steps into a corridor of rough wood, forcing her to go either left or right. The boards have been nailed to the walls, covering what was once a finely gilded entrance hall. She cannot think why her mother would go to such lengths to build a corridor within the hall. The boards blocked both light and air, they made it impossible to go directly into the house . . .

And then she understands: this is not her mother's work. She would have no knowledge of building such walls, much less the skill to accomplish it.

Her father did this.

Arianne eases off her clogs and places them carefully by the door; she feels a sudden need for caution. She goes to take the key from the lock, only to find there is no key; a close examination reveals the lock has been sealed on the inside. Locking her mother in.

How, then, did the door open for Théodore?

Arianne can think of no answer, save a growing sense of dread.

Slowly she steps to the left, following the corridor through what she remembers as a parlor; the next room was the library. From there you turned to the right, towards the bedrooms at the back of the house, passing through the pretty little conservatory where her mother taught her to sew and draw...

A rush of grief wracks her body, and she finds herself weeping, as she has not done since those first few months. The windows and doors are nailed shut; through the boards she can glimpse the empty shelves of the library, every book gone as though they never existed. All these years of listening to her father pray: was it for himself, not her mother? For his rage which made him seal her in this tomb?

She moves deeper into the house, tears running down her face. The rough wood and nailheads catch at her skirts, there are moist patches on the floor that seep into her stockings. *Maman!* Now that she is far from the front door she can smell the house, smell the damp and the hints of rot, but beneath it all is a faint odor that she only knows as *home*.

Maman!

The conservatory is a forest of webs, thick clouds of them tumbling from ceiling to floor where they end in drifts of grey dust. Dust casts a haze over the game tables, the settee; it gathers on the harpsichord whose lid has staved in from rot, its keys covered in a sludgy pulp of sheet music. Yet Arianne's vision keeps doubling, showing her what used to be, as though it all lies behind a scrim of decay and she need only draw it aside to return everything to as it was.

Past the conservatory and the hall is black now. She moves forward by touch, trailing her fingers lightly against the wood until they graze a strange bump, and another; she pauses in the darkness, feeling the protrusions, trying to make sense of them.

They feel like young grapevines.

Another few steps and her path narrows, hemmed in by both the wooden boards and the thicket of vines growing over them, how can they be growing without light? Yet they cling to the boards as if in the strongest sun, they bend beneath her hand without snapping. They even smell the part, green and fresh in the midst of the heavy mildewed air.

She must push now to get past the grapevines, shoving and twisting. No leaves, but she can feel the fine buds, can almost sense them waiting for the first ray of sunlight. The walls thicken around her until she finds herself turning to the side, stretching arm and leg through and then dragging the rest of herself after, breath rasping in her ears and her heart hammering, if something comes upon her now she will die trapped in this cage—

And then she hears someone whimper.

The sound fills her. She pushes blindly through the vines until at last she sees parallel gleams of light and she throws all her weight against the door, knocking it open.

It is her mother's bedroom. Arianne halts on the threshold, her mouth hanging open. Her bedroom, but untouched by decay, by dirt, by time itself. Every drape and covering pristine, the walls glowing in the candlelight from the sconces, the paintings bright and unsullied.

There is a body on the floor.

Slowly Arianne walks towards it. Every detail seems to etch itself upon her eyes: the bowl of water on the side table, the fortune-teller's cards that have tumbled across the floor—and oh she had forgotten the water and the cards, how her mother would peer at them and simply *know* things, while little Arianne would stare and stare, desperately hoping to see something, anything, and win her mother's approbation at last.

When she reaches the body she lets out a long, deep breath. For it is her mother, though older than Arianne remembers, and why did she never imagine this? She herself has aged from girl to woman, why did she think time would halt for her mother?

She wants to weep, but no tears will come.

There is a deep red line across her mother's throat and the floor beneath her glistens. The red line, the wet floor, Théodore's wet sword—and when did the air become so cold? For Arianne is shivering, she feels chilled to the bone, yet she can only look and look. The red line of congealing blood, how it matches the crimson damask of the dress. The unfamiliar wrinkles, the streaks of grey in the brown hair, all seemingly painted over her mother's familiar face.

At last Arianne wrenches her gaze away and goes to the bed, thinking to use the coverlet as a shroud. Now she sees what was hidden by the door: a pile of small, clean bones, the skulls marked by the thick curving teeth of rats; beside them, incongruously, sits a pyramid of wax tapers. Behind the piles, bursting through the wallpaper as if springing from the very beams of the house, are more young vines, their tiny leaves a bright, vivid green among the pinhead sprays of new fruit.

Between the vines is a smeary drawing of what appears to be a man's silhouette, the edges disappearing and reappearing between the green tendrils, the whole almost familiar.

Her mother's lover. *He's here at last.*

Arianne takes a step without realizing, and another. The

image seems to beckon to her. Her lips part, her body shudders, and she finds herself reaching for a hand that isn't there and yet, perhaps, in the shadows—?

Her fingertips touch the smudged wall and it is as soft and warm as Théodore's kiss, and she feels certain that she can go *into* the wall, and what lies beyond is wondrous.

A cry breaks the silence, a high-pitched wail rising to a shriek. Arianne's heart leaps; she looks to her right, her fingers resting on the softness, and gapes at the small figure that darts from behind the door. The room dims and she is no longer inside but outside, she is on the hill, she looks down at little Arianne running towards her and the body is hers and the hand clutching a broken piece of ribbon is hers and the face is nightmare.

"Down in hell," someone says, and she realizes the voice is her own, and the world vanishes.

3.

When Arianne awakens a candelabra is burning before her, so close she is momentarily blinded, and she pushes it aside before sitting up and staring at the child staring back at her.

Though perhaps *child* is not the right word for the creature, clad in a too-small shift and rocking back and forth on his bare, dirty feet, his breath coming in audible snorts from the calf's head that sits atop his thick neck.

There will come a point, Arianne thinks, a point when she will truly understand that this is real—her murdered mother and the monstrosity watching her with large black eyes—and in that moment she will probably go quite mad.

The creature opens his broad mouth and she recoils, but he only utters two small noises with such seeming earnestness she cannot help but lean forward, listening, mouthing the sounds until at last she understands.

"Maman," she says.

The creature flings himself at Arianne, moaning and whimpering, wrapping chubby arms around her neck and pressing his brown, downy face against her cheek. She nearly screams, but manages to smother her cry behind clenched teeth. Instead she takes a deep breath, willing herself calm; only then does she feel the creature's violent trembling. Slowly she rubs his back with one hand, cradling his head with her other, but as soon as she touches behind his ear he yelps.

Hushing him, she twists until she sees the dirty, scabbing weal running across the back of his head. As if struck by a sword, perhaps, while fleeing from a monster?

A monster that Arianne visited upon the child and her mother both.

Still rubbing his back, she takes out her handkerchief and wets it with her tongue, then dabs at the wound. As she works his shudderings lessen, then quiet altogether, and she finds herself humming and rocking him like any little boy.

When she draws back, the boy makes a high-pitched noise and pushes his wet nose against her lips, and for the first time in years she finds herself truly smiling.

Ϟ∞ϟ

She drapes the coverlet over her mother's body, the boy making lowing noises as her face disappears. He clings tightly to Arianne's skirts, nearly wrapping around her leg. Whatever he is, whatever will happen, she cannot leave him here. What would become of him in this dreadful place? All his sweetness eroding until only the monster remains, waiting for another Théodore to finish him. She has enough on her conscience.

They move around the bedroom in an ungainly crab-walk as she gathers up the cards, the discarded piece of ribbon. She needs to find better clothes for him, and a large hood; with the calf's head hidden from view he'll look like any other boy, three or four years old.

She pauses, looking down at the dark eyes gazing up at her. Three or four years old. If he is her mother's child, then he might well be four now—nine months after her father had removed them to the cottage and sealed the house for good—

Did her father imprison her mother knowing she was with child?

The thought fills Arianne with a fresh, bright pain. She cannot bear to think on it, she cannot bear any of it. The very air tastes of deceit and sorrow and she longs to leave. The boy nudges her and she rubs the soft hair between his ears. The feel of it quiets her, filling her with the same sense of calm as when she kneels among the grapevines.

She looks once more around the room. Beside her the boy sniffs, his large nostrils flaring, and whines uneasily. A moment later she too smells it, just a hint in the stale air of the bedroom.

Smoke.

Arianne goes to the window, peering through the shutters. She can just make out the rows of grapevines, some already scorched, some bright with flames. People run past the window, she sees familiar faces contorted with rage, she sees torches and farm tools and she lurches backwards in fright.

The villagers have come at last.

She slings the boy into her arms and hurries out of the room, shoving and kicking her way through the vines. As she draws close to the open door she sees orange-tinged smoke drifting in; she hears a roar of anger and an answering yell and quickly darts to the far side of the door, ducking into the deeper shadows there. As she passes the open doorway she glimpses dozens of angry faces crowded outside, and before them a broad back clad only in a shirt, a pistol in one hand, sword in the other.

"You're acting like primitives," Théodore shouts. "There is no bull god, there is no devil! You're killing an innocent man for the perversions of a madwoman."

"Blood answers blood," someone says, and many voices break out in chorus, making Arianne's hair stand on end. *Blood answers blood! Blood answers blood!*

"Listen to yourselves! My life for hers, to what end? Her unnatural offspring still lives."

"Not for long," a man says, and Arianne knows his voice: the shopkeeper. "You killed the witch; now we must appease her lover. If this child exists as you claim? The fire will take it, and this as well."

Someone begins howling in the night like an animal to slaughter, and the chorus shouts in response. A body tumbles through the open doorway of the house, crashing against the boards to land in a heap on the floor.

Arianne stares at her father's unmoving body, and then she starts walking backwards, hushing the boy who whimpers against her neck.

"You're murderers, all of you," Théodore says; she can see his shadow in the doorway. "I tried to help you—"

"On the contrary, Citizen," the shopkeeper replies. "We're philosophers. An Englishman once said: that which brings happiness to the greatest number? That is the definition of good." He pauses, then shouts, "now!"

The rushing feet sound like a thunderclap; a mass of bodies strikes Théodore all at once, shoving him back into the hall where he trips over her father, sword and pistol flailing. Before he can right himself they slam the door shut, dousing the hallway in darkness.

Arianne keeps stepping backwards, trying to keep her panicked breathing silent; she steps once too often and hits another wall. Only then does she realize she's on the wrong side, she doesn't know where these corridors lead.

"I can hear you, you little beast." There is the hiss of a sword being sheathed; a match sparks in the gloom. "I know you're close. You won't escape me again."

At the last she turns and runs, the boy snuffling in her ear as she hurries down the new passage, one hand held before her; she runs into another wall, her fingers jamming painfully, and feels on either side, trying to place herself in the house. There must be a way to get back to the front door. If she keeps turning?

"Arianne?" There is a tremor in his voice; it is also closer than she thought. "Arianne, is that you? We must stay together. There's something monstrous in here, I tried to kill it but it was too fast. Arianne, stay where you are, let me find you!"

At the last his voice rises to a yell, tinged with fury. She turns and keeps moving, her hand waving wildly before her; her foot catches on a thick root and she falls to her knees, just managing to keep herself from landing atop the boy. He screeches in her ear and she presses his face to her neck. "Please," she whispers. "Please be quiet, you must be quiet now."

"Arianne!" Théodore yells. "Arianne, don't go near it! Stay away from it!"

Another match sparks, then dies away, but she glimpses the light in the gloom—as if at the end of a very long hall, yet didn't she just turn? Is he ahead of her now? She staggers to her feet, swinging the boy against herself. From the curve of her neck comes a soft squeaking noise; the boy is trembling again, but she has no time to comfort him. Her hand slides along the rough wood, splinters catching in her skin; at last she feels the wall end and open space to her left.

She turns, quickening her pace once more. A few steps down she inhales and tastes smoke; her heart leaps. Eagerly she presses forward, pushing against fresh vines that are tangling around them. "Nearly there," she whispers into the boy's hair, "we're nearly there."

But as she speaks she walks headfirst into smooth, solid wood. The boy yelps as his head bangs against the door, followed by her elbow and knees, the blows and the child's wails echoing in the quiet.

"Arianne!" The roar makes her jump, nearly upon them and full of anger now. "Stay still, you idiot! We have to find a way out!"

Panicking, she feels the smooth wood, the boy nearly falling as she shifts him from one arm to the other; at last she seizes a handle and turns, pushing as hard as she can, her mouth opening to call out: *don't hurt us, we mean no harm—*

but she steps not into the burning vineyard but her mother's bedroom again.

Her eyes well with tears of frustration as she shuts the door behind them. The room is warm and hazy with smoke. Looking around wildly she tries to think: where can we hide, how can we protect ourselves?

And then she sees the smoke drifting towards the far corner of the room, towards the drawing of the silhouette.

Drifting *into* the drawing.

Arianne shifts the boy from one hip to the other and moves towards it, her fingertips just brushing its center. Soft and warm. She pushes harder and her fingers slide in with a puckering sound, like a kiss.

Outside the room Théodore thrashes and curses as he makes his way through the vine-choked hall. Not a moment to lose. Arianne looks at the boy, searching for any sign of refusal or fear. But he meets her gaze and blinks once, a slow lowering of his bristly eyelids.

She seizes the nearest grapevine and pulls it free from the wall. Gripping it firmly, she stretches a leg into the drawing. Like stepping through the skin on hot milk—

The door flies open; she just glimpses Théodore's enraged face and raised pistol as she goes completely into the wall.

And finds herself blinded by sunlight. Her feet slip on gravelly dirt and she skids to her knees, holding both boy and vine tightly. A great weight spills over them as Théodore lunges through, stumbling over her hunched body and falling headfirst down a steep hillside. Halfway down the pistol goes off, the shot reverberating around them, making the boy shriek in fright.

Arianne raises her head and blinks and squints, separating whiteglare sky from graygreen blotches that congeal into a vast expanse of walls and paths that run to the horizon. They are crouched before a crevice in the rocky hillside, at the start of a lacework of switchbacks leading down to the largest maze she has ever seen. She looks and looks and she cannot take it all in. She sees hedges taller than a house; she sees the façades of city streets with nothing behind them; she sees country lanes intersecting between fields that end a few feet from the road. She sees people too, people walking and running, embracing and grappling, and everyone's faces are alight with a wild, mad joy and their mouths and hands are stained crimson.

At the base of the hill Théodore rights himself and looks around, his one leg kinked unnaturally. Even from her vantage Arianne can sense his bewilderment and fear. Then he looks up, and his face contorts once more with anger.

"Stupid cow!" he calls up to her. "You nearly broke my neck!"

At the sound of his voice the people in the maze stop moving. A thousand bloodstained faces turn in his direction.

"No," Arianne whispers.

"Arianne, please." He spreads his hands wide, hopping on his one good leg. "That child is an abomination, you must see that. Leave it and help me!"

The maze shifts behind him, rearranging itself so its paths converge upon an empty space like a city square. People file in, dragging with them what looks like a large frame atop a wagon. A fountain bursts into life, gushing red liquid, and the people crowd around, jostling to scoop it up in handfuls, their faces ecstatic as they drink.

"Hide," Arianne says, but her throat is tight with fear. She tries again, straining her voice. "Théodore, you must hide."

He peers up at her, cupping his ear. Can he not hear them coming? She stands up, pressing the boy behind her. "Hide," she calls, her voice echoing now. "They're coming for you!"

Below her the boy suddenly cries out, "Maman!"

Arianne cannot see, she squints and strains—and then she sees her, climbing onto the wagon and swinging from the frame like a child. Her mother; *their* mother. Her naked body gleams red as she cavorts around the wagon, her hair coiling wildly about her face and her mouth hanging open in an endless cry, an unending scream of joy or anger.

The boy lurches forward and Arianne catches him around his little belly, pulling him against her as he squirms and bleats. "Not Maman," she whispers in his ear. "You mustn't go to her. You mustn't."

The crowd reaches the edge of the maze. Slowly Théodore turns, throwing up his hands before the sea of faces. They flow around him, drawing him among them until he stands before the wagon. Her mother pulls up the blade and Arianne wants to vomit, she wants to scream and vomit and run down the hillside and hit her and hit her, pummel her into the ground until she is as dead as the body in the bedroom.

"What have I done?" Théodore cries. "Why me? Tell me what I've done!"

Arianne's anger fills her. It makes her eyes well and her heart pound, it expands without end, enveloping the whole of the maze, until everything is happening at the rhythm of her rage, Théodore bellows *why me* in time with her rage, the crowd roars and hoots and howls in time, they drag Théodore onto the wagon and embrace and drink and pump their fists all in time, while around them the maze forms and reforms at intervals as regular as her pounding heart.

And then Théodore is held down, and the blade drops, and Arianne screams. Her cry echoes through the endless valley, coming back to her as a chorus of a hundred Ariannes screaming in terror and regret.

The boy starts howling. The crowd turns and looks up at the hillside. Arianne is backpedaling even as she weeps; it will be her next, she's certain of it. She reaches for the boy but he moves away, looking from her to the crowd and back again with half-lidded eyes.

"No," she gasps.

"Maman," he says, then makes a string of garbled noises, waving a chubby hand at the maze.

"Not Maman. It's not her." She catches his hand and he pulls back, digging his heels into the dirt, and something wrenches deep in her gut.

"Please," she says. "Please stay with me."

The boy looks at her and his eyes are as vast as the night sky. All the paths that brought her here. She can leave the boy and her mother both, go back and try to create some kind of life for herself—

Or.

She crouches down, bringing his hand to her lips and kissing his fingers. "I am Maman." Tugging him closer, she taps her chest with their joined hands. "I am Maman now."

He tilts his head, considering her, and she meets his gaze as best she can, tries to mutely express everything she needs him to understand. *Always. Maman. Yes.*

Rocks tumble free below them; they both peer down and see the crowd filing onto the switchback, tripping over each other as they fight to be the first up the hill, their eyes bright against their red-stained faces.

Arianne seizes the boy and follows the grapevine back to the crevice, only to gasp in dismay, how could they have come through something so narrow? But the crowd is upon them, they are moving now with a goat-like sureness. Gritting her teeth, she shoves the boy forward and he seems to slip between the rocks like they're slick with grease. Pulling on the grapevine, she wriggles after him, the space so tight she panics and nearly falters, but strange hands stroke her leg and she pulls and shoves and she is through, falling face first into the smoky, desolate ruins of the house.

She looks behind her, but there is nothing but the remains of the wall, the silhouette indistinguishable against the scorched wood; she touches it and the blackened surface crumbles beneath her fingers. The whole of the bedroom is a mess of smouldering, charred beams and heaps of ash. Her mother's body is ash and bone—and which one is her real mother, the body here or the madwoman in the maze, who gleefully decapitated a man without cause—she quickly looks for the boy, but he is standing stockstill in the center of the room, his snout pointed at the sky, staring openmouthed at the great sprays of stars.

Smoke clings to the scorched vines like fog. She takes the

boy's hand and leads him into the vineyard and up the rise, pausing at the top to look back one last time. A wave of sorrow fills her, for Théodore, for what might have been, but it quickly sours into a bitter regret: that she wasn't there to watch her father's monstrous work become visible at last, that she wasn't there to watch it all burn.

V is for Vendémiaire

Pete Aldin

HERE lies a wonderful child. Here lies a beautiful boy. Blood of my blood. Flesh of my flesh. My own heart made real.

The tot sleeps soundly beneath deer skins, woollen blankets and fleece while the fireplace burns its last log of the long night. There's enough light from the fire's glow to make my way about the cabin without cracking my shins – and enough for me to make out the shape of his nose, the curl of his hair. This, my son. This, my gift to a world that will never want him.

A world that hates us both.

I drag the fleece to his chin. He murmurs, wriggles until it slips back down. I smile.

He is *everything* to me, just as I am to him.

But I won't always be. He'll grow up. He'll become as I am, a man hating his own father.

This thought is fresh, a dagger's thrust to the heart. I've often thought of the day he'll no longer sigh *Papa* upon awakening; that will sadden me but I will survive it. Every father does. But how will I bear the day when he no longer wants and needs my arm, my advice, my company? The day when dark thoughts cloud his expression as he sees me for what I am and himself for what I've made him?

Did my father once think this way? Did he stand above my bed and grieve for something he was yet to lose? No, my father deserves no sympathy. He didn't take his son to a place of safety such as I have found for mine. He dragged me from settlement to settlement in order to avoid discovery, until the day came...

I turn toward the fire and prod the log with the poker, turning the handle over in my hand. Not much iron in this cabin, besides this poker. Two knives. A spoon. My short sword, a relic of my father's brought over from the Old Lands. An arquebus rifle, nothing but a decoration with my powder and shot used up. And the shackles I keep deep in my pack, where their occasional rattle and jingle reminds me of the things I have suffered at the hands of humans, the reasons I brought my son here, what I must teach him to fear, what I must teach him to fight.

I touch the tip of the poker to my palm, gasp in echo of the hiss of burning flesh. I turn my hand to catch the firelight and watch the burn fade to scar and then to healthy skin. Fire is no more danger to me than iron. Silver and gold are what I fear, the metals of high currency. The metals no longer offered in worship to the gods are now the only metals with the power to maim and kill their grandchildren.

A foot scuffs the mulch of pine needles downslope from the cabin. Somewhere further down the mountainside, a horse whickers.

Damn it! I've been so lost in thought, so full of self-pity, I didn't sense them coming. I pause, halfway to the door. I was raising the poker in a two-handed stance, but I drop it to my side, careful to avoid singeing my kilt: my clothes, after all, aren't made from the stuff of gods. I concentrate: there is no them, just a her. What in the four doors to eternity is a lone woman doing all the way out here? To my knowledge, no one has ever sent a woman *bravo* to kill *custodes*. I have certainly never faced one.

But there is always a first time.

"Hallo, cabin!" comes a high voice, thirty or forty paces away. I have let her get far too close. I close my eyes, Marking her. I am relieved; for a moment I wondered if she'd worn gold to hide her presence.

I stride to the door, whip it open and close it fast behind me, preventing backlighting from the fire. No sense inviting the pain of an arrow or musket shot if she has friends in the woods, friends masked by gold...

The lower half of her body is little more than a suggestion against the snow, and her upper half a blur against the treeline below.

"What do you want?" I challenge.

"Shelter." She draws the word out as if I am a simpleton. What else would someone want after travelling across mountains and through the tail end of this long and miserable winter?

Neither of us speaks for a long time. The winds—an ever present companion up here on my mountain—are strangely quiet this night, a whispering of twig on twig from nearby trees the only sign of moving air. The scents of pine and larch and fir are thick, as if swelling from the woods downhill. Not much grows upslope behind me but the wilted remains of last year's crop of rye and carrots and berry bushes. With the snow yet to thaw, I won't be able to cultivate these for some time. Each year, the winters grow longer. And yet still mortals refuse to—

The horse shifts nervously where she has tied it within the trees; perhaps it smells me, perhaps there's a wolf nearby. I was told my great-grandfather could Mark animals, and that his great-grandfather could speak with them. Me, I can barely ride a horse and I'm no better at sensing animals than the average huntsman. Worse maybe, if my larder is anything to go by.

Eventually she sighs. "You need not your weapon. I am here alone and unarmed."

She lies about that: hidden within the tang of pine carried uphill on the barest of breezes, I catch a whiff of gunpowder. Perhaps, then, she intends to spray a fistful of golden shot at me. But, I Mark no pistol on her; perhaps she carries a musket in her saddlepack for hunting. It makes little sense for her to have hunted me. Mortals have nothing to fear from me. And it has been years since shackles adorned my wrists and I had to fight for my life.

"I've some dried walnuts," I say. Though it's little more than a lump in the darkness, I glance at the hutch draped with thick skins beside the door. "My chicken lays few eggs, so I can only give you one. That's all I can spare, but I'll give it to you if you keep on moving."

"I said shelter, not supplies," she reminds me and puts one foot forward against a rock, leans her hands on her knee. Her accent is odd: heavy on consonants, light on vowels, as if she has pebbles in her mouth. If she is from one of the Banic settlements far south, then she is certainly a long way from where she started.

I should kill her. I should go back into the cabin, draw my short sword from the shelf above the fire, chase her through the snowdrifts and hack off her head. I should slaughter her horse; gods know we need the meat.

She clears her throat, continuing, "I can trade food for a roof above my head. I have some cheese, some hardbread. A little wine."

She has done well to have so much food left. The shortest journey from the nearest settlement would be four weeks, possibly five or six. I could slay her and take all of it. But what would that make me?

She gives a sigh and straightens. "While you stand there judging me, the night grows no brighter and the air no warmer."

"Then walk your horse across the mountain. There's a pass about a league to the west. The exercise will keep you warm and the activity will make the dawn come quicker."

"You would turn away a lone woman in need?"

"I would turn away intruders. I value my solitude."

"Long and hard have I travelled."

It's my turn to sigh. She won't be budged, this one. "What are you doing up here?"

"Breaking," she says, inching closer.

I frown at the word. "Say again?"

"The land. It breaks. I search for a way to heal it."

My stomach turns at this. Once that was *my* quest, *my* duty. My father had turned his back on it, but I wanted some sense of purpose, dull-witted enough to imagine I could bring a measure of health back to this land.

I nearly died trying.

Many want an end to the long winters, the failing crops, the harsh conditions, but few are willing to follow the one true way. The simple way.

I glance to the skies, moonlight and stars in patches between thick clouds. The winters have gotten longer and longer—for centuries, it is said. And now the nights are longer too. I remember the earthquake that near destroyed Tuvalos—as well as the way the locals blamed me for it. It's not this land that's broken, but the mortals who dwell in it. The land merely follows their lead.

The scent of rain is thick upon the air; the snow will soon turn to slush. The air out here is cold enough to turn piss to icicles before it hits the dirt and I'm wearing a tunic, kilt and rabbitskin slippers. Iron and fire mayn't kill me, but the lung fever will if I stay out here much longer. And no man, god-descended or mortal, enjoys the feeling of his manhood numbing and shrinking. I shove the door open and beckon to her, returning to my place by the fire. I toss on two small logs. The bark catches and flares and I hold my hands toward it, capturing the fresh heat.

Moments later the door closes. I turn to get my first good look at my guest as she shakes her cloak and hangs it by mine on back of the door.

She is undoubtedly the most beautiful woman I have ever seen. Younger than I expected from her voice. Tall. Graceful curves. A hard jaw and soft sapphire eyes. Hair the color of straw and the lustre of spun silk. Full lips that curve in a coy smile as she straightens her cloak on the hook: she is used to men staring—perhaps she enjoys it.

From a pocket in the cloak, she frees a small bladder that sloshes with the movement. It's been a long time since I've tasted strong drink. Perhaps there's some good in her arrival, then.

She has hung her cloak over my son's and she nods toward the pile of blankets and skins. "How old?"

I move to a point between the small table in the centre of my home and the bed where my son lies, blocking her view. My palm itches for my sword. "Four years," I murmur.

She moves toward the table. "His name?"

How does she know the child isn't female? "Keep your voice down. He needs his slumber."

She sniffs and flips a chair around, dumps herself onto it, legs sprawled. One hand snags her thick braid and strokes it like a pet upon her shoulder. The other tosses the wineskin on the table before her. "His name is a secret?"

"His name's none of your concern." I shift closer and press my thighs against the opposite side of the table. It's only big enough to seat two because two is all I made it for. "For your cheese and some hardbread, I'll trade a few hours sleep in my cot plus that handful of walnuts, an egg and some dried plums. That's it. Your horse will have to find its own provisions."

"You have no hay, in any case." It's a statement; she peers left and right, squinting as if she can see through the very walls. "You have no animal. You must be a strong man—and brave—to bring your son so far. To build this cabin. To provide for him." She dips her head to peer at me from beneath those perfect brows. The blue of her eyes brings a warm flush to my chest and belly, as if I've stepped suddenly into summer sunshine. The low light of a fireplace has been known to make women appear more comely than the light of day and perhaps it's this at work. But then, it's been a very long time...

I shake it off, avoiding a guilty glance toward the bed. My love of women has created enough pain already.

"I accept your trade," she says. "With one small change. Rather than sleep, let us speak a while."

One of my hands finds the back of the other chair and squeezes it. Women always want to speak. And speaking brings complications such as discovery. "I don't need talk."

"Sometimes one speaks not for need, but for pleasure. And for gain." Her fingers caress the wineskin. She raises her eyebrows, waiting for something.

"What?" I ask.

"Do you have cups? Or shall we take turns sucking from the skin?" The words are mocking, but her expression is more teasing, playful.

I growl and go to the box by the fire for mugs. I give her mine and accept five fingers of blood-red liquid into my son's.

"Your health," I mumble as she takes the first sip.

She smacks her lips and replies, "Our health and our world's."

I frown, but raise the cup to my lips. The wine is full and a little sweet. Its warmth spreads from my throat to my chest, like seepage from a leaking roof. The warmth alarms me. *Damn it all!* What if it's poisoned with ground up gold or silver?

But there's no pain. No sensation that I've been fooled. And why in the four doors would anyone go to this much effort to find and kill me? I'm sure mortals are happy enough that I'm simply out of their way.

"What's brought you up here?" I ask, and place the cup on

the table.

She sips. "I could ask you this same question. There was a time when only gods lived upon mountains."

"I like the quiet," I reply with meaning.

"Subtle. Well, then, perhaps I am a settler looking for my own space like you. Perhaps I am escaping from brutal men. Perhaps I heard rumors of gold in the valleys beyond this range." If she notices me stiffen at the mention of gold, she doesn't show it. "Although I would be foolish to seek such treasure since no one—but you possibly—has ever explored those lands. You have found yourself some virgin territory here, good sir." She sits straight and pulls off her thick overshirt, revealing a thin tunic beneath. The material rides across her bosom.

"We were speaking of you," I remind her, averting my eyes. "And you didn't actually answer my question."

She straightens her overshirt across her knees, folds it. "Perhaps I look for a way to bring an end to our long winters and failing crops."

I laugh at that, gesturing toward the lowland settlements far away from my mountain. "Isn't everyone?"

"No. They are not." The lightness flees her face. Her eyes cloud, her lips press together and her hands enclose the cup, fingers lacing. She stares into the depths of her wine for some moments before clearing her throat. "Especially not men who are not true men, who dwell on top of mountains rather than fight for the gods' honor and the world's wellbeing."

So this is it after all. She knows me. The shelf bearing my sword is two paces away. I can have the grip in my hand and the blade in her back before she gets out the door.

Slowly, I place my son's cup on the table. "What do you want with me?"

"Your help."

That answer, I did not expect. "Help? To heal the world?"

"You think that impossible?"

"Besides the fact people aren't interested in the gods who can repair it, the *world* is too far gone anyway. These winters will grow longer and longer until there's nothing but snow and ice, and days too short to be called days, and nothing grows anymore."

She nods. "The fate of the Old Lands."

"So it's said. So it's written. And now you mortals are doing it to the New Land as well. Destroying it with your unbelief."

"Unbelief indeed." She sips more wine and wrinkles her nose as if it suddenly tastes sour. "You know of the Naturalists?"

I nod again without speaking. Naturalists: vendors of "material philosophy", laboring to understand the workings of the world without finding any answers to its disease.

"They have a saying," she continues. "They call it a law: 'all things erode without intervention'." She huffs a laugh. Behind me, my son blows out a breath as if in response and turns within his tangle of blankets. "Their words describe exactly what the world has always needed—intervention—and yet they deny the gods a means to it."

I rub a hand across my face. I've had these same thoughts many many times and I'm sick of the weight of them. And now— now when the world is centuries past the point where *custodes* could actually turn things around—*now* a believer appears?

"If you know what I am, then you know what little I can offer. Even if they let me." I wave a hand toward the lowlands again.

"I understand your feelings. Your father and his father must have felt the same. We are long past the days in which each *custos* was sired directly by a god. For generation upon generation, demigods have bred with women, diluting their strength. In seven centuries, no true Custodian has been born–"

"Don't you think I know all–?"

"–until now!" she finishes.

My heart skips a beat. "What are you talking about?

She shakes her head and changes subjects. "Tracked you for three years, I have. Your name is Cassian, is it not?"

What harm is there now? I grunt a yes, impatient.

She makes a sympathetic face. "Cassian. 'Empty' in the old tongue. Your father had a sense of irony then."

My teeth grind together, my voice a low growl. "And yours?"

"Jasa."

Again, I am put in mind of the Banic settlements and the odd dialects and customs they reportedly brought with them from the Old Lands. She reads my face. "An odd name, certainly, as many have delighted in telling me. My father told me my mother named me. But she would not tell him the meaning."

I lean forward, fists clenching. "Enough about names. Tell me what you meant a moment ago. The gods have sired a child?"

"Indeed."

"Ridiculous! Where? Who?"

"Easier to show you than tell you," she says and raises a hand, making a fist.

We are plunged into abject darkness as the fire snuffs out like a candle flame. Smoke cloys and spreads through the blackness. I cry out, my chair crashing to the floor as I shoot to my feet and stumble backwards, calves butting against my son's bed.

I am about to grope for my sword when the fire flares to its former glory. She sits exactly where she was and as she was, except that her fingers are unclenched.

I gape at her. "*You?*"

She places the hand on the table, carefully as if it is a pistol already cocked. "If we work together..." she begins.

"You're a woman!" I blurt.

Her teasing smile returns fleetingly. "Your eyes work then."

"But... but *custodes* are... are men."

"Because only the male gods sired children. The male gods have lost both their power in this world and affection for it. But the goddess Dima decided she would at least try."

The name is familiar: Dima, Mother of Rains. I wonder just what her manifestation cost her, not to mention the rigors of a human-form pregnancy and birth?

"If we work together," Jasa is saying, "we can place this world on a path toward restoration. We can demonstrate that the gods still care, the gods can still heal, if mortals will only return to them."

Folding my arms across my chest, I find my voice. "If you want to choose such a numb-brained quest, you have every right. But why would *I* help mortals? What have they ever done but hound me?"

"A mortal gave you your son."

"Best you never mention his mother again."

"Spit! In those words lies the weakness of every man, even he who carries the seed of the gods. So quick to anger, so quick to battle. Even when he may be overwhelmed."

Overwhelmed? She's right, of course. It's been centuries since any Custodian commanded fire or any other element. Who knows what other powers she owns?

Fear flares fresh in my belly, clenching it. What's to stop her from slaying me and taking him?

"Leave here," I snarl and gesture to the bed. "Neither of us is strong enough to help you."

"I have heard the tales. You survived numerous–"

"I won't aid you! I won't help mortals."

She blinks at me for some time before asking, "So content are you for the boy to inherit a decaying world?"

"He will survive."

"And his son? And his grandson?"

"Leave. Please. Leave us in peace."

"For what purpose will any of them live?" she persists.

"For...? For life."

"A life as yours?" She sniffs. "He was meant for more than that. As were you. I will tell you something you know not, Cassian. It looked as if you and your father would be the last of your line, of your kind. The very last hope for this world. First he and then you deferred that hope by rejecting your true purpose, leaving Dima no choice but to create me."

More eager than ever to hurry her along, I move to the set of shelves where I keep our food. I unstop a jar. "What would you have me do? Yes, I've fought and bested dozens of mortals. I'm stronger and faster. I heal from my wounds. Fire and iron don't harm me in any lasting way. And I can *see* things, Mark things." I return to the table and dump the jar of walnuts there, shove it towards her. She can take my food. She can be on her way. "But I don't command the elements. I can't breathe new life into seedstock or the very earth itself."

"You can *give* 'seedstock'," she says. "You can give me a child."

The offer should warm me, should arouse me, but it's as if I'm back out in the snow.

"I want no part in this."

She rises and rounds the table. I tense, but her expression is gentle, as is the hand she lays on my shoulder. I smell sweat and stale breath along with something else, something ancient calling to me. The warmth of her skin reaches through our shirts and spreads against me as the wine did within me.

243

Her voice is a murmur now. "This is the purpose of your life, Custodian."

I edge away, just a little, looking to my sleeping son. "There lies my purpose. Just him and nothing else."

"You owe him, certainly. But he is the result of your selfishness."

I bristle but her hand tracks down to the hard muscle of my chest, and something like treacle moves from her hand to my heart making me settle. The only magic at work here is that which all women are born with, that native authority that a woman holds over a man simply by virtue of her sex.

I should resist, but I find I no longer have the strength to pull away.

She continues, "You wanted someone to love you. Understand you, and fight with you if the need arose. These are mortal wishes, Cassian. You – we – have a higher calling."

She is set on this course, but for all her power—and for all her beauty—she cannot bend me to her will. Her hand falls to her side but the treacle around my heart oozes lower. Her eyes glitter with reflected firelight.

I consider the curves of her, the lure of her like blood to the wolf. I also consider the consequences of taking her, as she watches me deciding.

What if she can do it, she and her child? Our child. What if she can make a world where my son can plant and harvest without fear? Where he may love and be loved, honoured for who he is, rather than hated for his heritage.

A world where he won't have reason to hate me.

I make my choice and reach for her, plunging into a sea of pleasure. We tear off shirt and tunic. She meets my hands with hers, raises them to fill them with her breasts, the feel of her skin like mystery, like a call to worship. She reaches beneath my kilt and ignites me. The warm pressure of breath and hands, of mouth and cheek and throat—these fast overpower the chill in the cabin.

She kicks off her boots. I bunch the fabric of her trousers in my fists and yank them down, drive her back on my bed and press myself to her, finding resistance at the entry before it gives and she cries out in a moment of pain. She is a virgin then, and this is almost enough to stop me. Almost, but not nearly enough.

Warmth flows from the wound I have inflicted, and her nails
ravage the skin of my back in response, one elbow crooked tight
around my neck to anchor her, her teeth in my shoulder. I don't
know if any of it is from agony, ecstasy or sheer bloody-minded
determination to complete her gods-damned quest. My cot is
barely big enough for us, but we make do. We buck and slide and
writhe, our love a tumult, a storm breaking, while the lad sleeps
on, oblivious, three paces away. This passion lasts for an
eternity—and far too soon she is leaning over me and kissing my
brow.

"Time for me to leave," she whispers and disappears from
sight, searching the floor for her clothes.

I can't believe the words issuing from my mouth. And yet
they come. "You could stay a few days. I can find more food:
hunt, check my traps."

"Food won't be an issue for you, Cassian. Not anymore. You'll
find your traps full when next you check them. And..." Dressed
only in her overshirt, she moves to my shelves on pale-gold legs,
rummages in the rabbitskin bags and poorly-made pottery until
deciding on a jar painted in ochre by my son. She reaches in and
brings the fist out, full of rye. For a spate of heartbeats it seems
there is a new glow in the room, soft and subtle and coming from
her hand. She sighs and returns the grain to the jar and the jar
to the shelf. "You will have a better crop this year."

She returns to the bed and picks up her trousers. The cot
leans dangerously as she sits to get her feet into them.

"Why?" I ask her. There are many ways to complete the
question, but I can't decide on any.

It's a few moments before she answers, while she wrestles
her trousers, stands and ties her belt. "Not just for the world.
But for you. And your boy."

As she hunts down her boots and drags them on, I watch
patterns of firelight flicker across her throat, her hair, her hands.
The fire is much lower now, the temperature falling. When she
slips her cloak from the door, I rise and twist a woolen blanket
tight around me. It is scratchy but it holds in some of the
warmth she lent me.

She smiles. "When you feel ready, come find me."

"How in the four doors would I ever find you?"

"I found you." She pauses a moment longer, holding my gaze

with those blue eyes of hers, smiling without hint of mockery now. "Thank you, Cassian. Thank you, *custos.*"

The door closes softly behind her. The lock clicks. Moments later, her horse whickers and I Mark their movement through the woods, heading back the way they must have come. She reaches the gully, the lip of the next downslope. And she is gone.

Outside, robins and jackdaws chatter: dawn is coming. She—Jasa—has flown in and through and out of my life like a bird through a clearing. But like the light of a new day's sun, she's changed everything.

I exchange my blanket for wool stockings, kilt and tunic. I toss a log onto the fire. I drain the wine from my son's cup and place it beside hers. The wineskin remains where she left it; I stroke it with one finger.

Wrapped in his nest of furs and skins, my son sniffs and groans, surfacing from the well of sleep. I move to his side in time to watch his eyes pry open and focus on me.

He smiles and sighs, "Papa."

He climbs into my arms and, for now, all is well with the world.

W is for Woman

Gabrielle Harbowy

FOR three nights Azrid slept with the gold coin under her pillow in her little hollowed-out room at the top of her family's home tree, imbuing the coin with her wish. Wishes were secret things, so she didn't worry that she might have to share it, but she had heard from her older sister's friends—and they knew everything!—that if someone found your wishing coin before you gave it to the wish-granters, they could put it under their pillow and *their* dreams would show them what you planned to wish for. That didn't sound entirely leaf-green to Azrid, but all the girls had sworn to it, so she wasn't ready to just assume it wasn't true. She couldn't ask her parents, either, because grownups stopped climbing down the home tree to the forest floor when they lost their tails; anything they could tell her about the wish-granters would be, like, a *dozen* tree-rings out of date.

On the fourth day, coin clutched in her hand, Azrid made the downward climb. She had no path picked out, so she simply clambered over the side of one of the sturdy rope walkways that connected the treetop village together, and made her way from bridge to branch to branch, all the way down toward the ground.

Azrid had been to the ground before. All the younglings got curious eventually. It was fun to play in the shed leaves, or trace the connected tree roots until they became hopelessly tangled, or swim in the sun-dappled pools. There were brightly colored berries that grew near the ground, and she had been taught which ones were safe to eat. They were considered to be children's treats, so at Azrid's age it wasn't seemly to eat them anymore. All of her age-mates lied and said they'd lost the taste for the sweetness of berries, that ground-food was beneath them. Azrid told the lie too, so that no one would make fun of her and say she was still a youngling, but she didn't worry too much about it. She knew that all the youths snuck berries when no one was looking. Just like she always did.

Not today, though. Everyone knew the wish-granters were more likely to take your wish if you left it in the morning. Azrid figured she had just enough time to place her coin and then rush back up for class.

There wasn't any one specific place to leave your wishing coin. Any crack or hole in the trunk would do. Some people left notes instead of coins, maybe because they didn't get gold from their parents on their tree-ring days, or because they wanted to wish for things that were too complicated for just a coin to convey and they thought the wish-granters needed a full set of instructions. Or maybe because they had trouble dreaming into a coin. Azrid wasn't sure. She just knew that, coin or note, if you left yours in a crack in the tree and it was gone when you came back the next week, it meant that the wish-granters had taken it and your wish would probably come true. Not necessarily in the way you wanted, and not necessarily right away, but eventually something would happen that you could tie somehow to the secret wish you had made.

Azrid was bad at figuring distance in the numbers she learned in class, since she had always just thought of it in terms of her own body's length. By her measure, the wishing cracks started about two Azrids up from the ground. They were easy to see because they were filled with coins and paper and scraps of anything that could be written on. She was kind of amazed at the sheer number of them. There didn't seem to be this many younglings in school, but maybe her school was just for her trunk or even her branch. Maybe it represented all the wishes in the entire sky-village. Being a wish-granter must be tiring work, with all these wishes to sort through.

Azrid circled, looking for the most likely place to wedge her coin. Too loose a spot and it might fall out. Too tight a fit and the wish-granters might not be able to take it. Too crowded an area and it might get lost among all the other wishes.

Time was growing short, and Azrid didn't want to be late. She found a spot, kissed her coin and wedged it in, and followed the crack up the trunk to the network of branches that would carry her swiftly home. She was in a little bit of a hurry, but not the big sort of hurry that invited carelessness. Still, when her foot pushed through the bark and plunged into the trunk, there was a brief stomach-dropping moment in which she was certain it was her fault.

But no. A whole section of bark was gone, revealing a ragged, spongy hollow that wound all the way to the ground. Insects the size of berries trotted over and around and through the holes in the structural substance of Azrid's home tree. They each had three feelers protruding from their foreheads, a blur of tiny legs, and a round carapace that was a lovely gold-speckled brown. Azrid set her jaw, resolutely refusing to think of them as lovely again; they must have been what weakened the tree, eating away at its core until a thin shell of bark was all that remained.

Eating away at the tree.

Destroying her home.

She could pretend she hadn't noticed. She felt the strong tug against her conscience that told her to keep climbing, to let someone else "discover" the hole her foot had made, but she already knew what she was actually going to do.

She swung over to the next tree, and then the next. Each time, it didn't take her long to find the weakness. On some of them, the bark had already fallen away, leaving similar holes to the one Azrid had created. It was an epidemic, and it was affecting the entire village. Her stomach sank even as she climbed. Someone had to be told.

Azrid went first to the elders, but they greeted her with laughter and a pat on her head. A fine prank, they said, but it wasn't enough to get them to make the climb. Her sister didn't believe her either, but at least her eagerness to prove Azrid wrong made her want to see for herself. She gathered a half-dozen of her friends and they swarmed down the tree, leaving Azrid to trail along behind them.

The hole was still there. Not that Azrid thought it would go anywhere, but a small part of the back of her mind had been trying to convince the rest of her that it really had been her imagination; that they would arrive back at the scene and nothing would be nothing there but Tazrid's mockery.

The older girls fell into a hush. One stuck her head inside the hole and looked around. No one accused Azrid of breaking the tree. The damage internally was much too great for that, and the girls were all too awed by its scope.

"Look!" Gendira hissed. One of the golden-backed beetles had dragged in a slip of paper at least five times larger than itself. Others descended on it, all nibbling inward from the edges until all their mandibles met in the middle.

"That was a wish, wasn't it?" another girl asked—Azrid thought it might have been Sendri.

"Now the wish-granters will never get it."

Tazrid shushed her. "No... I think these *are* the wish-granters. They take the wishes, and they eat them."

"Then what about the gold? Do they eat that, too?" Azrid asked.

"Gold is heavy. I bet we'll find it inside the trunk, near the ground."

Jelize let a beetle climb up onto her finger, and brought it close to study it. "Do you grant wishes?" she asked it. "If you do, please make my parents grow me a bedroom all for myself."

The beetle, being just a beetle, waved its three antennae at Jelize, but made her no promises.

৯৵৶

The gold was piled in the trunk of the tree, a cascade of it that filled all the spaces where wood and growth should have been. It was a wonder the bark hadn't caved outward from the weight of it, and a shiver ran down Azrid's neck at the thought that a single jump or shake or shift far above might collapse the fragile structure of their whole village with no warning at all.

They brought the beetle, along with handfuls of gold, back up the tree as proof; first, they made even little Jelize agree that none of them would keep any of it.

The elders crowded around the beetle as if they'd never seen one before. Azrid had not, either, but she thought the elders, alive for so many rings, would have already seen everything. They muttered quietly to each other, and retreated into the community hut to talk amongst themselves. Azrid and the other girls waited, fidgeting with the ends of their tails or settling into distracted games with acorn caps and feathers.

After a time, Mizra the Elder emerged and summoned the girls into the hut. It was where village meetings took place, and none of them, not even Tazrid, were old enough to ever have been inside before. A nervous hush settled across them.

"Many rings ago," Mizra began, "we learned the art of making paper from fallen leaves." She had so many wrinkles in her skin that she could have been a tree many rings old, herself. The golden beetle perched on her open palm as if her hand existed to be its throne. "When the ground-folk, our distant cousins, discovered our village, we discovered that our paper was of value to them. In return, they trade us their gold, which we save to purchase other goods from them, things which are more easily made or grown on the ground. Do you understand?"

Some of the girls nodded their heads. Azrid thought she understood, and supposed that thinking so was close enough to knowing so. She nodded, too.

"In the days before wishes, it was common for a tree to crack and weaken. We would harvest the wood for our structures and reinforce them, so that we would not suffer at an individual tree's loss. This weakening from within was what formed the cracks that began the tradition of leaving wishes in the trunks. Before the time of the trading, before the gold, we used to write all our wishes on paper. Wish-granters were residing in our trees even then; there was enough paper to sustain these creatures, so that they stopped eating the insides of the trees. The transition to gold wishes has starved these creatures, forcing them to feed on the trees themselves for sustenance once again."

It made sense, in its way. Except for the part where they were bugs and not granters of wishes. And the part where the elders could apparently communicate with them. Had they known that the wish-granters were bugs all along?

"Don't worry, young ones. We have a solution. But we need a volunteer to go to the ground-folk and bring them here to meet with us. This plan will require their aid."

Most of the girls stepped forward around Azrid. The elder picked two, and the rest filed out of the hut.

"Azrid," the elder said, "why did you not volunteer to go?"

Azrid toyed with the end of her tail. "I would rather stay and learn the language of the wish-granters."

❦

The language of the wish-granters turned out to be a complicated thing. Azrid began to wish that she had wished for antennae. Instead she had to learn the gestures with her fingers, with only a few chitters or clicks to modify the meaning of certain signs. Fortunately, the vocabulary of wish-granters was rather limited, so Azrid didn't have too many words and phrases to learn. By the time the others were back from their journey, Azrid was ready to return to the gaping hole at the base of her tree.

The elder of the ground-folk was a tall, solid man dressed in the hides of animals. He had brought a second with him, a quiet youngling boy who watched everything but spoke little; he seemed to be more of an official observer than a tag-along child. The boy didn't have a tail, but otherwise he seemed normal enough.

At Mizra's nod, Azrid wiped her damp palms on her leaf-spun tunic, took a breath, and peeked into the gash in the tree.

"Hello?" she signed with her middle three fingers. "Will you send a leader to speak with us?"

She heard faint chitters and clicks as the tiny wish-granters relayed her message. After a few moments, she felt antennae against her finger. She flattened her hand for the beetle, and lifted it carefully from the trunk.

"Please tell us the history of your people," she signed.

Azrid was surprised to see that she could mostly follow the story told by the three waving antennae. All the other girls stood around her in a loose ring, watching her wiggle her fingers at the bug. No one made fun of her.

"She says that most of their kind live in the upper branches. They eat leaves and new green shoots, and convert them to the fiber sacs we use to make our paper. When a storm shakes them free, they return to the trunk to make their way back up to the leaves. Or, they used to, until we built our homes in the trees. They can't pass by our structures because of the way we coat our bark, so they started to nest in the trunks instead. If we can give them safe return to the leaves, they won't have to eat our trunks anymore. They don't like the old wood, anyway. That's why they like the paper. It's the most like the green wood."

Everyone was silent for a few long moments. It was a lot for Azrid to take in at once, too.

"If they move to the leaves, what happens to all their gold?" one of the girls asked.

A flurry of voices replied at once.

"It was ours first, we should get it back."

"But what will happen to all the wishes in that gold? Will they all be reversed?"

"No, sapling, haven't you been paying attention? They don't actually grant wishes. They're just bugs. They've always been just bugs."

"Wait!" someone shouted, and they all fell silent. It was Tazrid. She spoke haltingly, still putting her idea together as she spoke it. "What if... What if we did something for the whole village with it. Something so big it would use all the gold."

Mizra rested a gnarled hand on Tazrid's shoulder. "Something like repairing the trees?" she asked, then turned to the ground-folk. "You have equipment that can melt gold?"

"Of course. We would be pleased to assist. If you tree-folk can no longer live here, we suffer as well."

And thus did the Gleaming Forest get its name. The grand, tall oaks did not grow with gold veins in their bark. No, it was once known to us as the Broken Forest. The gold was poured, in order to save and stabilize the trees. If you look very closely, you might catch a glimpse of a rope bridge high above us, or see the tawny tail of a tree-folk youngling as they scamper back up to their home. Or, it might just be a squirrel foraging for the gold-shelled beetles that still live on these leaves to this day.

X is for Xylophage

Lilah Wild

THE 1963 Trotwood RV peeked out from an alcove of trees. Its
rounded roof was lovingly blanketed with tapestries and old
quilts, the original Americana color scheme painted over in
scrolling purple and black. It sat at the back of the lot, its lawn a
worn Persian carpet, its fence a line of card tables. Overhead,
branches were strung with temple bells and decaying lace from
lonely farmhouse attics.

A dazzling avalanche of rescued yesteryear lay scattered atop
the tables, tied about with little white price tags. Czech glass
twinkled within a cluster of long necklaces, perfect for a flapper's
trousseau. Satin jewelry boxes awakened tiny ballerinas when
opened. Orphaned sugar bowls were adopted into gaily
mismatched serving sets. And teacups were perched everywhere,
their gilt shining in the midday light.

The proprietess sat before the camper's open door, occupied
with crochet. She was dressed in garnet velvet, waves of bronze
hair pinned up in jewelled chopsticks. Beside her sat an ever-
present cup of darjeeling. Towards the front of the lot, just
behind the tables, her daughter was settled on the carpet,
reclining on a pile of tasseled pillows. Ribbons were knotted in
her wild hair, pulled back from her pale face. Her dress was
fashioned from all her childhood petticoats slashed apart and
sewn back together, cascading down into a magnificent peacock
tail of dresses past, the hem yellowed from market dirt. She was

busy with a seam ripper, carefully trying to salvage the ruffles of a moth-eaten scarf. A small radio brightened the air with Ella Fitzgerald.

"Ouch!" Black lace fluttered to the carpet.

Lillie immediately dropped her crochet in her lap. "Charla. Let me see it."

Charla shook her head. "I stabbed myself with the needle, it's not serious. I'll wash it off."

She got up, stepped into the camper. Her bed was buried in a pile of chiffon – they frequently found abandoned clothes by the market's trash cans, their owners giving up any hope of profit, and last night had yielded a crop of vintage floral dresses that were wrecked beyond wearing but could be dissected for patchwork. She turned on the faucet, wrapped up her finger in a soaked washcloth. No bandages in the first aid kit. She'd have to wait until she healed up so she wouldn't bloody the merchandise.

A truck honked in the distance. A couple of voices grew loud. She leaned in the doorway and peered out. Two women in high heels and designer handbags had walked up to their tables, and the brunette one was delightedly running her hands over a babydoll's face. Charla was ready with a firm word – accidents usually meant a mad embarrassed dash into the crowd. And there were always those who ignored the polite calligraphy of the PLEASE ASK FOR ASSISTANCE signs.

The brunette picked up the babydoll and held it out to her friend. Charla opened her mouth, but Lillie beat her to it.

"Ma'am, I appreciate your interest, but we don't allow the dolls to be touched. They're very delicate."

The woman didn't even look up. "Just a minute. I'll put her down in just a minute. Kathy, I had this doll once! Oh my God!"

"Ma'am, please—"

A boy on a BMX came whizzing past the table, grazing the woman and startling her. Charla jumped out of the camper, helpless as the babydoll tumbled from the woman's hands. Her pink bonnet struck the table before shattering both ivory arms upon the ground.

"Oh, God. Oh my God. I am so, *so* sorry." The woman flung her hair, bent down to scoop up the babydoll. Lillie sighed and rose from her chair.

"Ma'am, that doll is eighty dollars."

"Okay, okay, that's fine. I wanted to buy her anyway." She dug in her purse, pulled out a little brown wallet covered with a pattern of linked C's. "I am *so* sorry. Here – here's a hundred bucks," thrusting a bill at Lillie so casually, as if apologizing with money was something she did a lot. "Keep the change. Kathy, let's go." The women walked off, the broken arms sticking up out of her purse like a panicked kidnap victim.

Lillie put the hundred in the cashbox and settled back in her chair, shaking her head in disgust as she resumed her crochet.

The kid on the bike came gliding back from the other direction. He was about six, seven years old. He smirked at Charla as he sped by.

The little brat did it on purpose.

Charla watched him ride off and disappear into stalls full of vinyl cellphone cases. T-shirts printed with badly bootlegged cartoon characters, silvertone earrings inside clear plastic wrappers, endless aisles of the same old junk, easy to hide in.

The broken babydoll had lost her bonnet. She picked up the scrap of pale pink satin and turned around to rearrange the dolls across the newly-vacated space. The porcelain clattered nervously as she worked, living in perpetual terror of a three-foot drop. A row of small glass eyes watched her from beneath spit curls and pigtails.

You all need a better babysitter.

She walked around the back of the table to straighten the velvet they sat on, and for just a moment, her face joined theirs: the raggedy teatime damsel among the china children.

And that was when her eyes met his.

He was about her age, maybe a little older. Long black hair fell in tight curls. A leather vest, necklaces of pewter. Engineer boots creased with dust. Something about the way he stood in front of their tables made her feel like he was tracking mud on their floor. In another era, he would be the outlaw riding up on horseback, a rifle slung across his back.

Her breath quickened.

Dark tan fingers were gentle across worn gilt, painted flowers. His eyes were hazel. She couldn't open her mouth to tell him *please don't touch the merchandise*, not when it felt like he was stroking her skin.

He stepped between the tables, onto the carpet. His build

was slender, and the light caught the down of his forearms as he paced along the restored antiques. He winked at Charla before calling out to her mother.

"Hey."

Lillie looked up. Disapproval strained her features, ever so slightly.

"Yes, can I help you?"

"Did you ever know a woman named Marithe?" Soft-spoken.

"Marithe?"

"Yeah. She did stuff like this, but with crystals. I mean, it was years ago, but she sold stuff around here too, back in the day."

"Marithe, Marithe…" Charla watched her mother mull over the name, prayed there was some thread in their network of vagabond friends that would connect her to this beautiful stranger.

"No," Lillie finally said. "I'm afraid I haven't."

"But we also travel the coast," said Charla. *No, don't go.* "It's possible we weren't here when she was around. How long ago was it?"

"Oh, like twenty years." A grin of futility.

"Ah. *I* was hardly around, that long ago." She smiled back at him.

Thin, wraithlike, but somewhere in there, muscle that could command a snarling machine, eyes as cool and calm as the sky as he did it. She, keeper of the dolls… she couldn't imagine having that kind of control. Especially not over something so dangerous.

"Ever been riding?" he asked. As if he'd been reading her mind.

"No." Everything was turning golden.

"I'll come by later, if you wanna."

She nodded her head once, caught herself, and glanced at Lillie.

That look was back in her mother's eyes. She'd first seen it long ago, when she'd wanted to play in the swamp with the hempseller's kids from the lot next-door. It appeared most recently when she'd begged Lillie to teach her how to drive the camper a few months ago. The forbidding governess face, rare yet severe, that was all *No.*

But this time it was crossed with something strange. Apprehension.

Charla looked back. He was already walking away. With her nod in his pocket. He'd be back later.

"Mama..."

Was that sadness, in her mother's face? Fear, even? Lillie spoke slowly. "I—I think that... I would rather you not go."

It wasn't *No*.

Gleaming chrome. A life that moved as fast as the wind.

His smile, like dancing light.

She was dizzy.

Yes.

Charla passed by Lillie and stepped inside the camper.

She moved the pile of dresses aside and sat crosslegged on her bed, pushing aside the small gingham curtain to gaze out at the back of the lot, into the woods that bordered the market. Summer sunlight warmed the trees. Birds' nests dotted the branches, holding tiny families.

So much traveling she'd done with her mother. Tarot readings told by candlelight, long skirts held up to wade along the edge of a lake. Gathering flowers, or bundles of magazines left on city streets. Grimacing over the drab, ugly coffee cups of highway diners. Market to market, sleeping on the couches of Lillie's herb-dabbling friends or parked beside a field on some quiet road.

She closed her eyes. There was an argument over lawn furniture a couple lots over, the jingle of bells on a water ice cart. She ran her hands over her arms, felt the sting from her finger. Bruises. She thought about that poor babydoll, probably wedged in the back of an SUV somewhere. And that nasty little kid.

She lay back on the bed, pulled a knotty chenille throw over herself. *A chopper could annihilate a pathetic little BMX*, she thought, as she fell into a light sleep.

When she woke, the sky had faded to purple, and the other vendors were rolling up their blankets. She pulled on her boots and went outside to help Lillie. The dolls and teapots had been packed up and they had gotten through most of the jewelry when an engine growled through the dusky air.

The outlaw pulled up in a flash of sculpted metal. His leather jacket was a wild mosaic of pins and patches, intricate with embroidery and the memento mori of tiny grinning skulls.

He had come to steal her away.

"You ready to go?"

Yes. She looked back at Lillie. Brown eyes faced her with a soft despair, so much like the night she'd left her mother's arms, old enough to sleep on the other side of the camper.

Trust in me, Mama. Please.

Charla tore herself away and jumped on the back of the bike, knotting her peacock tail safely away from the wheel, taking the helmet he offered her. She wrapped her arms around his waist as he merged into the line of cars. Willed herself not to look back, as they crossed the market exit.

೪ଛ

His name was Adrian, youngest in a family who all rode.

He turned them onto the road, and quickly lifted them into exhilarating speed. Wind cooled her skin, and the yellow dashed lines passed directly beneath her feet, breathtakingly close after years of glassed-in travel. And the vibrations... like shooting stars.

He wound through the countryside, a long drive to savor the deepening twilight, the warmth of summer-baked earth. Overhead, the skies faded from violet to black, and little houses lit up across the fields. The world looked so different when you went riding just to ride. Not to haul things around, not even to head towards a destination... just to enjoy the sheer rush of movement itself.

They pulled up to a weathered ranch set back from the road by a garden long gone to seed. Tools and bits of machinery were flung everywhere across the yard, as if the flowerbeds were being watered with nuts and bolts. What a luxury, she thought, not having to clean up every night. Just leaving whatever you were working on spread out on the lawn, for the next day.

"It's never clean. We don't bother," he said, mistaking her gaze for judgment, shameless where Lillie's friends had always been a little embarrassed by clutter in their living rooms, treating sprawled laundry and unwashed dishes like dirty secrets.

"No, it's not that. This is all like... puzzle pieces. I'm always trying to recover things, make them fit back together into something useful, or at least pretty. This," she swept her arm across the yard, "I can't imagine how this all turns into a *bike*."

"It's not that hard. But I've lived around it my whole life," an unmistakable undertone of pride beneath his soft voice as he opened the front door.

He rummaged in the refrigerator while she looked around the house. Aesthetically, it was barren. A couple of leather trenchcoats were draped across a worn tweedy couch, and gleaming cycles flashed across the flat screen of a computer monitor. An acoustic guitar sat in an overstuffed armchair. Not much else.

It was weird. *Everybody* had some kind of bric-a-brac lying around. Fancy little handpainted boxes, vases of frosted glass, those nauseating dewy-eyed angel-children she and Lillie loathed with a passion. Here, not one ceramic kitten.

Decoration was a kind of language, she realized. A starting point with strangers, a polite tearoom tactic of getting to know someone. *So your husband got you this snowglobe in New York City, in 1969? What a cute stuffed dragon, yes, your mother is very talented with a needle and thread. Wow, that's quite a collection of owls, did you do all this macrame yourself?* She searched for some point of reference from which she could begin to understand him, but the wood paneling revealed nothing.

She was about to give up when she saw something sparkling down the hall. Without waiting for permission—look, her manners were eroding already, in his company—she walked towards it.

A curtain of crystals was strung across a bedroom window. Etched glass fallen from chandeliers, amethyst briolettes, prisms of aurora borealis like frozen rain – Charla slipped her fingers behind the lowest shard, a furious slice of kaleidoscope. She held the magnificent teardrop in her palm.

"It's a mooncatcher."Adrian came up behind her, six-pack in hand. "That was what my mother called it. It's been there since I was born."

"Marithe?"

He nodded.

The crystal winked prettily from her fingertips. A small wind blew in from the dark, struck the curtain up into a delicate cacophony.

"Come on," he said, leading her out. "It's a great night for a fire."

Out back, thick stumps surrounded a fire pit, and an ancient grill rusted nearby. She circled the yard while he lit the kindling. Wildflowers grew in clusters at the edge of the grass, mowed down here and there by tire tracks. She peered out through the woods. No other lights close by.

"We have it all to ourselves. My brothers are down the shore and my dad's over his girlfriend's place."

He spread out a Navajo blanket near the flames. She could hear the crystals chiming from the window as they sat down and popped their cans open. She grimaced at the first swallow; she'd never liked the taste of beer.

"So how long have you been doing the market thing?" he asked.

"Oh, forever. My mother and I have always been travelers."

He'd seen a lot of the country, too. Riding in packs with his family, and all their friends, heading off to gatherings of thousands. Magazines, fashions, millions of dollars thrown behind a world that had never died out or needed a revival. She envied him as they juxtaposed maps, compared the places they'd been as the moon rose in the sky. Tipped each other off to cities that were safe for overnight parking and unconventional dress, and which ones were much too fast to call the cops.

"It all looks the same, though, after awhile. Every town we go to, my dad's got stories about bars that got torn down, places that don't exist anymore. It's all gotten built over." Adrian finished the last can and crushed it in his fist.

She flashed on an image of her mother, alone outside their camper, bravely raising one lone teacup against a tidal wave of beige.

"What was Marithe like?" she asked.

He answered with a grim little smile. "My mother went when I was so young, before I had a chance to get to know her. You know, as a real person. Your parents are just fairytales when you're a kid, these mythical people, right? And she was a witch.

261

She rode, but she had a real artistic side, spiritual. The whole house was covered in those chimes, she started selling them at the market when we had no room left. After she passed, my dad cleared out everything of hers. Had to get rid of it all, it was killing him to have it around. But I wouldn't let him take the mooncatcher. She made that one just for me, it's all I have left of her. That whole world that died with her."

The crystals edged the silence with soft bells. Charla thought about her tables at the market, the unknown histories behind each piece: the polite clinking conversations of silver cutlery against fine china. The whisper-drip of wax making its way down a pewter stem, pooling in a scalloped dish. The satisfying click of a lock sliding into place, keeping secrets inside a carved wooden box.

Vintage things held souls; these were the voices of the dead.

She thought of careless women plucking at babydolls, angry children coming to smash them.

I'm breakable too. And I can't be.

The promise of transformation awed her from the moment it surfaced in his brilliant smile; the night would be sweet, but it demanded sacrifice. No turning back to what she'd been, but there was no telling what she'd become, either. She hid her breathlessness behind bitter sips of beer.

Leather could shield from what the road could do, wouldn't shatter against it. She wanted to streamline it into her skin, all that confidence to handle such a wicked machine, make it part of herself to keep all the antiques from bursting apart, be a better guardian of an ever-trembling world. Of Lillie.

The alchemy itself would be severe, she knew. But the warlock? A notorious ancestry of roadlust, the blood passed down through the branches of his family, his dead honored in a lunar shrine that sang at every breeze... honored in the sparkling graveyard of her market table. She flashed on his ringed hands dancing along the porcelain.

She looked up at him. He was still staring into the fire, quieted by grief that had lain dormant for a long time, until today. Muscle was hidden within his slim body... teeth too. He was just choosing not to show them to her.

She brought her fingertips to his jawline, and he looked at her with surprise. Smiled, as she pulled him into a kiss. Her ribbons skimmed his face as she ran her hands over his back, down the patchwork and up under his jacket, gliding across his flesh. Tender and smooth inside his armor – just as vulnerable as she was, but better protected. And his hands, warm, strange and delightful across her senses. She savored this last sweet spell in her old skin before the moment came, when she'd take one deep breath and shed her petticoats forever.

She climbed on top of him, unzipped her dress, and he arched an appreciative eyebrow at her black lace bustier, tap panties, the prettiest of the vintage underclothes she always wore. Slowly, between kisses, they stripped down until she grabbed his jacket, whispered softly, *leave it on*. When he curled his arms around her and lifted her to be as close as they could possibly be, the leather brushed her cheek. Tough and soft, upholstery from the gentleman's den stolen and refashioned for the road. The earthy fragrance melted her open.

Pain. She willed it aside and breathed him in. Thought of accidents, all the spills and breaks one could live through and keep going, keep flying down the highway. Absorb the impact, roll with it, ride it. The sting gave way to hunger, the way the engine had pulsed her on from below, steady vibrations against the asphalt, reaching up into her hammering heart. Tangled hair, ragged breath as she rocked against him.

She'd never hurt like this again. She could not be so easily broken, now.

Her skin was turning golden.

∽◦≈

The soft morning light fell across silver compacts, cocktail rings. Lillie was sitting in her chair, needlework in her lap, teacup in her hand. Bessie Smith kept her company. Only the blues, today.

"Mama."

Lillie looked up.

Charla stood in front of the tables, completely dressed in leather. The pants were almost too big for her, and her lace bustier peeked from beneath the vest, but it all fit, just enough. Her hair was combed completely straight and fell down past her shoulders, with only two ribbons left, trailing down the sides of her face.

Her eyes glowed.

She walked onto their lot, unfolded a wooden chair and faced Lillie. The teacup settled back in its dish with a little clank. All around them, other merchants were busy setting their wares out for the day, drinking coffee, chatting with each other.

"Were you afraid I would leave?" asked Charla.

Nearby, on another lot, a child began to cry. Lillie didn't answer.

"I'm still me. You must believe that. I wasn't going to leave you. I just needed..." *To change? To become something else?*

"...I needed to become stronger." *Yes.*

She had crept out of Adrian's bed at dawn and started to put on her clothes, but caught sight of his riding gear. It was tossed around his bedroom in plentiful piles of beaten black. Careful not to take anything emblazoned with his family's symbology, she dressed in his warrior armor. She brushed her hair out, gathered up her ribbons in a clump and knotted them to the string of crystals. Barefoot, she had walked back to the market along the side of the road, the sand warm on her soles, the breeze playing with the two remaining ribbons in her hair.

Her peacock dress lay crumpled on his floor. The pretext to see him again.

Lillie stared at her, took it all in. Charla watched the storm of emotions within her mother's eyes: gladness, and acceptance, maybe even admiration... but a trace of unmistakable anguish. The teatime sprite was gone forever.

"I'll get you something to drink." Lillie went into the camper and brought out one of Charla's favorite cups. Orange and pink roses tangled beneath the rim, with a couple more blooms hiding inside, just waiting to be discovered as the tea was sipped away. She placed it in Charla's hands and filled it up, just as a man in a polo shirt called out to them.

"How much is this picture frame?"

We'll talk later.

Lillie walked over to handle him, and Charla settled back on the chair, looked out over the market. The early birds were out in full force. The start of another work day.

A small figure blurred by the table.

Something occurred to her that wouldn't have, yesterday,

before that thrilling ride. Charla got up, grabbed a crate of soda bottles from beside the camper. Nothing truly valuable—just glass recycling.

"Hey! Hey kid!"

Surprised, the boy turned around, pedaled back. He stopped in front of her.

"You're bored to death, aren't you?"

Silently, he stared at her, before nodding a little.

"You like breaking things. Alright. Here—smash all this instead, as much as you want. But in the dumpsters, OK?"

He blinked at her. Being encouraged to do something most adults yelled at you for? Unheard of, she could see. He took the box from her and balanced it on his seat, looking unsure of what to say.

"You don't look like you did yesterday," he finally managed, as he walked his bike away.

Hopefully that would be the end of it. If not... well. He'd find out what kind of teeth were hidden behind her smile.

So would she.

Charla went back to her chair and sat down, picked up her tea. Lots of milk and sugar, just the way she liked it. She watched a couple of teenagers try to haggle with her mother over a vanity set as she sipped the sweet warmth.

Thought of kisses.

She ran her lips over the edge of the cup. Last night. *Last night.* She shuddered, bit lightly on the gilt. Firelight. Adrian's skin beneath her fingers. His hands on her hips, in her hair. The crystals calling from the window. The grind of his body beneath her. Inside her.

In the distance, a cycle roared.

The china shattered between her teeth.

Y is for Yesterday

KV Taylor

I.

I didn't expect it to look like a pumpkin exploding. I suppose when you see it on television they cut out the gorier bits, even on HBO—or they go the opposite direction and make it look as if human blood and guts are under twelve-thousand pounds of direct pressure. The truth is that when someone is shot in the head, it's generally like something in between. And reminded me of our brothers lining up pumpkins on the fence for shooting with their air rifles on cool fall days.

I lost my mind; that's what the courts decided, anyhow. It didn't help that the woman who shot Marisa got off on a technicality. No, I said, no, *Marisa* lost her mind because she rolled down her window to give a stranger directions. But the mind and the brain aren't the same thing, are they? I was just confused. That happens a lot.

For a long time, I wondered why they couldn't just put her back together. Scrape up the brain, mend the pieces of skull, make her smile and laugh again. For an even longer time, I wondered why she didn't shoot me too. Why she left me in the passenger seat, just sitting there with the right number of holes in my head. I wondered why she didn't shoot me instead, if she wasn't even interested in taking the car. Or maybe she was and she panicked and pulled the trigger instead. I don't know and there was a mistrial. All I could think of over and over was a pumpkin sitting on the fence out back and how the bits exploded out of it.

I don't even know her name, the woman who shot my Marisa. I know where she lived. I know she was supposed to be taking a taxi to the airport. I know everyone thinks she's on vacation.

But she's not. She's in my basement.

II.

"It's okay," I lie. "I'm a nurse."

Maybe it's not a complete lie, maybe I'm a self-trained nurse. Stitching up dolls and dresses and teddy bears since the age of three, since my clumsy little fingers could pull thread through an eye. Marisa always broke her toys, the wild twin, my free half. I always mended them, the quiet twin, her conscience. It's like learning to walk with one leg and no crutches; I know I can do it, but I keep thinking something's missing.

No one else should have to go through this suffering, this pain, so I'm here to make sure. And so is the woman who shot Marisa in the head. She's crusty with dried mud from outdoors and dirt from the unfinished basement floor, chained to the hot water heater. She screams when I take a step closer.

I say, "There's no one here. Marisa's gone now. If I'd known how to put her back together she'd be here, but then, you wouldn't, would you?"

I'm amazed she hasn't burst into tears, but maybe there's no water left in her to make them. I crouch to hand her a bottle of water and she cringes, even though I haven't laid a finger on her since dragging her unconscious body down here. Finally she snatches the water and swallows it down, and I shake my head. I tell her, "Not too fast. You'll vomit."

"Fuck you, bitch." She spits like a cat when she talks. Like a mean cat, not Marisa's cat Spartacus, who sits on the stairs watching us with interest. The woman adds, "You fuckin' monster."

I nod, because she's not wrong. "At least my monstering is for a good cause," I say. "You can't say that, for yourself."

"I'm gonna cut your fucking heart out," she promises.

I doubt this very much, but don't see the point in telling her.

I know how dangerous she is. I've seen my twin sister's brains blasted all over the front of her Chevy. I was willing to let the State have her, but they lost her, and now she's mine.

I go back upstairs and look to my closet for inspiration. Spartacus follows on his silent padded feet and asks me what I'm doing, so I tell him. (Not really, of course, I know cats don't speak; I haven't lost that part of my mind. Yet.) I ask him what he thinks would work better. Could I use buttons? No, that would leave gaps. Velcro would become messy.

Well use a zipper, dummy, Spartacus doesn't say, with an indolent lick of his paw.

I have to admit, he has a point. I pick up Marisa's old Teddy Ruxpin and stroke his matted fur, smiling. The zipper on the back broke when we were ten, and I'd replaced it all by myself. Of course, of course, it was perfect. "I don't know if silk will hold," I admit.

Wire, suggests Spartacus.

So it's just a trip to the hardware store before I'm ready, at last.

III.

The woman's blood mingles with the dirt of the floor, dirt some pioneer woman once trod while stacking her potatoes and canned goods for winter. There was a log house here before Pappy built this one, and this one is ours, mine and Marisa's, now our brothers are all long gone. Shooting pumpkins in other states. They'd be appalled, I think with odd detachment, as I watch the red and brown mix into a thick, muddy black. Look at the mess in Pappy's basement.

I brought a pile of towels, but now the time's near I can't wait. I shovel some new dirt over and lift the woman's half-smashed head—yes, like a pumpkin, too, except when our brothers would run around the neighborhood on Halloween smashing jack o' lanterns. The sound had been different, but also better, so I didn't mind. There's too much blood to work on the back, where the smashing is really good, so I start at the front with the silver wire. It'll be congealed soon and all I'll have to do is push in the wet, pinkish-grayish brain and sew it up tight, silver wire and shiny new zipper. That'll hold it in. That'll hold it all in and stop it from looking like our brothers were in here with their Louisville Sluggers.

I used my own, not theirs, anyhow. I don't like guns.

The light fades through the tinted windows and the blood turns to jelly and the piles of red-turning-brown towels beside me grows. It's soaked through my jeans now but it's going to be worth it when it all comes together. Smears of red fingerprints on the bright new zipper, just like Teddy Ruxpin's when I pricked my fingers trying to sort him out. I have to stand and pull the cord on the naked bulb overhead to really get into things, but the wire's working beautifully. A bit of bone here and a tuck of brain there. "Now who's the monster?" I ask into her open skull.

Even when I hear someone ring the doorbell, even when I hear footsteps overhead, even when Spartacus comes flying down the stairs, I don't stop. If I can just finish. If I can just show them.

They say my name and the footsteps come down the stairs. My fingers are shaking, cold and stiff with drying, clotting life. But all I have to do is put all the stuffing back inside, just to prove it works, and no one will ever have to feel this pain again. "It had to be her," I say reasonably. "It had to be her because she shot Marisa. Who else should help develop the technique that could've saved her."

Someone throws up, and I look up from my work at the retching sound. "Oh," I say.

There are two men and one woman in uniform. When I notice the gun pointed at my head, I'm carried out of myself. Floating up to the ceiling, looking down at my body with the mess of her head in my hands, the remnants of her misshapen skull decorated by tiny silver teeth.

I don't know, comments Spartacus from the stairs where he sits watching and lashing his tail. *I think some of her can still get out through the gaps between the metal parts...*

I don't think that's right, but if it is... I'll do better next time.

Z is for Zipper

CONTRIBUTOR BIOGRAPHIES

BRITTANY WARMAN is a PhD candidate in English and Folklore at The Ohio State University, where she concentrates on the intersection of literature and folklore. Her creative work has been published by or is forthcoming from *Mythic Delirium, Jabberwocky Magazine, Ideomancer, inkscrawl, Cabinet des Fées: Scheherezade's Bequest*, and others. Her story "Q is for Queen" appeared in *A is for Apocalypse*. She can be found online at BrittanyWarman.com

❧

MILO JAMES FOWLER is a teacher by day and a speculative fictioneer by night. When he's not grading papers, he's imagining what the world might be like in a dozen alternate realities. His work has appeared in *AE SciFi, Cosmos, Daily Science Fiction, Nature, Shimmer*, and the *Wastelands 2* anthology. His novel *Captain Bartholomew Quasar and the Space-Time Displacement Conundrum* will be available later this year. www.milojamesfowler.com

❧

C.S. MACCATH is a writer of fiction, non-fiction and poetry whose work has appeared in *Strange Horizons, Clockwork Phoenix: Tales of Beauty and Strangeness, Mythic Delirium, Murky Depths, Witches & Pagans* and other publications. Her poetry has been nominated twice for the Rhysling Award, her fiction has been nominated for the Pushcart Prize and it has also received honorable mention in *The Year's Best Science Fiction: Twenty-Sixth Annual Collection*. You can find her online at csmaccath.com.

❧

SARA CLETO is a PhD student at the Ohio State University where she studies folklore, literature, disability, and the places where they intersect. Her work can be found or is forthcoming in

Goblin Fruit, Cabinet des Fees: Scheherazade's Bequest, Ideomancer, Niteblade, The Golden Key, and others. Her work has been nominated twice for the Pushcart Prize.

SAMANTHA KYMMELL-HARVEY's stories can be found in *Spark: A Creative Anthology, Every Day Fiction*, and *Waylines* just to name a few. She is a 2012 graduate of the Odyssey Writing Workshop. You can follow her adventures on her blog: http://samanthakymmell-harvey.blogspot.com/

MEGAN ARKENBERG lives in northern California. Her work has appeared in *Asimov's, Lightspeed, Strange Horizons, Ellen Datlow's Best Horror of the Year*, and dozens of other places. She procrastinates by editing the fantasy e-zine *Mirror Dance*.

GARY B. PHILLIPS is a writer and software developer surviving in the desert wastes of Arizona with his wife, three children, three cats, and four chickens. His work has appeared in *Daily Science Fiction, Flash Fiction Online*, and the *A is for Apocalypse* anthology, among others. He reads slush for *Flash Fiction Online*. Find him on Twitter @garybphillips.

ALEXANDRA SEIDEL is a writer, poet, and editor. H is for Hanging Man (aka The Hanging Man Who Does Not Heal) is her second story in the Alphabet Series. Other than that, her writing appeared in *Strange Horizons, Lackington's, Stone Telling*, and elsewhere. If you are so inclined you can follow Alexa on Twitter (@Alexa_Seidel) or read her blog: www.tigerinthematchstickbox.blogspot.com.

JONATHAN C. PARRISH is known by many other names. He goes by Jo because of a poem by A. A. Milne and by Jopa because of an email address he received in 1990 (and a blissful ignorance, at the time, of the Russian language). He spent most of his life in Canada, particularly in Alberta and Nova Scotia and he once made the mistake of taking the train from Halifax to Edmonton and back again.

SIMON KEWIN is the author of over 100 published short or flash stories. He lives in England with his wife and their daughters. His cyberpunk novel *The Genehunter* and his fantasy novels *Engn* and *Hedge Witch* were recently published. Find him at simonkewin.co.uk.

BETH CATO hails from Hanford, California, but currently writes and bakes cookies in a lair west of Phoenix, Arizona. She shares the household with a hockey-loving husband, a numbers-obsessed son, and a cat the size of a canned ham.

She's the author of *The Clockwork Dagger* steampunk fantasy series from Harper Voyager. The newest book is *The Clockwork Crown*.

Follow her at BethCato.com and on Twitter at @BethCato.

CORY CONE lives, works and writes in Baltimore, MD. He studied painting at the Maryland Institute College of Art, where he met and married his wife. His work has appeared in a handful of fine journals, including *Niteblade, Grim Corps, The Colored Lens*, and *Every Day Fiction*.

CINDY JAMES lives in Edmonton, Alberta with her husband and two children. After twenty years working as a court reporter and listening to other people's stories, she decided to engage the right side of her brain and tell a few of her own. She is pursuing a degree in English and History, and is committed to one day write something truly great. She now works as a broadcast closed-captioner, volunteers at the local art gallery, and agonizes in what remains of her free time over whether she should be writing or painting.

ALEXIS A. HUNTER revels in the endless possibilities of speculative fiction. Over fifty of her short stories have appeared recently in S*himmer, Cricket Magazine, Flash Fiction Online*, and more. To learn more, visit www.alexisahunter.com.

MICHAEL M. JONES is a writer, book reviewer, and editor. He lives in Southwest Virginia, with too many books, just enough cats, and a wife who translates geek into mundane. His short stories have appeared in Clockwork Phoenix 3, A Chimerical World, and at Inscription Magazine. He is the editor of Scheherazade's Facade and the forthcoming Schoolbooks & Sorcery. Visit him at www.michaelmjones.com.

STEVE BORNSTEIN has made his living fixing broken things, much to his chagrin. He currently works in an industry where things break all the time in ways they're not supposed to break. He lives in Central Texas with his wife and four cats. He blogs infrequently at stevebornstein.com and can be found on most major social networks.

BD WILSON is a writer from Edmonton, Alberta, Canada whose work has appeared in the anthology *Dark Pages* from Blade Red press, *Liquid Imagination Online*, and *Niteblade Fantasy and Horror Magazine* among others. A firm believer in a virtual existence, BD's home on the Web is located at http://www.bdwilson.ca

❧

MICHAEL KELLAR is a writer, poet, and occasional online bookseller living in Myrtle Beach, SC. He has had fiction appear in *Metastasis: An Anthology to Support Cancer Research*, *Bones II, Bones III, Side Show 2: Tales of the Big Top and the Bizarre, A is for Apocalypse*, and the recently released *The Grays*. He has also had fiction appear on the *Dark Futures Fiction* website, and had poetry published in *Gothic Blue Book III: The Graveyard Edition*. Upcoming pieces will include stories appearing in *Pure Fantasy and Sci-Fi 3* and *The Temporal Element II*.

❧

DAMIEN ANGELICA WALTERS' short fiction has appeared in various magazines and anthologies, including *Year's Best Weird Fiction Volume One, The Best of Electric Velocipede, Strange Horizons, Nightmare, Lightspeed, Shimmer*, and *Apex*. "The Floating Girls: A Documentary," originally published in *Jamais Vu*, is on the 2014 Bram Stoker Award ballot for Superior Achievement in Short Fiction.

Sing Me Your Scars, a collection of her short fiction, is out now from Apex Publications, and *Paper Tigers*, a novel, is forthcoming from Dark House Press. You can find her on Twitter @DamienAWalters or online at http://damienangelicawalters.com.

❧

MARGE SIMON's works appear in publications such as *DailySF Magazine, Pedestal, Urban Fantasist*. She edits a column for the HWA Newsletter, "Blood & Spades: Poets of the Dark Side," and serves as Chair of the Board of Trustees. She won the Strange Horizons Readers Choice Award, 2010, and the SFPA's Dwarf

Stars Award, 2012. She has won three Bram Stoker Awards ® for Superior Work in Poetry and has poetry in HWA's Simon & Schuster collection, It's Scary Out There, 2015. Marge also has poems in D*arke Phantastique, Qualia Nous* collections, and *Spectral Realms*, 2014. www.margesimon.com

MICHAEL R. FOSBURG, a recent Pushcart Prize nominee, is a senior Literature major at the University of South Florida Sarasota-Manatee. His work has appeared in *Star*Line, Niteblade, MindFlights, Illumen*, and elsewhere. He can be harangued through email, fosburg@gmail.com, or through his perpetually-neglected blog, http://m-roderick.livejournal.com/

SUZANNE is a tattooed storyteller from South Africa. She currently lives in Sweden and is busy making friends with the ghosts of her Viking ancestors. Although she has a Master's degree in music, Suzanne prefers conjuring strange worlds and creating quirky characters. When she grows up, she wants to be an elf – until then, she spends her time (when not writing) wall climbing, buying far too many books, and entertaining her shiba inu, Lego.

L.S. JOHNSON lives in Northern California. Her fiction has appeared or is forthcoming in *Strange Horizons, Interzone, Long Hidden, Fae, Lackington's, Strange Tales V*, and other venues. Currently she is working on a fantasy trilogy set in 18th century Europe.

By day, PETE ALDIN manages a program for people with disabilities; by night, he sits at a laptop and writes. His short fiction has appeared in publications including *Orson Scott Card's Intergalactic Medicine Show, Andromeda Spaceways Inflight*

Magazine, and *Niteblade*. His non-fiction has appeared in parenting and business magazines. He is a big fan of alcoholic ciders, the FIFA franchise on xBox and (being Australian) Vegemite. He is a member of the Australian Horror Writers Association and the Chelsea Dark Fiction Writers Circle.

GABRIELLE HARBOWY has edited for publishers such as Pyr, Lambda Literary, and Circlet Press. She is the managing editor at Dragon Moon Press and a submissions editor at the Hugo-nominated *Apex Magazine*. With Ed Greenwood, she co-edited the award-nominated *When the Hero Comes Home* anthology series. Her short fiction can be found in anthologies, including *Carbide Tipped Pens* from Tor, and her first novel is forthcoming from Paizo. Check out Gabrielle's personal site: www.gabrielle-edits.com.

LILAH WILD's dark fiction is an ongoing search for hidden cauldrons within the modern landscape. Her work explores the urban fantastic through contemporary witchcraft, from the grimy dive to the glittering dancefloor. When she's not elucidating on Old Hollywood screen goddesses or the blood and fire quotient of metal videos that purport to be evil, Lilah can be found dabbling in tribal fusion bellydancing, hiking the deco puzzlebox of Manhattan, or running away to the beach. She lives in Queens amid a clamor of doom metal noodling and four cats.

Visit LeopardMoon.com for the full bibliography and upcoming releases.

KV TAYLOR is an avid reader and writer of fantasy and dark fiction, even though the only degree she holds is in the history of art. (Or, possibly, because the only degree she holds is in the history of art.) In her spare time she enjoys comic books, Himalayan Buddhist art, loud music, her Epiphone, and Black

Bush. Her fiction can be found at kvtaylor.com.

RHONDA PARRISH is driven by a desire to do All The Things. She has been the publisher and editor-in-chief of Niteblade Magazine for over six years now (which is like 30 years in internet time) and is the editor of several anthologies including (most recently) Fae and B is for Broken.

In addition, Rhonda is a writer whose work has been included in dozens of publications including Tesseracts 17: Speculating Canada from Coast to Coast, Imaginarium: The Best Canadian Speculative Writing (2012) and Mythic Delirium.

Her website, updated weekly, is at
http://www.rhondaparrish.com

Thank you for reading

B is for Broken

We would appreciate it a great deal if you would leave an honest review on Goodreads and wherever you purchased this book.

Your stars and a couple sentences mean the world to us!

Truly.

The importance of reviews cannot be overstated—they often make the difference between a book's success or its utter failure.

Always Be The First To Know!

Whether it's a new release, a call for submissions, cover reveal, super sale or I just want to share a new story I've written, you will always be among the first to know if you sign up for my newsletter.

I promise to respect your privacy and your inbox. I will only email you when I have something exciting to share, probably about twice a month.

Subscribe now and you'll receive a free download of my award-winning post-apocalyptic short story, "Starry Night" as a welcome-to-the-newsletter present!

Subscribe to Rhonda's Mailing List!

http://bit.ly/StarryStory